USA TODAY BESTSELLING AUTHOR
Dale Mayer

SIMON SAYS...
FORGIVE

A KATE MORGAN NOVEL

SIMON SAYS… FORGIVE (KATE MORGAN, BOOK 7)
Beverly Dale Mayer
Valley Publishing Ltd.

ISBN-13: 978-1-773367-89-7
Print Edition

Books in This Series

The Kate Morgan Series

Simon Says… Hide, Book 1

Simon Says… Jump, Book 2

Simon Says… Ride, Book 3

Simon Says… Scream, Book 4

Simon Says… Run, Book 5

Simon Says… Walk, Book 6

Simon Says… Forgive, Book 7

Simon Says… Swim, Book 8

About This Book

Some cases stay with you longer than others. This is one of them for Detective Kate Morgan. That poor child was the worst part. Plus it's one thing to desecrate a church, but it's quite another to commit murder in one—particularly in this manner. Confused, but knowing she must understand the psychology of this killer before she can understand where his next killing ground will take place, Kate buries herself in the case.

Simon is trying to be there to support Kate, but his own world shifts when he's asked to step in to analyze issues in a poker buddy's company, only to have the guy commit suicide soon afterward. Or did he? Between his buddy's issues and the horrific nightmares Simon's dealing with—surrounding Kate and her latest investigation—Simon's life is slowing unravelling too.

Finding the killer is paramount. … Finding him before he annihilates another family? Well, that's a much harder job. Kate has no choice. … She must stop him before he kills yet again …

Sign up to be notified of all Dale's releases here!
https://geni.us/DaleNews

CHAPTER 1

Second Week of October

KATE WALKED INTO the office one week later. Sergeant Colby barked at her, "Meeting in five minutes in the conference room."

She nodded, grabbed a coffee, and headed into the conference room. "What's going on?"

"We have three ritualistic murders that we caught today," he stated, with a somber tone.

Her eyes widened. "Three, now, all at once?"

"Three," he emphasized. "Three bodies, one scene, all last night. Bodies were found at 6:00 a.m. this morning inside a church."

"Inside a church?" she repeated, her gaze widening.

"Yes, exactly," he confirmed.

"Do we know who the victims are?"

"They're all members of a polygamous group, that has a self-professed leader," Colby related, with a disgusted tone to his voice.

"So a cult," she said.

"I don't think they consider themselves a cult," he murmured, "although you and I probably would. A large group of them used to be in California. They moved up to BC a good ten, twelve years ago. They've been relatively harmless. We've never had any issues with them, until now."

"Do we know whether the issue is with them or they're having issues with somebody else?"

He gave her a proud nod. "And that is a very good question, Detective, and you will get a chance to find out for yourself soon."

"In what way?"

"Well, first off, these three bodies have been put on crosses." Colby brought up the images that had been prepped for the meeting.

She winced when she saw two bodies, arms spread and nailed, crucified style, to a cross. "Jesus Christ," she whispered, staring at it. "How is it people have time for this shit?"

"It's not even about time. It's all about motivation, and these are the first two." He took a moment, and then he said a bit crossly, "And this next one will get you." And there, in front, was a child. "The only thing I can say about the child is that he appears to have died first and was crucified afterward."

Kate's heart sank, as she stared at the young boy spread-eagled on a cross. He was still in his Mickey Mouse pajamas. Under her breath, she whispered, "Fuck. These people are animals."

"As I said, he was killed first, crucified later. Unfortunately for the parents, … I don't think they were given that mercy."

"What church were they found in?" Owen asked.

She looked over at him and nodded. "Yeah, and what location?"

"Inside the Catholic church of the Kerrisdale neighborhood in the city of Vancouver."

"Interesting," she murmured.

"Yeah, also what's interesting was the carving on their

bodies."

And, with that, the next image flashed on the screen. *Forgive* was written on the chest of each of the three victims.

Kate sat back, shook her head, and recapped, "Three people dead, left in a church, and a message to forgive," she murmured. "Christ, this one doesn't sound like fun."

Rodney looked over at her, and his lips quirked. "They aren't supposed to be. Remember that."

She rolled her eyes, nodded, and said, "Let's get to work, partner."

CHAPTER 2

KATE MORGAN SLAMMED the car door shut, then turned to look at Rodney, who'd driven her vehicle. Probably wise, considering all the emotions going through Kate right now. They both turned as one to stare at the massive church in front of them. Her frown was instinctive. She'd never spent any time in a church, either good or bad. It just hadn't been part of her upbringing, and it certainly hadn't been part of her adulthood.

Given her profession, maybe her views of good and evil, right and wrong, heaven and hell, all might have taken a slightly tainted turn. But, given Simon's gift, which she didn't think resided in the scientific realm and which she still struggled with, her whole vision of how religion worked was completely skewed.

She didn't have any answers and didn't think anybody in the church did either. She was still willing to be open enough to see just what would come.

It was a cold blustery day, and thankfully she had on a jacket. Pulling up the collar, she shoved her hands in her pockets.

When Rodney approached, she asked in a lowered tone, "Are you ready for this?"

He gave her half a smile. "Hey, it'll look bad, but we've got to get on this one."

"Oh, we'll get on it all right," she declared, as she strolled toward the massive stairs, shaking her head. "I'm not impressed with anybody who would take out an entire family."

"The good news is it looks like the boy died from natural causes," he pointed out.

"Natural causes, my ass, as in he was beaten to a pulp," she muttered in a blistering tone. No matter how hard she tried, it was all too close to her heart.

"Sure, okay, I'll give you that. He died not from natural causes but likely from previous beatings. The point is, he wasn't killed by this murderer."

"So why did the little boy have 'forgive' carved on his chest then?" she asked, turning to her partner. "Better yet, why was he put on a cross, like the other two? Are we assuming that the other two were done in by beatings?"

"We're not assuming anything at this point in time," Rodney stated firmly, as he pulled open one of the massive front doors.

For a church to normally be a place of peace and reverence, today was the exact opposite. At least a dozen white-suited forensic staff, as well as several policemen, were scattered throughout the space. A trio of members of the clergy stood in a tight huddle off to one side. Kate knew she would need to speak to them as well, and soon. She eyed them, then turned her gaze back to the victims.

As always, her job was the victims. They took and always would take precedence, and all else be damned.

As she strolled forward, Dr. Smidge looked up and glared at her, and she glared right back. He relented a bit as he always did, with her and only her. "What the hell are you doing about this?" he barked.

Several of the other forensics staff gave her a quick glance before sliding away to continue working elsewhere.

Kate answered him just as strongly as he had called her out. "Everything I can."

And, with that, he glared at her for a moment longer, then his shoulders slumped. "Let's hope it's enough." He gave an exhausted headshake, as he pointed to the boy. "This is child abuse, long-term sustained child abuse. … I don't even need to do a full autopsy to see that. Stunted growth, broken bones. Look at that." He pointed to part of the little boy's arm that looked askew and fingers that were the same.

"Damn," she murmured, in quiet sympathy for the child who could no longer hear her. As she stared down at the boy, her heart ached.

Dr. Smidge groaned. "It breaks my heart to see this."

"Mine too," she whispered, as she looked at the other two bodies on the crosses. "Anybody ID these three yet?"

"Roger and Mary Brown," he snapped, "at least that's what the IDs on the bodies said."

"And the little boy?"

"He apparently is Daniel Woodward, or so his ID said."

"What ID was on the kid?"

"That would be his school card." The coroner pointed out the evidence bag on the side. "You'll have to see if he was in foster care, adopted, or something else. Who knows in a screwed-up mess like this." Smidge waved her off. "Now get out of my way. I've got work to do."

But she didn't move, neither did she talk to him again, and yet she made sure to keep out of his way. A case involving a child always hurt. But for Kate? … Remembering her younger brother was personal, how he'd been about this age when he'd disappeared. It was devastating, even all these years later.

Kate shook her head to clear those painful memories. She could still learn a lot about this case by just standing here and surveying what had been done to the bodies. So she let Smidge be and just continued her own observations.

None of the crosses were mounted to the wall. The father, or the male victim anyway, wasn't tiny, but he wasn't a big man either. She would have put his height about five seven or eight maybe, slim build, approximately 120 pounds. His face looked a little bit punched up, as if he'd had a tough time growing up somewhere along the line. The female victim was smaller. Her face was pristine though, not a bruise visible on her.

Kate walked closer and stared down at the woman who had been pierced with a stake through each palm, into the cross constructed with 2x4s that she'd been placed upon. Again, her body lying flat, and no blood was anywhere. That meant she hadn't been staked here, at least not while she had been alive. And, with that noted, chances were, they'd been killed elsewhere and had been brought in along with the crosses, and then crucified on site.

She faced Rodney and asked him, "How the hell do you get two large crosses inside this place?" She turned back to the crosses again. "What are they, six feet by four or so?"

He nodded. "Approximately that, yes, but really they're just two-by-fours, so they're more symbolic than functional crosses."

"Thank God for that," Kate murmured in a heartfelt whisper. "Imagine if these were intended to be functional." As she looked around the church, she was aware of other people all around, yet noted the quiet hush. The shock that something like this could happen at a place like this. The blasphemy of it. "I wonder if he expected the crosses to work upright, only to get here and realize that there really wasn't a wall where he could hang them."

"Not to mention," Rodney pointed out, "with their body weights, he would need something quite substantial to get them hoisted up and to keep them fastened to the crosses. Bodies are heavy, and their weight alone would have torn their flesh from the wood as they collapsed."

"So, what then? Chains to hoist them?" she asked.

"Maybe, but how do you throw a chain around something in here?" He pointed to the massive beams that held the cross beams up. "Not possible."

"Which is the problem," she agreed, with a nod. "Maybe lying them down in the church was enough." She stared at the dead woman. "She's also small-framed, like the man, but not a bruise on her face," she muttered.

"You're thinking bruises are somewhere else?" Smidge asked, stepping beside them.

She nodded slowly. "We only saw the upper chest of each victim, with the word *Forgive* cut in each. So, yeah, I wonder what the rest of her body looks like. If the little boy was abused," she suggested, shaking her head, an expression of deep sorrow on her face, "what are the chances that she was abused as well?"

"I mean," Smidge began, "it's not unheard of for a mother to abuse her child, though it's rarer. But for husband and father to abuse both? That is common."

"Unfortunately," Kate added. "However, from our preliminary findings, this couple was part of a polygamous group. So multiple sex partners could be involved." She eyed the clergy again, who were solemn but huddled together, as if trying to keep the sins of man away from them, keeping them untouched by the evil that had entered their holy space. She looked over at Dr. Smidge. "Anybody talked to them yet?"

He snorted. "I'm not," he declared, pointing at her. "You've got to be good for something." And, with that, he went back to his work.

She looked at Rodney and nodded toward the clergy, but he shook his head.

"This will need a woman's touch."

She rolled her eyes at that. "I'm pretty sure you're Catholic."

"Exactly," he agreed quietly. "*Also* why I'm not the person to be talking to them." When she looked at him in surprise, he shrugged. "It would be hard for me to go against a lifetime of upbringing about how to deal with these priests," he explained in a businesslike tone. "I can't *not* talk to them in a certain way or even be objective about it. You, on the other hand, won't be encumbered by my beliefs and can interview them with zero reverence or respect."

She stared at him in shock. "I'll respect them," she stated in protest. "Why would you even think that?"

He shrugged. "You'll treat them with respect as *people*, but you won't necessarily respect their position in the church or feel that they should be kept untouched by all this."

She gave a hoarse laugh at that. "You've got to wonder why the hell their church was targeted." And, with that, she turned and strolled toward the three robed men. As she approached, she identified herself and held up her badge, but they didn't even look at it. They stared at her, each holding something in their hands.

The one in the middle had a Bible, and she thought the other two held a rosary, but she couldn't be sure. "I'm sorry that this crime has entered your house of worship," she noted calmly. "However, I do have some questions that I need to ask."

The priest with the Bible nodded his head. "Ask your questions, and the sooner you can remove these poor souls from our church, the sooner we can go about cleaning up the vestiges of evil having walked our hallways."

With that, she understood what Rodney meant about how to talk to them. "I can do my part in that," she replied briskly. "However, the forensic team will likely be here for several hours, if not longer. Don't expect to have this place back anytime today."

At that blunt end of her tongue, the priests looked visibly shocked.

She nodded. "If you have any services or events planned for the rest of the day, you'll need to cancel them."

"Impossible," the same priest noted in a strident voice. "We have choir practice and, of course, our evening service."

She looked back at the forensic techs, then shook her head. "They'll be at least six if not ten hours," she shared. "I don't know exactly how much time, but there will be no curtailing of the time they need to properly do their jobs," she stated, her voice firm.

That tone of voice earned her myriad protests from her onlookers.

"I'm sure, as caretakers of this beautiful space, you also want to ensure that these poor souls are taken care of and that whoever did this to them is also caught and held accountable."

The man holding the Bible nodded. "Absolutely we want him caught," he replied, "but we are not about revenge or retribution. Whoever did this is another poor soul."

"Maybe so," she agreed, "but there was a reason for anyone to do this. I also need to ask you if the word *forgive* carved in the chests of these poor victims means anything to you." When they looked at her in surprise, she shrugged. "Is it a part of your holy message or some ritual? Some word this killer would feel as if he needed to remind us of … in order to send his victims to heaven or something?"

"Ah," said the priest on the left. "You're a nonbeliever."

She looked at him with a calculated gaze. "Can you answer my question, please?"

He nodded. "Outside of our fundamental belief that everyone should be forgiven of all sins, especially of our own," he began, "*forgive* is a part of any of our religious teachings and likewise is a part of many religious sacraments."

"Right." She then asked, "Do you happen to recognize any of these victims?"

All three priests shook their heads.

"No? You're sure you've never seen them at a service? They aren't part of a choir? Anything?"

And again all three shook their heads in unison.

"Do you help the homeless? Do you operate soup kitchens? Do you do anything like that?" When they looked at her oddly, she shrugged. "Look. This is not my area of town, and I don't attend your church," she added. "So I do need some idea if these victims could have come here at another point in time, maybe when you were reaching out to help the poor?"

"How would you know if they were poor?" asked a priest, with a pointed look. "They are well dressed, and it doesn't appear that they are suffering."

She frowned at him. "I guess that depends on your definition of *suffering*, Father. Look closely at that little boy. He has suffered and suffered tremendously for a very long time."

Rodney stepped up behind her just then.

The priests turned to him, with almost a visible sense of relief on their faces, perhaps at the prospect of speaking to a man instead.

Rodney introduced himself and again apologized for this tragic deed left in their church, then murmured, "We do have names for them. Let's see if they are familiar to any of you." As he read off the names, all three priests shook their heads in unison.

"No," stated the man in the middle with the Bible. "Those are not names I know." He looked at the others, and they shook their heads as well.

"Okay, so on to the next question," Kate said. "We don't have a time of death established yet, but do you have CCTV cameras that would allow us to see when these crosses and the bodies were brought into the church?"

The priests gaped at her in surprise and shook their heads. "No, of course not," replied the priest holding the Bible, with a quick shake of his head. "There are no cameras or security of any kind. This is the house of God."

Kate's gaze froze on the main priest, who always seemed to be nodding or shaking his head, while the others seemed to follow his lead. "So, there's nothing such as surveillance here?"

They shook their heads.

"What about when the doors are locked? What time is that?"

Again the one in the middle smiled. "The doors are never locked."

She frowned at that, but he still gave her a bland smile.

"Is that common for all churches?" she asked.

"I don't know about all churches," he replied. "It has never been an issue for us, and we like to leave the house of our Lord open and accessible for everyone's purpose and need."

She nodded. "I'm sure that, for some, … it's a great comfort," she murmured, "and, for others, a great opportunity."

At that, their smiles fell away. "I think your work must give you a very dark view of life," the Bible holder suggested, and she gave him a thin smile. Rodney also gave them an apologetic look.

"To some extent that could be true," she admitted, "but they're all God's children, are they not?"

He nodded. "They all are, indeed."

She asked a few more questions and then returned to where Smidge was working.

He looked over at her as she arrived and glared at her again. She glared right back. "So, the Fathers know nothing about whoever might have done this. They know nothing about the victims. They don't recognize the faces and neither do they know the names," she shared in a singsong voice. Smidge rolled his eyes, and she nodded. "Same as always, isn't it? Nobody knows anything. Nobody saw anything, and nobody heard anything. … And yet it could not have been a very quiet process to have brought this in piecemeal, first the three bodies, not to mention the lumber for the crosses, and especially to put this together so they were left this way. So, I find it all hard to believe. Wouldn't they have needed a drill to put those stakes in?"

Smidge shook his head. "Chances are they were delivered with a sledge hammer, and, as you can see, there's no blood."

"No blood, I get it, meaning they were not killed here," she declared, with a nod. "And the two-by-fours, even with just one stake to begin making the crosses, they would collapse and be quite easy to carry in."

Smidge smiled up at Kate and nodded. "Exactly. I will start with an autopsy on the woman first."

She eyed him. "Why?"

His gaze was assessing as he replied, "You tell me."

"Because I think she's been abused beyond that pristine face of hers," she shared quietly. "I think she's been as abused as the boy was."

He nodded. "Hence the reason I'm starting with her. What I don't know is whether her husband's the abuser of one or both. Or whatever other partner was allowed into their polygamous group," Smidge added.

"And that," Kate noted, "is something I will work hard to find out."

***

SIMON HAD LEFT several messages, but he hadn't gotten any response, which usually meant that Kate was busy. Simon would just have to wait his turn. Most of the time he was totally okay with that, but, when she caught a new case, particularly if it were a fresh one, it could be hours upon hours before she got back to him. He sat on his couch with a glass of wine, staring out his big picture window in his penthouse at the glorious view of Vancouver, feeling an odd sense of peace inside. Although a sense of peace was an understatement, since it was more of an eerie feeling that he had from time to time.

The last of Kate's cases that he'd helped on had given him a very strange feeling. To know that somebody had held something against Simon or had seen him as an excuse to attack people whose lives he had touched briefly wasn't a great feeling. However, now that the case was over and would wind its way through the courts, at least he had that sense of closure.

He knew that, for Lisa Sands, the horror would continue, not to mention that Helen had been very much Lisa's right-hand person, somebody Lisa had depended on to get through the days at the shelter. So Helen's absence and Helen's guilt would never be any easier on Lisa.

Simon shifted on his couch, checked his watch, and, just as he was relaxing, his phone rang. He snatched it off the coffee table, wincing as he realized how eager he was.

"Hey."

Kate's tired voice came through the phone, and he winced a second time. "I've got food."

She snorted. "I'm really glad to hear you know how to get to a girl's heart."

"I have opened a brand-new bottle of wine. I have food, and I have a shower that is big enough for the both of us, plus a very cozy bed," he added calmly, his voice gentle. "Why don't you come here?"

"I'm sitting in my car outside a church," she murmured.

"A church?" he asked, as his eyebrows shot up. "Is there something I should know about?"

"What? You're asking if I came to pray or something?" she asked, a note of humor in her voice.

"I'm not too sure of the reasons that would take you to a church," Simon replied, "but, given your job, it could be both good and bad."

"I'll come to you," she said abruptly. "We'll talk when I get there." With that, she hung up.

Simon quickly sent a message down to his doorman, letting him know that Kate would be on her way. And then Simon got up, double-checked that the wine bottle was open to breathe, and brought out the food he had picked up earlier. He quickly set out a platter. He'd planned on a charcuterie board, hoping she would come. This time it worked out; it certainly didn't always with her. He cut big thick slabs of the French bread, buttered them, and set them off to one side, as he started to lay out meat and pickles and assorted fresh vegetables.

By the time he was done, and it was arranged to his satisfaction, the elevator opened, and there was Kate, leaning against the doorjamb. He just opened his arms. She walked into them, and he closed them around her, holding her. After a moment, she tilted her head back and smiled up at him. "This is definitely more soothing than the church."

"I don't know," he said, with half a smile, as he flicked her nose gently, then helped her out of her coat. "For a lot of people, a church is a place of solace, a place of healing."

"Today," she stated quietly, "it was a place of murder."

He stiffened, but that was the only way he let her words affect him. With her coat off, he led her into the kitchen and handed her a glass of wine. She sniffed the top of it, inhaling the aroma, and smiled. Then she had a sip and looked up at him with a happy sigh. "This is pretty nice to come back to."

"Sure it is," he agreed, "particularly after what you are dealing with in a church, but here? You can forget about it. Here you can just park it and can keep your thoughts on the present instead."

"Particularly," she pointed out, looking at him from the corner of her eye, "as this one has nothing to do with you."

"You have no idea how grateful I am," he replied, as he

led her to the couch. "I was just thinking how glad I am to have that last scenario over and done with."

"Yes, that one is over, and now I have this one," she murmured. "At least we had a few days that were calm, quiet, and peaceful, outside of the usual stabbings, gang shootings, and drunk drivers killing people." She shook her head. "It's bad enough with the full team at work, but Andy's still out on medical leave. I haven't even had a chance to see about his current status." She sighed.

"Do you want to tell me about the church case, or will that just make it worse?"

She hesitated, then shrugged. "You'll hear about it in the news soon enough anyway." So she slowly, interjected with lots of wine, explained what had happened.

He stared at her through the whole thing, wondering how she could possibly cope with the dregs of society like this. He had the heebie-jeebies just hearing about the shit that she saw on a daily basis. "That sounds incredibly ugly and very sad."

She nodded. "I didn't want to go into the church when I realized a child had been involved. And yet it's a small mercy that he was dead before being staked. ... It seems better somehow, at least for now. Putting them on the cross didn't kill any of them." She shrugged. "There was no bleeding from the bodies at that point in time, so clearly that was done post-mortem."

"That's something at least."

"They were also laid down on the floor instead of standing upright or hung on a wall, whether because the killer lacked the knowledge or the ability to manhandle that weight or was simply incapable of it. I don't know," she admitted. "I hate to say it, but it could have simply been their first time doing this."

Simon looked at her sharply and wondered out loud, "Why would you hate for that to be the case?"

"Because, when I see something like this," she explained, with a quick glance at him, "I always worry that something else will follow."

His wince was quick and furious. "Damn it," he swore, as he put down his glass of wine, hopped to his feet, and paced, his way of working off stress.

She nodded. "See? It doesn't help if I wear off my stress by coming here and adding to yours." He stopped, and glared at her, and she threw up her hands. "I don't want you getting upset over all the craziness in my world."

"If you can handle the craziness in my world," he stated pointedly, "I think I can handle the craziness in yours. But, as somebody who had a difficult childhood, as you well know, I really don't want to deal with thinking about some asshole beating up a young boy to the point that he died."

"Rodney said something about the child dying from natural causes, and I got pretty upset because, of course, it's never natural causes. However, what Rodney meant was that the boy didn't die at the hands of this murderer—or at least I don't think so—and neither do I think that the actual beatings were close enough to the child's time of death for that to have been his cause of death. I really won't know until Smidge gets through the autopsies," she murmured. She dropped her head back against the couch and closed her eyes, still holding her wineglass.

A bit of wine remained in her glass, so Simon gently took it from her hand.

She opened her eyes and muttered, "I'm fine."

"Sure, you're fine," Simon agreed, "but, if you want to

just sleep, you can do that too."

She shook her head. "No way, the images are still way too close in my mind. If I go to sleep with that, I'll wake up with nightmares."

As somebody who understood nightmares all too well, Simon wouldn't argue with her. "Come and eat then." He reached out a hand to help her up from the couch. She stood up in a smooth, graceful movement, something he found surprising when she was so tired. Yet her body somehow kept her in a loose and yet strong stupor, and that he was amazed to see.

She strolled into the kitchen, then stopped when she saw the board. "I've seen things like this before," she said. "I just never knew what you were supposed to do with them."

He chuckled. "I think the general idea is that we eat what's on it." She frowned at him, and his grin widened. "Come on and sit down." He pulled out a chair for her, and she sat. Then he carried over the plates and the board. "Now it's pretty simple. Just pick food off the board any way you want. Put it on bread, don't put it on bread. … I really don't mind."

She reached for the largest piece of the French bread and loaded it with meat.

He chuckled. "Look at that. A girl after my own heart."

Then she slathered it with pickled onions and placed tomato slices on top, folding over the bread to hold it all in.

He stared, opened his mouth, and wondered if he should mention the idea of savoring one flavor at a time. Then he decided to not say a word, as she picked it up and started munching. She obviously enjoyed it, so he didn't really have anything to complain about.

Keeping his smile tucked firmly in his cheek, he chose a

slice of the bread himself, layered with a little bit of onion and a slice of meat. Then he cut that into quarters and proceeded to make himself four small sandwiches, all different.

She stopped and looked at his, looked at hers, then shrugged and continued to eat.

He burst out laughing. "There's no right or wrong way, Detective," Simon muttered, with an eye roll.

"Good thing because I have already messed it up."

"No, not at all. No messing up happens here," he explained. "What you're eating is just fine."

They ate in silence, and, when they were done, Simon gently placed a second glass of wine beside her. "Now, do you need a shower? Do you want bed? Do you want to go for a walk?"

She frowned and then nodded. "I would like a walk."

Simon nodded. "Sure, let's go. Anything that would help change the images and the activity happening in your brain."

"I've put a little bit of distance between me and the crime scene already," she noted. "The meeting with the clergy was a little uncomfortable too. Not from my perspective maybe, but definitely from theirs."

He flashed her a smile. "I can't imagine what they would even begin to think of you," he admitted.

"I don't know either," she murmured. "They didn't like my questions, and I didn't like their answers."

"Such as?"

She told him, and he burst out laughing. "I'm surprised that they don't lock up the church," he shared, nodding in agreement, "but I guess the idea is that it's supposed to be a place of sanctuary, a place of healing, a place of maybe a heaven-on-earth type thing. Therefore, if they leave the doors unlocked, for people to go in and out all hours of the night, how would somebody know that nobody else was there?"

She stared at him in surprise and nodded. "That's a good question. How would our perp know that nobody was around? I was assuming that the killer had somehow found his way into the church after-hours, and nobody would be there, but I also forgot to ask if anybody would have come through the church yesterday evening …" She stopped and frowned at the thought. "They had an evening service set for tonight, and they weren't happy when I made them cancel it."

"Oh, ouch, now that probably would pretty-well upset them."

"Forensics, you know," she said, with a shrug. "They need as long as they need."

"Oh, I understand your point of view," Simon noted, "but I also understand theirs."

"Did you ever go to church?"

He sighed, then shook his head slightly. "No, my grandmother used to take me every once in a while, but more as a case of, … I don't know, a ritual more than anything. You have to understand that these priests don't know what life is really like. They think of evil completely differently than what most of us understand it to be," he shared. "I never really understood what my grandmother meant for me to get from church. However, I did go to church myself a couple times, a couple different churches actually," he noted, with a smile, "more out of curiosity than anything. I had friends who attended regular events, so I used to go with them, but I couldn't say I ever felt the need to return to any of them."

"I'm not so sure I've ever been inside one before today," she quickly shared. "Maybe that's why it seemed a little on the intimidating side. It was foreign and something I have no experience with." Kate looked up at Simon. "Rodney, being raised a devout Catholic himself, may have been a little disturbed that I didn't have the same sense of respect for the building or what it represented. I mean, honestly, the building itself was glorious. I don't think Rodney's mad at me. It just reveals yet another difference between us."

"Differences are fine too," Simon pointed out. "Nothing wrong with that."

"Maybe not," she murmured. "At the same time, I didn't want to go in there. I didn't want to see what was in there."

"You still want to go for that walk?"

"Yeah, let's do it," she replied, "and see if I can clear my head."

CHAPTER 3

OUTSIDE, ALONG THE water's edge, Kate and Simon sat quietly on a bench, watching the sun slowly go down. She stretched and rotated her neck and her shoulders. "That feels better."

"Sometimes you just need to get out and to forget about life for a bit," he said.

"And sometimes, when you try to do that"—she smirked at him—"it doesn't work."

He smiled, then nodded. "That's very true."

"So, how was your day?" She turned to stare at him intently. "God, I'm a terrible person. I forgot to even ask you."

"Oh, you're awful. Absolutely terrible."

"Hey," she muttered, as she punched him lightly.

"Ouch, ouch, ouch, that's abuse too, you know?" he teased.

She laughed. "It's nice that we can laugh and joke together, even after the day we had."

"It *is* very nice," he agreed. "Sometimes that's what both of us need."

"So, it wasn't a good day for you?"

"It wasn't a bad day either," he noted. "I mean, some of the buildings are going fine, but some of them? Not so much."

"Are you back up to full staff again?"

"No, we're still looking for more skilled tradesmen, but we're getting there." He gave her half a smile. He looped an arm around her shoulders and tucked her up close. "This is a particularly nice spot, don't you think?"

"You're lucky you have this." Kate motioned at the False Creek harbor and all the beautiful lights and buildings, enjoying the twinkling of the city around her.

"I know," he replied. "Believe me. I know."

"And that's one of the differences between you and a lot of people," she added, with a smile. "I don't ever really get a sense of arrogance, of being better than others, because you've got all this." She looked from him to the view around them. "At least I feel as you really appreciate this."

"I absolutely do." Simon nodded. "I'm glad you picked up on that because it always pisses me off when I see people being arrogant about what they have. They could lose it all in a blink of an eye. Even if it isn't about money, you could lose your health or even people who are important to you. So it's really not a smart idea to take any of it for granted." He shifted on the bench. "Are you okay, or do you want to keep walking?"

"I wouldn't mind walking a bit more." She stood and shook out her legs.

"Time to do more workouts?"

"I need to," she agreed, "if for nothing else but the stress relief, not to mention staying fit."

"And you have department physicals you have to pass too, don't you?"

"Yeah, we sure do," she stated. "I haven't had any issues over my fitness, thankfully. But you know that, if you let it go too far, it's harder to come back from," she murmured.

He nodded and looped his arm through hers. "I think

you're a long way from that."

She smiled, and, as they walked, she began to feel a sense of peace. "Now if only this calm would last," she muttered. "The second team is working on this case, so I can sleep tonight. However, if they catch another case tomorrow, I might not see you for a few days."

"Yeah, let's just hope you get some rest while you have a chance."

KATE WOKE UP the next morning, stretched, and yawned happily. "Wow," she murmured. "Coming here last night really was a good idea. Thank you."

He rolled over, gave her a gentle smile and a quick kiss on top of her head. "And it never hurts to have a little exercise to go to sleep with."

She smiled and hopped up. "Race you to the shower." As it was, he beat her there, but that was okay, since he proved that being a winner in the shower race was equally great for the loser. By the time she came out, delightfully relaxed and destressed, she quickly dressed. As she walked into the kitchen a few minutes later, he was pouring a hot cup of coffee for her.

"Look at all this attention. You're spoiling me." She checked her watch. "I can't be late," she muttered. "Too many things I need to get going on." She yawned, and he frowned at her. "I'm fine. I got as much sleep as I'll get and a whole lot more than I do on many other nights."

Simon frowned. "That's one of the things that always worries me. You're constantly burning the candle on both ends."

"Of course I am, but I'm used to it."

"That doesn't mean it's a good thing."

She smiled at him. "See you tonight? If …" He nodded. "How about back at my place?" she asked.

"How about not?" he replied, with an eye roll.

She frowned. "It's not *that* bad, plus I need fresh clothes."

"Fine. … We'll go to your place, pick up fresh clothes, maybe head out to dinner and spend some quality time together. Unless you need to work the case," he clarified, as if suddenly remembering the number of times she'd had to cancel.

"I'm sorry." She sent an apologetic glance to him. "It goes along with the job."

He just waved her off. "Have a good day."

She gave him a big kiss and raced out. Waving at Harry at the door, she called back to him, "Have a good day." Edgar was obviously not on duty yet today. She only ever saw him when she came in late, so Edgar must be the nighttime doorman, while Harry was the face she saw most mornings, when she left Simon's place.

She jumped into her vehicle and headed for the station. She stopped and froze at the doorway to the bullpen, the office noise filled with excitement, yet not in a good way. She asked, "What did I miss?"

"You didn't answer your phone," Rodney said, looking over at her. "Where were you?"

"I was over at Simon's. Why?" she asked. Pulling out her phone, she groaned. "Sorry, it looks like I forgot to charge it."

"That"—Rodney shook his head—"is definitely not a good thing right now."

"Why is that?"

He looked at her and, in an exasperated tone, replied, "Another church."

She repeated, "*Another* church?"

"Another church, with two victims this time." And, with that, Rodney gestured toward the exit. "Let's go. Hope you got sleep because it doesn't look like you'll get another chance for a while."

As she walked into the second church, her heart ached when she saw a repeat of yesterday. Another woman and another man. Thankfully no child. "We don't even have all the details on the first victims yet and now this," she muttered.

"No, and the media will be all over this soon, and we'll be in for it big-time. "We need"—Rodney looked at those gathered around—"a liaison to put out messages to the press to keep people off our backs, so we can do our jobs."

"I'm not holding my breath." Inside the church she stopped and took a moment to just assess. It was calm—too calm for her taste. She looked around at the doors, at the huge stained-glass windows, and whispered to him, "Another Catholic church?"

He nodded.

"I wonder if that's deliberate."

"You don't think it is? I just assumed so."

"I wonder whether Catholic churches provide the best opportunity for something like this—with their unlocked doors policies—or our perp's still sending messages that may or may not mean anything in this case."

Rodney seemed to ponder that as they walked forward.

Smidge bounced to his feet and snapped, "There you are."

"Yes, here I am," she replied in a mild tone as she

stepped up beside him, only to look down at the woman and to wince at the sight of her. "Good God, did the killer do this to her?" Her face had been beaten, and it very much resembled hamburger.

"I don't know," the coroner replied, "at least not yet. I'll have to get back to you on that."

Kate nodded but didn't say anything, even though she was desperate to ask him when he would get back to her on the other three victims he already had. However, it was one thing if they gave him one victim, but giving him three and now two more? That would make it hard to get answers at all. She had to wonder if that wasn't part of the killer's plan. She looked over at Rodney. "Why pile up the number of victims? One would be enough to make a statement."

"But not enough to punish the others," he stated.

She frowned. "Pardon?"

He shrugged. "I mean, I could be wrong, but this feels very much like our killer's punishing somebody. He is punishing these people for some twisted shit. Are these victims part of the polygamous group too?"

"But who's being punished though?" Kate asked quietly. "I mean, look at this. ... The woman's face has already been beaten to a pulp. So our killer's punishing someone who has already been abused?"

Rodney tilted his head. "And yet we don't know whether our perp did it or somebody else did."

"No, I get that," she murmured. "Still, it doesn't seem as if forgiveness would be part of this. If the message were *repent*, I might understand it more. But to carve *Forgive* into every dead body ..."

Smidge stopped and looked at her. "Why do you say that?"

"Because that would suggest the victims had done something wrong and that the murderer wanted them to repent, maybe to carve out their sins. But to add *Forgive* to these victims, yet see them in this shape? I don't understand."

Smidge nodded. "I have an idea on it, but I'm not willing to share just yet."

When she glared at him, he smiled at her. "Not yet," he repeated. "I want to get into these autopsies first."

"Yet, what will that have to do with it?" she asked, staring at him.

"I'll tell you when I'm ready to tell you," he declared.

She had to be satisfied with that. As she walked beside the body of the male victim, she crouched and pulled the sheet off his face. His face was also bruised, and yet she wasn't sure how recent that was either.

She stood and turned to look for anybody from the church she could talk to. Off to the side was an elderly man, sitting in the first pew, wearing a robe and a cleric's collar, staring up at the cross and obviously praying. She walked over, sat down beside him, and waited.

When he finally took a heavy inhale and released it, he looked at her sideways. "Thank you."

Surprised, she asked, "For what?"

"For allowing me a chance to finish."

She nodded. "I have to ask a lot of you, Father, and I'm hoping it will be easier for you if we can work together."

"In what way?"

"The forensics people will need your church for a while," she explained in an apologetic tone. "In other words, the church will need to be closed to the public, and, if you have any sessions, services, kitchen help, I don't know—whatever programs you might have set for today—they all need to be canceled." He just looked at her, and she nodded. "When evil comes to the heart of us," she noted quietly, "you must let those of us who fight evil do our jobs."

"Is that how you see yourself?" he asked, his tone soft.

She thought about it for a moment and nodded. "In some ways, yes. What I do is not easy, and it's not something I would wish on anybody." She added, "I've seen things that I would hope that most of the world never sees."

"I can imagine," he replied, as he held his gaze from going back to the bodies.

"But still, there must be a force that deals with people who can do something like this," she stated. "While you have your own ways, I have mine."

At that, a glimmer of a smile crossed his face, and he nodded. "Understood."

He slowly got up, and she wondered if she should reach out and help him. He was a little on the creaky tottering side, but he took several sure-footed steps toward the church's cross hanging above the altar, so she held back the urge to help him.

"The Lord works in mysterious ways, and a reason is behind all this," he began, "even if only to bring one extra soul to this church." He nodded, turning to look at her. "So I accept His methods for what they are."

"What are they?" she asked.

"Strange, unusual, but still His," he stated firmly.

She didn't say anything to that, just nodded, as he walked into an office farther up the aisle. Kate returned to Smidge. "Do we have an ID on the victims?"

He nodded. "Found in the back pockets, same as the first time." Pulling them out, he added, "I'll send you photos of these when we're done, but it looks like we have Mary

Holley and Jacob Holley."

Kate nodded but winced at the name Mary. "We're a little overwhelmed with *Marys* lately."

The coroner nodded. "And yet it's a good strong stalwart name," he noted, "so we can't blame those with the name."

"No, I can't blame any of the victims."

"Hold that thought," Smidge said, rolling his eyes. "You may also want to stop and to take a moment because, if you're not associating the victims here as also being perpetrators, you might be missing the bigger picture."

And, with that, something clicked in the back of her mind. *A polygamous group of abusers?* "Wow, that's your working theory regarding these two couples so far?" She took another look at the battered faces, coming at it from a different perspective now.

"Don't mention this yet. Not until I see more on these two bodies." He raised his chin to a group nearby. "Meanwhile, you need to start talking to them. I saw that group of people here earlier. If you come back to me in a bit, … I might have a little more for you."

Taking that as a dismissal, she turned and headed over to the group who had found the bodies. As she approached, she noted six women, sitting together in a huddle, tears in their eyes, all in one pew. Kate walked to the pew just ahead of the group and turned to face them. "Ladies, I am Detective Kate Morgan," she stated. "I need to ask you some questions about what you found this morning."

"We found evil," one of the women replied, tears in her eyes. "Evil like I have never seen before."

"And hopefully," Kate replied in a firm voice, "you'll never see it again."

The woman stared at her. "I don't know how you could

even begin to do this job."

Kate gave her a small smile. "Somebody needs to catch a killer, and sometimes it takes those of us with our own calling to do it," she replied. "So, maybe let's keep the conversation to the questions at hand."

"Maybe," the woman grumbled, and then she shuddered. "Ask your questions, so I can go home. I feel the need for a hot cup of tea, then maybe I'll go back to bed."

Kate understood the sentiment, but it wouldn't do her any good right now. As she looked at these women and carefully asked each of her questions, it quickly became apparent that they had walked in as a group, several ahead of the others, all talking and laughing, until they saw something up at the front by the altar.

"I was the one who raced forward," one woman admitted, "because I thought I saw a foot, and I was afraid it was Father Macmillan. He's at that age, you know. … Instead it was this." She pointed deeper into the building.

"Indeed." Kate asked, "Did you recognize the victims?"

All six women shook their heads. "No," replied one of the elderly women. "I've never seen them before. I can't imagine anybody would have done anything to deserve this."

"I can't imagine anybody deserving this either," Kate noted, "and I'll do my best to find out who is doing this. If you recognize these names, please let me know." She read off the names of the five victims to date, and the women shook their heads.

The same elderly woman spoke again. "No, those aren't names I know." She looked at the other women with her, and every one of them shook their heads.

"So, none of those names mean anything to you?" Kate asked again.

"No."

The youngest of the group, who looked to be in her early twenties, jumped to her feet. "Why are you asking us these questions?"

Kate turned to her. "Because these two were found here in this church, and one would think that maybe they were members."

"But following that thinking," the young woman argued, "you would then be thinking that we had something to do with it."

Surprised, Kate frowned at her, then slowly shook her head. "No, I'm not thinking that at all. Look. You are witnesses, the first to find the bodies. You are upset at that, I'm sure, … but it's far too early to even consider who might have done it," Kate explained in a calm tone.

The other woman shuddered. "I don't know them."

"Thank you." Kate looked over at the others, and they were all just huddled together, arms wrapped around each other. She got all their names and contact information. When finished with her questions, she let them go.

As a group, they basically picked up their feet and raced away. As they headed outside, Rodney walked over to Kate. "Anything?"

"No, nothing," she said, "nothing useful anyway. The six women came in together. Crap, I didn't ask what they were here for." Kate shook her head in frustration. "Damn it. Anyway, as soon as they arrived, they found the victims at the altar, where they are now. Of course they took off and called for help."

"We can be grateful that they returned," Rodney stated.

She eyed him intently.

Rodney shrugged, then added, "Particularly in cases like

this. I mean, a lot of innocent people would be terrified and would run for help and would not come back."

"I don't know that they ran for help, but they certainly didn't want to stick around, … even now."

"Would you?" he asked, with a note of humor, and she smiled at him.

"Hey, I'd go home now if I could. Is our shift over?" Kate teased.

"Oh, I don't think this shift will be over for a while," Rodney said, with a sad smile. "Not until we get some answers, that's for sure."

Seeing Father Macmillan returning with a thick mug in his hand, she walked to his side. "May we ask you to leave, please, and to let the forensics team do their jobs?"

He looked at her with a steady gaze. "Surely my being here isn't hurting anything."

"I'm not certain about that," she replied. "They work better when they're not being watched, as we all do."

He studied her and then nodded. "That is true. … I'm not here to judge. I was trying to find a way to ease the suffering of the souls on the floor in this holy place."

"And that is definitely your job, not mine," she noted quietly, "but, for now, please let us do our jobs, and maybe you could do yours elsewhere, *huh*?"

He nodded. "I'll try."

"By the way, I do have a couple other questions." She asked about security and whether any clergy from the church would be here in the middle of the night.

He frowned at her. "Not unless we're called. The doors remain open to this public area, and, yes, in the past we have had some people who have desecrated the church." He took a moment to think it through. "In the end it was thought that the church provided solace for enough people that we should keep it open."

"Do people come in the evenings?"

"In the evening, yes," he confirmed. "In the nighttime? Not so much anymore."

"Why so?"

"We used to have quite a few people here in the middle of the night to deal with grief, but after two of the older ones in that group passed away, it is less of a habit now."

"And the younger people?"

"We're lucky if they even come to church anymore," he said sadly.

She wasn't sure what to say to that because she was pretty sure he would put her in that same category. She pondered anything else to ask and then added, "If you don't have any security, I'll have to check out the street cams." He looked at her silently, and she shrugged. "I hope we find some vehicle that may have come through in the evening," she explained, looking around the church. "These people didn't walk here themselves." Then she stopped and frowned. "Or did they?"

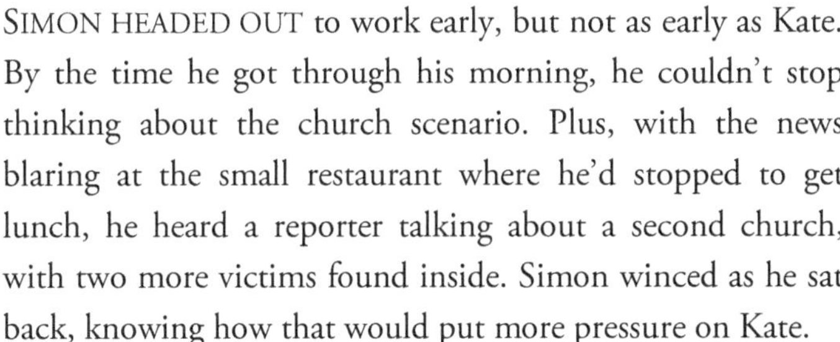

Simon headed out to work early, but not as early as Kate. By the time he got through his morning, he couldn't stop thinking about the church scenario. Plus, with the news blaring at the small restaurant where he'd stopped to get lunch, he heard a reporter talking about a second church, with two more victims found inside. Simon winced as he sat back, knowing how that would put more pressure on Kate.

One of the frustrations of her job, he knew, was the lack of progress in a timely manner. Autopsies and forensics both took time. There was this time period before there could even be any forensic determination, and fiber analysis, tox screens, and things like that could take far longer.

He sent her a quick text, with a small heart emoji. **I heard on the news about the second church.**

She sent back a thumbs-up, which essentially confirmed that she got his message, and that was all she was prepared to say at the moment, something so typical of Kate.

Hearing his name called, Simon looked back to see an old friend walking toward him with a smile on his face.

"Simon, damn, I haven't seen you in forever."

"And yet I'm still here," he replied, with a wry look at his friend. "Can't say I've moved very far. How are you doing, Bartlett?"

"You're still in Vancouver, *huh?*"

"That's where you find me now. Where are you living?"

"Here." He grinned. "I'm not sure staying was the best decision, but, hey, it's where headquarters is based and the family so …"

"As long as you're happy." Simon pointed to the counter and said, "I'm having lunch. Why don't you grab something and join me?"

Bartlett quickly walked up to the front counter, ordered soup and a sandwich, then returned to sit with him. "So, tell me. What's new and different?"

"I don't know that there's anything new or different," Simon said, with a shrug. "I'm still rehabbing buildings. What about you?"

"I invested in a couple startups that are doing well. Other than that, it seems like it's the same old, same old all the time." He laughed. "You hooked up with someone worthy or still on the lookout?"

"I'm dating a cop, so that's different." His friend blanched, then looked at him in shock. Simon nodded. "Right? Who would have thought it?"

"Not me," Bartlett admitted. "You've generally avoided romantic entanglements with anybody like that."

"Apparently I'm a sucker for this one," he shared, with half a smile.

"As long as you're happy," he said doubtfully. "I guess that brings up the point I was wondering about when I saw you."

"What's that?"

"Are you still playing all the time?"

"Not all the time, but some. Sure," Simon replied. "Why?"

Bartlett winced. "I could use some cash."

"Ah." Simon nodded. "I'm not sure that a poker game is the way to get cash, that's for damn sure. When you get on a losing streak, it can be brutal."

"But you never seem to have losing streaks, like the rest of us, do you?"

"Sure, I do," Simon noted calmly, having an idea where this conversation would go and wondering if their meetup was as random as it had first appeared. "Besides, I haven't been at a game in quite a while."

Bartlett didn't say anything at first, just nodded. "You're welcome to join the game tonight, if you want to though."

"No, I'm good." Simon shrugged. "I haven't been for a while, not feeling the inclination."

"That's the thing, when you feel the inclination, you get lucky, and the rest of us back off because we know that'll be a bad deal for us."

"Ha. It's never a bad deal for you guys because I never

go in for the jugular, like some do."

Bartlett winced. "Is that jab at me?"

"No, sure isn't," Simon declared, "but playing really isn't what I'm into right now." They finished their meals, and then Bartlett stood.

"Nice talking to you anyway." He dropped a card on the table. "If you feel like you need to get that game going again, give me a shout."

"How come you're short on money anyway?" Simon asked, as he picked up the *investment broker* card and toyed with it. "Money problems don't really go well with your title—or successful startups."

"No, it sure doesn't," he conceded, with a quick shrug. "I made a few bad decisions," he muttered, "and it's having a pretty ugly effect on my life."

At that, Simon studied him closely, trying to figure out what Bartlett expected of Simon. "When you say, bad decisions, what does that mean?"

"It means, *bad* decisions." Bartlett waved his hand. "Don't worry about it. It's not that bad."

"And yet you came looking for players for a poker game to recoup some money?"

"You know that, once you're in that mental frame, these guys at the poker table? They always know. They know, and they come, and they clean up. I was hoping not to lose very much," he admitted. "I was hoping to maybe gain a whole lot."

"Ouch, poker games are not the way to replenish a fortune."

"And yet you seem to do it just fine."

He stared at Bartlett, not really sure how to respond to that. "I don't use it to replenish anything," he stated.

"Maybe that's the difference."

Bartlett sighed. "No, you're probably right, but sometimes you just don't know what you're supposed to do. Therefore, not anything you can do except try."

Simon watched him walk away, more than a little worried at how that conversation had gone. It wasn't the thing he liked hearing, and it sounded a whole lot more dire than Bartlett was willing to let on. At the same time, it wasn't Simon's business to get involved if he didn't have to. Frowning, he paid for his lunch, left a tip for the waitress, and headed out.

He hadn't walked very far when another poker buddy he knew, but not all that well, stepped forward and blocked his path. "So, how come you won't play with us anymore?"

Simon frowned at him. "It's not that I won't play with you anymore. I haven't been playing at all lately." Simon couldn't remember the guy's name, but he was fairly adamant about something. Though unsure of what that was, he sure seemed pissed off to think that maybe Simon didn't *need* to play. "I play when I want to play," Simon stated, giving the guy a verbal pushback, not for any other reason.

"Not everybody can survive without playing."

"That's your problem," Simon declared, wondering at both him and Bartlett turning up like this. "Bartlett is looking to play, but I'm not." And, with that, Simon walked around the man, who was still obstructing his path. "When I feel like it again, I'll come knock on your door."

And, with that, he was gone.

CHAPTER 4

KATE PINCHED THE bridge of her nose and just let her eyelids drift closed for a moment. She'd been staring at street cam footage for hours, determined to see who and what could possibly be showing up at the church. However, with just so much traffic, it was almost impossible to sort it out, and that just pissed her off even more. Somebody had to know if anybody would be there before depositing and posing the victims. The murderer had to know if this place would be effectively empty, and that meant he had to be casing it.

She wanted to think it was somebody who worked at the church or volunteered or even attended the church, but given the popularity of both churches, it had been a heartbreaking discovery to realize that, even with these street cameras, way too many people were involved to even begin to track.

Rodney sat down beside her, his tone low as he asked, "Any luck?"

She shook her head. "Hell no. That would make too much sense, wouldn't it?"

"These killers do this shit for a reason, and they won't make it easy on us to catch them."

"They never do," she muttered, as she looked up at him. "It's frustrating because there must be a record of this guy out there. Yet for all intents and purposes, … I can't find a thing, and, yeah, it is pissing me off."

"Sure it is," he agreed. "You like results."

She snorted. "Don't you?"

"Of course I do." He gave her a wave of his hand. "However, our search area is way too wide."

"I know."

Just then Sergeant Colby walked in. "Okay, let's get ready for the meeting." She looked over at Rodney, one eyebrow raised.

He shrugged, and Colby sighed. "Maybe you didn't get the memo," he said, with exaggerated politeness.

Frowning she checked her emails, but nothing was there.

Colby sighed. "About the church cases." He clapped his hands together. "Let's go." She followed him into the meeting room and sat down beside Rodney.

By the time they'd analyzed all the evidence, and the various theories had been kicked around, Colby turned and looked at Kate with a searching gaze. "What's your take on it?"

She frowned at him, then shrugged. "Other than possibly polygamous couples, related to some religious sect, engaged in abuse and with the need for forgiveness, I don't have a take yet," she admitted bluntly. "I don't like anything about this, especially when there are no street cams to show the same vehicle casing out both churches. Plus, there's no security, and our killer's obviously got some religious bent to deliver these five to Catholic churches." She groaned, dropping her head in her hands. "Five victims in forty-eight hours, and he's probably not done, and we haven't got a thing to go on."

"Any witnesses?"

"Nothing. The clergy are all calling his acts evil, and, when asked, apparently it's all God's will to just bring one more believer into the fold." She gave an eye roll. "I get that a lot of you probably follow the same thought process, but, for me, it's a load of crap."

Rodney snorted. "Way to let us know how you really feel, Kate."

"Give me a little bit longer and I will," she snapped, glaring at him. That shut him up, but she didn't really mean to get on anybody's case. "Look. I just don't get how anybody would have had this access, yet nobody saw anything."

"I think that's the biggest issue," Rodney confirmed. "These churches are wide open, yet we have absolutely nothing to go on."

At that, Colby looked over at their department's head analyst, Reese. "Do you have anything?"

She shook her head. "I've been pulling files, looking at anything that might be connected, but I don't really have much of a parameter. I haven't found any other cases like this, where the victims are displayed as if crucified on a cross."

"Were there any crucifixion-theme crimes in the last, I don't know," Kate thought about it and said, "fifty years?"

Reese frowned at her. "Did you just pull that number out of your ass?"

"Sure," she replied, with a smirk. "That's about as far back as generations would go."

"Meaning?"

"What if their father was killed this way? What if their grandfather did time for something like this? I don't know. I'm just throwing out ideas, and I'm thinking in terms of generations."

"It's a good thought," Colby stated, staring at her. Then he turned to the others. "Anything to add to that?"

"It's just typical that we have another sicko," Lilliana noted, "and that Kate would be thinking of something like that."

"I'm *not* thinking of something like that," Kate corrected quietly, understanding where Lilliana was coming from. Her tone toward Kate had always been harsh, but regardless Lilliana respected Kate's opinion, and that's what mattered. "I would cheerfully never choose to think in terms of sickos and serial killers again. However, we do have a serial killer with these five victims. And some sickos are involved with the prior abuse we are seeing in most of these victims too. … Plus our killer's not done, or, even if he *is* done, how is he choosing his victims?"

"I think that's one of the interesting things," Rodney pointed out, as he looked at the whiteboard of these recent victims. "We have five victims, though the little boy was deceased already, as far as we can tell, and, yes, we're still waiting for the coroner's reports." He shook his head. "But we also appear to have one beaten child, two beaten women, and two relatively untouched males. Why the *Forgive* message? Is the killer asking the victims to forgive themselves of their sins, so God will forgive them?"

Kate remained silent, while looking at him with a narrowed gaze. "You're thinking of it in terms of salvation?"

"Of course." Rodney gave a wave of his hand at the whiteboard. "It's a church."

She pondered that and nodded. "Okay, I'll give you that, but what if our killer is asking his victims to forgive him?" At that, there was silence.

Lilliana looked at her and then shook her head. "I mean, that's quite possible too. Not exactly the way I would have interpreted it though."

"How would you have interpreted it?" Colby asked, turning to look at Lilliana.

"I'm not exactly sure I can at the moment," she muttered. "This case is definitely an odd one, and yet, at the same time, the religious connotation can go both ways."

Colby nodded. "Do you forgive the person who beat you? Do you forgive the person who killed you? Are you supposed to forgive other things in life or is the killer asking for forgiveness for having killed these people?" With that, a heavy and lively discussion broke through, and finally Colby faced Kate. "Guess where I'm sending you?"

She glared. "Send somebody else," she replied.

He gave her a big smile. "Nope, you're the one who struggles the most with this, so you need to deal with it."

She rolled her eyes. "You know anybody else could deal with the shrink, not just me."

"But you appear to have a special knack for this mentality," Colby stated in a not-so-teasing tone, "so this one's yours."

She groaned. Absolutely no point in arguing about it, though she certainly didn't agree with him. She didn't agree with the shrink most times either, but she also hadn't given the new shrink much of a chance.

"You keep finding ways to get out of it," Colby noted smoothly, "which just means that you need to face it and need to deal with it. Besides, this shrink isn't a pedophile."

"And I suppose you told him that was my problem with coming in and talking to him?"

He gave her a ghost of a smile. "I should, shouldn't I?"

She rolled her eyes at that. "You'll do whatever you'll do," she muttered, "but that's hardly giving me a clear-cut and neutral take on talking to the shrink."

"Either way," Colby noted smoothly, "I want you down there talking to him today. Present all the facts and bring a profile of sorts back, and you'll be the lead psychoanalyst for the team on this one." He looked at his watch and frowned. "I told him that you'd be coming about now, so you'll probably be back here in, say, forty-five minutes." Checking his watch again, he nodded. "We'll reconvene then." With that, he got up and walked out.

Rodney tapped her on the shoulder and muttered, "Better take the glare off your face, before you get in trouble for it."

She closed her eyes and sank back. "Why is it so hard to go there?"

"You do have a bit of history, and, in some ways, we all do, but you're the one who's holding it against the new guy, so this is probably a good thing. You'll get a chance to work out the kinks in your attitude."

She stared at him, shook her head, and asked, "How can that be a good thing?"

"Because you have to get past your own judgments and fears," Rodney noted quietly. "Otherwise it'll impact every other case going forward. The department shrink's just a tool. Use him."

KATE PONDERED RODNEY'S words, as she headed down to this meeting she did not want with the new department psych. When she knocked on the open door, the admin looked at her and nodded her head, while staring her full in the face. "You can go right in."

Kate didn't say anything, just headed on into the inner room.

As she walked in, Dr. Dudley looked at her and smiled. "Ah, the woman who hates shrinks."

Her back stiffened, and she glared at him.

He held up a hand. "Sorry, not exactly guaranteed to put us on the right footing."

"No, it sure isn't," she snapped in a hard voice. "So now I will just put it out there that if you turn out to be a pedophile, like the last department shrink," she stated, with a stern look, "believe me. I'll throw your ass in jail too." She heard the admin gasp in horror out in the other room, but Kate was locked in a stare-down with the doctor in front of her.

He sighed. "Sit down," he said, with a clipped nod. "Obviously we'll have to work out a few issues before we get anywhere."

"You can start by apologizing for that comment as I walked in."

He looked at her and nodded. "You're right. I shouldn't have done that," he admitted, with a casual smile, "so I definitely apologize. I'm sorry."

She frowned, as she stared at him. "As long as I don't hear it again," she noted, "apology accepted."

"How can you accept an apology with a future condition on it?" he asked curiously.

She continued to stand there and stared at him. "If you're psychoanalyzing me already, I'm gone. But if this will be about the case, then I'll stay."

He laughed. "Are you always this prickly?" When she just glared at him, he nodded. "I'll take that as a yes." He shrugged and again pointed to the chair. "Sit down, Detective."

She took a seat, then waited for him to start.

"Obviously we've gotten off on the wrong foot," he repeated, with a knowing smirk. "I'll blame my predecessor for that because I can't believe I did anything to piss you off, outside of my profession," he clarified.

She shrugged. "Outside of being a shrink, no, you probably didn't." His smile was wide and infectious, and she found herself almost responding to it.

"I'll take that for the moment," he said. "It sounds like a compromise."

"I don't know about a compromise," she corrected, studying him closely, "but I won't necessarily rat your ass out for shitty behavior, at least not at the moment."

He swallowed and nodded. "I will take that under consideration." Then he gave her a broad smile. "Wow, you drive a tough bargain."

"No, I don't," she said, "not really. How about you stay in your lane, and I'll stay in mine."

At that, he looked at her, and a slow grin lit up his face. "You know what? I can do that. Can you?"

"I'm working on it," she shared bluntly.

He burst out laughing again. "I can appreciate that too." He nodded. "Now, let's get down to business." And, with that, she told him about the case they had. His questions were hard and furious, and a lot of them she couldn't answer.

"I have no idea on the forensics yet. I just told you that," she snapped, her tone sharp. "When we get them in, I'll send them to you. Right now, we have, from the first crime scene, three victims, with one word carved into their chest. ...

Forgive. Done with something crude, like a knife. The boy was dead first, and we aren't sure about the other two. They weren't killed at the church, though they were staked and strung up on site. Same thing with the second crime scene, except no child involved. Two victims, *Forgive* on their chests, staked to and strung up on crosses at another Catholic church."

Dudley nodded, thinking about it. "What's your take on it?" he asked suddenly.

"I don't have a take on it yet," she replied.

"Yes, you do," he disagreed. "Your mind is running a mile a minute on it."

"I came here to get a word from the pro," she replied, "and that would be you in this instance, so what I think at this point is irrelevant."

"And yet, at the same time, you don't really have any faith in anything I have to say, so you're a little hard on my ego."

"I don't think your ego needs any help," she muttered, and again that grin of his flashed in her direction. In spite of herself, she found herself analyzing him in a completely different way. He didn't look to be more than in his late thirties, with curly black hair and an almost playboy manner about him. Almost instantly she tossed him into the bin of *useless*, only to drag him back out again when he started talking about the case in a way that she hadn't considered.

"So, we need to consider a couple things. History of the victims, history of the killer, and then obviously how did they connect, and how did they intercept. My immediate take will be a middle-aged white male, quite likely with family issues. He most likely bears some hatred against either his mother or father."

"How do you figure that?" she asked, frowning at Dudley. "I mean, it's not as if he's given us any idea about all that."

"No, he hasn't," Dudley admitted, "and obviously, until we get the full forensics, I won't know for sure. Even then, this is always a best guess, but it's a best guess based on a lot of years of experience."

"Keep talking," she muttered, her gaze narrowed, as she assessed what he was saying.

Dudley continued. "The whole *Forgive* angle could be his own way of saying, *Forgive me*, as in *Please forgive me*. Yet he still feels the need to do something like this. It could be seen more along the line of forgiveness needed for the victims' own sins, but then what sins does an eight- or nine-year-old have that our killer is asking forgiveness for?" Dudley asked her curiously.

"I have no idea," she said. "I wouldn't have thought any at that age, though it could also be about *forgive the sins that were done to you*."

"Meaning?"

"Meaning that the boy had been beaten for years before his death, possibly abused, and maybe the murderer is asking the child to forgive, … say, his father."

"You're thinking his father doesn't deserve forgiveness?"

"Do not analyze me," she snapped right back.

He shook his head. "Hadn't realized how easy it was to slip into that mode with you."

"You can just slip the hell right out of it."

He nodded. "Sorry, it's a professional habit."

"So, when I look into your history and see any association with young boys, it'll be just a professional habit on my part to instantly think *pedophile*?" she retorted smoothly.

He froze, his eyes wide.

She just continued to glare at him.

"Wow, I really hadn't expected that."

"Yet why not? You just used that excuse on me." She still stared at him, with zero give.

He pinched the bridge of his nose. "I can tell you this, but you won't believe me. However, I have never participated in anything quite so horrific as what you're suggesting, or as what my predecessor was involved in." Dr. Dudley sighed. "Obviously it will take us a bit of time to work out our own professional relationship. Yet I promise you. I would never do what you're accusing me of."

"I promise you that, if there is any hint or scent that you ever did, or are doing such a thing," she declared, staring him down, "I'll be on your ass faster than you can think it."

He gave her a wan smile and nodded carefully. "Thank you for that. At least we know where we stand."

"We do," she confirmed. "You don't cross any of those very basic moral tenets, and neither will I."

"Do you have any bad habits?"

"Yes, I drink far too much coffee." And once again he flipped from a professional to a way-too-attractive male, as he burst into laughter and smiled at her.

"You are definitely somebody I'll have to stay on top of," he noted, "and you're very fascinating to talk to."

"Forget that," she replied. "Not interested."

He looked at her in surprise, nodded, and added, "It's not as if I was asking."

"Good," she stated, her tone short. "That way you won't go wasting either your time or mine."

Still chuckling, he nodded. "Don't believe I've ever been turned down quite that fast."

"Yeah, get used to it."

Again he broke into outrageous laughter. "Oh my," he said, with a smirk. "Anything else I can help you with?"

"Not if you don't have anything else to go on," she replied.

"As I get the forensics, I'll add to my hypothesis."

"Fine." Kate stood. "I will email you the information as it comes in. Dr. Smidge is on it."

Dr. Dudley stood too. "And, by the same token, I will email you any changes or additions to my diagnosis."

"Good enough." With that, she turned and walked out.

⚬⚬⚬

SIMON WALKED THE streets, sensing the day was slowly winding down as he checked his watch, noting it was almost 5:30 p.m., heading to the six-o'clock mark. Vancouver was still busy, and rush-hour traffic remained, yet half of the town had emptied, while the rest of the city was desperately trying to get home, so they could enjoy the balance of their day, something Simon understood completely.

He was in a similar boat most of the time himself, but today was a little different. Today was a little bit more laid-back, mostly because of his own mind-set, that curiosity in his head that wondered at Bartlett's opportune arrival at lunchtime, and, soon afterward, with the appearance of a second poker player in Simon's life.

It made no sense in some ways, yet Simon often found residences weekly, where nobody was in, and yet next time suddenly several people were. He had the same thing happen with real estate. There would be a completely unloved piece of property, and then, as soon as somebody showed an interest in it, three or four or five people showed an interest in it. Sometimes the property would bid at a much higher level than they were worth.

Simon was usually pretty good about not getting caught up in a bidding war, unless it was one of the properties he was emotionally attached to, and then sometimes it was hard to back off.

He hopped on the aquabus that traveled up and down Vancouver harbor, and, instead of getting off at the next stop, he went around, all the way around, until it came back to his penthouse, which was just prior to the stop he'd gotten onto. He could have walked, but one of the things that he liked to do was to see all the architecture from the harbor side, from the water.

To be honest, he would also say that, particularly since meeting Kate, he liked to people watch. Not exactly something he ever thought he would do, but maybe it was the happenings today. Maybe it was seeing Bartlett. Maybe it was realizing that other people weren't necessarily handling everything in life quite the way that Simon would like to see them handle it. People were still out there, making decisions all on their own. If they crashed and burned, it had nothing to do with Simon. As long as he kept reminding himself of that, maybe, just maybe, he'd let the Bartlett discussion go.

He could certainly help Bartlett out with some cash, but that wasn't probably the best answer, and Simon also didn't know how much money the guy needed. Some of these poker games played deep, and Bartlett could easily lose $25,000 in a night and some of them a lot more than that, especially those private games in little back rooms all around the city, though the ones Simon particularly liked to play were the ones on the cruises. They often had limits, and, if you were winning too much, you would be politely asked to leave. He always thought that was an odd thing. I mean, if you were winning too much, you're asked to leave, but if you were losing too much? … Well then, nobody gave a crap. It was like, *Stay, bud, stay*.

Yet just some things about Bartlett today gave Simon an odd feeling and put him in a really off mood.

For all intents and purposes, it was foolish on Simon's part. Bartlett was a grown man, and he'd been doing this for a long time. He had his own business, and he'd been running it more or less successfully for a very long time, so it wasn't Simon's fault or responsibility. However, Simon still couldn't toss off the feeling that he should do something about it this time. As he wandered toward his apartment building, his phone rang.

He looked down and smiled. "Hey, Kate. Where are you, and what stage in life are you at for the day?"

"Two steps from dead," she muttered.

He burst into raucous laughter at that. "Honey, that would never be you."

"I hope not, … but I'm still in the office."

"Oh, crap," he muttered. "Another difficult day?"

"Just a day of nothing, and I'm so afraid that I'll wake up with yet another one of those calls."

"I'm sorry," he murmured. "Are you coming over?"

"I'm heading out right now, or at least I will be, as soon as I can get out of this building," she muttered. And he heard doors opening in the distance, people calling out to her. "I'm heading over for a workout."

"Then get going and come over to my place afterward."

"Honestly, I'll be too tired."

He hesitated, then asked in a casual tone, "Shall I come to your place then?"

After a short silence, she laughed. "That's quite a concession, knowing how you don't like my place."

"No, I don't like it, but I will certainly survive," he noted. "Why don't I show up with dinner?"

"I won't say no," she mumbled. "I might even feel better by the time I'm through this nightmare workout. I'll talk to you in a little bit."

"I'll meet you at your place," he stated, knowing it was better to go with the flow than to bring up any previous plans they'd made.

And, with that, he stopped, took stock of where he was and of what he wanted to do. He would need to drive to her apartment. Therefore, he could pick up whatever food he wanted. He quickly ran up to his penthouse and grabbed a few things for the night. As he headed downstairs, he called out to Edgar, "I'm heading over to Kate's."

"Good enough," Edgar replied. "Say *hi* for me."

"Will do."

It always amazed Simon that Kate had somehow made herself so popular with Edgar. He wasn't the kind to put himself out, but he'd certainly taken to her. But then she was also a person who was hard to ignore. However, as long as you played straight with her, she would play straight with you. Edgar was very much the same type person.

Then again, she had also worked hard at keeping Simon alive at various points in time, and he knew Edgar appreciated those attempts. Loyalty couldn't be bought, but it sure could be earned, and Edgar had earned Simon's, and it went both ways. Now, whenever Simon needed something, he knew Edgar and Harry would get it for him, earning a hefty tip afterward.

And tonight, Edgar would keep track of Simon's place,

making sure nobody who didn't belong went up and down the special penthouse elevator. It shouldn't be an issue, but one never really knew, particularly when you had ex-girlfriends like Caitlan. She'd been much better of late. Every once in a while, she still called to see if there was any chance of rekindling their relationship. The answer would always be no, particularly after finding out exactly who she was as a person.

Yet they'd been friends once, and he would like to think they could be friends again, but he highly doubted that such a thing was even something that Caitlan understood. Simon figured, if he were friends with Caitlan, she would escalate things to a more sexual relationship. Simon knew Kate would probably have a lot to say about such a friendship. And he didn't really care enough to go in that direction.

Caitlan was one of those people he was better off staying away from. It wasn't always that easy though, and sometimes he wondered at the mistakes he had made in life and how the punishment hadn't even seemed to fit the crime. Conversely he didn't know what he'd done to deserve a blessing such as Kate either, so he'd take that one with a smile on his face and with gratitude in his heart. She was one of a kind, and thankfully she was his kind.

He drove to one of Kate's favorite restaurants, ordered dinner for two, waited for the order, then headed out. As he pulled up outside of Kate's apartment, he looked up and noted no lights were on at her place, which meant she was still at the dojo, getting beaten to pulp, albeit willingly. Hopefully she wouldn't be too much longer; these workouts were serious business, and she got very, very tired. When he heard a whistle behind him, he turned, and there she was, limping very slowly toward him. He shook his head. "You look like death warmed over."

"Wow, that good, *huh*? I feel worse."

Gently reaching for her arm, he helped her up the stairs. "What happened?"

She shook her head. "I went in fully prepared to get a hard workout, but I wasn't really prepared to get my ass beat."

"Your master did this?"

"No, it was a new master, not our usual one. I think I pissed him off when I took him down in the first go-round. So, after that, it was a hardcore fight."

"And yet it shouldn't be."

"No, it sure shouldn't," she agreed, with half a smile in his direction. "He did apologize afterward. My master came in and put a stop to it, but I tell you. … In the meantime, it was hard and fast, and I will say that I gave as good as I got, and I think that just pissed him off."

Simon laughed at the thought. "Yet he's supposed to be the master and to not lose control."

"Yeah, and he failed at that too," she muttered. "Not sure I did any better in that department though."

"And that's not necessarily your fault."

"Maybe not," she acknowledged, "but I've got to tell you. It did my heart good to whip his butt, since a little too much ego showed on his side. However, my master did point out to me that conquest was not always the best result, but he still told me that I had done very well."

Simon smiled as they walked inside her tiny apartment.

Kate pointed at dinner. "I don't know what's in that bag, but it smells absolutely divine. I haven't even looked at the logo because my eyes are so damn tired. I'm heading in for a shower, and I'll be out in a few minutes."

And while she went in and had a shower, Simon quickly dished out the food on plates, wondering at her constant need to punish herself physically. He knew that if anybody had mentioned anything to her that made her feel like she was doing anything less than a majestic job at whatever she was trying, it would have just pissed her off. He wondered too at the master who could so easily lose control.

When she came back out, dressed in a simple nightie, her still-damp hair down her back, and her skin flushed pink from the hot water, he smiled, seeing her fresh yet so tired in her demeanor. "You look like you're eighteen."

She glanced at him. "Wow, … it's been a hell of a long time since I was anywhere close to that."

"I know, but it's the way you look right now."

She shook her head. "After the beatdown I just took, I doubt it."

"I'm surprised he lost control so quickly."

"I don't even know if it was quickly or not," she replied, "but, when I took him to the mat right off the bat, I think it was a matter of pride."

"Ah, but pride goes before a fall, as they say," Simon muttered.

"Yeah, particularly after my master got a hold of him."

"Is he new?"

"He is," she confirmed, "but I'm not entirely sure he'll be there the next time I go."

"Would you go against him again?"

She pondered it and nodded. "It was tough, and it was hard to swallow in a way. I took a beating, part of which was my fault," she admitted. "At the same time, I'm alive, and it was one of the hardest workouts I've ever done."

Simon didn't say anything, just frowned at her.

She smiled. "I'm fine."

"You are," he stated. "You're better than fine because you're always better than fine. That doesn't change the fact that you shouldn't have to work that hard and that a master should never lose control."

She nodded. "Yeah, and I suspect he'll pay for that, whether he's aware of it or not."

"Good. That level of skill comes with a certain responsibility, especially when you have reached dominance in the sport," Simon noted. "And it's not okay to turn around and to beat up the next student who pisses you off."

"No, it sure isn't," she agreed calmly. "On the other hand, he didn't beat me up, not at first, not until after I whipped his butt and put him on the ground. ... Hence the immediate retribution." She gave Simon a weak smile. "Now let's forget about that. What about this food?" She walked toward the kitchen, her nose sniffing the air around them. "Gosh, I hadn't realized how damn hungry I am," she muttered. "Or how damn easy it is to lose track of the reality that I should be keeping more food around here." She sighed. "Honestly, if you didn't show up tonight, ... I would probably just have toast."

He stared at her, and she shrugged. "I haven't had any time to get out and shop."

"It's a theme," he noted, with a sigh. "Now sit down, and we'll eat, and you can tell me where you're at on the case."

She snorted. "Don't you have anything you want to talk about instead of murder and mayhem?"

"I never would have thought that murder and mayhem appealed," he shared, "but I have to admit that, when it comes to a conversation with you, it's pretty fascinating stuff."

CHAPTER 5

KATE WOKE UP very sore the next morning, more so than she'd expected, and groaned when she slid out of bed, surprising even herself. Immediately Simon popped his head around the door, reminding her that he'd spent the night.

"You okay?" he asked, concern in his tone.

She nodded. "Yeah, just really sore from that workout last night."

He raised an eyebrow and gave her a one-arm shrug. "I can't say I'm surprised, based on how you looked when you got here. I'm still not happy it got so out of hand."

She shrugged. "I won out, didn't I?"

He smiled and nodded. "Yes, it sounds like you held your own, but you'll be paying for it today." She lost her smile and glared at him. He just laughed. "Come on. I've got the coffee on."

Moving slowly, she made her way into the kitchen, where she collapsed into the nearest chair and muttered, "Good Lord, it'll be a long day at this rate."

"Do you want to take anything for it?"

"No, I just should have been up and moving already," she noted. "It would have made it easier."

"Maybe, but, on the other hand, it's not as if you're going anywhere right this minute, are you?"

"Not fast anyway," she muttered, with a laugh.

He looked at her and nodded. "I hear you. You should at least eat some breakfast because I suspect that you'll still have a long hard day ahead of you."

"But the good news is that my phone didn't ring in the night, so it's not likely that we'll have any new victims in a church," she noted, with a shake of her head. "Honest to God, that's worth everything."

———※———

OUTSIDE, KATE QUICKLY picked up the pace and caught a bus on her way to work. She was sore enough that she didn't want to walk all the way, plus she tried very hard to go on the bus several times a week, just to keep connected with the way the city hummed. When you had a vehicle, you forgot how a lot of people in the world lived, and she intentionally tried to remember. With Simon in her life, she was often reminded of how different his world was from hers, both the good and the bad, yet, at the same time, it could be frustrating.

She didn't ever want to lose sight of where she came from, and, with Simon around, that wasn't a danger, but it was definitely something she should always be aware of. She didn't think she could ever get smug about his money, since it was his money, not hers. Though she stayed at his place frequently, she didn't want to live in his place, despite all the comforts of it. She couldn't imagine that it would be an easy place to live either, yet who knew? Just enough was going on in her world at any time that those comforts were a welcome relief and made her smile, and usually in a very big way.

As she walked into the office, Rodney looked up at her and announced with a heavy sigh, "I guess I'm driving today, *huh?*" When she frowned at him, he nodded. "You look like shit."

She winced and nodded. "That's because I feel like shit."

Sergeant Colby entered the room at that moment and heard that comment.

Kate shrugged. "Let's just say that my workout with a master last night didn't quite go the way I planned."

The others had a good laugh, but a little later, when they were headed out in his vehicle to go to the morgue, Rodney asked her in genuine concern, "What did you mean about your workout?"

After she told him, he whistled. "That is very unusual behavior. It's also shitty. Surprising too."

"I already had a conversation with Simon about it."

"I'm surprised he didn't go down there and have a talk with them."

She gave Rodney a wide-eyed look. "Don't even say that. He still might."

Rodney laughed at that. "I'm half tempted to go over there and see what is going on myself." He looked at her sideways for a few minutes. "Does the owner of the club know about it?"

She nodded. "He's the one who broke it up, when things got a little heated," she admitted. "Once I took out the new master, he was just looking for payback and lost that lovely detached air of a true master," she noted, with a wry look in his direction. "Something about me set him off, and it got pretty ugly for a bit. On the other hand, I got a really hard workout, one of the hardest I've ever had in my life. Mostly because it seemed like I *was* fighting for my life," she added on a broken laugh. "The bottom line is that I'm definitely feeling a little worse for wear right now."

He whistled at that. "That could shut down his dojo,

you know?"

She nodded. "I certainly won't shut it down, and I think you know that's part of the fear in a place like that, when you overdo it. It's unfortunate that it happened, but it's better that it happened to me and not to one of the other people there."

"I'll be surprised if he's got a job after this."

She thought about it and nodded. "I suppose you're right, but, as I said, no harm done—no lasting harm— though it was quite a fight for a while." She gingerly touched her jaw, still sore and swollen, and she hoped it was not too colorfully bruised because the last thing she wanted was to listen to everybody laughing at her for the next several days. Yet Rodney didn't appear to be interested in laughing at all. He seemed more concerned that she might be seriously hurt.

"I'm fine," she told him, waving off his concerns. "It's probably my fault for going into it a little too heavy."

He laughed. "Of course you would blame yourself." With that, he pulled up to the morgue. "*Ugh*, here we are. I really wish we didn't have to go in there."

"Oh, I'm looking forward to it," she stated cheerfully, as she hopped right out.

"Why, because you just missed winding up in here last night?"

At that, she burst out laughing. "You know? There could be some truth to that."

As they walked in, Dr. Smidge was muttering over his desk, but it didn't seem to be at paperwork. When Kate cleared her throat, he looked up, a bit startled. "There you are," he said in relief and then frowned at her. "You're late." When she didn't say anything, he added, "I see you were in an altercation. I sure hope the other guy looks worse than you."

With a touch of pride, she nodded. "He does."

When he snorted at that, Rodney looked at her too, a grin on his face. "You're proud of that, aren't you?"

She shrugged. "Not necessarily, because letting emotions get in the way of everything else is a surefire way to lose a fight," she explained. "You have to stay calm and cool under pressure, and I didn't do that last night," she admitted. "So any lickings he got in on me, I pretty well had coming."

"I'm sure you did," Smidge said, with exaggerated politeness. "Now, can we get back to the matter at hand?" He pointed to one of the bodies on one of his tables.

She walked over to the body of the young boy and sighed, as she stood near the small shrouded form.

Smidge nodded. "A good place to start." He came up beside her and removed the sheet, exposing a very scrawny body—so scrawny, in fact, that it was all she could do to hold back a hoarse cry. He nodded. "You wouldn't be human if you weren't affected by this."

"It's terrible," she replied flatly, biting her lip. "What animal does this to a child?" His body was emaciated to the point of complete starvation, and she saw more bones that had healed incorrectly and joints that didn't sit quite right on his already malnourished form. "My God," Kate muttered, "his life must have been one of complete pain and agony."

"I think you're right about that," Dr. Smidge agreed, with a frown. "Unfortunately, nobody was there to save him."

She didn't know what to say to that but nodded quietly, as the coroner went through the litany of injuries the boy had. It was a very long list of painful injuries that the young lad had endured before his death, which death had brought his suffering to a merciful end.

Smidge looked over at her. "Do we have any idea who did this to him?"

"Not yet," she admitted, "but we will look at the usual suspects, and I will find out."

"Chances are," Rodney said carefully at her side, as if realizing how heated the space would get in a few minutes, "it's way too easy to assume that we know the kid's abuser was the mother and or the father, who both were killed at the same time."

"I know that," Smidge snapped. "I'm doing my job. You do yours." And, with that, he launched into a similar litany of the injuries on the mother. "Now, her injuries aren't as severe or as prolonged, but that's only because the comparison is so shocking," he noted, as he motioned with his hand toward the young boy. "In fact, if she had lived, her life would also have been one of extreme pain and most likely terror."

"Terror ... because?" Kate asked.

"Because she'd never know when the next blow was coming," Smidge replied bluntly.

Kate didn't say anything to that, and just nodded quietly as she looked around. "What about the man, her husband?"

"Nothing," Smidge stated in disgust. "His body is perfectly fine and fit. It doesn't look like he had suffered a day in his life."

She winced at that. "If he's the one responsible for all this damage to that young boy and to the mother," Kate suggested quietly, "then I hope he suffers in whatever is on the other side of death."

Smidge nodded. "I'm not one to sit here and bitch about

what happens to people," he began, "but, in this case, and in all cases involving children like this, we share the same mindset."

Kate studied the boy once more. "But, if the father used his fists, you would have seen evidence on his own hands, right?" Kate stared at Smidge.

"Correct. None found."

Rodney added, "Doesn't mean he didn't use a belt or a whip or a skillet or a two-by-four or whatever."

Kate nodded.

"Now, the father was drugged, based on indications of a puncture wound. Hard to find a puncture wound on the other two," Smidge added. "However, I asked for rushed tox screen results on this trio. All had been drugged. Same drug used on each. Probably the father was overcome first, I would presume. He would have been a much harder victim to subdue than the others."

"How did they die?"

"The parents overdosed," Smidge stated, "painless deaths."

"Interesting," she muttered, staring at Smidge. "I would have thought that the father at least should have gotten a beating from whoever beat the mother and the child."

"You would think so, but maybe, … maybe the killer thought death itself would have been enough of a punishment."

She looked from the little boy's abused body to the mother's abused body and back to the little boy, then shook her head. "It wasn't."

They got back to the discussion, where Smidge clarified that, while the method of death for the mother and the father were, indeed, drug overdoses, the little boy apparently died from something completely different. "Cause of death wasn't an overdose in his case. On the up and up, … it looks like starvation."

"Oh, Christ," Kate muttered, feeling all the air sucked out of the room at his words.

Smidge nodded. "I know how you feel, and, at this moment, there's very little to redeem whoever did this."

She nodded, not even sure that redemption was possible. "When you say that he died, most likely from starvation, how do you know?"

"He was put on the cross afterward."

"And these two?"

"They were drugged, probably barely alive when they were put on the crosses, and wouldn't have known what was happening," he shared. "One thing to note. It seemed our killer planned to transport them on the crosses, but it didn't seem to work."

Kate asked, "How do you see that?"

"Two different holes for the stakes in each palm."

She stared at him. "So, somebody didn't have any sympathy for the mother, who was also apparently battered, and yet the little boy, who was already dead, was also given the same message and was also placed on a cross?" she noted, with a raised brow. "That's an odd combination."

"Is it though? I'm not sure anything's odd about it. I mean, when you're dealing with a mind this twisted, it seems to me there's no rhyme or reason."

"Maybe not," she acknowledged, "but the killer had a reason. The killer had something in his head that made him think this was a good message to send."

"Or perhaps was even driven to send this message," Rodney pointed out. "These aren't the actions of a sane mind."

"No, I wouldn't think so," Smidge agreed, "which is why you need to catch him." Smidge pointedly stared at Kate.

She nodded. "On it." She looked back at the boy. "I want your report as soon as you've got it typed up for these three."

"Of course." Smidge nodded, his tone almost as formal as hers.

With that, she turned and walked out of the morgue. Outside, she stood still and took several slow deep breaths, trying to calm the churning fury in her system.

When Rodney joined her, he studied her with concern. "Are you all right?"

"I will be," she claimed. "Just something about seeing that level of violence, especially in the case of an innocent child. I mean, I know I'm supposed to feel some sympathy for the mother, for what she obviously endured, but that anybody would allow the child to be damaged to that extent, to be starved and tortured?" She shook her head. "That's just completely unacceptable."

"Do you blame the mother?" Rodney asked.

"It's easy to blame the mother," she replied, "yet she's just another victim. Though we don't know the circumstances. Was she beaten every time she tried to protect the little boy, or was she a part of beating Daniel?" Kate shrugged. "It would be nice to think that we would know the answers to all these details, but the truth is, ... we may never know."

"That's the hardest thing, isn't it?" Rodney asked.

"We want answers. We desperately want to find the answers, but we won't always get what we want."

"Let's go find the bastard who did this," Rodney said.

She stopped and looked at him. "What if he's the one in the morgue? I mean, who else would it be? That was long-term abuse."

"Maybe, but let's not rule out anything yet," Rodney noted. "Let's go talk to the neighbors and the family."

She shrugged in faint disgust. "Yeah, let's go talk to all the people in that little boy's life who did absolutely nothing to help him."

⌘

SIMON STEPPED IN and physically worked that morning on one of his rehab projects. He swung a sledgehammer just as well as the next guy, and, unfortunately right now, it seemed his skills were needed in that department too. He never said anything to anyone. He just got in line and got busy. Some people would know he was the boss. Others wouldn't, and he didn't care either way. The work had to be done, and, as long as each employee did theirs, Simon was good with it. If they didn't do theirs, that was a whole different story.

However, by lunchtime he was feeling it, since it wasn't a job he did on a regular basis, and his muscles were starting to scream.

When the foreman walked up and handed him a bottle of water, Simon gulped it back with relish. "Been a while, hasn't it?" the foreman quipped, with a knowing smile.

"Too long in some ways and not long enough in others," Simon replied, looking over at him with a wry expression. "You can jump in here yourself too."

"Oh, don't worry. I have been," he confirmed, with a nod. "I've been working on the other side. The good news is, I have two extra men coming in tomorrow."

"I'm glad to hear that," Simon replied. "It seems like we're not getting anywhere some days."

"And yet, other days, it seems like we're doing just fine."

"I wonder," Simon muttered but didn't say a whole lot more. With the water gone, he went back to work, and, by the time he was done with that particular job, he knew he needed to be done for the day.

Picking up his things, he left the site and walked over to a street vendor, grabbed a cold bottle of water and a cup of hot coffee. He sat here on a nearby bench, with his laptop, waiting for his body to cool down and for his muscles to ease up. He would need a hot shower tonight and would potentially take something to stop everything from seizing up. If he was lucky, he'd miss all that too.

He hadn't heard anything from Kate all day, so, on a whim, he sent her a quick message. When he got a **Hey** back, he smiled and kept on working on his laptop. When a shadow crossed his face, he looked up to see Bartlett again. Frowning, Simon took a hard look at him. "This isn't a coincidence."

Bartlett shrugged and sat down. "I need help."

"What help?" And with the question phrased plainly, he waited.

Bartlett flushed. "I would say money, but money between friends is never a good deal."

"We're friends," Simon pointed out, "but I haven't seen you in ages."

"I know," Bartlett admitted, his tone harsh, "but I didn't know who else to turn to. You have the dandiest luck when it comes to cards," he murmured, "and I need some of that luck."

Simon sat back, unsure what Bartlett was asking for.

"You better clarify that statement," he snapped, and Bartlett flushed all kinds of red.

"Look. I'm not saying you cheat. I'm definitely not saying that, man. I'm just saying that, when it comes to cards, you just, … you have the devil's luck. You win."

Simon studied the other man carefully. "Where is this going?"

"I was hoping you would come play a few games with me and either show me how to win or how to play a few games on my behalf, you know, to help me pick up some winnings. That's all."

"Why the hell would I do that?" he asked, staring at him.

Bartlett flushed. "Because I'm desperate, Simon, and you know nobody in their right mind would be here talking to you like this unless they really were."

Simon pondered that for a few moments and nodded. "Okay, so you're desperate, and that's my problem, why?"

"It's not your problem. It's my problem, but it's also a problem where people are counting on me," he admitted, pale in the face, "and I don't know what else to do."

"What about the banks?"

"Tried that," he said bitterly. "My house is mortgaged to the hilt, and they won't give me anything more, even though all the prices have gone up."

"Sure, but nobody's feeling very confident about that at the moment, so they won't lend you more than they think is safe."

"They don't think I'm very safe at all at the moment apparently," Bartlett replied, bitterness in his voice.

"Why don't you tell me what got you into this trouble?"

Bartlett looked at him in surprise and then nodded. "As

I mentioned, I made a couple bad business deals. I bought some properties, thinking I could sell them at a profit, and instead it seems I bought a couple lemons."

Simon pondered that. "Did you take somebody else's advice?"

"I did." And when he mentioned a name, Simon's glare deepened. "Now you'll tell me that I should have known better, right?" Bartlett asked, with a shrug. "I was already losing money at that point in time, and I have to admit that I was getting rather desperate, and it sounded like it was a sure thing."

"There's no sure thing when it comes to property."

"No, I understand that now," he replied. "However, I owe money on the properties, and I owe money outside of it."

"Damn, and how much did you expect to make playing poker?" Simon asked, bewildered.

Bartlett hesitated and murmured, "I don't know. I really don't know. I don't even know what the options are at this point. I don't know what else to do, but I can't go home."

"Whoa, whoa, whoa," Simon said, for the first time getting really worried. "Let's not have any talk about doing anything stupid."

Bartlett looked at him and muttered in resignation, "You know there was a time for stupid, and that's long past. Now it's just looking more like a hell of a good deal."

Simon groaned at that. "Look. I've spent way too much time recently dealing with suicides," he shared, "and I really, really don't want to be in this position right now."

Bartlett looked at him. "I didn't say I would commit suicide."

"No, but you're talking like it."

He hesitated, and then his shoulders sagged. "I just don't know what else to do. I believe I've done everything right, but obviously I trusted the wrong person."

"I do know something of this person you trusted," Simon noted.

"Yeah? He's a shyster, I suppose."

"Not sure about that, since I haven't done any business dealings with him, and I don't know about anybody who has."

"That's because you're smarter than I am," Bartlett replied bitterly.

"Or is it more a case of the real estate needs more time to grow?"

"Maybe that's what it is," Bartlett agreed, "but I just don't have any more time."

"Why not?"

"Because I need an influx of cash to keep the business going, and I need cash on a regular basis to maintain my business operations." When Simon frowned at him, Bartlett continued. "I'm in investments, but really it's been property developments. That's the main focus of where my money is at. I generally buy buildings, rent them out, lease them out, do something. And you know, or maybe you don't," he added in quick succession, "that my business came from my father-in-law. But he passed away recently, and apparently I don't have the same damn nose for business that he did."

"I'm not sure it's a nose for business as much as it's learning the business," Simon corrected. "Why don't you sell some of your buildings?"

"I would sell the bulk of my holdings if I thought I could get a decent price for them," Bartlett replied, "but the minute anybody knows that you're in trouble, they'll just move in and take everything you've got." Bartlett studied Simon intently. "And that won't leave me anything."

"So exactly what is it you need? What are we talking here?"

The six-digit figure had Simon raising his eyebrows. "Right."

Bartlett nodded, sighing loudly. "So don't bother telling me that I'm stupid. Believe me. I already know."

"I don't know about *stupid*," Simon clarified, "but what buildings do you have? What buildings do you want to sell?"

"Are you interested in buying buildings?" Bartlett looked at him, confused.

"I buy buildings all the time," Simon declared. "Then I fix them up and rehab them, usually for low income or various other purposes that have potential," he explained, with a smile. "I'm not saying I'm interested in any of the ones you have, but I'm not saying that I'm not interested either."

Bartlett hesitated, then gave him a couple addresses on the same block. Simon brought them up on his laptop, and he pointed them out. "These ones?"

"Yes, those are the ones." Bartlett nodded. "I've got this one and this one. They were supposed to make me money, but instead they're bleeding me damn dry." He shook his head bitterly.

"They're decent properties," Simon noted, "and, if you could hold them, you would make money in the end."

Bartlett frowned at him. "I just don't have the time," he said in exasperation. "It was supposed to be a short thing and quick."

Simon shook his head. "No such thing as a short thing that's quick in a legitimate business." He'd had his eyes on one of the properties for a while but didn't want to get involved in something like this. "If you sold one of them, would it get you off the hook for a while?"

"If I sold it at a decent price," he hedged, his voice suddenly cagey, as he stared at Simon, frowning.

"I'm not interested in taking you for a ride, but neither am I interested in being taken for a ride myself," Simon declared.

"Right, and that's always the problem when it comes to business, isn't it?"

"It can be, yes," Simon agreed. "There's absolutely no reason you can't sell these properties, but that does take time. What did you pay for it? And, before you answer, remember that it's public information."

"It is, indeed." He named a figure, and Simon nodded.

"That's a decent price," he replied, "and then your expenses would have been …" Simon thought about it for a moment. "Property transfer tax, legal fees, and the like." Then Simon gave him a figure.

"Yes, it would have been somewhere around there."

"So, what if you got that money back? What would that do for you?"

"It would hold me for a little while but not for very long," Bartlett said. "The whole purpose of going into this was to try and make some money to get me out of trouble. I have another building that I would be more than happy to sell you."

Bartlett started to sound like he had an ace up his sleeve, and Simon didn't like where this was heading.

"I bought it quite a while ago, and I was developing it with my father-in-law. However, he passed away before it could happen, and," with emotions choking him, he whispered, "now I don't have the heart for it."

"It's not a property that you could sell on the open market?"

"Sure, it is, but again it's a time issue."

"How much of a time issue?"

"I need money like now," Bartlett stated, "like seventy-two hours max."

Simon considered that and shook his head. "There's no way. We can't even do a real estate deal that quickly."

"I know." Bartlett dropped his head into his hands.

"Although I could give you a bridge loan against the property that was in process."

At that, Bartlett raised his head. "Do you have that kind of money?"

"If you're talking the half-million you mentioned, then yes," Simon confirmed. "Obviously I'd have to move some things around. It's possible but ..." Simon put a bit too much emphasis on the *but*. "Only if I'm getting the property in question."

The conversation then took a much harder and faster turn, and, at the end of it, both men looked at each other in delight.

Bartlett sighed. "Man, you have no idea how much you've saved my ass."

"I've had my eye on that property you've been hanging on to for quite a while," Simon shared. "So I'm okay to take it off your hands. I'm always looking for a couple more to work on."

"You really take them on and fix them up just because?"

"Yeah, I'm a bit of a weirdo that way," he quipped. "Properties have a bit of a soul to me, and some of them need a bit more work than others." He gave Bartlett a chuckle, seeing the expression on his face. "I do want to come and take a look at it in person and make sure things aren't as bad as they potentially could be."

"Got it," Bartlett agreed. "Let's go now."

They jumped up. Simon hailed a cab, and they spent the next two hours walking properties and discussing prices. At the end of the day, they reached an agreement that had Bartlett floating moneywise again, at least for a little while, with a promise that he wouldn't head back to the gambling tables. When they were done and the initial paperwork had been signed and then passed off to the lawyers, Bartlett said, "I really do need a bridge loan now."

"You need it for the full amount?"

"No." He thought about it for a moment, then added, "I could probably get away with about $75,000 for now." Simon picked up the phone and contacted his lawyer. "I'll acknowledge the release of that," Simon stated, with a hint of warmth and warning, "as long as you acknowledge the release of the property."

It took a few more steps, but Simon finally got off the phone with a smile on his face. "The courier will have the money in your bank at the end of the day."

Bartlett let out a slow breath. "I was really just hoping you'd take me out gambling and win me a few million dollars," he shared, with a stuttering laugh, "but this? ... This is much better."

"This is also legal, aboveboard, and you forget that I also lose money while gambling. It's one of the reasons I never gamble with other people's money. I stop when I get to the point that I can't handle any more losses, and I walk."

"Yeah." Bartlett nodded. "I get that. Besides, gambling's not something I've done in a long time. With so many sharks out there, chances are, I would have been completely wiped out."

"Yeah, and you still could be, if you're not smart with what you've just done. Have you ever considered getting somebody to take a look at your books, particularly now that your father-in-law is not there?"

"You think it's necessary?"

"Yes. I presume he was the head of the business?"

"He was, and believe me. ... I'm already worried that I've screwed up to the point of no return."

"I don't think that's the case, but you might want to consider getting somebody to take a closer look at things."

"Is that something you do for people?"

Simon hesitated. "Yes, I've done it from time to time ... but not as part of my regular business."

"Why not?"

"It takes a lot of time for one thing," he shared, as he'd learned the hard way, "and people don't generally like my suggestions. I'm not one to gamble too much money. I have a formula I use that I stick to, and it's worked for me."

"So how much would it cost to have you do an audit on my business?"

"It's not an audit," Simon corrected. "That's something much more formal, but I could take a look at your business and could figure out what your father-in-law's strategy was and maybe find a way to keep you from getting into this position again."

Bartlett looked at him and nodded slowly. "That's truly what I need, you know? Somebody who'll give me that roadmap. I was working with him long enough that I thought I had it, and then he died suddenly, and all these bills and things started coming out of nowhere, and I had no idea how to keep it all from spinning out of control." They sat down on a nearby street corner bench. "Sometimes I just wonder if I should, you know, find another job."

"What job would you do?" Simon asked, with a smile. "When you've been working your own business for a long time, it's pretty hard to turn around and all of a sudden decide that you'll work for somebody else."

"Maybe," he agreed, with a nod. "But, if I don't have the wherewithal to make this happen and to keep everything floating, … I can't face the employees, who will all lose their jobs because of me."

"That's one of the reasons I've agreed to help you," Simon shared. "However, in order to help you, I need to have complete access."

"Good enough," Bartlett agreed. "I'm not sure what all you need, but I can make information available to you."

"Where is your corporate office?"

Bartlett gave him the address, and Simon nodded. "I'll be there tomorrow morning at eight, so make sure you're there too."

Bartlett looked at him in surprise, then nodded. "That's pretty fast."

"You really can't afford to waste any time. The faster we identify the problem and map out a solution, the better your chances. Basically you don't have time to screw up anymore," he pointed out. "The world is unkind, and you'll get maybe a year of respite from this real estate deal we just brokered. However, if you get into a cash-strapped situation like this again, nobody'll be there to bail you out, including me. So let's fix it so you won't need help, and, maybe by this time next year, you'll have enough confidence to continue on your own."

Bartlett winced. "Who would have thought that would ever be an issue?"

"It happens. The minute you have other people's lives in your hands," Simon stated, with a shrug, "that's a huge responsibility and, with that responsibility, comes the need to make things work."

Bartlett and Simon shook hands and confirmed the meeting the next morning.

Long after Bartlett had gone, as Simon now sat at a waterfront café, he wondered if he'd gotten himself into something he shouldn't have. He was perfectly comfortable having picked up the properties, especially the one that had been on his wish list for quite a while anyway. The other one he knew of, and he was okay to take a gamble on. He could fix it up enough that, even if things got bad, he could just sell it and make enough money to bail out of it.

As for Bartlett, Simon wasn't sure the guy knew how to do that business. His father-in-law had been the strong one in the business, but even he'd had a bit of a shady reputation. Simon wasn't sure many would miss the old man now. Bartlett would be on his own to get himself in and out of trouble, if he didn't get himself straightened away very fast, so tomorrow should prove interesting, if nothing else.

With that thought, he sent Kate a message. **Heading home to my place. Hope your day is going a hell of a lot better.**

CHAPTER 6

HOURS LATER KATE looked down at her text messages to see one that she'd missed from Simon. She read it and snorted at the sentiment about her day going well. Shaking her head, she walked back outside into the cool of the evening, wondering just how this day could continue to go so wrong. But wrong it was, with just no ending in sight, at least not as far as she could see. That was a pisser in itself because they needed action, and they needed a break with this case.

She had spent a lot of time at the first church today, talking to regular people coming and going. She had attempted to get through to the family, but apparently the husband's parents had just come in on a flight. Kate was about to go meet Roger Brown's parents at the hotel.

As she exited her car at the station's parking lot, she heard a shout and looked up to see Rodney coming toward her. "I thought you had to leave."

"I canceled."

She frowned at him, and he frowned right back. "We don't know what the hell we're dealing with here," he explained, raising his hands in peace. "It's not smart for you to go alone on something like this."

"I'm meeting the victim's family," she pointed out. "How risky can that be?"

"Yeah, you are, but who the hell knows who else our killer might have a grudge against," Rodney pointed out. "Let's not have it be one of us or anybody who's working to help solve this case."

She shrugged and nodded. "I'm sure Simon would agree with you."

He snorted at that. "I'm sure he would. Now, let's get you into the thick of things, so we can get back out again."

She snorted. "How about we avoid the *thick of things* and just solve it?"

"That works for me too," he replied, "though I highly doubt it'll be quite that easy."

"It hasn't been yet," she agreed, as they drove toward the hotel. "We also have to find more family members or neighbors because this just isn't adding up. So far, finding anybody at the church who even knew the Browns is tough. Then among those people, everybody says the Browns were a lovely couple."

"Yet not many people knew anything about them, and the ones who supposedly did had only met them once or twice."

She frowned at that and nodded. "And almost everybody said that had been a while ago."

"What does that mean to you?" he asked quietly. "I mean, did they get off the beaten path and lose their way in some sense?" Rodney frowned. "Or does it mean they changed churches, and they found another one more conducive to the way they wanted to live?"

"Maybe you're the one who should be telling me that," she noted, looking at him sideways, "because all this church stuff is pretty foreign to me."

"Yeah, but pretty foreign to you is still a whole different

story than for a lot of us." He shook his head at her reference to his religious upbringing. "I'm close with my church and with everybody who's in it. I've been to who-knows-how-many baptisms and all kinds of special events, all involving multiple people at my church. Yet I'm not sure any of this is quite the same thing."

"I wouldn't know," she muttered.

Pulling up at the hotel, she got out, and, showing her badge at the reception desk, she asked for the room number of the victim's family. The woman hesitated, earning her a steely look from Kate. "Your cooperation is being noted."

The other woman flushed all kinds of red. "I don't have any permission to give you a room number."

Kate looked at her in astonishment. "Seriously? I'm here to meet somebody, and you can't tell me what room they're in?"

The other woman stammered, and the manager walked over, asking if there was a problem. Kate introduced herself, explained why they were here, and then turned back to the front desk clerk, frowning. "But apparently that's a problem."

"We do take our visitor's safety into account at all times," he replied smoothly.

"That's nice," Kate snapped, her expression going from cold to dead. "But what has that got to do with the fact that I'm here to speak with them about deaths in their family?" she asked.

He flushed and then stammered, "Let me just tell them that you're here."

"You do that," she muttered, staring at him, her gaze going from the front desk clerk to the manager. She didn't understand why so many roadblocks delayed her access to the people she needed to get to. That they existed was obvious, so what was the point of stonewalling what should have been a simple request? Instead it was now at a whole different level.

At her side, Rodney nudged her gently, and she looked over at him and shrugged. If they wanted to be difficult, that was fine; she would make note of it and keep it in the back of her mind for later. She didn't know who was involved in this mess, and already she wanted to look a more closely into several people right here.

As she looked back over at the front desk clerk, she found the woman staring at her, but her bottom lip was almost trembling. With that noted, the manager came back in a hurry. "They're waiting for you."

"Funny how I told you that in the first place," she murmured, giving the front desk clerk another death stare, as she walked past the manager.

"It is our standard procedure," he called out behind her.

"*Uh-huh,*" she called back. "Interesting that you need it."

And, with that last jab, she headed up to the room in question. She took the stairs instead of the elevator, still more than a little pissed at the trouble from the hotel staff. When she knocked on the door, Rodney at her side, it opened to reveal a woman with tears in her eyes, still sniffling as she pulled the door open wider.

"Come in. Come in," she muttered anxiously, as she looked around to see if anybody had followed Kate and Rodney.

That struck Kate as strange right off the bat. As she stepped inside, she couldn't help but ask, "You appear to be afraid that somebody might be following me."

"It's not so much that they might be following you," Mrs. Brown clarified, "but it's not as if we have a very good relationship with any of Roger's in-laws. That family was always trouble, and it's been a problem since Roger married that woman," she stated in a harsher tone. "So, whatever this is, it's quite likely it involves them somehow, and we just want to stay free and clear of that family."

"Interesting," Kate said, eyeing the woman. "Obviously we have even more questions now."

The other woman flushed, then looked back at her husband, who stepped up to her side. "That's why we agreed to see you."

At his wording, Kate rounded on him. "Meaning that, if there was any other reason, you wouldn't have?" She didn't know whether she was being particularly ornery today or people were just pissing her off or something underhanded could be going on here. If there were some underhandedness going on, who are the receivers of that behavior—the Browns or Rodney and her?

Mr. Brown flushed. "Look. We need to explain."

She nodded slowly. "That might help."

She was shown to one of the couches, where she took up a position that faced the victim's parents squarely and waited. Rodney took the seat beside her and did the same. The couple looked at each other once more, and then Mrs. Brown addressed Kate.

"This is very difficult for us."

Kate nodded, but she didn't give any quarter on it. "Apparently we need to understand some things here. No matter how you feel and or how you look at it, we need to know anything there is to know about your son and his wife."

"Yes." The woman looked over at her husband, then

took a deep breath. "Frankly we haven't had very much to do with Roger since he married that woman," she replied, a particularly spiteful tone in her voice.

"Okay, and why is that?"

"Because we didn't like her, and my son took offense to that. She's a drug addict and has a lot of mental issues. She was abused as a child and God only knows what else. My son wanted to make her life easy—perfect in any way he could. He let her have complete control."

"That's how families generally have issues," Kate noted calmly. "Go on."

Mrs. Brown flushed, as if not terribly happy that she wasn't getting the sympathy she expected. "Once they got together, there just didn't seem to be any pleasing him, and we weren't sure what to do anymore. We ended up just slowly backing off," she explained, pursing her lips. "We just didn't feel right about any of it."

"But, rather than listening to you, I presume Roger went and did his own thing."

Mr. Brown's face turned beet red with anger, replaced immediately by sadness. "That's exactly what happened," he replied. "Maybe we didn't handle it in the best way, but it was truly because we were so worried."

"And we were obviously correct about that," Mrs. Brown declared, pointing that out to her husband. "We weren't trying to hurt them by any means, and we wanted to have a relationship with them, but it just seemed almost impossible. We could never do anything right, and everything we said seemed to be taken the wrong way. It was all just very, very frustrating."

"Understood," Kate stated, as she looked from one to the other. "What about the boy?"

Mr. Brown let out a deep sigh and shook his head. "We didn't quite understand why they would want to take in a child like that, when she was having so many issues. Not that we're terrible people by any means, but they were planning on having a family of their own," he shared, "so it seemed rather odd that they would want to do this so quickly."

Kate suggested, "Maybe they were just happy to help."

"Maybe," he agreed, with a nod. "I don't know, and we can't ask them now." His tone had turned brisk, as if trying to regain some control of himself and the conversation.

Kate watched and waited, while he seemed to cast about for some sense of control again.

"We understood the boy was well-loved and well-looked after," Mr. Brown added, "but now horrible things are going around. Why, we've already heard rumors that the boy was mistreated in some way. We are hoping you can straighten that out and could put the rumor to rest through the media or something."

She looked at him, her gaze turning steely. "Unfortunately we cannot negate the rumors because that's not our role. However, what I can tell you is what we know to be true at this point. While we don't yet have a final report from the medical examiner, it is apparent that the boy died of starvation, and his body bears evidence of systemic abuse. What I mean by that is, many beatings and bruising over the years. Broken bones and dislocated joints that were never allowed to heal properly. He was lucky to have survived as long as he did, though I use *lucky* in a facetious tone, since he obviously suffered, ... and he suffered a great deal."

Rodney laid a hand on her shoulder, letting her know that her tone was probably far-less-than polite and likely harsher than necessary. However, the grandfather was asking for the attitude he got by pressuring Kate to correct these supposedly false rumors of abuse, assuming everyone was spreading lies about the boy's condition, before the grandfather had even heard the facts that they had.

As her words sank in, the couple just stared at her in shock, eyes wide in disbelief. "Our boy would never do that."

She looked at the couple intently, trying hard to control her anger. "I hear you, and I understand your desire to believe that, but what I don't have is evidence to the contrary. Your son's body did not show he had been beaten. However, I have a little boy who had been starved and beaten and a wife who had also been badly battered. These conditions and injuries occurred over some extended period of time and prior to the crime that brought us all here."

At that, Mrs. Brown stifled a cry, her hand on her mouth, staring in horror at the two detectives. "No, no, no," she wailed. "Roger never would have hurt her."

Kate studied them, from one to the other and back again, as Mr. Brown repeatedly shook his head.

"You've got it wrong," he muttered. "You've got it all wrong."

"How can you know this, when you told me yourself that you've had little to do with your son?" she asked.

"Because he's gentle, a gentle soul," they both replied, their voices overlapping and becoming incoherent.

Kate raised a hand to stop the gibberish. "One at a time, please."

Mr. Brown shook his head. "Roger would never do something like that."

Now, if Kate had a dollar for every time somebody had protested the innocence of someone they knew who could *never do anything like that*, only to find out afterward that was exactly what had happened, she could probably rival Simon's riches.

She looked from one to the other and replied, "That's not what you *want* to believe," she began, raising her hand once again to stop their protests, "but all I can do at the moment is rely on the evidence, which suggests the woman and the child were badly beaten."

"Surely by the killer," the father stated, staring at her in hope.

Kate shook her head. "Again, the injuries occurred over an extended period of time, as in many years."

Shaking and pale, the husband sat beside his wife, who grasped his hand, as if he could make this nightmare go away.

"Roger wasn't the kind to ever beat a woman," Mrs. Brown whispered quietly, "and he would never have hurt a little boy." She turned to look at her husband, tears in her eyes. "Dear God, what happened to him?"

"That woman," he snapped. "It was that woman."

"You mean his wife, who I just told you was badly beaten?" Kate asked, trying to keep the ironic tone out of her voice, stunned that they could even contemplate that would be the answer. Kate had seen a lot of strange things in life, but she highly doubted that a woman who would endure that level of beating would be the one behind it.

Mr. Brown faced Kate, his gaze turning furious, his jaw ticking. "Obviously we don't want to believe our son beat his wife," he replied painfully. "But, just as obvious, we know something was very wrong with that woman. However, you don't know that because you don't know anything about her," he said, his voice getting more strident. "But we can tell you there was something wrong."

Rodney asked the next questions. "When you say *wrong*," he began quietly, "just what does that mean?"

Mr. Brown looked at his wife, who looked back at him and shrugged. "It's hard to tell you in a way that would make you understand," he replied, his hands brushing his forehead.

Kate noted the tremors in Mr. Brown's hands.

Whatever this was, they firmly believed in what they were saying. Kate didn't have any proof of it, and they didn't either, but they were fully convinced that whatever had happened had somehow involved their son's wife. "Did he join a certain religious group with her? Was it hers to begin with?"

"It was her family," Mrs. Brown replied. "She belonged to a very strict religious … I don't know what you want to call it." She showed her palms. "But the woman's family was very strict, and her father was the ruler above all else. Honest to God, I can't think of anything other than the fact that that family was somehow responsible for what happened to that little boy and to our daughter-in-law." She turned to Kate. "That will be your job to sort this out and to determine who and what happened to them. I just can't imagine in my worst nightmare that my son would ever have participated." Mrs. Brown took a deep breath, then continued. "In your mind it's already pretty clear," she told Kate, "and all I can ask is that you keep an open mind when you find out more details because this is not who my son was."

"It may not be who he was when you knew him," Kate replied quietly, "but it's obvious that's who he became by the end of the day."

At that, the other woman broke down into tears, then heavy sobs.

❧

THE REST OF his evening went way too quickly, as far as Simon was concerned. He was also constantly looking for some response from Kate but assumed that it would be another one of those evenings where he didn't get to see her.

The next morning dawned bright and clear, and he hopped out of bed, surprisingly eager to take a look at Bartlett's business and see just what was going on. Simon wasn't sure that he had any information to help the guy, and that was a concern because Simon was obviously hoping for some answers to Bartlett's mess. And, if there were answers, Simon might find them, but it depended on how badly the business had been running.

As he approached the corporate office, Bartlett was already there, talking to somebody ahead of him. Bartlett opened the door for Simon and waved him in. "I was just explaining to the staff here who you are and what you'll be doing and to give you whatever access you need," he said easily.

If it were that simple, it would be nice, but, chances were, it wouldn't be that simple. It never was. Everybody always wanted to hold back when it came to sharing information, but regardless Simon smiled and nodded at the clerk. "Do you have a desk for me? A space where I can sit down and start going through paperwork?"

They set him up with an office, and Bartlett stood nervously in the doorway. "Honestly, I'm really hoping you can help out."

"Me too," Simon replied, looking up at him. "Go and let me take a look."

Bartlett still hesitated to leave, but he didn't say a word.

"You're obviously very nervous," Simon added. "Maybe you need to come in and tell me why."

He looked behind him at the staff, quickly stepped in, and closed the door. "I'm not sure if my father-in-law was completely legit."

Simon sat back and then gave Bartlett a searching gaze. "Now's not a good time to find that out."

"I know," Bartlett admitted. "It's a shit time to find out. I just don't have too many options right now."

Simon thought about it and nodded. "The only thing I can tell you is that I'll keep it in mind, while we go through things, but honestly, if he wasn't legit, … this is the time to sort it out."

"But what does that mean?" Bartlett asked in a hoarse whisper. "I don't want to do jail time for something he did."

"If it was just him," Simon noted, "then there should be some way to get clear of it. If not, that's a different story, and, worst-case scenario, … you could very well need a lawyer. However, we aren't there yet."

"Right." Bartlett took several deep breaths and then gave a forced smile. "Can I get you anything? Coffee?"

"Coffee would be good."

And with that and a log-on, Simon headed into the databases of the computers. It didn't take long to sort out the filing system. It took a whole lot longer to figure out what he was looking at. When Bartlett returned several hours later, Simon was still sifting through online documents.

"You're making me nervous."

Simon looked at him. "Why is that?"

"You haven't said anything."

"I haven't said anything because I haven't gotten very far yet," he stated. "I'm seeing all kinds of business deals, and potentially decent business deals, but it depends how they were made, whether they were made willingly, or if a lot of pressure was involved."

"I don't know," Bartlett admitted.

"You mentioned your father-in-law handled the business. Where's your wife in all this?"

"She doesn't have anything to do with the business," he replied.

Simon sat back and looked at him, relaxing in his seat. "So, does she only take part in spending the business's earnings?"

Bartlett winced and nodded slowly. "Unfortunately, you could say that."

"You'll have to shut her down real fast," Simon declared, with a definitive tone. "You guys are bleeding money, and, before you lose the home you're in, you need to make some pretty strong financial turnarounds here."

At that, Bartlett's face fell. "I was really hoping you wouldn't say that."

"Meaning, she won't take it kindly?"

"No, not only will she not take it kindly, I doubt she'll even listen," he stated bluntly.

"Then it's time you brought her in, so she can hear it from somebody else," Simon declared equally bluntly. "Because you are bleeding money. I'm not even a portion of the way through, but it's already very clear the activity in the bank account is not in sync with the cash flow, so you better bring her in," he ordered.

At that, Bartlett stared at him in horror.

"Yeah, I'm serious, unless you *want* to end up in debtor's jail," Simon added, with a frown.

"Do they even call it that anymore?" Bartlett asked, as his face fell.

"Does it matter? It is prudent that you get this under

control, before you get in bigger trouble than you are expecting or can handle. Somebody needs to give her a talking to, and believe me. I don't have a problem doing it."

At that, Bartlett winced. "Nobody's ever had a chance to talk to her."

"Yeah? How does she feel about losing the house, the status, the cars, and everything else? Because, based on what I can see here, absolutely everything you own is about to be sold, just so you can stay out of jail and can pay your taxes."

"What?" Bartlett asked. "What are you talking about?"

"Oh, come on. You knew you were in trouble," Simon stated, sighing, looking at him.

"Yeah, but is it that bad?"

"Oh, it's that bad," Simon snapped, "and yet you're still not leaving me alone long enough to sort out just how bad, but I can already tell you that it's bad, and now I need some time."

"Right." Bartlett took a deep breath.

"Get your wife in here," Simon ordered, his tone firm.

He winced. "You don't know my wife."

"No, but lots of women are like your wife," Simon explained, his voice hard. "She's got a couple choices right now, but one of the things that she won't do is divorce you over this."

"Why not?" he asked.

"Because her name's got a lot of the debt too," Simon pointed out. "She's just as likely to be in hot water as anybody else."

"That was her father's doing then. He wanted to make sure the assets stayed with her."

"Yeah? In the process, he also made sure the liabilities stayed with her, so, as I said, get her in here."

And, with that, Bartlett took off at a run.

Simon wasn't even sure what to say to anybody who could be this blind as to what was going on around him. Obviously the father-in-law had been running the business, probably pretty much kept it in the red. Maybe he didn't care. Maybe it was all about lifestyle. Maybe he didn't particularly worry about the end result, since he didn't live all that long, after all. Although, without a clue how old the old man was, or how he died, Simon couldn't make a judgment call on that.

When Bartlett came back a little later, Simon asked him, "How old was your father-in-law when he passed?" He asked the question as he searched through documents, looking for some of the information that was a little harder to find.

"He was …" Bartlett thought about it and said, "I think sixty-eight, sixty-nine, or thereabouts."

"Now, the tough question," Simon said, looking at him directly. "How did he die?"

Bartlett took a deep breath. "I'm afraid he killed himself."

"I am afraid of that too," Simon agreed, looking at him. "He's been bleeding the company dry. This was heading for a major crash, whether you were aware of it or not."

Bartlett paled. "Oh God, it'll be bad, won't it?"

"Yeah, it sure will," Simon muttered. "But there's bad and then there's bad, and, right now, if we can get some of this sorted and pay off some of these taxes"—he quickly tallied the figures in his head—"you might not need to declare bankruptcy."

Bartlett gave a half squawk.

Simon looked up at him, frowned, and asked, "Why do you think you contacted me?"

"I know," he muttered. "It's just that my wife will hit the roof."

"Yeah, she probably will," Simon agreed, "but, if you don't listen, you're heading for some major financial trauma in your life. So, it's up to you guys. In the meantime, I'll get a lawyer on this right away and see where your liability starts and stops."

At that, Bartlett sagged into the chair beside him, just staring at Simon.

Simon nodded. "Sorry, man, but I'm calling it the way I see it, and you guys are in trouble."

Bartlett sat here, sipping something from a mug that Simon was pretty certain was a whole lot stronger than coffee.

A woman, her voice strident, called out from the nearby hallway, "Bartlett, where are you, damn it? You knew I was off having a day with the ladies." She stomped closer to them, looking for Bartlett.

Bartlett seemed to shrink farther into the chair, and Simon shook his head. "Seriously? That's what you're putting up with?"

Bartlett nodded. "The thing is, I mean, she's really not that bad."

"Right, until you disturb her *ladies' day*."

"Exactly."

"That's not all she's about to get disturbed about," Simon added, a smirk on his face.

The door flung open, and a woman stepped in, her fury obvious in the way she let the door crash behind her.

Simon stood and reached out a hand. "I'm Simon. Mrs. Morris. You need to sit down, and you need to listen."

She glared at him. "Who the fuck are you? And better

yet, why the hell should I listen to you?"

Simon moved to shut the door, then turned to face her. "Because you guys are broke. You should have declared bankruptcy quite a while ago, and, if your father did commit suicide, it's because he knew what the hell was happening, and he dodged it," Simon stated bluntly. "That bullet now has both your names on it, and it's about to go off now."

She stared at him in shock, then turned to look at Bartlett in more shock, then sagged into the chair beside him. "What?"

"You heard me," Simon stated, with a careless shrug. "You've been ripping money out of this company, like it was your personal bank account," Simon told her bluntly, "and that not only has to stop but you have to give back a whole pile of it, right now to the tax authorities, and the sooner, the better."

She went silent.

Simon continued. "We have a lawyer coming in to see about the indemnity of your personal status, considering that your father was likely embezzling money and not paying taxes that should have been paid." Simon stared at her. "And please don't waste my time by telling me that it's not possible because your daddy would never do such a thing because the evidence is right in front of me."

She took a deep breath, but Bartlett reached over and grabbed her hand. "We're past that now."

She looked at him in shock. "Seriously?"

He nodded. "Yeah, according to Simon, we'll quite likely lose the house, the cars, everything."

She stared at him. "But we own all kinds of properties," she wailed. "Sell that."

"All that is potentially possible," Bartlett replied. "I sold several pieces to Simon himself, in order to stay afloat long enough to see if we can fix this."

"Declare bankruptcy," she snapped, "but give me a chance to move the money first."

"There is no money to move," Simon declared from the desk. "That's what I'm trying to tell you. There is no more money for you to pull out of the company. You've already stripped everything there is."

She stared at him like a viper. "I didn't do it."

"Oh, you're clearly an old hand at it yourself," Simon declared. "You've been bleeding the company dry, right along with your daddy, and that stops now."

"And if it doesn't?" she asked coolly.

"There isn't any more money," Simon repeated, "and I've just frozen your accounts, so that your bills and your staff can be paid."

She turned to glance at the shut door, where at least thirty people were beyond there in the office, and then back to look at him.

Simon nodded. "Don't even begin to tell me that you'll strip out whatever money is left in the account," he snapped, his voice harsh, "and leave every one of these people trying to pay their own rent because you decided that you were more important than your responsibilities. You don't get a free ride for life, Mrs. Morris, and your free ride just stopped."

She turned and looked at Bartlett. "What the hell have you done?"

"What have I done?" he asked, looking at her in astonishment.

"Daddy had this completely set up to run autonomously. He told me that I would be looked after forever."

"How long ago was that?" Simon asked her curiously.

She flushed all kinds of red. "It's been a while. So what?"

"Oh, I'm sure it has been," Simon agreed. "I'm sure it's been *quite* a while." She glared at him, and he nodded. "I don't give a fuck who you are, where you live, or what you do, but I was asked to look into this and to see if there was any possible way to save your company, to save your properties, and at least give you something to keep over your head." Simon shook his head. "Right now the answer is clearly no." He looked at the bag she carried and smiled. "What did that bag cost—$7,000?"

She flushed and pulled it tight against her. "Somewhat around there, yes."

"And the jewelry you're wearing, another $40,000?"

She reached her hand up instinctively, touching her earrings and necklace, then nodded. "Maybe."

Simon nodded. "Guess what? That money was taken from the company, with no taxes paid on any of it," he explained. "Your dad just assumed that, somewhere along the line, things would work out. However, once he hit a bad patch, … he just kept on assuming, hoping things would work out." Simon looked at her and added, "Things won't work out any longer."

She shook her head in denial. "Somebody else can take a look at this," she snapped. "I don't like you."

"Of course you don't like me. I just told you that your free ride is done," he repeated, with a knowing smile. "Something Bartlett should have told you a long time ago, and something your father should never have let you do in the first place. Absolutely no way should you be spending the company credit cards the way you are. So those have been frozen too. Plus we'll look at your personal taxes, pay down whatever we can, maybe declare bankruptcy, and see what we can salvage afterward." Simon gave a shake of his head. "And, if you're lucky, maybe, … just maybe you'll still have a place to live."

"Not just a place to live," she wailed in horror. "It must be *my* place to live. We just finished the renovations."

"Yeah, and what did they cost you?" he asked, with a sardonic smile in her direction.

She flushed and shrugged. "I don't know. I didn't pay it."

"And that's one of the questions I need to ask. Who did pay it?" Simon asked, turning to look at Bartlett, and it was his time to flush red.

"My father-in-law told her to do it before he died."

"So, it's been ongoing for months, and you've been just giving the bills to Daddy?"

She nodded slowly.

Simon asked her, "Are you telling me that he's been taking it out of the company?"

"Of course he's been taking it out of the company," she snapped. "That's what the company is there for. That's what it makes money for."

Simon groaned, shaking his head. "Yeah, it makes money all right, but you're also supposed to only take out profits, after expenditures and taxes and payroll, so the company is still solvent." Simon snorted, sending a harsh look to Bartlett. "And any money you take out … is taxable."

She rolled her eyes at him. "So, pay the tax on it for Christ's sake. Why are you bothering me with this stuff?"

"Because there's no money to pay the taxes," Simon repeated, looking at her. "There's no money to pay any of it. Your house isn't even paid off, and you were still blowing all that money on renos, when you've got a very hefty mortgage.

You don't even have the money to pay next month's payments."

She stared at Simon in shock, then slowly turned to Bartlett.

Her husband nodded. "I've been trying to figure out what to do ever since your father died."

"He told me everything was in great shape," she whispered.

"Yeah, he told me the same thing," Bartlett agreed, "but then remember that letter he left us? ... The one that said he was sorry?"

Her eyes widened, as it slowly sank in. "Oh my God, we're really broke?"

"No, you're not just broke," Simon corrected, "you're bankrupt, and there's quite a difference."

"What is ... what ..." She could hardly get the words out. "What does it mean when you say, *bankrupt?*"

"I mean that you're about to lose the house, the cars, your jewelry, and everything else you own. It will all need to be sold to pay your debtors. If we can get this done quickly and efficiently, and, no, I'm not sure how fast yet," he added, "we might save the business but no guarantees."

She glared at him. "My father would never have done this. You're wrong."

"If I'm wrong," Simon replied, "you go home and do whatever you want to do. Go home and see how long all this lasts. First, your credit cards—that were already way overdue—have stopped working. Then soon the bill collectors and the tax agents will be coming and calling because, jeez, somebody's been making minimum payments on how much is this current balance on just the one credit card?" he asked, turning to look at the screen. "Ah, a balance of $32,000."

She shrugged. "That's nothing. I mean ..." She turned to Bartlett and said in a much harsher tone, "Just pay that."

Bartlett looked at her and for the first time seemed angry. "I can't. That kind of money isn't in the accounts."

Simon asked her, "What did your father live on when he was alive?"

"Well," she winced and said, "he could spend money pretty well."

"On what?" Simon persisted.

She glared at him, and he just stared right back. "Let's just say he was a little free with his money."

"But it wasn't his money, was it?" Simon stated.

"It was the company's money, so it's the same thing. It's his."

"No," Bartlett disagreed quietly, "it's the company's money, and he didn't pay his debts either. Apparently Simon confirmed that his house isn't paid off, and neither are any of his own properties."

"But that's all supposed to be mine." She turned to look at Bartlett in horror. "You can't take that from me."

"There's nothing to take," Bartlett explained. "I already had his house appraised, and it's worthless. Your father took out a second mortgage, and he even did some reverse financing, and, with the way the market is struggling at the moment"—Bartlett shook his head—"it's now worth less than is owed on it."

At that, she sat back, tears in her eyes, and whispered, "My God."

"Yeah," he muttered, with a look at Simon. "Now you understand why I brought Simon in. I'm trying desperately to find a way to save this, so we can go home tonight and have a place to sleep."

She didn't even seem to know what to say.

Simon looked at her intently. "You may not want to hear it, but this is your wake-up call. Whether you like it or not, everything you own and thought you owned isn't yours." Simon shrugged. "Now we have to find a way to pay it back—or pay enough of it back and restructure the company so that you can keep something."

"If not?" she asked.

"Otherwise the easy answer is to declare bankruptcy and lose it all," Simon replied. "In that case, you need to get a bankruptcy lawyer and accountant in here and see what they can do for you."

She was almost trembling as she stared at him, but it seemed she finally understood.

Bartlett looked over at Simon and added, "We need a few minutes."

Simon nodded. "You can do whatever you want to do," he said, as he looked down at his watch. "I have to deal with other issues in my own world. You know where to find me."

And, with that, he got up, not unaware but completely devoid of emotion at the devastation he'd left behind.

CHAPTER 7

EVEN AFTER KATE had finished interviewing the family yesterday, she still had nothing to go on. These people had been kept out of the loop for long enough that they didn't really have any current information on their son's family's lifestyle, where they lived, or how they lived. Kate wanted to canvass the neighborhood but the street cops did that the first night.

However, they didn't get much. Kate wanted to check it out in person. She was having a very hard time staying neutral after seeing that little boy's body, especially with the Browns so adamant that their son Roger would never do such a thing. Yet Kate knew from experience that everybody out there would like to think their son would never do that. Still the fact of the matter was that it had happened.

And somebody somewhere knew something.

So this morning, they headed out to canvass the Brown neighborhood early. She'd also left orders for both sets of the victims' last days to be tracked. Jobs worked at, companies visited, bank accounts used, friends, and anything else to be brought out into the light, so Kate and her team could take a look and could analyze where the Brown family and the Holley couple had been. Kate didn't know whether somebody had kidnapped them for an extended period or this was seriously just the way that their lives had ended up.

That didn't sit right with Kate either.

So many things could go wrong in this world, and this just seemed to add another layer that didn't make any sense. She kept focusing on the Browns, what with the little boy involved. Unless the father was rich in terms of finances, he must have had a job somewhere along the line. A job that required him to show up and to perform some task. That's what jobs were, and yet nobody knew where Roger worked or what he did.

"And yet, on the first canvass, everybody in the neighborhood said good things about them, how the Browns seemed like the nicest people," Kate muttered, her tone full of irony, as she got back to her car, Rodney right there with her.

"We can't hold it against them. They just didn't know," Rodney pointed out. "How many of your neighbors do you know?"

"The little old lady down at the other end of the hall," Kate stated, with a nod. "And mostly only because, every once in a while, I give her a hand carrying groceries. Plus she has this habit of getting locked out of the building," Kate noted, with half a smile.

"Exactly. I'm surprised that you're ever there enough to help out."

"It happens," she said, "not very often, but it does happen."

He nodded, and, as she pulled into the Browns' driveway, her phone rang. It was Lilliana.

"Hey, we found out where Roger worked," she updated Kate. "We'll check it out."

"Sounds good. Otherwise we'll hit it today."

At the Browns' family home, Kate deliberately walked

around outside the house several times, to see whether anybody would look, would be bothered, or would even check out of a window, but she saw nothing. Finally she walked up to a nearby house and knocked.

When a woman finally answered the door, she held a cranky baby and looked fairly unhappy at seeing Kate.

She smiled and nodded at her. "Sorry to disturb you, but we're investigating the murder of your neighbors."

The neighbor lady winced, and a visible shudder rippled down her body. "God, it's all I can think about."

"I'm sorry. It's always hard when violence comes to your neighborhood."

The other woman started to sob gently. Kate held her ground, and then, when the tears dried up, she asked, "May we come in?"

She shook her head. "Please, please, no, I just need this to go away."

"The sooner we can ask you a few questions," Rodney added, his voice gentle but firm, "the sooner we can leave you alone. Plus the neighbors won't see us standing here on your stoop."

She stared up at him, looked down at the baby, and then groaned. "Fine, but make it fast, please. My husband will be home soon, and he won't be happy." She let them into the entry foyer, but no further, shutting the front door behind them.

As these were shades of what this neighbor may very well be going through, Kate looked at her intently. "I presume this stuff is bothering everybody."

The woman just nodded and didn't say anything.

Kate cast a glance at Rodney, and he'd caught it too. As she smiled at the woman, Kate asked, "How old is the baby?"

She looked down and muttered, "Fourteen months."

"Do you only have the one?"

She nodded and then looked at Kate and then to Rodney. "Is this really relevant?"

"No, not necessarily," Kate replied. "But I do need to know if you saw anybody in the neighborhood, especially anyone at the victims' house. We would also like to know what type of people they were."

"I didn't really have anything to do with them," she muttered.

"And yet you told the officers who interviewed you earlier this week that they were really nice people," Rodney noted immediately.

She looked at him and shrugged. "What else was I supposed to say? Of course they were nice people. Everybody is when you get murdered," she snapped and then started to cry again.

Rodney looked over at Kate, as she winced. "So, you didn't really know them, is that what you're saying?"

"You make it sound like I was lying before," she replied, staring at her in horror.

"We come here asking questions because we're trying to solve three murders," Kate snapped in a flinty tone. "The Browns died in an extremely violent way, possibly here in your neighborhood, and we need to know more about what these people were like. So, when we ask questions, there is a purpose behind them. We aren't looking for platitudes or something that makes you feel better, and definitely not *Oh, they're such nice people.* If they weren't nice people, tell us, and, if they were nice people, then tell us that too."

The woman seemed more panicked from one second to the next. "Do I have to?"

"Yes, you do. Did you ever hear them fighting? Did you ever hear the little boy crying? Did you ever hear anything that bothered you?"

She stared at Kate and took a deep breath. "I didn't even know that little boy lived there," she cried out in frustration. "When I first heard it, I thought it couldn't be my neighbors because we never saw the little boy, not once. That's partly why I'm so upset because I never even knew he was there," she wailed painfully.

"That's a start," Kate noted. "Would your husband have seen him?"

"I don't think so," the woman replied. "He's gone most of the time at work, and, when he's not working, he's ..." Then she stopped and winced, not sure how to say it out loud.

"Drinking?" Kate asked. The other woman looked at her in horror, as Kate shrugged. "Believe me. We've seen it all."

"You might have seen it all, but if my husband had any indication that I told you anything—"

"We're not telling him," Kate stated.

The other woman looked immeasurably relieved, leaving Kate to wonder just what kind of a world this woman was living in, when the first thing on her mind was to protect herself from her husband. Kate looked over at Rodney, who was staring at her with a worried look on his face.

Rodney added, "Ma'am, I know you don't want to hear this, but domestic violence can erupt over the slightest thing."

"Oh, I know." The woman shook her head in a panic. "But when you don't have any other means of support and when you're stuck in a scenario like this, it's not as if there are simple answers."

"No," Rodney agreed quietly, "but there are answers, simple or not."

She stared at him for a long moment, then nodded. "Fine. I hear your point, and I get it. Now, can you please leave?"

Kate looked over at Rodney and nodded. "Outside of not having seen the little boy, did you see Mary and Roger Brown much?"

"No." Her tone appeared to be a little desperate, as if really hoping that, by answering, they would move on faster.

At this point, Kate was itching to see this husband who had such an impact on his wife. "Did your husband have anything to do with the Brown family?"

"No, of course not," she said, looking at the detective in surprise. "Why would he?"

"I don't know, but the fact is, the Brown family was badly beaten, and your husband is an abuser," she stated. "So, it's not that I'm looking at him as a suspect, but I just wondered if maybe they belonged to the same club or something."

The woman appeared shocked, puzzled and slowly shook her head. "It's not as if there's a wife-beating club, you know."

"I don't know about that," Kate countered. "Believe me. I've heard and seen enough things in my lifetime that the existence of such a thing would not surprise me in the least."

The woman winced. "I couldn't do your job," she muttered.

"Not many can," Kate stated, "but I do what I do to try and keep people like you, safe."

The woman nodded. "Believe me. … I am grateful." Yet she spoke in an urgent tone. "However, right now, keeping me safe would mean you guys leaving. Please."

Such a note of desperation filled her tone that Kate nodded. "Okay, we'll leave. But is there a better time we can come back?"

She hesitated, then added, "Look. I have to go to the nurse tomorrow for the baby to get her shot," she explained. "I could meet you someplace then."

"Good enough," Kate agreed. As she stepped out, she looked over at Rodney, who was obviously unhappy about leaving this woman alone. Kate called him over and said, "Come on. Let's go."

"I don't like it," he muttered, staring back at the young woman.

The woman just shook her head, but her desperation was getting stronger.

"Don't worry," Kate told her. "We're leaving. We're going right now." She pulled Rodney along the walkway. "Come on. Walk quickly, and head over toward the next set of neighbors."

"Why?" he asked, then turned and looked behind at the woman.

Kate grabbed him by the arm. "Stop it."

He hesitated. "Why? What's going on?"

"She's terrified—in case you hadn't figured that out," she snapped, frowning at him.

"Of course I figured it out. But why is she still there?" he asked in frustration.

"Because she doesn't have anywhere else to go."

He looked at her in surprise and then groaned. "I guess there's not really a whole lot of options for some of these women, is there?"

"If she doesn't have parents or a sibling to help out or a

safe place to go or even a way to get to that safe place, then, no, there isn't a whole lot of options."

He swallowed and nodded. "Damn it."

"Yeah, *damn it* is right, but we can't force her to leave. And we're limited in man-hours, and we have to stick to what we're doing."

"Can't we do anything?"

"No," Kate replied. "Not unless the baby was injured. The mother is an adult and is willingly staying there on her own."

That just seemed to upset Rodney even more.

"Rodney," Kate said in a warning tone, as they walked up the sidewalk to the next house. "Remember why we're here."

"Yeah." Rodney shook his head. "Apparently we're in a wife-beater neighborhood," he stated in disgust, but he held his tone in check. When they knocked on the door at the next house, an older man opened the door, glaring at them.

She nodded, as she held up her badge. "We're here to ask you about the neighbors, Mary and Roger Brown, and the boy, Daniel."

"I don't give a shit about the neighbors," he snapped. "The cops were already here once. Don't you guys talk?"

"I'm the detective on the case," Kate replied smoothly, "and I don't like to listen to anybody else's interpretations, so I came myself."

He stared at her and then slowly nodded. "At least that's something," he muttered, "but I don't know anything."

"No? Nobody ever really knows anything, but some-times the tiniest little bit of information that can help is huge."

"Which means, you've got nothing," he stated, staring at

her.

"Which means, we have very little to go on, yes," she replied, grudgingly admitting the truth. "That doesn't mean we don't have anything, but everyone deserves to have a fair trial, so, when we get this guy, we need to make sure we have a solid case."

He groaned. "I was a security guard for many years, and there's just nothing quite like having a scenario like this happen so close to home," he shared. "It's bullshit. That's what it is. It's all just bullshit."

"That may be," she acknowledged, with a nod, "but, if you were a security guard, you also know that there are a lot of rules, a lot of things that don't go the way you want them to, even though you think they should."

"Yeah, I know," he agreed quietly, as he stared off into the distance. "I didn't even know that boy was there." The former security guard seemed lost in his own thoughts. "It makes me feel like a piece of shit to know that a little boy suffered like that."

"I've heard that from other people as well, so I presume he was kept in the house and away from everyone."

"I guess so," he said listlessly, "though it makes no sense to me. I mean, why have a kid at all if you'll just use him as a punching bag?"

"But then why have a wife at all," she added, "if you'll just use her as a punching bag?"

He looked at her in surprise and nodded. "Never did make much sense out of that either," he noted, as he glanced over at the other house. "Did you just come from over there?"

"I did," she confirmed, her tone soft. "You've seen or heard some things over there, have you?"

"I sure have, and it would be nice to think that she would take some advice and leave, but …" He just shook his head. "I never understood that whole punching-bag mentality myself."

"It's not a punching-bag mentality," Kate corrected. "It's an abuse-victim mentality. Somebody who thinks nobody is out there to help. Somebody who doesn't believe that anybody gives a crap."

He groaned. "I know. I know. I shouldn't have put it quite that way."

"Yet you've seen it before. So, in your mind, … that's just what it is."

"I have seen it before." He nodded. "It makes me just as angry now as it did then."

"When did you see it before?"

"My daughter," he said. "I couldn't get her to leave him, not for the longest time. She kept saying that she'd be fine, that he would change, and that he was a different man when she was around." The former security guard raised both hands. "It's just bullshit." He glared at her in frustration. "You know that woman next door won't leave either."

"I can only offer her the opportunity to leave," Kate stated, "and, after that, it'll be up to her. It's not easy being a single parent, and I'm sure that weighs heavily on her mind."

He nodded. "I still think we're a messed-up world when that's not a priority."

"Nobody said it wasn't a priority," Kate pointed out. "I'm just telling you that, right now, I'm here to ask you questions about your neighbors."

"Yeah, but will you ask about the right neighbor?"

"We'll talk about that one lady in a little bit, but, first off, how about the ones who wound up dead?"

"As I told you, I never saw the boy at all," he muttered. "I didn't see anything like the mess that apparently was visible on their bodies." He shook his head. "It's a hell of a thing to hang up somebody like that in a church."

She didn't say anything and just let him ramble.

"He wasn't exactly church-going material."

"How do you know that?" she asked.

He looked at her and snorted. "You should have heard that man swear. You should have heard his attitude about life. It had nothing to do with being a law-abiding citizen. I can tell you that," he declared, almost in disgust. "It was all about him looking after himself and keeping anything he wanted for himself too. He didn't give a shit about that wife of his, so no way he gave a shit about that kid."

"I'm sorry to hear that," Kate noted quietly. "That must have been tough for the family."

"And yet she stayed," he snapped, staring at Kate. "She stayed."

Kate nodded slowly. "And again, maybe she didn't know how to do any differently."

"Maybe," he muttered, "or maybe she just didn't give a shit either."

"I don't know. … I doubt that we'll ever find answers to that question."

Rodney asked, "Did you ever see him hit his wife?"

He shook his head. "No, I heard the crying though."

"Did you ever hear her scream *Stop, get away, help*, or anything like that?" Kate asked.

He shook his head again. "No, I never did. Maybe I would have done something about it if I heard her asking for help." He stared back at the victims' house, frowning. "I just don't understand, unless she was drugged or something," he muttered, his gaze sliding back toward Kate.

"No idea," she replied, "and, no, I won't tell you if she was."

"No, of course not," he muttered. "It still sucks though."

"It absolutely does still suck," Kate agreed.

"I don't want to see the other neighbor lady and her kid end up the same way."

"No, none of us do. On the other hand," Kate reminded him, "there is still such a thing as free will in this world."

He shook his head. "How is any of that free will?"

She smiled. "How's your daughter doing?"

"She's better," he said, brightening up, "much better actually."

"Good. So, keep your focus on that, and we'll see what else we can find out to make sure whoever did this to the Browns goes down for it."

He nodded. "I don't really have anything to offer." He shook his head. "I wasn't a very good neighbor, and, because of all that shit going on over there, I didn't want to get involved," he muttered. "I didn't really get to know them."

"I think that's probably how they preferred it too," she suggested, nodding in agreement. "So any efforts could quite possibly have just been rebuffed. So, I get that you might want to blame yourself, but I wouldn't waste your energy on that."

He nodded. "Thanks for that. It's a shitty thing to think that you've got somebody out there pulling these kinds of stunts, and you have absolutely no idea it's even going on."

"I know," she murmured. "But again, stick to what you know, to what you can deal with, and let us work on the rest." And, with that, she turned and walked outside.

She groaned, when she got back to the street, and turned

to Rodney. "Cases like this tend to make everybody rethink a lot of things in their lives."

"Hell, and so it should. We shouldn't be going around innocently into the night, when a family suffered like the Browns did."

"Oh, I agree," she murmured. "But how are you supposed to tell, from one day to the next, the good from the bad and how to make it all into something that's doable?" she asked, looking over at him. "I mean, obviously a lot of people could have gotten involved, could have helped, and nobody did. ... I don't know that it's so much that they didn't care to help, as much as ..." She paused.

"Nobody really wants to get involved. Nobody wants to call the cops. Nobody wants to see how bad it actually is, and nobody wants to turn that kind of attention onto themselves," Rodney muttered.

She nodded, then continued with the canvass. The people living in the next three houses didn't appear to be any different, with the same type of responses. Nobody had seen the little boy. Everybody seemed to know that there was some sort of abuse going on, but nobody had told the police because, well, ... she'd stayed.

"It's interesting to me that everybody thinks that, because she stayed, she didn't need or couldn't have used a little help in getting out," Rodney stated in a hard tone.

"Whether it was a case of not being able to do something about it, I don't know," Kate replied, "but it is an interesting insight, isn't it?"

"Yeah, and it sucks," he muttered. "I would really like to think that she could have gotten out and could have stayed out."

"You and me both, but not this time around."

After they headed back to their vehicle, they sat in the car for a long moment, exchanging thoughts, when the last guy they had talked to came out and rapped on the window. She rolled it down to look at him expectantly.

"Look. I don't know that it means anything," he began, "but the Browns had a regular visitor, and, whenever that guy came over, it seemed like, … like it was much worse."

She frowned at him. "You think the visits incited more violence?"

"I don't know if it incited more violence," he replied, then hesitated and lowered his voice. "Maybe this guy … wasn't part of it."

"As in actively beating her too?"

He nodded, then turned, looked around, and added, "But I don't know anything about it." And, with that, he quickly left.

Kate hesitated, then looked back to a couple other places where they had already asked questions. She pointed out the first house. "How about you go and ask about this visiting man over there," she suggested. "I'll go ask at the other house."

Rodney raised an eyebrow and nodded. "That would be pretty twisted."

"We've seen plenty of twisted," Kate noted. "Let's just make sure we aren't dealing with something *extra* ugly here."

"It doesn't even have to be really ugly," he muttered, as he turned to walk away. "Everybody has different sets of beliefs, and, just because they're not yours, it doesn't automatically make them wrong," he said pointedly.

"Oh, absolutely, but you're the one who brought up *ugly*, so you're the one who may have to deal with the fact that whatever is going on here is not something you would approve of."

He winced and nodded. "Yeah, that's how we've spun, isn't it?"

She chuckled. "Let's at least get this question answered. Then we'll move on from there." She walked up to the one house where she'd already been. When the middle-aged woman answered, she glared at her, and Kate nodded in an apology. "I just have another question that came up, and I hope it's not a bother."

"What if it is?" she asked bitterly, and Kate nodded.

"Have you seen another man over there at the Browns' house at times? Particularly when there may have been incidents?"

The woman looked at her and frowned. "Incidents?"

"Yes, and you know perfectly well what I mean."

She flushed. "Look. I don't want to get into any trouble."

"Why would telling us get you into any trouble?"

She shrugged. "We like to keep to ourselves around here," she whispered, nervously looking around.

"I get that, but what we don't want is to have anybody else hurt."

Her frown seemed to pull down her entire face, and finally she nodded. "I have seen a stranger around. I mean, I'm not saying he was a stranger. … Well, no, saying it that way implies that I knew him." She frowned, then stopped. "Look. I don't even know what I'm saying," she muttered. "All I can tell you is that there has been somebody over there at odd times. I don't know what, if any, involvement he has with the group."

"Good enough," Kate said, "and I suppose you couldn't give me any description, could you?"

The woman frowned at her. "I'm not sure I could actually. He always seemed to come wearing a dark coat. That's how I would know him. A dark coat, you know? Like a trench coat, those long ones, and he always had a hat on."

"Okay, and what hat do you wear with a trench coat?" Kate asked, with a note of humor.

The woman shrugged. "Whatever it is, I think he was very comfortable over there because he rarely knocked."

"Oh, that's interesting," Kate replied. "That implies a pretty high position in the family, doesn't it?"

"It does in a way, and yet I don't know if that's how I would put it," she replied cautiously. "I don't know."

"No, of course not," Kate said, "and that's fine, thank you." Kate walked away, and the woman's relief was almost palpable.

When Kate got back to the car, Rodney looked at her and nodded. "Mine certainly noticed but didn't know anything about it."

"Yeah, mine did too, and she told me how he always wore a long trench coat and a hat, but she couldn't really describe the hat."

"Or she didn't want to describe the hat."

"Either way, we do have another character we need to talk to, though finding him will be a challenge."

"Next we better head over to the brother, George Brown's place, and talk to him."

She winced because talking to the families was always one of the hardest things, but she also knew it needed to be done.

As they pulled up in front of the brother's home, she watched two men talking in the driveway. When they saw her and Rodney approach, they frowned and separated, one going around the house and the other one heading over to the neighbors. She snorted at Rodney. "Isn't it nice to know how welcome we are?"

With a smile, Rodney muttered a reply, "We're only welcome if we're bringing them good news, and when do cops ever bring good news?"

She walked up to the front door to knock, and it opened right under her fingers, and there was the man she had seen on the driveway. She nodded. "I could have just talked to you outside. But, now that you've answered the door, may we come in?"

George shook his head. "I really don't want you inside. It's already a very upsetting time for us."

"Absolutely it is," Kate agreed. "So Roger was your brother, right? Your parents didn't say much about you."

"No, they are pretty upset over Roger's death right now. And we've never been close. But they are coming over for dinner tomorrow. Hopefully my brother's death can help bring us closer," he shared.

Kate did detect a tremor of emotion—or fear. She studied him closely for a long moment and asked, "Any idea just what was going on in Roger and Mary's relationship?"

He looked at her carefully and then shook his head. "No, I didn't really have anything to do with him. Remember?"

"That's what your father mentioned."

"It's true. I don't know what all my father had to say," George added, "but it was sad that the family lost touch with Roger the way we did."

She asked, "What was Mary like?"

"It's hard to say," he replied briskly. "It's not as if I had a chance to get to know her."

"Were you at the wedding?"

"No, we weren't invited." When Kate's eyebrows rose at that, he shrugged. "Right? Just like everything else about them, that was another very strange thing. There was no need to keep our family away, but my parents certainly felt they should do something along that line, and they did." George shook his head. "So, what am I supposed to say about it?"

"You don't have to say anything?" Kate asked. "Obviously, losing your brother right now is hard, but we now have two families affected by very similar incidents, and quite possibly the same killer, so I'm trying to make sure there isn't a third family who goes by the wayside."

His eyes widened at that. "God, that's a shitty thought." He frowned and added in a harsh tone, "You should be out there looking for the sadistic son of a bitch who killed Roger."

She gave him a droll look. "That's why we're here asking questions, so anything you can tell me about your brother and his wife's relationship, where they worked, what they did, how they spent their free time, anything could possibly help us." She took a deep breath to add, "And whether your brother was known to beat his wife."

Her words came out of the blue and shocked George to the core. He shook his head. "No way, he wasn't the kind to beat anybody."

"These autopsies of the five victims are happening as we speak, but there was clear evidence of long-term physical abuse of both Mary and Daniel." George stared at her blankly, and she realized it was the first time he'd even considered the thought.

"My brother would never have hit a soul," he stated, his

voice hoarse. "Never." He stared off in the distance blankly. "I can't even imagine what she could possibly have done that would cause him to resort to violence." He turned to face Kate, visibly shaken.

A woman came up behind him and slipped her hand into his and whispered, "Georgie, what's going on?"

Absentmindedly his fingers curled around his partner's easily. "It's the police. They're asking questions about my brother."

She winced. "It's such a terrible thing to have happened," she shared. "Just doesn't bear thinking about."

"And yet," Kate stated, "do you have any idea of what might have happened?"

She stared at her a bit coolly and asked, "No, why would I?"

"I don't know. We're just asking everybody who might have had anything to do with the family if they knew about anybody who might have hated them, anybody they had problems with, any conflicts at work, that kind of thing."

She shook her head. "You'd have to check at work. We didn't have any anything to do with them. That's the way they wanted it. Right, Georgie?"

George nodded. "Yes, I was just telling her that," he said, his tone heavy. "Apparently"—George turned to his wife—"Mary was badly beaten over a long time." His wife's mouth opened wide in shock, but she held back the scream, even as she clapped a hand over her open mouth.

"Good God." She looked around and in a hoarse whisper turned to Kate and asked, "Are you saying that his brother beat his wife?" She looked back to George. "There's no way."

"That's what he just said too," Kate murmured, "and

we're still struggling with the no-way part."

"If you know anything about their history and what Roger was like when they were younger, I mean, he was thoroughly traumatized by some family affliction, and he kept to himself."

Kate nodded. "I get that. What I don't understand is, … in what way does the past excuse him from violence today?"

They both just stared at Kate in shock, even as George's head shifted back and forth, gaining in momentum. "Roger just wasn't like that."

She sighed. "Okay." And, with that acknowledgment, he seemed to relax somewhat. "Do you have any idea where he worked? What he did? Friends or anyone in his circle, things like that?"

"No, nothing," he replied.

"We're still checking into everything in the family."

He nodded and stared at her. "God, I'm sorry. I am not much help but, … it's just this whole thing is a bit of a shock." He turned and looked at his wife, then just wrapped his arms around her and pulled her close, kissing the top of her head. "I can't even imagine. It's so foreign to the brother I knew, and this brother you're painting this godawful picture of … is not somebody I recognize at all." George went silent for a moment, then took a deep long breath. "I mean, you might say it's true, and maybe it is, but I'll remember the brother I knew, the one who needed lights on because he was so scared of the dark."

"This really is not making any sense," his wife added, turning to look at Kate. "Can you keep us in the loop, when you find out something?"

"I can let you know if and when we get to the bottom of this," Kate said. "I just don't have anything to tell you about it right now."

"No, of course not." George's wife nodded. "It's such a shock though. I need to get him inside."

It was obvious that George was fading quickly in front of her, so Kate nodded. "That's fine." She handed over her card. "We will be in touch, particularly if we have any other questions."

"Just remember. Georgie hasn't seen his brother or had anything to do with him in quite a long time."

"Why is that?" Kate asked.

"Roger wanted it that way. Roger was a troubled soul, and I think seeing us, seeing Georgie, tended to emphasize the fact that Mary didn't really have it together. Roger told Georgie that he was trying to keep his life together and didn't need the pressure of family expectations," the wife explained, with a roll of her eyes. "Roger said he'd found a soulmate and planned to live happily ever after. I don't see how that worked out to their advantage now either."

"Maybe it didn't," Kate acknowledged, "but let's hope that he did have at least a few years of happiness before this happened."

"And yet how much happiness can anybody be having," she argued, "if he just turned around and beat up his wife?"

"That's what we're still trying to figure out," Kate noted, "so give us a little time to sort through things."

The woman nodded and pulled George back. "Come on, Georgie. Let's go sit down and relax for a bit," she suggested, her voice low. It was soothing, calm, and clearly effective.

He looked at her, nodded, then back at Kate.

She smiled back at them both. "We'll talk later."

And, with that, the door was closed firmly in her face.

She looked over at Rodney, who'd been silent through the whole thing. "Thoughts?"

"You mean, besides the broken families, the damage these guys do to an ever-widening circle of people who they may not intend to hurt but somehow shatter their lives anyway?"

She nodded. "It's really sad, isn't it?"

"I don't know if that's even the word for it," Rodney muttered. "Heartbreaking, demoralizing, excruciatingly painful. I mean, how does anybody ignore something like this, with all the shit going on?" He shook his head. "It's just very, very … sad." As they walked back to the car, he looked up at the house and added, "You know, he seemed absolutely demoralized by that information."

"I got that feeling too," Kate confirmed. "Maybe he'd always hoped that he would reconnect with his baby brother and that they could work out whatever it was that had come between them."

"Maybe, but I also wonder if George somehow thought that maybe his baby brother was off on his own, just living the dream, and that George could be content knowing Roger was out there, doing his thing. By telling him his brother was an abusive asshole, we crushed what little peace George may have made with it."

"There are a lot worse things in life," she murmured, "and in a case like this? Absolutely no way to know just what went wrong. Particularly if people don't open up and tell us."

"Do you think George was holding anything back?"

"I don't know. He didn't seem to be. I wondered if the wife knew more, but that doesn't mean there's a hope in hell of her sharing it."

HAVING SPENT THE bulk of the morning at Bartlett's place, Simon was behind on his own work. By the time he got to his third rehab project, most of the workmen were gone, and his foreman stood around impatiently. "Sorry to keep you, Paul," Simon said, as he walked up, the fatigue in his voice evident.

The foreman looked over at him and nodded. "You don't normally come by this late." Paul eyed Simon in concern. "So I presume there's a reason for it."

"Isn't there always," Simon muttered, but he refused to get into a discussion about just what that reason was. They did a quick recap on the progress on this project, and thankfully there weren't a whole lot of issues to deal with. By the time Paul left, Simon was free to just sit back and relax a bit. With that in mind, he grabbed a coffee and hopped onto the aquabus, heading back toward home.

He got off a stop early and walked around the water, all along the seawalls on the beach area. When he found a bench, he plunked down and just sat here, taking several long deep breaths to try to ease up some of the stress nudging his shoulders and his neck. In his heart of hearts, he knew he probably should have walked away from Bartlett and that whole mess, but, having sensed that his acquaintance had been seriously in trouble, Simon had been open to helping. However, now it felt like something was off about the whole thing. Simon just didn't know what or how. One thing was certain. Bartlett's wife wouldn't accept Simon's strict position on budgets and bills going forward, and Bartlett would continue to have his hands full either way.

So many people spent money like it was their right, and they had absolutely no concept that taxes were owed on damn-near everything, nor did they care to pay the taxes or their other obligations, and that was something Simon would not get involved in. They could either take his advice or not, but it wouldn't yield an easy solution either way.

As Simon sat here by the water, he felt some of his tension easing back. If he could connect with Kate, that would do a lot for him too, but she'd been out on whatever duty she was hell-bent to do right now, regardless of where he was at, and he understood. He had more than a few of his own issues on a day-to-day basis that meant he couldn't always call her back or keep their plans. But, as he sat here, his phone rang, and he smiled to see it was Kate. "Hey," he greeted her, a grin on his face.

"Ooh, ouch," she murmured, "that sounds pretty rough."

He laughed. "And here I thought I was doing pretty well."

"Maybe you are, but that greeting? It sounded pretty bad."

"Great. It's awesome to know my lying abilities are crap where you are concerned."

"True," she agreed in a light tone, "but why in the hell would you want to lie to me anyway? Lying is for dumb shits after all."

"Oh, thanks for the lesson," he muttered, with a chuckle. "Most people consider me a good liar, I'll have you know."

"I don't think one good liar is out there," she countered.

Simon heard the smirk in her voice.

"Besides, if you're a good liar, it means you've had a lot of practice, and, if you've had a lot of practice, you're probably not someone I want to spend time with because I won't trust anything you say."

He had to love Kate. Everything was black-and-white for her, with no middle ground. As far as she was concerned, you were either on the good side of life or you weren't. Honestly it made things a little difficult when she was so adamant about being right. Her black-and-white attitude was often not quite as black-and-white as what he saw, and she often came to her conclusions very quickly, so it was hard to change her mind sometimes.

"So, what's going on?" Kate asked him. "You sound like you've had a hell of a day."

"That's because I *have* had a hell of a day," he replied, laughing. "As only someone in your position would know."

"Ah, are you pissed off at me over something?"

"No, absolutely not," he replied quickly. "Why would you get that impression?"

"I don't know. It just came to me."

He shook his head. "Nope, I'm not pissed at you at all. I'm sitting a couple blocks from my house, having a coffee," he shared, with a grin. "I made an attempt to help somebody, and I'm not so sure it's working out all that well."

"Ooh. ouch," she repeated. "If it's got anything to do with money or business, you're probably better off to leave them to their own failures."

"Yeah, but he came and asked me specifically, so I thought maybe I could lend a hand."

"How'd that work out for you?"

"Turns out things were much worse than expected, but it was still going pretty well, until the wife arrived."

At that, Kate started to laugh. "Oh, don't tell me. The cliché wife, with the overcharged credit cards, living the life of a diva and not giving a crap about the penalties."

He stared down at the phone at her too-damn-accurate analysis. "Sometimes I think *you*'re the psychic."

There was a shocked moment on the other end, and she gasped. "Wow, now you're really insulting me, aren't you?"

He grinned. "Only you would take it that way."

"If I'm a psychic, I don't want anything to do with that chaos," she growled, "and you know it."

"Maybe so," he agreed, already feeling immeasurably more cheerful. "Doesn't mean you're not damn good at it."

"And more insults," she groaned, as he burst out laughing.

"Hardly an insult," he corrected, still chuckling. "Are you coming over tonight?"

"I might, if I can get free and clear of this damn case," she muttered. "Unfortunately … we're running out of leads, and the time is whipping by."

"But no other victims?"

"Please don't even bring that up," she said quietly. "The answer thankfully … is, no, no more victims, but we also know that the chances of this being over are not great."

"No, I'm sorry," Simon replied. "I wouldn't wish something like this on my worst enemy."

"Good, then I don't have to worry about tracking you down and forcing your ass into jail."

At that, he burst out laughing again, his voice booming across the harbor. Several people nearby turned to smile, and he realized just how good she was for him, how she made his world turn, even if she didn't like the idea of it. He was suddenly feeling light and calm.

"What are you smiling about?" she asked suspiciously.

At that, he asked, "How is it you even know I'm smiling?"

"With a laugh like that, you would have to be," she muttered. "No way you wouldn't smile with that laughter going on."

"You could be right," he replied. "I mean, it's pretty hard to be upset when I've got somebody like you around to keep me entertained."

"Oh. *great*." She groaned. "Seriously? Am I that much of an entertainment to you?"

"Nope," he corrected, "but it's been a crappy day, so I'll take any smiles I can get."

"Ah, sorry, some of these days are pretty rough for you."

"They are," he agreed, "and some days aren't too bad, but today? Today was a shitty one. Anyway, dinner?"

"I probably can get free," she replied hesitantly. "I just don't know when."

He groaned. "So, maybe not at all then."

"It depends if you're in a rush. If you're not in a rush, and you can wait maybe an hour, then it's possible."

"I can wait an hour," he stated.

"It's nice to know you can be so accommodating."

He heard the smile in her voice when she spoke those words. "Hey, if I get to spend time with you, I can be very accommodating."

"You do say the dandiest things," she muttered.

"No, not the dandiest," he corrected. "I say what comes naturally. Especially when I am around you."

"And those are usually the dandiest things," she said.

He laughed. "I'm not arguing with you. Whenever you can get there, just come, okay?" And, with that, he rang off.

CHAPTER 8

W ITH THE LAST of the jobs ticked off on her mental list, Kate checked her watch. "What do you think? Any chance Roger's workplace is still open? Lilliana hasn't made it there yet."

"I suggest we go find out," Rodney replied. "The sooner, the better, as far as I'm concerned."

She agreed. "It will be a little tough to keep people in the loop, and everybody will want answers."

"Their families all want answers regardless," he noted, "and you can't blame them."

"No, I absolutely don't blame them," she muttered. "It's just a little more stress on our part to get them the answers that they're all looking for, particularly when we're having absolutely zero luck."

"That's the part that bothers me."

"Another reason why I'm wondering if this has happened before."

"We do have the cases from the analyst."

"True, Reese left those with Lilliana, who is working through them."

"But you want to take a look too, don't you?"

"Absolutely," she muttered, "but first we have to stop at Roger Brown's place of work."

"So, check it out, then back to the office, *huh*?"

"Sure," she muttered. "Chances are, we'll be too late for his workplace to be open anyway." As she suspected, when they drove up, she looked at the locked office, which was dark. "Dang, just as we thought. They're already closed."

He nodded. "Tomorrow then."

"Sure, tomorrow," she muttered, "bright and early." And, with that, they headed back to the station. When they got inside, she immediately went to her desk.

Rodney looked at her and announced, "I'm heading home."

"Good, go ahead," she said, her voice already fading, as she looked around, hoping to see the reports she was looking for. When her gaze landed on them on top of her desk, she smiled in relief. "There they are. I'll take these and read them over tonight."

"I thought you would be at Simon's."

"That's the plan," she noted, "but I do want to read these, so I have some good ideas to sleep on." He rolled his eyes, but she just shrugged. "Hey, I think it helps."

"It might help you," Rodney acknowledged, as he walked over and picked up his copies too, "but I think my brain will be completely on overload. Plus you need to be focusing on you and Simon when you are off duty, not sleeping on the ideas and the ways of murdering psychopaths."

"Nobody said you had to take them home," she pointed out, looking at him with a frown.

"No, you're not saying I have to, but, at the same time, it makes me feel that I need to," he explained in exasperation, as he glared at her, clutching his copy of the same reports. "I'll see you tomorrow." And, with that, he was gone.

She didn't want to take all the paperwork if she didn't have to, so she sat down at her desk and quickly skimmed through what had been found. It was seriously interesting, yet at the same time frustrating. A series of similar killings had been found, but they were a long time ago, and the victims themselves weren't tortured. Plus no history of long-term beatings were noted, so to even think that they were related was a big stretch.

The fact that they were found tied on a cross through? … Not a whole lot she could find on that in this old information, but she chucked the research into her folder and walked out of the building.

As soon as she got outside, she stopped, took several deep breaths of the thick muggy air, and smiled. Typical Vancouver weather. There were always some good things about it, but, man, there were sure some other issues. However, Vancouver wasn't anywhere near like the inhospitality of weather in other places. She hopped into her vehicle, then headed for home. It wasn't until she got out that she realized what she'd done and groaned.

She sent him a quick text. **I'm at home.**

He sent her a question mark.

She sighed and looked at the time. "I might be too tired to come over," she muttered to herself, just as her phone rang.

"That bad?"

"Kind of, yeah," she said in a grudging tone. "I wasn't really expecting to crash, but, now that I'm home, I'm fading fast, damn it. I'm sorry. I just wasn't thinking and drove straight here."

"I get it," Simon noted, "and believe me. I understand, particularly after my day."

"I'm sorry," she added. "I just don't think I've got it in me to drive over."

"Hey, it's okay," he said, "and, as much as I'd love to see you, I do understand."

She smiled. "Sometimes you're almost too understanding," she muttered.

He laughed. "If I'm understanding, it's a problem. If I'm not understanding, it's a problem," he pointed out. "You do understand what that makes you?"

"Yeah, a bitch," she admitted, and then groaned. "You can come over here if you want," she offered. Then, after a deep breath, she added, "I'm heading into a shower. I'm pretty done in."

"It's okay. I'll meet you in a little bit," he replied, and, with that, he hung up.

She felt bad, but, as she headed into the hot shower, she realized she was just worn out. It was one of those things that happened when she was on these cases that were just shit through and through, especially when there were no answers, even no bad answers. And that bothered her more than anything, to think that all this was going on around her, and she just didn't have anything to go on.

She put on a pot of coffee, then stepped into the hot water. When she came back out, with just a robe wrapped around her, she found Simon already inside, sipping a cup of coffee.

When she stopped in the doorway, he looked up, and a slow smile took over his features. "Damn. See? It's already worth the trip, coming over to see you."

She looked down to realize that her robe had slipped open. Rolling her eyes, she quickly retied it and said, "I thought you were exhausted."

"Honey, I'm never too exhausted for that," he declared, with a chuckle and a wink.

She smiled and shook her head. "You found the coffee, I see."

"I did, but your coffee sucks."

"Thanks for that," she replied, with an eye roll. "Next time you can buy the coffee."

"Oh, that's a great idea," he agreed, with a laugh. "I've often wondered about that, but I didn't want to insult you."

She raised her hands. "I'm lucky if I can even remember to buy coffee," she admitted, "so it's a gift that there is any here at all. Therefore, if you want better shit, you have to provide it."

"I can do that," he said, with a laugh, his gaze intent, as he studied her features. "It's not that you look tired, so much as it's"—he pondered it—"it's frustration, isn't it? You can't get anywhere, and there's nothing you hate more."

"You're right," she admitted, with a nod. "I'm still at that initial stage, where we're trying to gather all the information about the victims and looking for a perpetrator, but finding nothing." Kate walked over and poured herself a coffee. "I mean, you do everything right and just hope you come up with information that'll give you something useful, but too often it doesn't give us anything, and that's where I'm at right now."

"I'm sorry," Simon muttered. "I have to admit that being around you is showing me a whole different side to law enforcement that I've never seen before."

"Yeah, particularly if you've only ever seen the wrong side," she quipped, a twinkle in her eyes.

He grinned. "I might have had a slightly checkered past," he replied, "but it wasn't that bad."

"You wouldn't have been allowed," she stated, with a knowing smile. "Your grandmother would have had something to say about that, I'm sure."

"Oh, good Lord." He shook his head. "I don't even want to think about what she would have said about me going off the beaten path to that extent. Outside of the fact that my energy needed the goodness of positive energy or some crap like that," he suggested, with a roll of his eyes.

She nodded and smiled. "I figure, if nothing else, it probably kept you on the straight and narrow all these years."

"It has," he admitted, "whether I liked it or not."

"Exactly, so in a way her threats of perpetual evil, hell, damnation, and God-only-knows what else she used on you, it worked."

"It worked except for the fact that, when she was gone, she wasn't there to look after me anymore. … Only so much anybody can do to keep teenagers on the straight and narrow."

"Absolutely, which is why I don't have any kids."

He eyed her carefully. "Did you ever think about having any?"

"Never gave it any real thought," she shared. "With the line of work I'm in, the number of things I've seen, … I'm not sure I'm up for it." He nodded. She hesitated, then looked over at him, suddenly curious. "How about you?"

"Like you, I haven't really given it any serious thought. I mean, up until now, it's always been a case of hell no, mostly because of what it's like for a lot of people, so *hell no* covered it."

She smiled and nodded. "When you think about it, we've seen a lot of what life has to offer and most of it not in a good way."

"Does that make us potentially better parents," he asked curiously, "or worse?"

"I have no clue," she muttered. "If you think about it, just so many things can go wrong out there that I'm not sure I would be up for figuring it out anyway." When he didn't say anything and just studied her, she frowned and asked, "Now what?"

"Just wondering," he said, still with that searching gaze, "because, for the record, I think you would make a hell of a parent."

She winced. "And, for the record, … I think you probably would too, but I am so not ready to go in that direction."

"I don't think either of us are," he replied, "but that doesn't mean that we should rule it out entirely for all time, you know?"

"Maybe not, but it'll take a lot for me to go in that direction—at any point in time," she admitted, giving him a smile, "Besides, that would have to be quite a while away."

"Agreed." He nodded. "So, now that we've put children on the back burner, how about we spend a little bit more time practicing making them, you know, just in case?"

She stared at him, and, for whatever reason, his words caught her sideways, and she started to laugh and laugh and laugh and laugh. By the time he caught her and rolled her onto the couch, she linked her arms around his neck and whispered, "Considering that it's just practice …"

"Of course it's just practice," he said. "I mean, after all, we have to make sure we get it right, when and if we're ready."

"*When and if,*" she repeated, with an eye roll.

"Can't imagine it happening, but"—he tapped her gently on the nose—"we'll leave that unresolved in the realm of mystery and be totally open to whatever the world gives us down the road."

"Considering that we're talking *down the road*, maybe," she murmured, "but only if it's some possibly nameless future point of view."

"Absolutely." Simon smiled, then pulled her close and gave her a long hard passionate kiss, reminding her of all the good reasons he was in her life, and it wasn't just for the coffee.

THE NEXT MORNING, Simon woke alone. He looked around in surprise, as it was rare for her to ever get up and to leave while he was still sleeping. Plus he had slept soundly, at least he thought he had. He shifted to recollect through the night, wondering if something had happened that he didn't know about. He got up slowly, heading out to the kitchen, and noted that she'd set up a pot of coffee but hadn't turned it on.

Frowning, he hit the button and then caught sight of the note on the counter off to the side. *Called out at 4:00 a.m.* And that was it, except for a little heart on the bottom, and yet the heart said it all. He gave a happy sigh, feeling like a teenager all over again, just because that little heart made such a difference.

He went and had a hot shower, and, when the coffee was done, quickly helped himself to a cup. The pot only held a couple cups, which would be just about right, as he went through his laptop, taking a few minutes before starting his day. When his phone rang a while later, he picked it up, half engrossed in the work he was already doing, to hear Bartlett on the other end of the phone.

"Hey," Bartlett greeted him quietly. "Yesterday was a little rough on the family."

"I'm sure it was," Simon agreed equally quietly. "Coming to earth-shattering decisions isn't exactly easy."

"No, it's not. My wife doesn't believe anything that you said, of course."

"No surprise there." Simon chuckled. "Why would she? She doesn't know me. She doesn't know anything about me, and she loved her daddy and what he could do for her."

"Right now, she's rethinking the whole marital thing."

"She won't get anything through a divorce right now, so I don't know whether that's of any solace to you or not," Simon pointed out.

"It should be, but I don't know. Are you coming back?" Bartlett asked.

Simon hesitated, then replied, "You need a forensic accountant, and you need a lawyer. My being there won't be much help to you on those matters."

"Shit," Bartlett muttered. "Are you sure there's no other way out of this?"

"There are lots of ways out of it, but, if you want legal ways out of it, I don't have any others for you," Simon stated. "I mean, if restructuring the company is needed, it has to be done quickly. Otherwise your employees are all out of luck, and that's not the karma you want."

"It's funny to hear you talk of karma," Bartlett replied. "My father-in-law mentioned something about reaping what you sow."

"Oh, I tend to think that it's quite true," Simon declared. "A lot of people think I'm nuts for it, but, when you think about all the things that can go wrong in life, and the fact that you're still alive, still doing well, you have to wonder if it was dumb luck or if you were doing something right."

"I've often thought that I wasn't doing anything right," Bartlett admitted, with a sigh. "That I'm alive and doing what I'm doing because nobody's caught me yet."

"Then maybe it's time to face the music. I mean, if you've been doing some of this yourself, well then, that's quite likely something you need to deal with."

"Who else would I need to tell?" he asked, with a laugh. "I mean, you have the potential to absolutely destroy me right now."

Simon raised his eyebrows at that. "Anybody has the potential of destroying another person," Simon replied. "But that doesn't mean we'll do it. This is strictly business. ... I don't get involved in that other shit. Now, if you're smart, ... you'll find a way out that's honorable and do a full cleanup on the company business, and, in the end, you'll probably be just fine. I would think that the business could flourish, if you handled this part right."

"Do you think so?" Bartlett asked in hope.

"I do actually. I really do. I mean, your father-in-law had a solid business, until he decided he didn't want to play the game nicely anymore, right?"

"I'm not sure he ever played it that nicely," Bartlett said bitterly. "Anyway, I just wanted to thank you for what you did yesterday."

"I don't know that there's any *thank you* required," Simon noted. "Obviously you don't have any money to pay me for the effort. I don't know what you'll end up doing about the business, but at least you have a better idea of what your choices are."

"Yeah, none of them great."

"No, but at least you have some choices, and it's not a case of losing everything right now because the creditors are at your doorstep. That'll come soon, but you have a month or two to figure a way out."

"What if I sold everything," he asked, "just sold it all and ran?"

There was just enough tiredness in his voice that Simon knew it was one of those *shot in the dark* things, but he immediately told Bartlett that nobody would buy his business if they couldn't look at his books. And nobody looking at his books would have a problem sorting out all the discrepancies. "Honestly, get yourself a good lawyer, get yourself a good accountant, and make a fresh start. I don't know if your wife will stick with you through all this, but at least you can stop the bleeding."

"I guess it depends on why she's here in the first place," Bartlett replied, with a wry note in his tone.

"Sounds like it, and those problems I can't help you with, sorry."

"You never did marry, did you?"

"No. I came close a couple times, but it never worked out."

"I'm not sure that anybody should ever get married," Bartlett muttered, "because who you start with does not seem to be who you end up with."

"I'm not a marriage counselor either," Simon added. Then he took a deep breath before he continued. "I'm heading off to work, so good luck with your day," he said quietly, and, with that, he quickly rang off.

He stared at the phone for a long moment afterward, wondering. Bartlett sounded quite depressed but certainly not suicidal, and hopefully that wouldn't become an issue. Did he love his wife, and did he want to deal with whatever ugliness would come up when it came to curtailing her spending habits? But again that was Bartlett's problem.

Still trying to convince himself of that, Simon headed out the door and back to his building rehab projects. He needed to get caught up after losing a bunch of hours yesterday. So he dove into his work, going from one to another, ordering supplies, picking up the chaff, checking on staff, approving overtime, making phone calls to accountants and lawyers. It just never ended.

When his phone rang at noon, Kate was on the other end. "Are you okay?"

"I'm okay, why?"

She hesitated. "I just heard something involving a name I thought I'd heard you mention before."

"What are you talking about?" he asked, pulling his attention back from what he was working on.

"You mentioned a Bartlett Morris."

At the mention of his name, Simon's heart skipped a beat.

"He went out a window this morning."

Simon sat down hard on the bench he'd been in the process of standing up from. "What?"

"Yeah, I heard about it when the case came in," she said. "I'm right in thinking you knew him, aren't I?"

"Holy shit." Simon rubbed his face. "Kate, I just talked to him this morning," he stated in a clipped tone. "That is the last news I wanted to hear today."

"You want to tell me what it's all about?"

"Will there be some police inquiry?"

"He's a jumper," she noted, "and you know what that

means. These things always come with all kinds of complications."

"He asked me to look into his business dealings, after his father-in-law had passed away. He suspected they were in deep trouble, but he didn't know how bad. I spent all morning there yesterday, and they were in very deep trouble," he declared in a sorrowful tone. "I told him this morning that he needed a forensic accountant and a good lawyer. His father-in-law pretty well embezzled the company into bankruptcy."

There was silence on the other end at first, then she added, "It's not your fault."

"It's not my fault, but somehow it feels like it's my fault," he snapped. "I had a bad feeling this morning, Kate, but I ignored it."

"I get that," she said. "I need to report what happened though. Are you okay with that?"

"Sure, why not." He groaned. "It just adds to the guilt, to me feeling like crap. You should also take a look at that wife of his. She got pretty upset when I told her to cut back all the spending, to hand off the $7,000 purse she was sporting, and the like. The business credit card that she had been using is owed over $30,000. The house that daddy just put one-half-million dollars into still has a large mortgage, and the creditors will need to go in and strip it all out," he explained. "I mean, we're talking financial ruin, and I don't think she was the kind to stick around for the long haul."

"Ah, crap," Kate muttered. "Again it's not your fault."

He knew that, but, at the same time, it wasn't helping. "You're sure it was him?" Simon asked hopefully.

"I can tell you that the news said it was, but whether it was him or not? I don't have a confirmed ID yet."

"No, of course not. Can I go see him?" She hesitated, and he pleaded. "Please?"

"I'll get back to you on that," she said quietly, "but I really don't think you should go, not if you're emotionally overwrought about it."

"His wife sure as hell won't give a shit," he replied bitterly.

"I don't think that's fair either, and yet …"

"I know," he broke in. "Nothing is fair in love and war, but in this case? … I'm sure she took everything I had to say yesterday and turned around and blamed him for it."

"Maybe," she agreed, "but you also don't know what else was going on in his world. So let's keep that down and stay positive."

"He's dead," he snapped, "so it's pretty-damn hard to stay positive when the words that I had with him and his wife just sent a man to his death." And, with that, Simon hung up on her.

CHAPTER 9

K ATE FOUND IT hard to keep Simon's words out of her head all day. Still, she went from house to house, statement to statement, morgue to station, and finally sat down back at her desk at two o'clock, while she glared at Rodney. "Do we have anything?"

He shook his head. "No, we sure don't," he stated bitter-ly.

"Street cams for the strange visitor, can we at least find that?"

At that, Lilliana piped up, "Reese has been working on it, and, last I knew, she had it narrowed down to three possible vehicles, but we don't even have any real reason to go talk to these people."

"Do we even know who this guy is?" Kate asked Lilliana. "Do we have that much?"

"We have something along that line, but it's still pretty sketchy."

Just then Reese came in and announced, "Okay, guys, I do have someone you could talk to. I can't guarantee he's got anything to do with this though."

"No, none of us have any guarantees, but I'll take it," Kate said. "If nothing else, I could rule him out." And, with that, Kate asked, "So, what did you find?"

"Street cams and cars, back and forth, plus afterhours

footage, where I found one regular visitor over the last six months, and it all came from a neighbor's security camera," Reese explained, handing over the guy's home address info.

"Okay, good enough." With that, Kate looked over at Rodney, and he hopped to his feet.

"Oh yeah, I'm coming," he declared, "and I'm driving."

"Why is that?" she asked. "Did you get a paycheck so you can afford gas now?"

"Hey, hey, hey," he muttered, with an injured air. "We get to expense our gas, you know?"

"Sure, but it's just more paperwork," she muttered.

"Don't take that on yourself," Rodney said. "That's a really bad expense to get caught with."

She rolled her eyes. "It is what it is. Whatever."

"No, it's not *whatever*," he argued, glaring at her. "Make sure you get those expense sheets in. Otherwise you'll end up paying, and the department doesn't like that because, down the road, when they do their budgets, they think that they're in the clear. However, they suddenly realize that somebody hasn't been expensing, and it throws the budget all off."

"Oh, and I'm supposed to give a crap that their budgets are off?" she asked, staring at him.

"Believe me. They don't like it."

"Oh, fine, enough with the nagging." Kate shrugged. "It's not like this is easy on us, and the last thing we need is more paperwork."

"Nope," he acknowledged, "but, at the same time, we're all in the same boat."

She wasn't sure what boat that was because it often seemed as if just hers was sinking. But she wouldn't go there; there was time enough for that later.

As they pulled up to the driveway of this newfound address a bit later, a man was getting out of the vehicle and walking up to his place. She called out to him, "Excuse me, Billy Roy?"

He turned, looked at her, and immediately stiffened. "Yes. What can I do for you?"

"I believe you were a friend of Roger Brown."

"Yes," he answered, with a sudden change in his demeanor. "What a terrible thing to have happen."

She nodded. "We would like to ask you a few questions about them."

"What possible questions would you have to ask me?"

"Anything that might lead to helping us solve it," she replied, with a shrug. "So it might seem like some of the questions are odd, but we're doing our best."

"Must be tough when doing your best isn't very good," he noted in an odd tone.

She looked at him sharply, and even Rodney seemed to think that was an odd comment. "Which," she stated slowly, "is why we're out here, doing our due diligence."

"Of course. *Due diligence.* ... That's important," he replied, with a bit of a mocking tone.

She didn't like any of his tone. But knowing that a prior cop, now missing, had made Roy's life difficult for a time did explain Roy's attitude now.

"Come in. Come in."

She walked into a room that was so clean, it seemed as if the housekeeper had just come through, and it was ready for showing to potential buyers. It was antiseptic clean. She looked around and frowned.

"What's the matter?" he asked. "You don't like my house?"

"It's beautiful," she responded, although nothing was

particularly beautiful about it. It was just a house. It was fine. Nothing was special or fancy about it, but she didn't want to get into it. "The fact that it's so very clean just surprised me, that's all."

"Why? Do I have to be slob to live here these days?"

"Not at all." She sent him an odd look again. "You're doing a bang-up job of keeping it nice and clean. I'll have to give you that."

He shrugged. "I like clean."

"Good, I do too."

"Ah, you probably don't put in the time or effort to clean things, do you?"

"Oh, I try," she said, with half a smile.

"But there are no cigars for trying," he declared, with a nod.

"Yeah, I get it."

"Take a seat and ask your questions, so I can get to my dinner." He looked at his watch. "With the rate this is going, I'll be late."

"I'm sorry. Are you heading out?"

"No, not heading out," he clarified, "but I like to eat on a strict schedule."

"Okay, can you tell us what you know about the family of Roger Brown and Mary Brown?"

He looked at her in surprise. "What do you mean? What do I know about the family? You're the one who should know all that."

"And we do," she stated, with a clipped nod, "but we'd like to hear your take on it."

He shook his head. "*Tsk, tsk.* You really don't have very much information at all, do you?"

"We have quite a bit," Rodney interjected, his voice

hard, "but we're always looking for more."

"Yes, of course you are," he said, an odd smile on his face, then looked back to Kate. "They were a lovely family," he replied, "very loving, very caring." She looked at him in surprise, and he nodded. "I mean, they were not good on money, so that was always a problem for them. … Money, you know. They were always broke, it seemed, and always looking for ways to make money."

"Really? We spoke to people at both of their jobs, and neither seemed to have that impression."

"No, of course not, but then people don't really like to tell you the real story, do they?"

She wasn't sure exactly what *real story* they were talking about right now, but Roy obviously knew something she didn't. "Maybe you could explain that to us."

"I mean, what can I say? They were broke, always broke, and always looking to make money," he stated, with a shrug, as Kate looked at him expectantly. "So, you know, sometimes I would help them out."

"You mean, you gave them money?" she asked carefully.

"No, but I would hire them to do various things."

"Such as?"

He gave her half a smile. "You'll probably say it's illegal, and, of course, I'll deny it."

She narrowed her gaze at him. "What are we talking about here?"

"I like rough sex," he shared calmly, "and Mary was open to it. So I would use their situation to have a nice little sideline business for myself."

"For yourself?" she asked, her stomach churning. "Meaning, you used her as a prostitute for your own gain?"

"No, no, no," he stated, "not handing her out to anyone,

no. For myself. … It was only for myself. I quite enjoyed it, and so did she."

Kate thought about all the marks on the woman's body and just couldn't quite reconcile his words. "Are you sure she enjoyed it? Her body … was in pretty-rough shape."

"Of course she did," he declared. "It's not as if I forced her."

"No, but circumstances alone could definitely be construed as pressure."

"Oh, but putting pressure on somebody is nothing," he muttered. "Who cares? That's minor."

"Did you beat her?"

"No, no, no," he stated in quick succession. "You don't understand. Anything in sex, as long as it's consensual, is fine. It's not as if I beat her outside of sex." He laughed. "Honestly … I was totally okay to give the bi-side idea a try too, but Roger wasn't into it, so that was fine."

She slowly nodded. "So you're telling me that you paid the couple to have rough sex with the wife."

"Yes, and on a fairly regular basis."

"According to the marks on her body, that would match," she stated, "though I do find it hard to believe it would be consensual."

He shrugged. "It was," he declared forcefully, "so you can rest your mind."

But she couldn't, of course, because it just seemed so wrong to think that anybody would think that was okay.

He laughed at the look on her face. "You really don't like to hear that, do you?"

"No, I sure don't," she admitted. Then she pondered it and asked him plainly, "What about Mary Holley?"

He looked at her in surprise. "Oh, you have been busy."

"Is she another one of your consensual partners?"

"Indeed, she is," he agreed, with a benevolent smile. "Smart of you to notice."

"Not really." Kate felt incredibly sick. "You do realize that both are dead, right?"

"I do," he replied, with a sorrowful look at her. "It saddens me greatly."

"How greatly?" she asked, with a mocking tone. "Because the idea that you are now linked to two dead victims and possibly five is a little too coincidental for my liking."

He looked at her in surprise. "Oh no, no, no," he said. "Now you're looking at this the wrong way."

"What way is that?"

"I'm not connected to them. They're connected to me," he stated, with an odd smile. "I didn't do anything to them, and, if there's a problem right now, I can assure you that it's got nothing to do with me. Obviously the problem was them."

She blinked several times, trying to work her way through his very torturous logic. "So, you're saying that somebody is trying to make you look bad by killing them?"

"Oh, … exactly," he agreed and then smiled, like a predator. "You're not as stupid as you look."

She glared at him but managed to keep her mouth shut, as she pondered what he was saying. "So, in your mind you have absolutely nothing to do with these killings?"

"Oh, not only just in my mind, dear," he corrected, with a careless hand gesture. "Of course I had nothing to do with them. Why on earth would I want anything to do with their deaths, when it's so hard for me to find good people like that to give me my little pleasures, you know?" he asked in a gentle voice. "You really should be looking at it from that perspective."

"Should I? That's funny. I was looking at the victims and thinking it was about them."

"Right, and that's the classic police mentality, isn't it? But I'm not sure it was about them," he pointed out, "as much as it was about me."

Oh, boy. This is about police retaliation, harassment, or whatever his crazy mind has determined. Wow. "When did you last see them?" She deliberately changed the subject because, while she got his perspective, the twisted logic was something she needed a closer look at.

"Who?" he asked, raising one eyebrow. "If you're talking about Mary Holley," he replied, "two days before she was killed."

"And Mary Brown?"

He smiled. "The night before she was killed."

She sat back, looked over at Rodney, and back at Billy Roy again. "Any idea who killed them?"

"No, of course not." He then laughed in a booming voice. "Oh dear, you really don't have anything on their killer, do you?"

She just stared at him, waiting him out.

"No, I don't have a clue who would want to kill them."

He was still smiling, and that aggravated her.

He added, "I'm not at all sure who would want to make me look bad."

"Maybe you could take a serious look at that because, if people are killing those around you," she noted, smiling too sweetly, "what's to stop them from turning around and killing you?"

"It's not me they're after, not really. I mean, whoever is doing this is doing it because they don't like what the women were doing. You get what I mean?"

"So, in that case, why kill the men too?"

"Because the men were going along with it or allowing it to happen. I mean, it was what they agreed to," Bill Roy shared, with a shrug. "We did what we did with consent from both partners. So, you really should be looking at this upside down."

"Got it," she said in a clipped tone. "So maybe you can fill us in a little more on your life and why somebody would do this."

"Oh, sure," he agreed comfortably, as he sat back and dug right in. "I was raised by a Protestant minister father and a Jewish Orthodox mother, who both had walked away from their churches in order to have their time together. So, basically they were free hippy spirits. We were essentially a happy family, and I have been working in car sales for the last twenty-plus years."

"You are a car salesman?" she asked in complete disbelief.

He nodded, with a chuckle. "Yes, do you really think people who like BDSM only live and work in back alleys?"

"No," she said bitterly, but that was exactly what was running through the back of her mind. "But when it's somebody who constantly abuses women to that extent, it does seem a little far-fetched." She hated to admit it, but she was really having trouble wrapping her head around the idea.

"Ooh, so somebody who doesn't like car salesmen. You probably don't like politicians or even lawyers either," he noted, with a laugh.

She just stared at him. Sure, she and the coroner had thought some rough sex games were at play here, but surely Smidge thought just between the marriage partners, right?

This third-party involvement was a surprise. She was not at all sure what was going on here, but the truth was, Roy had completely flipped her entire theory on this case, and he was right. She did need to look at it upside down, with brand new eyes, but something here wasn't making any sense.

NO MATTER WHAT Kate had said, the guilt was driving Simon hard. He sat here, his head in his hands at the coffee shop, trying to focus on work, and yet all he could see was Bartlett's shock and dismay at his words. Yet, there was no way to know that Bartlett would take his own life. Of course that suspicion had been at the back of Simon's mind that Bartlett hadn't necessarily done this final act on his own and that maybe he'd had a little bit of help with it. Simon couldn't imagine that Bartlett would have chosen such an end.

Even if he were depressed.

He'd come to Simon looking for help, after all, and there was help. There was a way out of this, a way to move forward, and Simon had told him that. The fact that Bartlett didn't seem to see it was troublesome, and the fact that he had apparently taken a route that didn't make any sense was also troublesome.

It's not that Simon could surmise what was going on in Bartlett's world, but Simon was pretty darn sure that wife of his hadn't helped Bartlett at all. Then again, that was a judgment Simon had no right to make, but, from the little bit he'd seen of the wife, Simon was pretty sure she had been doing something completely immoral in terms of supporting her husband, yet another judgment. He gave his head a shake, and, when he looked up, his foreman walked toward him.

He sat down beside him, concern in his eyes. "You all right?"

Simon nodded quietly but didn't say anything.

"You look like you're a bit on the shell-shocked side."

"Yeah." Simon tried to force a smile. "You could say that. I just found out a friend of mine, somebody I was trying to help over the last few days, jumped out of a window."

His foreman's gaze widened, and he shook his head in dismay, "Ah, shit, man."

"Right? Just when you think you're getting somewhere in life, somebody like that turns around and jumps, and you realize that, for some people, … there is no getting any-where."

"That still sucks though. I don't know what you were doing to help, but at least he had you …"

"Yeah, but apparently I wasn't helping at all. The guy was completely broke. Broke as in very broke, and he needed to declare bankruptcy and to get a forensic accountant in to sort out where he stood and what would happen," Simon explained quietly, "but part of the problem was his wife."

"Ah." His foreman nodded. "We've heard that a time or two."

"I'm still just processing the aftermath of his actions," Simon admitted. Then, as if truly seeing him here, Simon looked at him intently. "Did you need me?"

"Nope, nope, you take all the time you want." His fore-man stood back up again.

"Yeah, that may not be something I have the luxury of doing," Simon admitted, with a casual shrug of his shoul-ders. "It's not as if we don't have our own problems and our own projects."

"Yeah, and that's one of the things I was going to mention." He hesitated and then shrugged. "I mean, it's shitty timing, but you need to know that we've got a plumbing leak and a big one down on rehab four."

He stared at him and swore. "Shitty plumbing up on the second floor, isn't it?"

His foreman nodded grimly. "Yeah, not sure if you wanted to come and see it or not."

"Hell no, I don't want to see it, but, yes, I need to come and have a look." Simon shook his head. "There won't be any easy way out."

With that, he allowed his foreman to pull him back out of the worry that he'd been responsible for Bartlett's death and to turn his attention to the worry about his own problems, and there were plenty of those. As he was finally easing back from solving that plumbing mess, something else broke on another project, and Simon had to race off to another rehab location.

By lunchtime he felt his blood sugar dropping and knew he needed sustenance almost immediately. Luckily right around the corner was Mama's Italian restaurant.

He walked inside, tired, worn-out, and completely sick at heart for Bartlett. Mama raced toward him, took one look at his face, and sighed heavily. "Oh dear." She put a hand on her heart. "You look like you've lost your best friend."

He was startled for a moment, then shrugged. "Well, Mama, he wasn't a best friend, but he was definitely somebody I knew, and the thought of him doing what they're saying he did …" And he just left it at that, shaking his head with a shrug.

She reached out her beefy arms and gave him a big hug,

then led him to a table in the back room and sat him down. "Not to worry," she declared. "Good food will help feed the soul."

He gave her a wry look. "Sometimes that's not always the answer."

She shook her head. "It's *always* the answer, son," she stated firmly. "You can't think or work yourself in and out of a situation if you're not fed, and, while you think about it, you just relax now, and I'll be right back."

And, with that, she disappeared, then reappeared almost like magic moments later, with a carafe of water and a cup of coffee. She placed them both down, disappeared again, then returned with a board of French bread and a big platter of butter. He smiled as he looked at it and nodded. "You know what? It might not be *the* answer, but it does bring a lot of comfort."

"Exactly," she agreed, with a mighty laugh. "From that position you can then solve your problems, but you can't do it if everything inside you is screaming for food."

"I wasn't even thinking I was hungry," he muttered.

"Because you were ignoring it," she stated serenely and then disappeared.

He wasn't even sure that he had ordered anything or that she would even listen if he did because she was like that sometimes. It seemed she always had a better answer for what people needed than they often thought they did, and he was quite willing to let her do her thing—for the moment at least.

When she came back about ten minutes later, he was surprised to see big, fat stuffed noodles heaped on a plate. She quickly served him and said, "There you go, boy. … That'll help." And she was gone once again.

He smiled as he stared down at them, not sure exactly what they were, but, as he studied the menu board across the way, he saw it was the special dish of the day.

He dug in with gusto, only realizing as he was partway through just how right she was about needing food for the body and mind and feeding the soul at the same time. With his meal mostly tucked under his belt, he sat back, cut another slice of bread and relaxed. It was probably the first time he'd relaxed since hearing the devasting news. Even the pain in his heart had dulled somewhat.

His phone buzzed several times, and, as he checked his emails, one came from somebody he didn't know, but it was a lawyer's office. He frowned as he opened up the message. A lawyer for Bartlett asking for a meeting. Thinking it had to be important, he called the number at the end. Once he was put through by the receptionist, Simon got to the point right away. "What's this about?"

The lawyer on the other end hesitated and then replied, "I would prefer to have this conversation face-to-face and in private. Is there any way you can come to my office, potentially this afternoon?"

Just enough anxiety filled his tone to make Simon quite suspicious. He replied in a low voice, "I'm just finishing lunch."

"Perfect, come on over right afterward, if you could." He quickly gave him the address and ended the call.

Simon stared down at his phone, disconcerted at the suddenness of the message and at the request for a meeting out of the blue, so soon after Bartlett's death.

Simon didn't know what it was all about, but he couldn't ignore it. After finishing his lunch, he walked toward the lawyer's office. Simon began to feel a sense of balance inside, a little bit of adjustment or acceptance about the end result. But, as he crossed the street, a wave of faintness overtook him. Frowning, he quickly hurried his pace, got across the street, and collapsed onto a bench.

As soon as he hit the bench, everything in the world around him went black.

CHAPTER 10

"OKAY, LISTEN UP, everyone," Kate announced, as she walked back into the office, Rodney at her side. "Based on some information we got from that rather colorful character that Reese located, it seems we have another angle to look at with these church killings."

Once she explained, everybody stared at her in shock and then disbelief, with Lilliana shaking her head. "No way, absolutely no way."

"That's what I'm trying to figure out," Kate replied. "Billy Roy is adamant that he paid for these services, that the women were willing, and that the husbands were as well, although he may have hinted that they were potentially less willing. No mention of the children—thank God. Then we didn't push that angle."

"Good Christ." Owen stared at her. "So, is this BDSM gone wrong or what?"

"Roy says he saw our Mary Brown the night before her death, not on the day of, and he didn't see the husband on that day either. For Mary Holley, Roy says he'd seen her two days before she was put on the cross."

They stared at her and looked over at Rodney.

He nodded. "Believe me. This one is taking some strange turns."

"That is not a strange turn," Owen stated. "That's just

absolutely wrong."

"I won't argue about that because I'm certainly in agreement with your take on it," Kate noted, "but it does give us something else to look into now. For all I know, Billy Roy is a flat-out liar, and he thinks we're idiots. Remember about the closed case Lilliana found, where one of our locals was all over Roy, probably about this same shit, then got reprimanded. And that cop is missing, so we won't get to ask him about his investigation. Regardless, we have to check out Roy's claims."

"But what do we check out?" Owen asked with an exasperated sigh.

"He's connected to both sets of victims, which is why he thinks somebody is trying to make him look bad, but, when we asked him for any names of somebody who would do this, he had no clue."

"Several BDSM clubs are around," Lilliana shared. "We should check into those." Everybody turned and looked at her. She widened her gaze and laughed. "Don't. … Don't even go there."

"No, we won't," Rodney said, still staring at her, "but you do have hidden depths, my dear Lilliana."

"No," she declared, "that shit is definitely not my scene. However, I have known a few people who really liked it. As in really, absolutely lapped up that shit."

Kate frowned at her, shaking her head. "It's such a foreign concept that sex should be purposely painful that I find it difficult to think that anybody would do this willingly."

Lilliana nodded. "That was my reaction too." She chuckled. "On the other hand, if it's the only way that you can orgasm, … I guess, for some people, the cost is worth it."

Kate shuddered at the thought. "Still sounds incredibly

off, but, if that's where this guy spends some of his time or finds his—I don't want to say *victims*—his *clients* or whatever, then maybe we need to know these clubs from inside out."

"I can draw up a list," Lilliana offered, "and I can contact my girlfriend about it."

Kate asked, "I don't suppose she would talk to us, would she? Like maybe help us understand a little bit more about it?"

Lilliana looked at her and frowned. "Maybe, … if I was there," she replied cautiously. "It's not a subject she's terribly keen to discuss."

"No, I can imagine," Kate said. "I mean, understanding this is one aspect of our work, and it wouldn't be an easy thing for her to discuss, I'm sure, so maybe just ask her and see, or maybe you figure it out and tell us," Kate added, with a flash of a bright smile.

Lilliana rolled her eyes. "I don't see where this is coming from," she muttered.

"It's not even so much that it's coming from anything. It's just a case of, we don't know where to go with this or how to proceed," she explained because Lilliana was no one to mess around with. They were getting on good terms and to mess it up was to take a step backward, which Kate didn't want to risk. The last thing she needed was friction with a colleague, not to mention one of the best detectives. "I just want a few key insights and something that can help in breaking this shit. Right now, we're just a little bit in the dark, and we need some light."

"More than a little bit," Lilliana muttered.

There wasn't anything Kate could say to that because it was quite true. It was definitely a case of more than a little bit in the dark, but something had to be done.

With Lilliana off on that, Kate sat down, updated her notes, then looked back over at Rodney. "How do you feel about asking the neighbors about it?"

"I doubt they know," he stated comfortably. "That's not exactly something you would advertise. Would you?"

"No, but if they heard the screams …"

He pondered that and nodded. "Still, I don't think we'll get any further and, if they didn't see who was there or can place our charming BDSM master on the scene, going back doesn't serve us any purpose."

"Maybe not."

At that moment Reese came in and walked straight up to Kate. "I do have more information." She held out several pages. "Job histories on our victims. Plus the little boy was apparently her nephew, Mary Brown's nephew, and, when Daniel came to them, it seems he was already in rough shape."

She stared at Reese for a long moment. "He was in rough shape already, so what then? We just continue to abuse him? He doesn't deserve a better life?"

Reese winced. "Remember. I just deliver this crap," she muttered, "and sometimes it's not all that easy to read about. I could do without the snarly comments."

Kate nodded. "Point taken. Sorry for the outburst, and all you do is very much appreciated. I just can't imagine what that little boy went through."

"Which is one of the reasons I'm bringing it to your attention," she pointed out. "I do have his birth father's address here for you."

"Excellent. I want to a talk to him." Kate bounced to her feet. She looked down at the address and nodded. "That's not too far away from here," she muttered.

As she started for the door, Reese called back, "I found a brother from the second set of victims as well. I'm running a deeper background check on him now." She handed over more pages.

"And the brother is?"

She shrugged. "Somebody fairly public, like a smaller-level politician."

"*Great*," Kate muttered, as she scanned that information too. "I'll go have a talk with him as well."

"I'm coming," Rodney said, as he jumped up and walked toward her.

She didn't say anything but just kept on walking.

He was trying to match her furious pace, as he patted her on the shoulder. "Unless … you want to do this one alone."

"No, not worried about doing it alone," she noted. "However, just too much filth is attached to this one for anybody to be comfortable."

"Oh, I hear you there," Rodney agreed, "particularly when we're talking children."

"Daniel had already been abused," she snapped. "What makes somebody take in a child like that and then sign them up for more abuse?"

"The only thing I'll take comfort from in any of this," Rodney shared, his tone low, "is the fact that the autopsy didn't show any sexual assault on the child."

She let out her breath in a heavy gush. "I'm really glad to hear that too," she murmured. "I was hoping but not really expecting to hear that. He suffered. He suffered a lot. So why did he end up going from his father to his aunt? What do we know?"

"Well, they're family."

"Sure, so what? Abuse seems to be something that runs rampant in their family."

"I don't know how this happened," Rodney said. "Let's go ask him."

As they drove to the first place, she went over the information on hand. "And, even with this, none of it makes any particular reference as to why the Browns were killed."

"Maybe they were killed because of the little boy. Maybe the little boy, in this case, was the trigger."

She looked at him, startled. "Oh, now that's an idea. Meaning, somebody knew the boy was there, whether somebody from that wife-beating neighborhood or from the BDSM club or whatever, although no one claimed to know about Daniel."

Rodney nodded. "Well, if you were part of a polygamous group of abusers who veered off into painful sex practices, would you call the cops? A social worker? A doctor? A priest? Well, a priest would keep your secret anyway. But the authorities? Would you call them?"

"Hell no, not if I'm partaking of all that other crap. Still, somebody maybe got pretty upset about what happened to the little boy."

"Like the biological father," Rodney pointed out. "Maybe the father had been in a rough relationship and got out of it but not fast enough, and he lost his little boy anyway, who then went to his sister, who maybe ended up abusing Daniel too, eventually killing him. After all, we do see where abuse is perpetuated in too many families."

"Doesn't make any sense for the abused to become the abusers, but yeah. We see that shit all too often." She pondered all that as they drove up to a small rundown apartment building, and then she sighed. "I suspect that we won't find anything good here either."

"Yet we don't know that yet," Rodney cautioned her. As soon as he parked, they got out and headed up to the fourth floor, noting the loud music and lots of reckless laughter coming from several of the apartments, some of it sounding completely off-color.

She looked over at him in dismay. "Popular location for drugs apparently."

He nodded. "So, maybe it'll shoot down my theory," he muttered, "but we still have to check it out." Sure enough, they knocked on the door.

Answering the door was a rough-looking bearded man, maybe in his midthirties, still rubbing the sleep from his eyes. He frowned at them. "Who the hell are you?"

She quickly identified herself, and he shrugged. "I don't know what the hell you want with me," he muttered. "I don't have nothing to do with cops."

"Yeah, and what about your son? You have anything to do with him?"

"Nope, I haven't seen him in a while," he said. "My own parents thought I was abusing him, which I sure as hell wasn't, but my sister ended up with him anyway," he declared, with a note of disgust. "What the hell does Mary want now? If it's child support, then forget it. … She can go fuck herself."

Kate winced, as she looked at him. "You haven't heard the news then."

He stared at her. "I don't have anything to do with any of my family, not since any of this started. So, I don't know what news you expect me to have, but I don't have any of it."

She nodded and asked, "May we come in?"

"No, you can't." He glared at her. "What the hell is this about?"

She looked over at Rodney and then added, "I think it would be better if we told you inside."

"I don't give a shit what you think," he snapped. "I am not *inviting* you in my house. No cops allowed." He chewed on the last words to stress his point.

"Fine," she murmured. Then, taking a deep breath, she began. "I'm sorry to tell you this, but both your son and your sister are deceased."

He just stared at her in shock, then simply fell against the doorjamb. Rodney caught him quickly and half lifted him inside the apartment. She quickly followed suit, and, once inside his apartment, they sat him down on a chair.

He looked at her, blinking constantly. "You're serious?"

She nodded. "Yes, I'm very sorry."

He shook his head. "I always figured that, when Daniel was older, I would have a chance to explain. I figured there'd be time, and I could tell him what really happened."

"You want to tell me what really happened instead?" she asked.

He blinked at her and shrugged. "You won't understand."

"Maybe I will."

"No," he replied, then looked away, trying to catch the tears in the back of his eyes. "Cops like you, you never understand. You don't know what it's like to be an addict. You don't know what it is to lose control and to try to get your life on track, only to have everything taken away from you so fast that there is no chance of ever being on track anymore."

He stared around his apartment. "I've been doing better lately. I was thinking that maybe … I could get him back again." He bit his lips. "I knew it was a faint hope because they never really let you get them back again. It's almost like they take great delight in holding that out as a stick, you know? The carrot and the stick thing," he muttered, obviously struggling to make sense of what had just happened in his world. "But they don't really ever give you that opportunity."

She let him ramble on, knowing that, at some point in time, he would get a hold of himself and would start asking questions. When he appeared to just sit here in a stupor, she asked, "When did you last see your son?"

He blinked, shook his head. "I have blackouts, so I'm not good with time. Maybe a couple months ago."

"How did he look then?"

He gave her a hard stare. "Better than he did when he was with me, if that's what you're trying to get at. Still, he didn't look all that great."

"When you say, *He didn't look all that great*, what does that mean?"

"He was really sad, really quiet. He didn't say anything, wasn't happy to see me. He was there but not present. It wasn't that he was unhappy to see me, more like he wasn't even there," he whispered. "It was like he was just a shell."

She winced at that description because, given what she knew of the abuse Daniel had endured for so long, chances were there was not a whole lot of resistance left in the child. "And you lost custody of him, why?"

He glared at her. "You already know. It's old history."

"Sure," she said. "Do you have a history of violence in your family?"

"Yeah ..." He let out a broken laugh. "You're not kidding. Abuse leads to anger." He leaned his head back, staring up at the ceiling, then looked from Kate to Rodney. "My old man beat me and my sister pretty good." He shook his head. "He beat the shit out of both of us, and we both had temper-control issues. So it was pretty ugly for a while, and it was probably the best thing for Daniel to get him out of this cycle." He again looked around the room. "Still sucks though, since I really had hope that, you know, maybe one day ..."

Kate didn't say anything because that one day quite likely would never have happened. "And your sister, you mentioned she had anger issues?"

"Yes, she did, and she was beaten pretty bad for a while there too. She had very low self-esteem, and my dad ..." He winced and then, collecting his thoughts, added, "Yeah, he was a sexually frustrated man, and she probably took the worst of it, but she seemed to do much better than I did."

"And why is that?"

"I think because of her husband," he suggested, with a shrug. "He really loved her and would do anything for her."

"How was she personally?"

He turned to Kate. "She took my boy rather than putting him in foster care and said that it might be something she could do right for once."

Kate frowned at that phrase. "So, did she struggle with drugs and anger too?"

"Oh man, yes, she struggled and struggled. Christ, she struggled. Hell, we both did," he replied, with a tone of defeat in his words. "And, until you've been up against something like that, ... you don't know just how much struggling it requires."

"I am sorry," she murmured. "It's hard for any of us to imagine."

He nodded. "It absolutely is. ... She was always so damn guilty, so torn. She loved our father so much and would do anything for him. I don't know for sure, but there's probably some psychological term for when an abused victim turns and loves the abuser because that was definitely it, ... but she hated it at the same time. She hated him, and she was always feeling so guilty about it."

"Feeling guilty about how she felt about your father?"

"Yes," he confirmed, "mostly because of the abuse. I think a part of her loved him for that too. He used to beat her, you know, and there was a part of her that felt she was so damaged that she could never have a normal life anymore," he muttered.

"So, she got her normal?"

"*Nah*, there's nothing for people like us out there. I don't think she could ever have children, which is why she was happy to look after Daniel," he muttered. "Hell." He scrubbed his face. "I can't believe he's dead." Then it all seemed to hit him. He turned and looked at Kate. "How did he die?"

She hesitated, then glanced at Rodney, back at the child's father. "It's hard to hear," she began hesitantly.

He fixed his gaze on her, staring like he was trying hard to refrain from saying anything. "It's all hard to hear, so you might as well give it to me."

She nodded. "Your son died from abuse." He blinked at her in shock, and she nodded. "He faded away into nothing, and, according to the medical examiner, he essentially starved to death."

He shook his head. "No, no, no, you see? ... *Nah*, man.

That couldn't happen. My sister was looking after him."

Kate nodded. "Yes, that's what you said."

He stared at her, not comprehending, as if not aware or not able to take in the details of the truth. Then he started to cry …

Those great big sobbing tears broke her heart, but Kate was also pissed at him. She walked over and sat down beside him and just held his hand.

When he finally could, he whispered, "God, that's not fair. Daniel went through so much with me … and then to …"

Kate nodded. "The only thing I can say is that, right now, at this moment, he's finally at peace."

And hearing that sent him off again in tears.

She looked over at Rodney, wondering if they could do or say anything that would make this father feel better, but how did you even begin to make somebody else feel better over the loss of their own child?

He took several gulping sobs and stared at her. "That's why you're asking about my sister's history?"

She nodded. "That's partly why I was asking, yes." She nodded. "Obviously your sister was dealing with a lot of trauma herself."

"But what about her husband?" he asked, looking up expectantly. Yet, at the same time, he seemed afraid of the answer she would give him. "I know he loved her."

"Maybe … or maybe he wasn't strong enough to deal with whatever she was dishing out. I don't know," Kate added quietly. "However, the little boy had been beaten repeatedly, and the last beating? … I guess he was already so weak and emaciated that he didn't survive."

"Damn it," he muttered, staring at her. "I always wondered."

"Wondered what?" Kate asked.

"I wondered if I was doing the right thing," he wailed, not able to control himself now. "However, I was such a mess, and I wasn't even capable of looking after me or him. So, when she said she could take him, she wasn't necessarily happy about it, but I didn't think she was unhappy about it."

"If she was tormented by guilt already," Kate suggested, "it could be that this psychosis was something that she struggled to stop." He just blinked at her, and she added, "Maybe abusing your son made her feel even guiltier, but he was not sexually abused."

At that, he closed his eyes, and she saw a tear escape from the corner of his eye. "Thank God for that. … I still don't understand how she could have done it, how the abused becomes the abuser."

Yet he didn't see how he himself had done the same thing. Kate shook her head. "I think that's one of the challenges we all have when we see cases like this. We don't understand the how." She hesitated and then asked gingerly, "Do you know if she was ever into …" Then she stopped.

He frowned at her quizzically. "After everything you've already said, you still hesitate to ask some things?" he asked bitterly.

"Yes," Kate acknowledged and then decided that she had absolutely no reason not to. "I guess the question is, do you have any idea about your sister being into BDSM?"

He stared at her, blinked, and shrugged. "That doesn't surprise me terribly, mostly because my father groomed her that way."

"Interesting," Kate replied, as she sat back.

"Why?" The question was so plain, until he saw the look

on Kate's face. He blinked. "Hang on a minute. You said she was dead too."

"Yes," Kate stated quietly, "she is dead. I don't know if you heard about the church killings?"

"Yeah, I did. … God," he murmured, "that's just beyond sick. Putting people on a cross, posting them in a church like that." He shook his head. "What the hell is wrong with people?"

She just waited, until all the color washed out of his skin.

"Jesus, no, no, no, no, not her. Was that her?"

Kate nodded slowly. "Her, her husband, and your son, all three of them."

"Holy Christ." His stare froze on her, as the shocks continued to reverberate through his system. "Okay, now this is just too much. You need to leave." He was now hyperventilating. "I can't handle this."

She stayed firmly in her place. "You may not be able to handle it, and I'm really sorry for your loss," she murmured, "but we have five dead people now. Your son died from the abuse inflicted on him before this, so either somebody found out what had happened to Daniel and decided that the parents potentially needed to suffer, or some other psycho's out there."

"Wait, wait, but her husband wouldn't have had anything to do with it."

"Your son died from prolonged abuse, or did you not hear me clearly?" she asked.

He winced at that. "Christ, I don't …" Then he stopped. "I don't even know what to say."

Kate didn't say anything, just waited.

After a prolonged pause, the father wailed, "It's so ugly. I can't even stand what you're telling me. … I swear Roger was not capable of harming another. Yet, if that's true, does that mean my sister beat my son to death, starved him to death? Oh my God …"

"It is ugly," Kate stated. "It's incredibly ugly, and it's something that we're desperately trying to solve. We need you to understand that we're doing everything we can to find their killer."

He frowned at her. "And yet you've found nothing, I suppose. So somebody just walks into a church, puts people up like that, and walks out. How does that even work?"

"Pretty much like you described it," she said. "In those churches, there's no security, no cameras, and the doors remain unlocked, so anyone could walk in."

"Why my sister? Why my son?"

"I guess part of what I'm wondering is whether your son was part of this because he died through Mary's actions."

"Meaning that her killer decided Mary needed to be crucified to make up for my son's death?" he asked in confusion.

"I can't answer that," she admitted. "All I can tell you is that we're working on a bunch of theories."

"And so far you don't really have anything, do you?"

"No, we sure don't, but believe me, I will figure this out and will find their killer. Which is why I'm here, talking to you."

He blinked several times, and then he started to cry all over. "She was a mess at the time. I knew she was a mess, but she was less of a mess than I was," he said, trying to explain. "And, for many people, that makes no sense, but until you're in that situation …"

She nodded. "I'm not judging you," she stated quietly. "What I am looking for is anything that you might know that could help us to find who would have done this."

He gave a brutal laugh. "We didn't run in the same circles. We didn't do anything in the same circles," he shared, "and, when you talk about BDSM, that could in a way be explained by some of the things that happened to her in childhood and beyond, but that's a result of my father. After we finally left his house, I hadn't had much contact with her."

"Your father is deceased?"

He looked at her with an odd look and nodded. "Yeah, good riddance to an abusive asshole."

"So, what do you make of your relationship with her, after that?"

"We were good, but we kept away deliberately. It was just not good for us to be around each other and to be reminded of the hurts. I still loved her. I knew what she'd gone through, and, of course, I didn't judge her for it. My sister was pretty messed up, but Roger? ... He loved her and took her exactly as she was, and she found him to be a gift that she could hardly accept, and I think that was part of her torment. I think she felt he was too good for her, and she couldn't ever do anything right or enough right to make it something where she could accept that gift." And, with that, he suddenly got up and moved to the door. "I need you to leave now."

She stood, left her card on the side table, and walked alongside Rodney to the door. "If you can think of anybody or anything ..."

He nodded.

"I don't know if you have any inclination to help, but three family members need to be buried."

He looked up at her and blinked owlishly, and the tears

slipped out again. "Oh my God." Then he started to bawl.

She winced, as they quickly slipped down the hallway and stairwell to the outside.

In the fresh air, she took several deep breaths, trying to find that cleansing sense of balance she so desperately needed right now.

Rodney stood beside her, taking big gulps of air himself. "Yeah, and then you go back to that source, the father of Mary," Rodney shared, "and you realize all the pain and torment he started because of his own evil nature."

She nodded, not even wanting to argue the term *evil*. "He ruined so many lives. I mean, how does anybody even come to terms with something like this?"

"Does that really explain the BDSM?" Rodney asked quietly a few minutes later.

"In a way, yes," Kate stated. "It might be part of that guilt and yet, at the same time, retribution, still doing what daddy loved, feeling guilty because it may have been the only way that she could find pleasure herself, and totally hating herself for it the whole time."

"What do you make of the husband?"

"God only knows how he handled this, especially if he wasn't responsible for any of this crap," she muttered, looking at her partner. "That is something I don't have a clue on and still can't quite imagine."

Rodney nodded, stared off in the distance. "Neither can I. So much damage, so much pain in one family. It is …" He groaned and added, "I need a shower."

She snorted. "As if that would help," she murmured. "But I get your meaning, anything to wash away the stench of what we just heard and the pain of what's going on in that apartment right now."

And together the two of them turned and headed off to the next name on their list. The day was off to a rough start, but, until she was done with all these interviews, there would really be no end to it. They still hadn't found anything that they could use to get a hold of whoever was killing these couples. Kate knew the countdown was already on, as it was highly doubtful that the killer would stop now that he had these under his belt. Chances were that enough people out in the world needed to find forgiveness for everything that had happened to them. At that thought, she stopped, turned, and looked at Rodney. "*Forgive*."

He stared at her curiously. "Yes? What about it?"

"I wonder if it's about the victims needing to forgive themselves for what happened to them. For example, … what if the killer was trying to save their souls by killing them or something?" she asked him warily. "Maybe, I mean, maybe it was a case of, *While you're in this state, we can get you to find some peace for what was done to you.* Maybe someone thought this could be a way to save their souls, and that's why he took them into the church—because they had already suffered so much—and this was his way of helping them to reach heaven."

"For Christ's sake." Rodney frowned at her. "So, you think that their murderer thought he was saving them by killing them?"

She gave him a twisted smile. "With what we just heard about the mother, Mary, yes, but, as far as her husband goes, Roger? I have no idea. I don't seem to have any grasp on him at all, and that is something we need to sort out."

Rodney shook his head. "How could Roger possibly allow that child to suffer, and what possible reason could he have to stand by and let that happen? I mean, I can see him trying to ignore his wife having rough sex with Roy, but wasn't Roger still in the house? Didn't he hear her screams? And, even if Roger was ignoring the torture masquerading as sex going on in his house with his own goddamn wife, how did he treat her wounds afterward without visualizing all that crap?"

Kate shrugged. "Maybe Roger was deemed worthy of death for just standing by, for doing nothing. Whereas our killers are being proactive."

Rodney raised both hands in mock surrender.

Kate added, "Let's keep after it and try to find out because I need an answer to that question too."

SIMON CAME BACK to the present with a hard tug, then somebody pushing his shoulder, plus slapping him across the face. A woman, speaking rapid Chinese, was beside him. When he slowly opened his eyes, he saw a look of relief on the older lady, with a young boy at her side.

She said in broken English, "You okay? You okay?"

He groaned but nodded, then reached up to grab her hand still shaking him, stilling her efforts. "I'll be fine." He gave her a small smile and whispered, "Thank you."

She crouched in front of him and just waited.

He took several deep breaths, knowing that he didn't dare lose it while he was out here, particularly since the little boy was looking more than a little nervous. "I'm fine," he told them both, with a weak smile. "Sorry, I just appeared to have passed out. My blood sugar," he tried to explain. That was BS, of course, but whatever worked, he didn't care, as long as it would get this lady to stop staring at him, as if he were some criminal, taking a break in the middle of the day.

Simon got up slowly, took several tentative steps, and smiled at her. "See? I'm fine." Thankfully she took off, jabbering in a constant stream to the little boy, and Simon called out behind her, "Thank you."

She lifted a hand, didn't say anything else, and continued to walk away rapidly. He hadn't meant to send her away at a run, and he should have certainly done something to show his appreciation and to help her out. He could have done something, though he didn't know just what at the moment, since his brain was still not even functioning. But, as it was, he sank back down onto the bench. He just sat here for a long moment, trying to figure out what had just happened.

It wasn't the easiest thing to process. Something was off in his world, and it didn't make any sense. As he sat here quietly, he kept hoping that whatever it was he'd just been a party to would make some sense and would come back to him. He felt part of it. He heard hymns in the background, like a choir singing, and yet it didn't make … He couldn't place it; he couldn't place the voices. He sat here for the longest time, but nothing else was coming. When he slowly got up again, he heard a whisper, almost in a holy reverence, as if emanating from the buildings around him, or the wind was calling it.

Forgive.

CHAPTER 11

A S KATE AND Rodney drove away from the last place on their list, a fatigue had settled so deep in Kate that she didn't want to acknowledge it. "God, this is all just so depressing," Kate murmured.

When her phone buzzed a little later, she looked at it and groaned. "It's Simon."

"Why the groan?" Rodney asked, throwing her a teasing glance. "You tired of him already?"

She shook her head. "Nope, it's an order to call him."

He looked at her in surprise. "Call him already. It's not as if we have anything else right now. If he can give us anything to point us in a direction," he added, "it could be huge."

Grumbling, she called him back. "Hey, Simon. You're on Speakerphone. Rodney and I are heading back to the station. What's up?" When he hesitated, she winced. "You want me to take it off Speaker?"

"*Nah*, that's fine. Hey, Rodney. How're you doing?"

"It's been a mighty shitty day, man. If you've got something for us, … I'll take it."

Simon sighed. "I do, but it's not helpful."

"What do you have?" she asked, suddenly realizing he didn't sound right. "What happened?"

"I apparently just blacked out on a city bench," he muttered.

"What? Shit," she said, leaning forward, looking around for a place for Rodney to turn. "Where are you now? Do we need to come get you?"

"No, I'm fine," he replied, his voice strengthening as he spoke.

"*Sure*, you sound really fine to me," she quipped, with an eye roll, but she also knew it would get a rise out of him and would kick him out of whatever slump he was in.

He snorted at that. "Even though I know why you're doing this, and I know that it's probably the right strategy in this situation, it's still pissing me off, which pisses me off even more."

She smiled. "That's fine. As long as you're not passed out drunk on some park bench, we can deal with it."

"*Great*, so that's what you think of me." She waited patiently, as he cleared his throat and added, "So, you'll love this then. An older oriental lady slapped my face to wake me up," he shared, with a note of humor. "I think she thought I was drunk and was upsetting her little grandson, who was with her."

"It would be upsetting," Kate agreed, with a laugh, "for anybody who saw you, but, I mean, anybody in various parts of the city will see that on a fairly regular basis."

"*Great*," Simon muttered, "dissing me once more, thanks. On second thought, maybe the kid looked so horrified because his grandma was slapping the shit out of me."

"So tell me what happened."

"I'm pretty sure that whatever happened," he began in a slow reverb, "had something to do with your case."

Rodney stopped and pulled over to the roadside, looking

over at Kate. "Why do you think that?" she asked, her voice hard and all business. "What came through?"

"It's not so much what came through. It's just that I woke up to a series of ... voices, and it sounded like hymns, like a choir, but not live necessarily," he explained, followed by a pause, as if trying to place what he'd heard, "but I definitely heard church music. Just as it started to disappear and to fade away—maybe because I came to rather abruptly from somebody slapping me, so it's not as if I could get the full message—anyway what I got was a voice, gentle, like almost in my ear, saying just one word. *Forgive.*"

"That definitely sounds like our guy," Rodney noted beside her.

She was silent for a long moment. "Of course you couldn't place the location or anything, right?"

"Don't be quite so dismissive," he said. "I wasn't even going to call you."

"No, I'm glad you did. I'm also concerned because you don't sound quite like yourself yet."

"It just happened, and I might have had more information except for the way I was brought back, but then I am in a public spot, and I'm sure it's not doing my reputation any good."

"I don't think your reputation is anything you need to worry about." She looked over at Rodney and rolled her eyes. "Maybe it's time to go home."

"Yeah, I was thinking of it. I'm just waiting to get my strength back."

"Whoa, whoa, whoa, what do you mean by that?" she asked, almost in panic.

"It hit me hard," he murmured. "I'm not exactly sure what it was. It just feels not so much that I got punched but

I'm drained, exhausted, like seriously exhausted. I am really tired all of a sudden."

"And is that fatigue yours or his?"

"Oh, now that's a very good question," Simon noted. "I hadn't thought of that."

"Because if it's his, you know you can throw it off, but if it's not his…"

"You want me to try and find information?" Simon asked.

"It's not that I want you to try," she corrected. "I can't ask something like that from you, and believe me. I'm still struggling with the fact that it's even a discussion."

He laughed. "And honestly that it is a discussion is something I love."

"Sure, you do," she quipped, "because you like tormenting me."

"Yeah, when it comes to this shit, I sure do. Why should I be stuck in this alone?"

At that, she had to smile. "Look. we're about ten minutes out from the station, and I'll be back on the road about ten minutes after that. Shall I come get you? Are you okay to drive?"

"I didn't drive. I've been walking between projects today." Taking a deep breath, he added, "I'll just head home."

"You do that," she said. "Go on home, and I'll be there in a little bit."

"Are you coming over then?"

"Yeah, absolutely," she stated. "I want to confirm you're okay."

"I'm fine," he repeated, his tone gaining in strength and outrage. "I wouldn't have called you if I wasn't fine."

"And that would piss me off even more," she declared.

"To even think that you wouldn't call me if you were hurt? … That is the wrong thing to say to me right now."

"Maybe, but suddenly you don't sound quite so worried about me." And, with that, he hung up.

She stared down at the phone and then laughed. "God, nothing quite like having somebody like Simon around."

"You do keep each other on your toes though," Rodney pointed out, as they pulled into the police station. "And he's right. You don't sound quite so worried now."

"I was trying to mask it before," she admitted, "but, if he'll routinely start passing out in public, that's not something that'll be all that easy to deal with."

"I think it'll be a whole lot harder on him to deal with than for you," he pointed out.

"I know. I know. Back to the fact that this is his nightmare, and I need to support him, rather than being critical."

"Particularly when he's been such a big help so many times."

"Got it," she said. "Believe me. I do know that, but it also worries me to think about it. I mean, what if he was in a crosswalk? What if it just overtook him while he was, I don't know, just walking along the river, and he ended up in the water?"

"Wouldn't it kick him back out again?" Rodney asked, as they locked the vehicle and headed up to the front steps.

"I don't know," she said, "since we really don't know how any of his visions work. Hell, I'm still on the outside, trying not to be too bitchy when something happens, when I can't get the answers I want," she explained, with a shrug.

"Because having him there means you think you should get what you need from him, but, of course, you can't because it's never that clear."

"Not only is it never that clear, it's never clear at all," she replied. "These visions seem to deliberately make life awkward and difficult for you, so you can't get very much at all from them."

"I can see how that would drive you nuts," Rodney stated, as they walked into the station.

"Oh, what's this?" Owen asked, looking up. "You driving her nuts there, Rodney?"

"Yes," she replied, grateful to have someone shift the conversation from where it was. "He is." As she walked to her desk, she turned to look back at Rodney, then to Owen and the team. "I'm heading out, unless anybody has any reason for me not to go?"

"No, you need to go," Rodney declared, before anyone said anything. "Go check up on him."

"Yeah, I'll do that." With that, she quickly escaped but stopped at the doorway and called out, "Look. I'll check in later. Just share those notes and see if something else comes up." She groaned, then added, "We didn't get anything decent this afternoon, at least not after the morning interviews, but still …"

"That was painful enough," Rodney muttered.

She nodded and quickly escaped, heading over to Simon's. She wasn't sure if he had any food, but she desperately needed something for when she got there and assumed he would too. She pondered about stopping to pick something up and then realized that, even if it was too much food, it didn't matter. They could eat it over the next day or so, if need be.

And, with that decided, she picked up two pizzas and a bottle of wine. By the time she made it to his apartment, she walked in to see Edgar at the front desk, getting off the phone. She looked over at him and asked earnestly, "Is he in?"

"Yeah, he came in just a few minutes ago." Frowning, he turned to face her.

Seeing his expression, she knew he had noticed.

Edgar noted, "He doesn't look very good."

She nodded. "That's why I'm here."

He quickly buzzed her up and helped her onto the elevator. As she made her way up, she tried to rehearse what she would say to Simon, but it was so hard to know how to handle it, and she had zero experience with this stuff.

As she walked through the apartment after putting down the pizza and wine, there was no sign of him. She headed into the bedroom, and there he was, crashed, his boots still on, sound asleep. She winced and walked closer, checking to make sure he was alive and not in the midst of an actual vision, but that was much harder to tell. Each breath was slow and steady, so she would take that to mean he was sleeping.

She quickly stripped down and took a shower, trying to scrub off the grime of the day, as Rodney had suggested. Some days were easier to handle, but death notifications were always tough, particularly in a case like this. With that done, she put on a robe and walked into the kitchen, where she popped open the bottle of wine, poured herself a glass, and sat down to stare out at the beautiful scenery below. Once again struck by the contrast between such an absolutely glorious city and the dark underbelly that constantly operated just beneath the surface, she felt melancholy and so disturbed. After the day's events, she felt the weight of it all.

She was working on her second glass when she heard a noise in the other room. She got up, raced into the bedroom, calling out, "Simon, I'm here. Take it easy. I'm right here."

He opened his eyes, but something was off about the look in them. "You must forgive," he thundered at her, as he sat up on the bed. "You must forgive."

"That's all right," she told him, reaching out—then realizing that she shouldn't touch him. "Why? Why must I forgive?"

"Salvation. You must forgive so you can go to heaven, so your soul can go to heaven. You must forgive, and you must ask for forgiveness as well," he declared in the same booming voice. "Two halves of the same coin."

"But are they?" she wondered.

Immediately his voice thundered back at her, "Do not doubt the rules. The Lord has rules for us, and we must abide by them." He didn't seem to be looking at her or was seeing her from a different purview. "You must forgive."

"I'm fine to forgive," she stated. "Forgive what was done to me?"

"Yes, you must forgive. Only then will you stop hurting others."

At that, something struck her, and she stopped and looked at him carefully. "Who are you?"

"You must forgive," he repeated, his voice intoning, as he now knelt on the bed, holding something in his hand. All of a sudden, he raised his other hand and pounded it down on whatever he held in his left hand.

She realized it must be a stake in his vision. She walked closer, studying his position, and dared not go any closer to him. "Why this church? Why would you choose this church, and who are you?"

"I am a sinner," he whispered, and this time around, as he looked back at her, his eyes were glossy. "A sinner who desperately needs salvation."

"If you're a sinner, why are you hurting others?"

He raised that blank gaze toward her and whispered, "Because I cannot forgive."

Like a string pulled up behind him, Simon rose up onto his feet in a movement that was way too smooth. And then, like the strings holding him were cut, he fell face down onto the mattress. She raced over to his side, her hands immediately checking for a pulse, but it was there, strong and steady.

She sat back, ran a shaky hand over her forehead, and whispered, "Oh Lord."

Almost immediately Simon whispered back, "I'm sorry, Kate. He's not here, not anymore. Will I do instead?" Tears in her eyes, she leaned over and gave him a gentle hug. His arms opened up, and he pulled her close. "I don't know what that was," he whispered, "I could only hear it on the outside."

"I'll tell you in a few minutes," she muttered, as she snuggled in close. "Just hold me."

And, with that, he wrapped his arms tighter around her and pulled her in, and she hoped he would never let go. God, what she had just seen, what she'd just heard, and what she'd understood, was beyond anything she could have imagined. There was only salvation in his arms, and even that thought could be enough to make her bolt from the bed and across the room, but she knew that, at the end of the day, Simon was the wholeness that she needed.

She just didn't know how or what to give him to make his world an easier place to live.

SIMON WOKE THE next morning, rolled over to see a tousled

Kate still sleeping, a gentle snore coming through her chest. He smiled, leaned over, kissed her gently, got up, and headed into the shower. He felt better, after an evening of heavy discussions, ugly thoughts, and so much more that he didn't seem able to handle or to control. It was the lack of control that was starting to really bother him, but he knew that to even attempt to control these psychic visions was something that could turn him into a basket case very quickly. So much was going on that sometimes it was almost impossible to sort through it.

That he had connected with the case she was working on was both good and bad. Good because he knew he might help, bad in the sense that it would torment her, and apparently also him. Nothing was easy about this one; he could sense so much guilt and so much pain. Too much was in there to process, yet none of it made a whole lot of sense, mostly because Simon hadn't connected enough with the killer to understand the motivations, and that may never come. Simon may never connect at that level. Maybe it wasn't even so much about connecting at that level as it was to even find a way to connect.

After his shower, he walked out and smiled at the cold leftover pizza. He put on a pot of coffee, then snagged several pieces and tossed them in the microwave. She didn't often bring food, and, when she did, it was usually pizza, mostly because food was something she just didn't think about or plan ahead for. If there was food when she got home, she was always pleasantly surprised, but it's not like a lack of good food bothered her, and that was something he could never understand.

To him, food was an art, and he loved it to boot, but it wasn't something that she worried about much. Food to her was sustenance, but it wasn't anything she was worried about doing without, whereas he appreciated good food, good wine, and the mood that was set around fine dining. So, although this pizza and wine wasn't exactly at the top of his list, she'd made a point of bringing them, and that had made them even more special.

And it was foolish to even think of it that way, but, hey, he would accept whatever he could from her and would enjoy it. Once the coffee was done dripping, he poured a cup, carried it in to her, then leaned over and kissed her hard. "As much as I'd like to keep you here," he murmured against her ear, "I think you have to go to work."

She opened her eyes and stared at him and groaned. "Did you say, *work*?"

"I did," he stated, with half a smile. "Not too sure you should be staying in bed."

"What time is it?" Rolling over, she stretched upward, wincing at the sore muscles she apparently was dealing with.

He nodded. "About seven o'clock."

"That's not too bad," she muttered, as she relaxed back. "I wanted to ride the bus today, once I drop off my car at home. So I was afraid you would say it was like nine or something."

"No, you're doing fine."

"Good, now for a shower and some coffee." She shifted slowly in bed, until she leaned against the head of the bed, then picked up the coffee and sipped it. "Thank you. I can really use this right now," she murmured. Then, as if remembering last night, she tossed a sharp gaze his way. "How are you?"

He hated that being her first thought, but, at the same time, he knew he should be grateful that she even gave a damn. He nodded. "I'm fine."

Her lips quirked, but she didn't say anything.

If being *fine* was a pat answer, she was guilty of saying that herself. He figured a lot of people in the world were. He didn't know too many people who liked being fussed over, although that was more a case with the men, he thought. But then again, maybe he was wrong about that, and he just knew the wrong men.

"How are you handling Bartlett's death?" she murmured.

He thought about it and then relented. "Sad, upset, and worried that it wasn't a suicide of course, though that is probably mostly your influence." He sent a pointed look in her direction.

She stared at him in surprise. "As far as I know, there's no reason *not* to consider it a suicide."

"But you don't know, do you?"

"Do any of us? I don't have the details. It's not my case. But suicides are investigated, and, if you feel the need to know for sure, I can probably put a word out on it, just to get some answers."

He smiled and nodded. "If you could, I would appreciate that."

She nodded slowly. "I can, but no guarantees."

"There never are," he noted, with a smile. "There never are. But maybe we can get something sorted."

"I don't know about getting something sorted," she said, with a snort, "but if we can get you some answers so you're more comfortable about it at least, that will be good."

He swore. "I forgot to tell you that I have to go meet Bartlett's lawyer. I was supposed to be there yesterday, and that's when I zapped out on the city bench. He did contact me later, and I pushed it off until today. So that's where I'll be heading first thing."

"Why on earth would you be going there?" she asked in amazement.

"I don't know, but that's one of the things I need to sort out. It was crappy timing yesterday, and I don't really have a ready excuse for it. He sent me a text, saying he had something to discuss. I called, but he wasn't comfortable talking about it over the phone. When he called me later, asking me where I was when I failed to show, thank God I had enough energy to say I had low blood sugar, so that worked for the time being."

"Hey, blood sugar always works."

"Sure, and then people think I'm a diabetic and just don't care enough about my health."

"Ouch," she replied. "That's a lot of judgment on diabetics."

He shrugged. "You know that's just how a lot of people think."

"Yet that's not what we think," she stated firmly. "Anyway, maybe say that you got called to the hospital or something."

He pondered that, then shrugged. "I'll think about it, but what I need to know is why he wants to talk to me."

"You can always let me know if something comes up," she said pointedly.

"Oh, I will." He gave her a big grin. "If nothing else, it's handy to have a cop around."

She rolled her eyes at that. "Not sure I want to be kept as somebody *handy to have around.*"

He laughed. "Regardless, there are definite benefits," he murmured, leaning over and kissing her gently. "But I do have to go make that stupid meeting," he said, as he checked his watch. "I should have scheduled it for much later in the day."

"No point in trying to get out of it," she noted. "It's not going away."

"Are you sure?" he asked, with a smirk. "It would certainly be nice if it did."

"Yet, if you want answers, dodging this meeting is not the way to get them."

"I get it," he agreed, holding up his hand. "I did just have some pizza, but, if I'm to make that meeting, I do need to get going.

"Go, go, go." She waved him off. "I'm fine. I'll connect with you later today."

"Good enough."

She added, "Let me know how the meeting goes. It's got me curious."

"Me too," he agreed. With that, he headed to the closet, got dressed, and, giving her a goodbye kiss, was gone a few short minutes later.

CHAPTER 12

KATE GOT UP to get dressed, then remembered the crazy events of the night before. She had seen Simon ripping into the bed with a stake—and heard the rips—but now that she looked at the bed, there was no sign of any such damage. It unnerved her, yet, at the same time, it was a mystery that she was thinking of discussing with Simon. Now she only had to figure out the best way to ask him about it.

She drove home, changed into a fresh shirt and pants, then hopped the next bus to the station. Walking inside, she felt a little bit better, until Rodney looked up at her, and the expression on his face changed. "How's Simon?"

She frowned. "He's okay, a little bit perturbed because he had very little warning. He got himself to a bench, and that was it."

Rodney winced at that. "That would suck."

"Yeah, a lot of it sucks," she noted, "and you don't really think about it."

"In your case, I didn't think you ever thought about it."

"No, I didn't," she admitted, "and I still don't want to either." And, with that, she checked her computer. After bringing up the case of Bartlett's suicide, she made a call to the morgue.

When the call was answered, she introduced herself and got straight to the point. "I was looking for information on

Bartlett Morris, believed to be a jumper from yesterday."

"Oh, yes, I have that case file right here. Any particular reason you're asking?"

"A friend of mine saw him the day before and is quite upset at the idea of him going out a window and wondered if there was anything untoward about it."

"*Hmm.*" Then apparently Smidge was put on phone.

"Interesting friend you have there."

"A good friend, and he's done a lot to help me out."

At that, his tone changed. "Are we talking about Simon here?"

"Yeah," she replied, relenting because Smidge would be more cooperative if he knew that, rather than not. "Bartlett had asked him to have a look at the books of his business and to see if they could come up with a way forward. According to Simon, there were viable options, but it was quite serious and might mean declaring bankruptcy and restructuring the company. He advised him to get a forensic accountant and a lawyer on it right away."

"But instead he stepped out of a window?"

"Apparently."

"You don't believe it?"

"I'm not sure what I believe," she admitted. "Simon told me that there's no way, and, of course, that just adds to the confusion. Simon thinks Bartlett wasn't suicidal, hence my predicament."

"Of course if Simon says there's no way," Smidge added, "we should definitely take another look."

Such an ironic tone filled his voice, it was all she could do to hold back a snappy response. When she did get a hold of herself, she replied in a calmer tone than she felt. "I think it's more a case of feeling terribly guilty about potentially having made his friend feel like this was the only solution."

"I've got the body here still, and it is a clear-cut case of going over from a great height. I don't have any evidence that would suggest he was pushed."

"Right, so would you typically have evidence of something like that?"

"Not necessarily," he replied. "I don't have much backstory on Mr. Morris either. Here's the case number. You can follow up on your own time." And with that, he gave her the file number, and that had to be enough for her.

"Got it, thanks." She ended the call and checked out the file and quickly phoned the officers who had responded to the call. Unfortunately their answers only gave her more questions. "I'm sorry. Did you say that the wife called it in?"

"Yes, she told us that her husband had jumped from the building, and, at the same time, we were getting calls from 9-1-1 about the body down below," he replied.

"Of course, and was anybody else there?"

"No."

"Did you take a statement from her?"

"Yes, he'd apparently been despondent over his business affairs, decided that there was no way out, and this was his answer."

"Okay," she murmured, "that's an interesting take."

"We see it quite often, particularly when it comes to these financial gurus." As he chewed on the last word, she realized the value and attention that would be given to this case.

"No, I hear you," she replied, trying to stifle an outcry that might land her in hot water. "I mean, I'm certainly not surprised, as I mentioned. I just wanted to see that in black-and-white. Would you mind sending me his wife's statement?"

"Sure," the cop said. "Any reason to doubt this?"

"I don't know," she hedged. "Let me have a look at the statement first."

"Okay," the cop replied, "but keep me in the loop, will you? As far as I'm concerned, this one is pretty clear-cut, but I'm open to any ideas you have."

"Oh, it's clear-cut he went over," she clarified. "What's not so clear-cut is whether he had any help."

"He was a pretty good-size man, although more tall and skinny than bulky," he pointed out.

"Yet his wife is no tiny weakling."

"That's true." He stopped and repeated, "No, that's also true. I can't imagine why she would want to throw him over though."

"I don't know," she admitted. "Again that's something I need to take another look at."

"I feel that you're not telling me something."

"The thing is, somebody spoke to him that day, earlier in the morning, and had seen him the day before. He'd been asked by Bartlett to have a look at the books and to help find a solution to save the company. They had settled on a plan to get a forensic accountant and an attorney on board immediately." She tried to make it sound casual. "So, the fact that he went over in that particular manner with that timing doesn't make any sense. He had other viable options."

"So, you've got a contact who was helping?"

"Yes," she verified, and she gave him Simon's name. "You need to talk to him to get the specifics, but my understanding is that they had discussed a path forward that would allow Bartlett to restructure the company, to retain certain assets, and to keep the business running, while they made the changes necessary to correct past problems. Apparently Bartlett was relieved to have a plan in place and sounded quite positive about it. But his wife, on the other hand, was not. Bartlett mentioned her crying about losing face, only to die in this mess where she wouldn't get anything out of it. So Simon was more than a little surprised when Bartlett ended up jumping. It's not a normal response, and that needs to be taken into account."

"So, you're thinking the wife might have had something to do with it?"

"I'm not thinking anything," she declared, cutting him down, "but who knows? Maybe they had a fight, and some things were said. I certainly don't want to put any impressions in your head. You need to make up your own mind and to consider the source."

"She was certainly distraught when we saw her," he shared. "I did take a statement from her obviously, and she was distraught but controlled."

"Right, too controlled?"

After a moment of silence on the other end, he replied grudgingly, "I don't want to say that either, but let me think about it."

"Yeah, that's what I'll do too," she stated, "as soon as I go over the wife's statement."

"Good enough."

With that, she disconnected, finding Rodney staring at her.

"What's that all about?" he asked.

She explained about Bartlett's suicide and Simon's involvement with it.

"And Simon doesn't think it was a suicide? Or are any of

his abilities involved?"

"I don't think that's ever come up. I just think he's afraid that he had more to do to with the mental state of his friend than he wants to deal with," she explained. "I mean, he's definitely feeling guilty, and yet he was just trying to help. Also, he told me how the wife was particularly outraged at the idea of curtailing her spending in any way."

"Which would have happened with bankruptcy."

"Sure, but now she's lost her husband, so who's to say exactly what went on. I mean, that won't change the fact that the business is in trouble. But what changed is the fact that she now has much more control over how it's handled and what she can do about it and what money she can move over the next few weeks, doesn't it?"

Rodney whistled at that. "You really do pick them, don't you?"

"I don't know about picking anything," she argued, "but this one's just got that nasty edge to it, and it was literally dropped into my lap. I didn't even have to pick it up."

He nodded. "But, if they ruled it a suicide, then what?"

She nodded. "Then nobody has any say in it. I get it," she acknowledged, "but I still don't have to like it."

He smiled. "What about our other cases?" Just then his phone rang, and so did hers.

She winced as she looked down at it. "*Great.*" Kate looked over at Rodney. In a way, she'd been expecting this notification. After Simon's episode last night, she had a sinking feeling in the back of her mind that something like this was coming. She didn't relish thinking about the fact that Simon was so connected to their church killer that he'd literally ripped into the bed and even those signs were erased. "Did you get the same message I did?" she asked Rodney.

He nodded, eyeing her grimly. "Third church."

"Right, God help us. The media won't let it go this time," she murmured. At that, the rest of the team galvanized into action, and they all raced out to the new location.

CHAPTER 13

KATE WALKED INTO another huge ornate Catholic church building, this one in Point Grey, commanding a certain reverence as she entered, which changed to shock and horror as she spied the couple staked to crosses, lying in front of the altar. She expected to see them like that, but it still gutted her from the inside out. They'd been half propped up, as if the killer was still attempting to figure out a way to get them to hang on the wall, as in a proper crucifixion.

She stared from down below at the two victims, one male, one female, and both appeared to have been recently beaten, if not at the actual time of the killing. Her heart was saddened as she stared at obviously another attempt to either get somebody forgiven for their sins or to forgive someone else for their sins. Obviously the killer had some penchant for the Catholic church, and some beliefs were coming into play. Either he thought the church itself would help or would hinder the process, depending on what his actual purpose was in all this.

Based on Simon's psychic episode, maybe this was a way to let the couple out of their misery, and that line of thought she was ready to explore. As she stood here, staring around at the small area where the bodies were, a certain quiet filled the space. It was peaceful, almost calming. She could see why somebody distraught and upset over circumstances in their life might come here, looking for peace, looking for that sensation of salvation or just even the calming serenity. The sigh that worked out of her chest when she finally turned away was heartfelt and agonizingly deep.

As she turned away from the victims, she caught sight of the priest standing there ever-so-still, watching her. She walked closer, and he smiled at her.

His smile was gentle, commiserating, yet full of love. "Your job, my child, is not an easy one."

Surprised, she considered that for a moment and then nodded. "No, sometimes it isn't. However, I do believe it's very necessary."

He nodded. "And it takes a special person to handle it, and, for that, I am grateful for your service." He looked around, and the sadness in his heart was almost more than she could bear.

She fought back the tears that were threatening to escape. "I'm so sorry."

He looked up at her and then nodded. "You do understand, don't you?"

"I understand much of it, though I can't say that I can possibly understand it all. But I do see a space of hope, joy, and serenity as being under attack in many ways. Yet I believe that our killer, the perpetrator who is doing this to these victims, is doing so for what he considers to be the right reasons."

The priest studied her. "What possible reason could that be?"

She gave him half a smile. "Salvation of their souls."

Startled, he looked at her, then back at the bodies behind them and whispered, "What dark mind could possibly think this is salvation?"

"A tortured one," she replied, her voice equally low, equally soft. "One who has most likely suffered a great deal in his life, which is what brought him to this point."

At her words, a certain understanding entered the priest's gaze. "I'm sorry for his pain and suffering, though I've never understood how making others suffer made it better."

"I'm not sure the point is making it better, as much as trying to save these victims from whatever fate the killer thinks they'll end up with."

The priest once again nodded and smiled at her. "You have a unique understanding."

"Sometimes I'm wrong," she stated, in barely a whisper, "but, when I see these acts, … so horrific and so painful, yet, in his mind, full of triumph because he's doing something. He's sending out a message, one that most of us abhor, and yet, for him, it's a calling, something he feels driven to do. Whether that is based on a sound mind and logic is no longer part of the equation. He's driven by an internal impulse that doesn't necessarily have anything to do with such simple concepts."

Rodney came up behind her just then, and she introduced both of them to the priest. "We'll be looking into this," she said, pointing to the crosses, without looking at the newest victims.

"Looking into it?" he questioned.

"Solving it," she stated firmly. "We will find the killer."

He looked at her for a moment and then nodded. "I do believe you will, and it will be interesting to see what it is that you choose to do with him."

"I will prosecute him," she replied, "to the fullest extent of the law, as I am beholden to do."

The priest let out a heavy sigh. "It's a hard time in our world when this is something that somebody feels driven to do."

"Absolutely," Rodney agreed. "On the other hand, the fact that he is driven to do it helps us find him."

"Does it though?" the priest asked, his voice sad and dropping, even as he spoke. "It appears to me that somebody like this won't just be out walking around, like everybody else."

"I think you're wrong there, Father," Kate noted. "His torment is on the inside. I think, on the outside, he'll look the same as you or me."

The priest shuddered. "I have no idea who would have done this," he muttered, forestalling the questions that were even now forming on Kate's lips. "I have absolutely no idea who in our circle could have done such a thing, if even he was of our church," he added in a soft tone. "I understand this is not the first case."

"No, it is not," she confirmed in the same tone. "Unfortunately this is the third time that he has done this, and we now have seven victims."

"And still you haven't been able to stop him?" His voice sharpened in outrage, only to immediately close his eyes and whisper, "I'm sorry. I'm trying not to judge you."

"That's all right," she said in a bitter tone, yet with a passive face. "I'm trying not to judge you for it either." At that, his eyes opened wide, and she gave him a small smile. "Somewhere along the line it is because of his beliefs that he is here doing this," she stated, looking at the cross to her side. "So, from my perspective, it's hard for me to not see the same blame."

He shook his head. "We can try to save as many souls as

we want," he explained, "but they still have to be willing to take those steps and to accept the Lord into their hearts, and that? That is an ongoing challenge."

"I have no doubt about it," she murmured and then shrugged. "Do you have anybody in this church who …" She hesitated and then added a bit carefully, "Obviously you wouldn't think he would do this because I suspect that nobody would think he's doing this. However, I tend to think of somebody who's gone through a recent trauma, somebody who may be on the verge of snapping or maybe has lost people close to him?"

The priest faced her fully and nodded. "Yes, of course, many people come to the church, when they hit that time of life. Many of my parishioners have hit rock bottom. Many of them, more often than not."

"Of course," she said, hiding her desperation. She hesitated once more, and yet knew she needed to give it a try. "A list of names would be very helpful." He shook his head, and she reached out, touched his shoulder gently. "Father, we won't accuse them, and we won't in any way disturb their world, beyond the fact that they're already in a great deal of pain. However, we do need some idea of who could do this."

"My people come to me for comfort," he stated with finality. "I cannot just give their names to the police because they're bereaved."

She pondered that, knowing what he was saying, knowing how he felt about it, and yet frustrated because how was she supposed to sort out who had done this if nobody was ever willing to talk?

Rodney broke in just then. "Any chance you have a security system or maybe hours when the church is closed? Are there places with cameras where we can see who may be coming and going?"

The priest shook his head. "No. Once again, we are one of the churches that have refused to do that. We haven't had any violence in our corner, and certainly no atrocities like this have happened before. So, no, we don't have anything like that."

She sighed and nodded. "In other words, anybody can come and go at any time."

"Yes. We have in the past closed for various times, but the whole purpose of the church is to be here for the people."

And again she understood that, but it sure didn't help in terms of an investigation. She asked a few more questions of the priest, before she heard a shout in her direction. She turned to see Smidge motioning at her. She quickly made her excuses and walked over to him. "Hey."

"I told you not to bring me any more of these," he snapped.

She nodded, understanding full well where his anger was coming from and agreeing with it mostly, just not that she had any control over it. "Yeah, apparently I have no clout in that regard," she murmured, with quiet sarcasm. "So, what can you tell me?"

He shook his head. "Not a whole lot. This killer's a little too anxious and a little too impatient, but he is meticulous and not giving us any chance to get ahead of him."

"I wonder if that's a part of it, you know? Like he's try-ing to process as many souls as he can, before such a thing happens and we do get in front of this."

He looked at her and nodded. "That could be. It could very well be what he's up to." Smidge pondered that, as he looked around. "But, in a world like the one we live in today, he'll be a very busy guy."

"And that's my concern," she noted, looking at him. "I mean, anybody attempting to save souls—or whatever it is he thinks he's doing here—will be a huge danger to the rest of us, until we get this solved. Unfortunately, until he gets put away, this is an even bigger issue than we first thought," she stated, as she stared at the bodies. "Please tell me that they were not tortured as part of the prior ritual."

"I won't know that until I get them back to the morgue," he replied. "I need time to do an autopsy, as soon I can get back." His initial ire had eased back, after unloading on her. "More to the point, you need the actual crime scene because what we don't have here is any blood evidence."

"And again you noticed, I'm sure," she added, making a circle with her hands, "that they're small in stature."

"I had noticed and wondered if you did as well," he stated, with a nod.

"I see it, and I'm a little concerned because unfortunately that could also leave us open to the killer being female."

"I wondered that too," he muttered. "This really is completely wide open so far, isn't it?"

"Yes, way too wide open and too much going on for us to sort through it all at the moment. So far, we don't have anything."

"I might have something forensically for you this time," he claimed, with suppressed excitement. "There are a few fibers in her mouth and a couple fibers on this male." Smidge picked up the dead man's hand. "It looks like something under his fingernails."

"That would be good news," she said in delight. "It may not help us catch him—or her—but it might help us lock him down in some way."

"It's a two-part job as always," Smidge noted, his tone

deepening in frustration. "The only thing I can do is give you the information and hope enough is there to do something with it."

"And all I can do," she added, "is gather as much as I can and hand it over to the prosecutors. It's all up to them at that point."

"Which in most cases isn't enough," Smidge snapped again.

While she understood his frustration, she wanted to point out that he ought to take it up with the prosecutor's office, but it was useless to start an argument here.

He rubbed at his eye, looking away, as if realizing by her silence that he was out of line. "I'll finish this one and head back to the office," he muttered. "Don't expect answers immediately, but I'll get to it as quickly as I can."

"Appreciate it," she said, quietly watching as the male body had been released from its wooden stakes and was loaded onto a gurney. She walked over and asked one of the guys lifting it, "Did you check his pockets?"

He nodded. "Smidge did, but I don't think anything was there."

She called out to Smidge, "If you come up with anything for an ID, let me know."

"I will," he said, with a nod. "The male does have some unusual dental work, so we might trace him from that."

That was also good news, more good news than she'd expected. Feeling slightly buoyed over it all, she headed back to where Rodney was talking to several of the other people at the church. She listened in as he questioned one woman, who had been in earlier cleaning but hadn't seen anything.

As soon as he fell quiet, Kate spoke up. "Have you seen anybody hanging around here recently, a little more often than usual?"

The witness shook her head. "I don't see very many people. When I come in, I try to be discreet and quiet as I do my work, then leave." She took a moment to collect herself, and, even then, she was teary-eyed. "I'm here all the time, so I see a lot of people, but I can't say that anybody in particular stands out."

"Right," Kate noted. "Thank you very much." As she walked away with Rodney at her side, she asked, "How is it that somebody can come in to all these churches and have nobody see him?"

"That is the big question," he replied, with a look around, "because, if he can do that, he's already casing his next place."

"What's to stop him from going back to one of the original ones?" she asked Rodney, while they inspected the rest of the sanctuary. "I mean, particularly once the police presence dies down."

"Do you think he would?" Rodney asked.

"I don't know. … I mean, when you think about it, he's got to keep up on locations at hand, and he had to be canvassing the area. Given his MO and handiwork up to this point, it will be Catholic churches. We know there are a lot here, probably a couple hundred in Vancouver, I suppose, but they all won't be as easily accessible or as devoid of people, which he needs to do this, without fear of being seen."

Rodney pondered that. "Do you want to set up some cameras?"

"I'm sure the budget won't allow it," she grumbled, "but I would absolutely love it if the churches would set up security—though of course that's something they're totally against. So, once again, this whole discussion is pointless."

"I don't know that the department heads are against it, but there certainly would be no budgetary money for it," Rodney explained. "You can guarantee that, for almost any church which is run on donations, there'll be even more people wanting to come to a church for the exact same reasons that our killer chose it. I mean, they're gaining comfort here."

"Will the people still come if the media finds out the killer was at this church?"

Rodney looked over at her and nodded slowly. "I would."

She stopped and stared at him. "Okay, now that surprises me. I would have thought that this would be the last place you would want to come and worship."

"Not at all," he replied, raising his shoulders in a casual bump. "I mean ..." He paused, trying to formulate his thoughts, then finally spoke. "You have to look at it from the church member's perspective. ... This is a place of holiness and prayer and worship and always that sense of salvation. So, if the church is under attack—which is what some people would say this is—I could see large groups coming in to hold prayers and vigils to keep it safe."

"Ah, crap, I never considered that angle, so thanks for putting that in my mind. That would explain why he'll have to continuously look for new locations to drop his victims then, right?"

"Exactly, and, as you mentioned, we probably have hundreds of Catholic churches in Vancouver. We could have a look at various locations and maybe pinpoint what the next church site will be." He took a moment to add, "It would literally be guesswork." He hesitated, then looked up, as if he had just thought of something, and maybe he had. "Unless, … you know, *somebody* had some indication as to what church would be next," he suggested, with a sideways look at her.

It took her a minute to understand what he was saying, and then her eyes widened. "Good God, are you suggesting I should ask Simon?"

He shrugged. "If Simon had any ideas, … I mean, no pressure or anything, but, if he had a name or an area for us, we could certainly check it out."

"Checking it out is one thing," she stated harshly, "but asking him for help for something like this? … I don't know if that's appropriate."

"It may not be appropriate," Rodney acknowledged, "but, if it catches this asshole, I'm all for it."

———

SIMON STARED AT the lawyer in shock. "I'm sorry. What did you just say?"

The lawyer looked at him, with a knowing smile on the corner of his lips, then repeated it again in a mild tone. "Mr. Morris left instructions that you were to handle the company from here on out."

Simon shook his head. "When did he do this?"

"Just before he passed away, he put it in writing and then had it signed and notarized."

"Good Christ," Simon muttered, staring at the attorney in shock. "Why in the hell would he do that?"

"I was hoping you would know," the lawyer stated. "I haven't even told his wife yet."

"Oh, *great*," he muttered, pinching the bridge of his nose. "You know how she'll handle that. She'll flip—and in a big way."

"Absolutely. I gather you've met then," he replied, a note of amusement in his voice.

"I've only met her once, and I can't say it was a pleasure." Then he winced. "I don't want to say anything bad about this whole scenario, but this is total BS."

"I mean, you have every right to say no, but Bartlett obviously felt that you had something to offer."

"Then why take his own life?" Then Simon hesitated and stared at the lawyer. "Were you surprised that he did it?"

The lawyer eyed him, then cautiously nodded. "I was definitely surprised, particularly after the instructions he'd just given me," he explained. "However, … if he was seriously tormented by something he'd done or would be dealing with, I guess it makes sense in some ways." He paced around the room for a moment. Then he looked directly at Simon, as if a switch in the back of his head had flipped. "Hell no, it doesn't make any sense at all." He threw down his pen. "I've known Bartlett for probably twenty years, and it's not what I would have expected of him."

"No, me either," Simon agreed, "and I haven't known him even a fraction of that. I'm not really even sure I would have called him a friend. Honestly he came to me not long ago because we've played poker off and on for many years, and he was hoping that I could help him to play enough poker to win back the money he needed to keep his company solvent. I shut down that idea immediately because, for one, that's not an easy way to make money, and I don't do things like that for other people. Plus he was implying that maybe I could cheat and help him out or something, which is ridiculous and not something I would ever be involved in," he declared, his voice thickening with emotions. "Instead, I suggested that I take a look at his books and see if there was a way to help him out. After we talked about it, he was very interested in me coming and doing that."

"So, did you?"

"I did," Simon confirmed, with a nod. "I spent the bulk of the day before he passed at his company offices, going over everything. The problem is, it appears that his father-in-law had done one hell of a job stripping the company before *he* committed suicide." Then Simon winced and added in exasperation, "*If* he committed suicide at all. Now with Bartlett dead under similar circumstances, ... that is also a concern for me."

"As in, you don't think Bartlett committed suicide?" The attorney's voice was low, as he leaned forward. "You know what you're saying then?"

"What I'm implying, yes, and, no, I don't like it, but, under the circumstances, it's definitely something that has to be looked at."

"So, what did you see as far as the company? Did you see anything there that would in any way send Bartlett on this suicide pathway?"

"The company's a mess. It's belly up, and his father-in-law embezzled a ton of money. They haven't paid a lot of their creditors, not to mention taxes. Plus he has some very large bills to pay off, for which he has zero funds to do so. Meanwhile, at no point in time, has anybody curtailed the wife from her ridiculous spending."

At that, the lawyer winced. "Yeah, she's another case altogether."

"Oh, I got that, and you can bet she wasn't very happy about what I had to say. I basically told Bartlett that, while I understood his challenges where she was concerned, if they weren't prepared to make significant changes, then no change would happen. I told him that it wouldn't be easy by any means, but he still had the chance to get out of this and quite likely still with the company by doing a restructure. That way, he could get the creditors paid off, keep the jobs of all the employees involved in the multiple companies under the umbrella company, negotiate a plan to address his tax issues, and, with some luck, he could come out of this okay and could rebuild."

"So, you met the wife then?"

"Bartlett seemed reluctant to share the information with his wife, so I had him call her in. Thus I could be certain she was told the gravity of the situation and the need for her to stop the spending immediately. I made it clear she had to give up her $7,000 purse, her out-of-control spending, and her $32,000 credit card, which had just been paid off only to see her charge it right back up again. I knew that, as soon as I left, there would be hell to pay, one for bringing in a stranger to look at their financial situation, another for having the temerity to say something about her lack of care for the company and for the money that she was blowing. It was clear that she'd been doing this for some time and believed the company was nothing but a cash cow to provide for her every whim."

The lawyer propped his chin up on his hands and nodded. "So, based on that, do you think what you just said had something to do with his death?"

"I'm afraid it did absolutely," he stated, "but it was the truth, and finding out that he already knew his father-in-law had pretty well embezzled everything to be had from the company, Bartlett was desperately looking for an answer. He needed an influx of cash pretty badly and soon. I didn't want to put any cash into it, certainly not while they were in that situation. I might have seen my way clear to do it somewhere down the road, but it's not the business I'm in. Before I'd even looked at his books, we had talked about the potential for me to buy some properties from him, which I was willing to do—since rehabbing buildings is what I do, after all. After I'd reviewed his books, I told him to get a forensic accountant and a good lawyer right away, and he needed to start looking at his bankruptcy options immediately."

"Oh good Lord, he never mentioned any of that to me," his lawyer noted in a concerned tone. "I'm not a corporate lawyer, and I certainly wouldn't have done any of those filings for him, though I could have helped him find someone. I just handle his personal business, you know— wills, finances, trusts for the kids, and the like. Still, he should have told me."

"And yet there are no kids," Simon stated, frowning at him.

The lawyer lifted his head and asked, "What?"

Still frowning, Simon looked up at him. "My understanding is that he had no children. Are you saying that he does?"

The lawyer pulled back to look at him in shock. "Yeah, we set up a foundation for two kids," he shared, as he shuffled through the paperwork on his desk.

"Are they his children, or were they hers?" Simon asked.

Frowning, he moved over to the computer, then quickly brought up several files. "They're supposed to be Bartlett's," he said, "so I'm not sure what's going on here, if you're saying they don't exist."

"My understanding is that he never had any children," Simon stated, looking at the lawyer, more puzzled than ever.

"But why would he lie about something like that?"

"I'm not sure. I'm not sure at all what's going on," he muttered. "However, you're right. That's a fairly innocuous thing to set up."

"What happens to the money if nobody takes control of it?"

"His wife has been assigned as the manager of the trust."

"Of course," Simon noted, with a sigh. "Now, answer this carefully. Did you get instructions giving her control by email or from him personally?"

He winced. "Email, and that was done more recently."

"So, even though there are no kids, we have a dead husband and a wife with trust fund accounts she now has access to and that she can spend from as she deems necessary. So, how does that impact his will and the estate?"

The lawyer shook his head. "I have no idea. … I'll have to look into it. I've never had anything like this happen."

"My suspicion would be that it's been set up on purpose to give her enough money to live off of, and it will be sheltered so the creditors can't touch it," Simon declared. "What are the names of the kids?"

The lawyer looked at him and shook his head. "He was supposed to send me the birth certificates, but then … he never did."

"Okay, and, now with his death, who would complete this process?"

"His wife," he replied, with a sigh.

"Are these trusts legal and binding?"

"They would be. I mean, we were just in the final stages of it."

"So, if this is fraudulent, or if there are kids, but she still is the trustee of all this, she would do whatever she selfishly decided to do, right?"

"A lot of money is in here," he noted, "as in a lot of money."

"Five million, ten million, twenty million?"

The lawyer winced and shook his head. "More than that."

Simon let out his breath with a *whoosh*. "So, I don't suppose this process was started by the father-in-law before he died?"

"Yes, exactly," the lawyer confirmed. "He was involved. He planned to use the money for something else. I don't remember what it was now, but then suddenly they set it up as a foundation for the kids, so that it could never be taken away, should anything ever happen to the business."

"Let me guess, and only Bartlett's wife was on there?"

"Yes, Bartlett was manager initially of course. Then at some point it changed to his wife."

"Yet you have no proof of the existence of children?"

"That's right. However, at the same time, I don't have any proof that they don't exist."

"Which must be infinitely harder to prove. But, if there aren't any kids, what happens to the money?"

"She has control, whether there are kids or not, I suppose."

"So, why go through all these legal meanderings?"

"Because the money is in this trust," he pointed out, "and the guidance can change regarding who benefits from the trust, and that was fairly specifically spelled out."

"So, she can now access all that money, even though the business is likely to go belly up?"

"I would suspect that's the case, yes," the lawyer confirmed, staring across the desk at him. "And now you'll tell me that's completely illegal."

"I don't know if it's illegal or not," Simon stated, "but it's certainly unethical and immoral. Beyond that, I couldn't tell you."

The lawyer nodded. "Of course I haven't finished anything involving Bartlett's estate, since the investigation into his death has not been completed."

"Then you also have a certain responsibility now, since you know that the business is belly up."

The lawyer looked at Simon and nodded. "That probably explains why Bartlett wanted you brought in."

Simon stared at him. "Meaning?"

"Meaning, that he probably thought, if you were to tell me what's going on with the company, then I would be compelled to get this stopped, and, you know, whatever needs to be done will get done."

"Ah, in other words, he would use me as his gatekeeper to stop his wife from gaining control of his fortune, which should have gone to his creditors and employees, not to mention the rest of his businesses."

"Exactly," the lawyer agreed, "which is also why I made no record of you coming in here right now."

After a moment of silence, Simon looked at him directly. "Meaning, I could be in danger?"

The lawyer sighed, as he looked around his office and added in a quiet tone, "I suspect I'll be shutting down my office very quickly after this as well."

"And doing what?" Simon asked.

"I don't know, but I think I need to disappear," he shared, "though I can't believe I'm even saying that."

"Neither can I," Simon said. "Presumably we must come to some solution on this, and I don't know how to do that."

"I think that's why it's in your hands, and you get to make a decision here. *That* paperwork did get completed, and I do have it on file."

"Which also means that Bartlett made these plans before he jumped. *If* he jumped," Simon corrected himself immediately. "If he didn't jump, he did it because he was afraid that he wouldn't survive anyway."

"In which case," the lawyer noted, "I would really like to find that out before the estate is settled."

"But that doesn't solve the issue of the foundation, does it?"

"The trust, no, and there's both a trust and a foundation, each to be managed by her."

"Interesting," Simon muttered, "and, therefore, they are untouchable, as far as the estate or the businesses are concerned, correct?"

"Yes." The lawyer nodded in agreement. "It's a much harder process to get money back out of those types of things, even with bankruptcy, which is why it's been done."

Simon sat back, then shook his head. "I really wish Bartlett had stuck around for this."

"You and me both," the lawyer said nervously. He looked around the room and then back to Simon. "This whole thing now has me very nervous."

"Unfortunately, with good reason," Simon declared. "Look. Ideally I would need a few days to sort this out and to figure out what options we even have."

"So, what if something happens to you?"

"I could ask the same question of you," Simon replied.

"There's really no telling what she could accomplish if we were out of the picture. I suppose she could work to get her hands on as much as she could, while no one was the wiser."

"*Great,* so we don't have a whole lot of time," Simon muttered. "Is there a place you can go and stay safe?"

The lawyer looked at him, clearly horrified.

"At least until we resolve this," Simon added.

"Jesus." The lawyer swore heavily.

"Friends, family?"

"They're all around the world," he shared, "and I doubt anybody would care for that danger being brought to their doorstep, nor would they put their life on hold on my account."

"You'll need to write out something, maybe send it to me and somebody else, in case anything happens to you," Simon suggested, "and I guess I'll have to do the same." He swore suddenly too. "I can't believe he dragged me into this BS."

"You do understand that he likely did it because he didn't know who else to turn to."

"Maybe, but this is classic case of passing on the responsibility for something that has absolutely nothing to do with me. I don't want it. I don't need it, and honestly I'm still trying to figure out how the hell to fix it."

"I'll give you until tomorrow by closing," the lawyer stated. "Then I'll get very hard to find. I'll email you." He handed a card to him. "I do have somebody else I can talk to as well. However, because you're on this list, he told me that it needs to be done with your permission."

"Fine, talk to him. Meanwhile, I just need to step outside for a moment." Simon stood up. "We need to move fast if we're to stop another travesty from happening."

"How do we know if one hasn't already happened?"

"As far as I'm concerned, it has. We just don't know how far the rot went." And, with that, Simon turned and walked out.

CHAPTER 14

W ITH ID COMING in from the lab on the victim, the day was long, wearying, as Kate and Rodney did next-of-kin notifications, checked on neighbors, checked back at the church, stopped in to talk to various coworkers for both of the two new victims, and, as usual, everybody had no clue. Frustrated and angry, Kate picked up the phone and contacted Billy Roy.

When he answered, his voice was jovial. "Look at that. The detective is calling me," he greeted her, with laughter in his voice. "Not into a little bit of BDSM yourself, are you?"

"No thanks," she snapped. "Do you know a Heather Michaels and John Shepherd?" The question was followed by silence on the other end, and she nodded. "You do, don't you?"

"I know of them," he replied carefully, "though they aren't clients of mine."

"But you know of them, so are they into the same thing?"

"Yes," he confirmed, his voice sounding heavy now, the humor gone. "What the hell is going on?"

"You can imagine why I'm calling," she said, "and the fact is, we found both of their bodies this morning at a church." Then she went on to name the church in the Point Grey area. "Have you ever been there before?"

"God, no," he replied in protest. "I've done my best to avoid churches for the bulk of my life. And I sure as hell won't go back to one right now."

"Yet our killer seems to be focused on churches."

"That's for you to figure out," he snapped. "I had nothing to do with it."

"Have you known any of these people from one of your gatherings?"

"Yes, they both … attend."

"How? What …" She stopped, not knowing how to proceed.

"I've never had a relationship with either of them, but we do have a club, where there are some partnerships that switch around," he explained in a cautious tone. "We're fairly open about our sexuality among ourselves, Detective." His tone was mocking now, as if he were laughing at some inside joke.

"I don't care what the hell you are," she snapped, regaining her voice. "All I want is to stop this asshole from going around killing people."

"I find myself in total agreement with you," he replied. "Look. I can't just hand out the names of who's in this club. That could throw me into hot water over revealing the names of the people who are supposed to be confidential members."

"Why not?" she asked, with mock laughter. "If you're so completely open about your sexuality, then you shouldn't have any problem with it."

He gave a bitter laugh. "Touché, Detective, but, no, I can't hand out names like candy, if they aren't mine to give. I will, however, talk to others in the group and have them contact you."

"Thank you. You know the last thing I want is to have any of them show up in a church, crucified for who they are."

"And is there still a message to forgive?" he asked curiously.

"Yes. Does that mean anything to you?"

"No. God, no. As I said, ... I avoid the whole church scenario."

"You may avoid it, but somebody is getting you quite involved over it."

"And that just sickens me," he stated, his voice rough. "Catch this bastard, will you?" And, with that, he abruptly ended the call.

She looked over at Rodney, who was sitting beside her in his parked vehicle. "So, this couple did belong to the same BDSM club as Billy Roy," she shared in frustration, "but he won't give me any names of other people in the club."

"Interesting."

"Yeah, something about privacy and all that good stuff."

"I can see how that might be an issue, but it's not helpful."

"Not only is it not helpful, it's a complete pain in the ass."

He gave her half a smile. "What about Lilliana? Any news from her?"

"No, but we need to check in with her." Kate scratched the back of her head, then added, "I would rather go home and get a shower, yet we need to stay after this."

"We're on it," Rodney said, with a casual shrug. "If you want to head out for a while, I'm sure we can manage without you."

"I want to do the street cams," she stated. "There must

be some in that Point Grey vicinity, maybe showing the same vehicle, the same *anything* as at the previous crime scenes."

"You're assuming the killer's using the same vehicle."

"If it isn't the same vehicle, he's got access to multiple vehicles, and that in itself would be very interesting."

"So, back to the office?" Rodney asked.

"Yeah, back to the office."

Once they arrived, Lilliana looked up and said, "I've got a list."

"Good," Kate noted. "Anybody willing to talk, you think?"

"I suggest we go, the two of us, and talk to the club organizers."

Kate put down the mug she had been about to fill. "Let's go."

"Do you want a coffee first?"

"No, I want to catch this bastard," she snapped. "We can pick up a coffee on the way."

And, with that, they headed out. Lilliana drove, and they ended up downtown in a seedier corner of the world.

Kate noted, "Pretty divey neighborhood. They must not find any normal place to do their stuff," she muttered, as she marched into the front door.

They had to go up several flights of stairs, and, as they walked into a room in the rear of the building, it was like taking a step back in time. There were no windows that Kate saw. The room seemed … muted, and, if people were in there, she couldn't hear them.

A woman sat at the front desk, and, when she looked up, Lilliana introduced herself.

The receptionist nodded and stood to shake her hand.

"Hi. I did get advance warning that you were coming."

"Good," Kate said. "We need to talk about your membership here."

"We're only one of several clubs in town," the receptionist pointed out. "I can understand you may need some help in order to assess whatever is happening with this crazy killer, but I can assure you that the killer is not one of our members."

"No," Kate hedged, "but maybe the killer was one of your former members or was somebody who knows somebody who does this."

"Maybe," she murmured.

At that, Kate provided her a note, containing two names.

The receptionist gasped, frowning at Kate. "Yes, they are both members of this club," she confirmed, her voice trembling. "Why?"

"Because they are our latest victims," Kate informed her. "So, do you think anybody here will want to help us now?"

The woman paled and sat down hard on the chair behind her. She looked over at Lilliana, who nodded.

"They were found this morning," Lilliana shared.

"Good Lord," the woman murmured. "Why would anybody want to kill BDSM people? We're harmless, and those who we do play games with are doing what they want as well." The receptionist had tears in her eyes. "Everything is consensual. It's not as if we're hurting anybody against their will."

"I'm glad to hear that," Kate replied, "but the fact of the matter is, I still need to talk to whomever may have been involved with all these dead couples." Kate provided the names of the other victims, and the receptionist shook her head.

"None of those people have anything to do with our club," she stated, with a note of relief. "I wonder if he's going from club to club or something."

"Maybe, or maybe he's choosing his victims based on other things, and these people just happen to fit those parameters."

"But from the club …"

"Yes, from this club," Kate confirmed, with a gentle nod.

At that point, a man walked in from the back, looked over at the woman at the front desk, and asked, "Laura, is everything okay?"

She looked up at him and smiled weakly. "Actually I'm glad you're here," she replied, her voice low. "These are police detectives." Then, turning to Kate, she pointed to the man. "This is Zaroon, the manager of this establishment."

Kate explained why they were there, and he shook his head.

"None of that makes any sense," he declared, looking at them in confusion. "It's not as if we're forcing people to be here. They're here because they have a different version of what sexuality looks like for them."

"I get that," Kate stated, crossing her arms over her chest. "But somebody has terminated their lives in a pretty abrupt and unpleasant display," she added, "and there appears to be a strong connection between the sexual lifestyles of all three sets of victims."

He shook his head at that and swore. "Christ."

She eyed him intently. "What about Billy Roy? Do you know him?"

Zaroon nodded slowly. "Yes, he is somebody … who likes to inflict pain. He's one of the most experienced Doms we have ever seen," he shared. "However, some of our patrons have a problem with his style, and some have chosen not to come if he's here. We ended up kicking him out of the club a while back."

"So, not everything is always consensual?" Kate asked.

Zaroon winced. "Sometimes, and I mean specifically in Billy's case, … it went a little far, and the people involved weren't happy." He hesitated. "You do realize that some people have very strong, very unique sexual needs, right?"

Kate stared at him and slowly nodded. "I do understand that, and I get that privacy is an issue. … My concern is that people are dying, and you're the connection between them."

"No, no, no," Zaroon argued. "I'm not the connection. This club isn't even the connection." He was beginning to panic, and it showed. "It's just that this killer has something against those of us practicing in a safe way. We've found a way to make this work for people."

"And still, in that safe way," Kate added in a bleak tone, "somebody else isn't happy, and that's where we need to step in and to see who has a strong opinion about what goes on here."

He groaned, then looked over at Lilliana and smiled. "Hey, Lilliana."

"Hey," she replied, with a cheerful smile of her own. "Sorry it's come to your doorstep."

"Yeah, me too," he muttered, as he looked back at Laura, still seated behind the desk. "We need to help them as much as we can."

"Oh, I agree completely," she said. "It's just such a shocking thing to even have to consider."

"Beyond shocking, but we must do whatever we can to help." He looked back at the detectives. "So, what is it that you're asking of us?"

"To talk to some of your club members," Kate stated. "We need to warn everybody that somebody out there is cherry picking and choosing his victims from clubs like this," she explained, for lack of a better way to put it.

"*Great*," Zaroon muttered, "and, of course, they will all be quite angry that you haven't done anything to stop it."

"Oh, I'm pretty angry myself," Kate snapped, "because the first set of victims was a couple, like the others, but there was also a child murdered. So, you can imagine how I'm feeling about that."

"Why the child?" Zaroon asked, the pain visible in his expression. "I mean, if this is child abuse, God, nobody here is involved in something like that. I can't tell you enough that we are all consenting adults, and this is literally a case of coming here because we have no other safe place where we can have these kinds of sexual experiences."

"I get that," Kate repeated, "and I'm totally okay to let you do your thing, but, if something else is going on here, then I need to know about it."

Zaroon turned to Laura and then nodded. "Fine. … If you want to wait here for a second, I'll be right back." Then he turned and headed into the back room.

Kate turned to face Lilliana, one eyebrow raised.

Lilliana shrugged. "Just wait, and I guess we'll see."

Within a few minutes, the doors opened, and Zaroon motioned to them. "Come back this way, please."

They walked in to see a group of people, sitting around, having coffee.

Kate looked at them and smiled, then introduced herself. Most of the people nodded, and Kate explained why she was here.

"I think it's absolutely disgusting," said the woman closest to her. "I mean, we're being persecuted for absolutely nothing."

"We're not here to persecute you," Kate pointed out quickly. "We're here, for one, to warn you that it appears that somebody is utilizing clubs like this to pick his victims because that is a common denominator in all the recent church murders so far. Plus this club itself has had two victims." When Kate mentioned the names, gasps came from all around, and one woman got very upset.

Lilliana walked over and quite comfortably gave the other woman a hug. Kate watched in amazement, as the woman leaned on Lilliana. Kate was reminded of Lilliana's superior people skills.

"Susan, I'm so sorry. You knew her quite well?" Lilliana asked.

"It took her a long time to really open up to becoming who she was," replied Susan in between sobs, "and this was such a safe place for her. It's just terrible that somebody would have done this, especially after all she's been through."

Kate looked up. "When you say, *after all she's been through*, could you explain that?"

The woman hesitated, then looked over at Lilliana, who nodded in an encouraging way. "I really don't want to go into it, not now."

"And yet," Lilliana pointed out, "if something here can help us find her killer, wouldn't you want to help us figure it out as soon as possible?"

Susan winced. "But it's not my story. It's hers, and it's private."

"The minute she was murdered," Kate explained, "nothing remains private about her world any longer, and unfortunately we have to go deep into the pain that she suffered in order to find answers. I'm sorry for that, but it's the only way we'll get to the bottom of this and can prevent more killing."

SIMON WALKED OUT of the lawyer's office once more, now happy to have a plan in place, and, with the lawyer's permission, Simon headed straight down to the police station, where he met the investigating officer on Bartlett's suicide. Simon quickly explained what was going on, and, at that, the police sergeant nodded. "Okay, so this is a whole different story now." He took a moment to add, "And it's an investigation that's well past the scope of what we normally handle."

"I understand," Simon replied in a careful tone. "I'm just telling you that I'm heading off right now to talk to another lawyer about making sure that everything is on the up and up in this case."

"Good luck with that," he said sincerely.

Simon nodded and quickly dashed out of the station, heading toward his appointment with yet another lawyer.

As he walked in, the lawyer looked at him and smiled. "Simon."

Simon looked at him and nodded. "Frank, I've got a problem, a big one. I'm not sure if you can help or not, but any advice that you have for me will be very much appreciated."

The smile fell off his face. "Let's see. Have a seat. Hopefully it won't be too bad." By the time they were done, Frank whistled. "Yeah, okay, so this is a whole different story now. … There have been rumors about the company being in trouble."

"There should have been quite a few rumors, and there should have been a lot of red flags because I'm sure that a hell of a lot more people know about this than even I anticipate at the moment."

"Look. I'll handle this, but don't tell the wife anything at the moment. For now, we need to keep the news to ourselves and to keep a close track of everything."

"Okay. To be honest, I don't know for certain whether she's actively involved in this or she's just an innocent victim herself somehow," Simon muttered, with an eye roll.

"You don't like her much, do you?" asked Frank, with a knowing smile.

"It's not about liking her or not. I just don't see her as someone who acted as a wife, as a partner in this instance. She didn't even try to participate in solutions to the problems Bartlett encountered. She was more of the problem than any solution."

"No, but then she's probably spent her entire life spending her daddy's money, without any consequences. So that has got to be a nurtured habit by now."

"The consequence this time ended Bartlett's life."

"Do you think he committed suicide?"

"I think there's a good possibility, but I also think it's possible that somebody may have helped him."

His lawyer winced at that. "Okay, that's way more serious then."

"I'm not trying to bring you in on something this ugly, but I didn't know who else to talk to."

"It's definitely in my wheelhouse," he acknowledged, with a nod, "and you've been given the okay by the lawyer at Bartlett's request, so let me take a look. I'll also need documents."

"This is the lawyer you'll contact to get them," Simon shared, handing him a card. "I also still have log-ins from my audit of Bartlett's business, unless anybody's gone and changed them." He brought out the laptop that he always carried with him and quickly signed in. "I've still got access." He was genuinely surprised.

"Good, start downloading anything that can help you take control of his estate, and let me know exactly what it is that we're looking at."

The rest of the day was spent downloading and sorting documents. The lawyer shook his head. "Okay, so we need to freeze these accounts. Court orders are in process for the trust fund, the foundation, and all holdings," he stated. "We need to immediately start a restructure." He paused for a moment, until Simon looked up at him. "You do realize that now that you've taken control, you've *taken control*, right?"

Simon winced. "*Great*. I sure as hell wish I hadn't been given permission to do that."

"And yet," Frank added, with a smile, "Bartlett was right in making that request because he knew that you are honorable, and, in this case, that, above all else, is what's needed."

"Maybe so," Simon agreed, "but it's still a shit storm that he's dumped me into."

"Luckily you're well used to shit storms then," his lawyer pointed out cheerfully.

Simon groaned. "You don't have to sound quite so happy about it."

"It's what I do. You do know this is like a multiyear process, right?"

"Which is also why I'm not terribly impressed that Bartlett died like this," Simon admitted in a frustrated tone. "I was quite happy to help him out, but then he went and did what he did."

"But did he though? Maybe keep that in mind. It's quite possible he had nothing to do with that supposed suicide."

"That's one of the reasons I'm here," Simon said, "just on the off chance that maybe Bartlett didn't commit suicide."

"I guess my next move is to call a board meeting, now that the paperwork is through," Frank added.

Simon added, "Bartlett's lawyer did give me these before I left, and Bartlett had signed the documents, handing over control of the company, so that'll cause its own set of problems."

Frank gently took the documents from Simon, glancing through them quickly, then whistled and nodded. "This is exactly what you need in order to take control of the company," Frank declared. "The board doesn't know it yet, but you're the best thing that could have come along."

"They don't know it yet, but I'm not impressed with a lot of what's gone on, so this won't be a fun job."

"No, but you'll take it on because of Bartlett."

"I will, but I'm also concerned about these children that he supposedly handed over a trust fund for, with an exorbitant amount of money that his wife was to have control of."

"Yet he deliberately didn't hand over the birth certificates, as I understand from the lawyer," Frank noted.

"Exactly. I didn't think Bartlett had any children. Yet his personal lawyer thought he did but didn't have any information, other than the fact that two were associated with the trust fund. I also found it odd that Bartlett's personal attorney was informed of all that via email, and recently."

"So, what are the chances that they're Bartlett's children,

but they're not in any way connected to his wife? Or vice versa?"

"That's probably the more likely of the two, but frankly I won't be shocked if there are no children at all. The lawyer suggested that the father-in-law may have been involved in starting the trust process before his death. That's all something we'll have to sort out and fast."

"No," Frank disagreed, with a cheerful look in Simon's direction, "that's something *you*'ll have to sort out pretty fast. The court order will help." Simon groaned, but Frank nodded and continued. "You and I both know that an awful lot must be dealt with here." Frank gave Simon a sideways look. "I can only deal with so much, and you'll have to deal with so much. Beyond that? … We'll have to hire a company to handle some of this. I suggest one of these." Frank handed over a short list. Simon picked one that he was familiar with and stood to leave.

"I'll get in touch with them right away," Frank replied.

"Do that." Simon nodded.

"I'll call a board meeting for tomorrow morning," Frank confirmed.

And, with that, Simon turned at the doorway, looked back at his lawyer, and muttered, "Thanks, Frank."

His lawyer just shook his head. "Don't thank me yet," he warned. "This one could get ugly."

"We'll know after tomorrow," Simon noted, "but freeze everything now."

"It's already done," he shared quietly, "but you know the shit storm you'll face for that."

"Yes, but more important than that, I must ensure that the staff and the creditors get paid," Simon stated. "That's not the way some of these boards like to work in a situation like this, but I won't tolerate anything less." And, with that, he slammed the door and walked out. He wasn't gone from the building yet, when his lawyer phoned him.

"Bartlett's made sizeable donations to a church," Frank began. "Do you know anything about that?"

"No, I sure don't."

"More on the previous subject, what if the kids aren't his?"

"His wife's?"

"Or, maybe he's, you know, paying for them to be taken care of."

"Maybe," Simon agreed thoughtfully.

"Anyway the church is one of those where the bodies were found," Frank pointed out. "I just wondered if you knew of any reason to be worried about that."

Simon stopped and froze. "What did you say?"

"The police case that's currently ongoing. Surely you've heard about it. It's all over the news."

"Yeah, the church crucifixion cases. I've heard a bit about it from the lead detective."

"Interestingly enough, Mr. Morris here has been making substantial donations to that Point Grey church for quite a while. He may very well be one of the biggest donors."

"But a lot of people tithe, don't they?"

"They do," Frank agreed, "but, when you're really broke, maybe it doesn't make so much sense."

Simon added, "But I don't think Bartlett understood how broke they were, not until after his father-in-law died."

"Looks like the donations stopped about a month ago."

"I wonder what triggered that?" Simon asked.

"Probably some financial hardship or something. I highly doubt any of this is connected to the killer."

Simon wasn't so sure, since he was connected to both. "Let's hope not," he muttered in an exasperated tone. "I'll mention it to the detective though."

"You think that's wise?"

With a note of humor in his voice, Simon retorted, "For certain. Keeping anything about her case from her is not wise, … not wise at all." And, with that, Simon stepped outside and headed to one of his rehab projects.

CHAPTER 15

K ATE LOOKED OVER at the BDSM group and stated, "Look. This is scary and a terrible invasion of privacy. That's not my intent at all, but I've got to ask you some questions. First of all, does anybody know this man?" She held up a photo of Billy Roy. Several of the women gasped, and Kate nodded in understanding. "Okay, I see you all have some history with him."

"Not all of us," snapped one of the women, "but those who do know full well that he doesn't know when to stop. He's somebody who likes to cause pain and knows that he's doing a hell of a job on it," she declared in a bitter tone.

"Very few of us are interested in literally having ourselves bleed to the point where it's hard to care for our body," another murmured.

Kate continued. "Roy knew our previous victims, including the latest two, and them? … He knew from this place. Apparently he hadn't had any relationship with them."

"He left quite a while ago," one of the women said, "but he's a right bastard. So, if he's connected to these murders in any way, you won't upset us."

"Meaning, if he's connected in a way that will get him in trouble?"

"Exactly," she agreed, with a nod. "There are assholes, and then there are assholes." She shook her head and shuddered. "He is one with a capital *A*."

Kate nodded. "Did you guys have trouble with anyone else in the club, outside of this Billy Roy guy? Anybody else you kicked out or refused admittance to? Anybody who's made troublesome comments, created negative publicity, social media trouble, anything along that line?"

She asked a few more questions, but nobody appeared to be willing to speak up about anything. Groaning, she sat back and dropped her head. "Thank you for the cooperation you've given, but honestly, I have to admit, you haven't given very much."

"We don't have any information that's not already out there."

"That may very well be true, but the last thing I want is to find any of you on a cross in some church in the next few weeks, while we sort this out." Kate stood. "If any of you want to talk to me privately, I'll leave some of my cards at the front desk. You're all welcome to call me anytime and any place. I do understand the need for privacy, and I'm really not here to judge you on your preferences, your lifestyle, or anything else. What I am trying to do is keep you from becoming the next victim."

She hadn't even made it to Lilliana's car when her phone rang. She identified herself and then asked, "Who is this?" Quiet breathing could be heard on the other end. "Presumably from the group I just left," Kate guessed, her voice soft.

"Yes," the female caller confirmed, with tears in her voice. "Yet I don't want anybody to know."

"I get that." Kate glanced over at Lilliana, as Kate put her caller on Speaker. Lilliana winced when Kate asked, "Do you want to meet somewhere?"

"No, no, I don't. I don't want to meet at all," she stated

in a panic.

"Okay, then tell me what this is about."

"He's an asshole, a right bastard asshole."

"Okay, I presume we're talking about Billy Roy?"

"Yes."

"Did he hurt you?"

"He hurt me a lot, and honestly I was up for it," she admitted in a meek voice, as Kate cringed. "At least initially. I didn't think it would be that bad. But we have safe words when it gets to be too much, when we don't want to go any further, and he, … he just didn't listen. He took way too much fun from all that pain, and he wouldn't stop," she shared. "I'm still coming to the club, but I haven't partaken in any of the scenarios since then. I just can't bear it anymore, always worried that, well, … what if the next person won't stop?"

Kate asked, "You didn't want to report it to anybody?"

"No, God, no. I mean, … first off, I'd gone willingly, so I knew that nobody would believe that he'd actually, you know, ignored the safe word," she said in a mocking tone. "Everybody already thinks we're all strange and stupid anyway."

"I don't know about that," Kate disagreed, looking over at Lilliana, wondering how to handle this. "The thing is, you were a victim, and, in that case, you didn't agree to a hard beating. You agreed to pleasure. … Also it's hard, very hard to go back to a pastime that you enjoyed before."

"I did enjoy it," she said, with a choked-up voice. "This is really hard, but, like, … I never used to enjoy sex," she shared in a rush. "Until this, until I came into bondage and all of it. I took pleasure in it but now? Now I can't enjoy it either."

"I'm sorry," Kate murmured. "That can't be easy."

"No, and the thing is, that bastard knew it," she declared, her tone gaining in strength. "He knew that I was touchy, knew that it would be hard for me, but I was interested and trying to deal with my problems, trying to get past it, you know?"

"It sounds like that attempt didn't go very well."

"No, it didn't," she agreed. "The bottom line is, if he's responsible for these church murders, nobody'll be upset."

"I get that," Kate replied, wishing she had more information about it. "Do you know any other women he may not have gotten along with? Did you tell anybody about him?"

"No," she replied quietly, "no way. I didn't want to involve anybody else, particularly not my husband."

At the word *husband*, Kate winced. "Is he an angry sort?"

"Oh, you could say that," she snorted. "He has established very specific parameters about what I can and cannot do, and I have to do it with him and with his permission."

"So, I presume your association with this club is secret then."

"Oh my God. … If he had any idea, he would probably kill me," she cried out.

Even just using that phrase made Kate wince. "I hope you're joking when you say that," she noted, with a question in her voice.

"No, no, no, I'm not joking at all," she stated in a panic. "My God, if he found out, he wouldn't understand at all, and he would make sure I never had access to my children again."

Kate didn't quite know what to say to that. "Let's hope that he doesn't find out then, and I certainly won't tell him," she shared instantly. "That's not part of my mandate here. All I'm interested in doing is trying to stop a killer from killing somebody else."

"Are you sure it isn't Billy Roy?" she asked, almost pathetically eager for it to be him.

"We haven't found any proof that he is our killer," she said. "We don't have any reason to suspect him, outside of the fact that he knew the victims and is one of several people we're looking at right now."

"God."

"I will need your name though."

She hesitated and then spoke. "Julie, Julie Lampard."

"Okay, Julie, I've got a rough question for you."

"What's that?"

"Is there any possible way that your husband would be involved in this?"

She gasped in horror. "No, no, no, he would never, ever do anything like that. He's, like, very religious."

At that, Kate stiffened. "When you say, *religious*, what do you mean?"

"No, you don't understand. He wouldn't do that," she repeated. "He loves me. He loves me and his children very much. He's a good man."

Unsure how to resolve the inherent conflict in Julie's statements about her husband, since she'd gone from saying he would kill people if he found out about the BDSM club to saying that he was a very good religious man who loved her very much. "What would he do if he found out about Roy?"

"Oh, he would have killed him outright, instead of going after any other people," she declared. "You don't understand. There's no forgiveness in my husband. Everything is black-

and-white. It's very much a case of *You've done wrong, and you have to be punished.* There is no forgiveness in his world at all."

Kate frowned into the phone as she asked, "Do you attend a local church?"

"He attends one, and I only go because I have to," she replied. "I mean, he insists, but it is hard for me because I have a very different viewpoint than the church. However, he seems to think that, if I go often enough, I'll eventually be saved or something."

"Ah." Kate nodded. "And yet it's not exactly working, is it?"

She gave a broken laugh. "No, but I didn't go there to be saved. I went along with it, trying to save my marriage."

"Right." Kate wasn't sure what else to ask, but she added, "Lilliana is here with me, and, if we have any other questions, we'll get back to you, okay?"

Julie replied, her voice faint, "Please, dear God, don't tell my husband. You don't understand."

"We'll definitely talk to you first."

"Not first," Julie cried out. "No, not first, not ever. Oh my God, oh my God. … I shouldn't have shared anything with you. I just knew it."

"Hey, calm down," Lilliana said into the phone. "We're not here to tell your husband. Remember that. We're just trying to find the killer."

"But if he finds out I talked to you, if he finds out anything about that club," Julie wailed, "I'm in so much trouble. You don't understand how much trouble."

"How do you keep the club secret from him?" Lilliana asked curiously. "He sounds very much on the controlling side."

"Yeah, he's very controlling," she quipped, with a broken laugh. "He checks my phone records, and he's always on my case about having the right friends, people who won't lead me astray."

Kate struggled with something there, and yet it seemed important. "So, he checks your phone. In that case, how do you contact the group?"

"I don't contact them, outside of our in-person meetings, and I haven't attended a session in quite a while," she explained, with a broken sob, "since Billy."

"Okay, and you're pretty sure your husband doesn't know about it, right?"

"No, I'm sure he doesn't know about it."

"How can you be so sure?" Lilliana broke in.

"Because I'm alive," Julie snapped, and, with that final cry of pain and terror, she ended the call.

Kate looked over at Lilliana before briefly closing her eyes and pinching the bridge of her nose. "The trouble people get into…"

"It's hard to hear all that." Lilliana nodded toward the phone. "I mean, we hear things, and it's so hard to understand how people are living in these circumstances, when they could just get up and walk away."

"And yet, as she suggested, walking away would most certainly cost her the children."

"Alternatively, if he found out that she was part of this club, surely he would hold it over her head, just to make sure she complied with his every wish."

Kate sat back in the passenger seat. "The more she talked, the more he sounded like a pretty good suspect."

"But to get a look at him without letting him know we spoke to his wife will be dicey," Lilliana pointed out. "We'll be putting her in danger if he finds out, so that would be a challenge."

Kate nodded. "Doesn't leave us a whole lot to go on, does it?"

"No, it sure doesn't, but we'll dig in the database and see who he really is." As Lilliana drove back to the station, she asked Kate. "You didn't drive to work today, did you?"

"No," she murmured, "I didn't."

"Where do you want to get dropped off?"

She looked at Lilliana in surprise, then realized how late it was. "Home." After another moment, Kate added in a whisper, "Just home."

"You're not going to Simon's tonight?"

"No, I don't think so." She rested her head back, but, once again, as if he had some inner knowledge, she got a text from Simon. Looking down at her phone, she sighed. "Maybe I am."

Lilliana laughed. "It'll be good for your soul if you do."

"Are you sure about that?" She looked over at Lilliana with a hard smile. "It seems everything is a shit show right now, but how can we take any time off?"

"The better question is, how can we *not*?" Lilliana pointed out. "We can only do so much, and now we have a whole new take on a case that's been a complete shit show right from the beginning. You need to keep your head on straight, and you can't do that by avoiding having your own life and avoiding someone who can take a load off you. Simon is a good guy, and clearly you need him, just as he needs you. We'll pull this together in the morning, so get some sleep. You've done a lot of good work today. Let it roll around in that magnificent brain of yours, and we'll see what pops up in the morning. I'm exhausted, so I'll go home, have a bottle of wine, and crash."

"A whole bottle?" Kate asked.

"Yeah, tonight will definitely be a whole bottle," she shared, rolling her eyes. "Just seeing those bodies, those people on the crosses in that church? … Damn, but I would love to erase that from my memory."

"I don't think it's possible," Kate muttered. "Something like that is permanently emblazoned on our brains."

"And here I keep thinking that maybe one day the world will be a better place."

"It will be," Kate noted, "but maybe not in our lifetime." With that, she fell silent. Just then her phone beeped with another text from Simon, asking where she was. She sent him a message back right away, saying she would be there soon.

He came back with an immediate response. **Good, I have something to add to your case.** At that, she straightened up in the passenger seat and read it out loud to Lilliana.

"Call him," she urged. "Just call him right now."

Hesitating, but knowing it was probably the better choice, she phoned Simon back. "Come on. You can't just send me a text like that, not when we're running around like crazy people trying to find something. What did you get?"

"It's not me," he corrected, "but remember Bartlett Morris?"

"Sure. Your friend who committed suicide."

"Maybe it's nothing. I don't know," Simon added, suddenly stopping in doubt.

"Let me decide," Kate stated. "What is it?"

"Apparently he's been making a lot of large donations to the church, the same church where you found the most recent bodies, and then about a month ago—I presume when he realized the company was in so much trouble—he stopped."

She stared down at the phone. "Ha, I wonder if that isn't fairly normal. I guess that's tithing, isn't it?" she asked Simon.

"It's a form of tithing, where people give a percentage of their income to the church."

"Would you have said that Bartlett was religious?" she asked.

"No," Simon replied. "I wouldn't have, but apparently I didn't know him all that well."

"Which you've also told me," she noted.

"Yeah, it's a little hard to even think about it right now. The church thing's probably nothing pertinent, but I just wanted to let you know."

"And that's good, thanks," she said quietly, as she looked over at Lilliana. "Not sure if it's significant, but I'll file it away because probably a lot of people tithed to the churches. We can look into it further."

"Good," Simon replied. "Tithing is got to be how the churches get a large share of their money."

"Good enough," she said. "I'll be at your place fairly soon."

"Fine, I'm walking that way myself." He stopped, and she heard the bustle around him, loud and clear. Then Simon added, "It's been a real shit of a day."

"Yeah, you and me both," she agreed, with a sigh, "but, on the other hand, neither one of us are staked to a cross in a church." And, with that, she hung up.

❧

SIMON WALKED INTO his penthouse apartment, tired, worn-out, confused, frustrated, and angry all at the same time. The anger was at Bartlett for having put Simon in this very uncomfortable position. He could handle the business side—particularly with a knowledgeable team—but the fact that there could be ugly shenanigans going on that would involve the cops, Bartlett's wife, and all sorts of debtors and employees wasn't happy news. That was a whole different story.

Simon quickly had a shower, as he waited for Kate to show up, wondering at her last words.

It was unusual for her to make a comment like that, and it just went to show how her day was going. As cases went, he couldn't imagine anything quite so rough as dealing with what she had right now. She was perfectly capable of handling it, and he knew it. However, at some point in time, he had to look at what humanity had become and had to wonder if any of it was even redeemable.

After a shower and finishing his normal after-work routine, he walked out to the living room, popped open a bottle of wine, then poured himself a glass. His phone beeped with an email. Frowning, he pulled it from his pocket and stared.

It was from Bartlett, probably sent on a delayed schedule.

As Simon sat down and read it slowly, it made his blood run cold. He forwarded the email to the lawyers, as well as the cop handling Bartlett's supposed suicide case. Just as Simon was done, the elevator door opened, and Kate walked in, with a look of complete exhaustion on her face. He walked over and enveloped her in a hug.

Resting against him, she whispered, "I hope I never see anybody impaled on a stake like that ever again. This asshole has hit three churches with seven victims by now, while I'm just running around like an idiot, trying to figure out who it is." She shook her head in frustration. "It just defies logic."

"I'm sorry," he murmured.

She pulled back, then looked up at him. "It's not your fault. It's got nothing to do with you really. Besides, you've got your own shit show happening at the moment, *huh?*"

He nodded. "Yeah, and that's taken a turn as well."

Her eyebrows shot up, and she looked at him expectantly. "In what way?"

Pulling up the email, he handed his phone over to her. She sat down on a nearby kitchen chair, while he walked over and poured her a glass of wine to match his, as she read the email out loud.

"Simon, I'm sorry. I always thought you had the devil's own luck or some extrasensory abilities to be so damn lucky at cards, and I really, really, really needed help. You offered help, and that too was more than I expected or deserved. I am so sorry to dump this on you, but I really have nobody else to ask for help.

I have two kids, twins from before my marriage to Eleana, but some shenanigans are going on. I tried to set up a founda- tion and a trust to look after them. Yet apparently the paperwork got hijacked somehow, and my wife's been given guardianship over them, though she has no intention of doing anything for the children. The amount I had initially put in has been quadrupled, and I've been taken entirely off the paperwork, and that money won't go to them at all. Instead it will all go to my wife.

And now that you've told me that the business is completely bankrupt, I can see that she may have had a hand in all of this from the beginning. I don't know if my life is in danger, but I am concerned, and I'm also wondering if her father committed suicide after all. So, if anything happens to me, I guess the answer is to look to her first."

Kate lifted her head and stared at Simon in shock. "Seriously?"

"Yeah, that literally just came in seconds ago." Simon pointed to the time on his phone. "That email is a fairly good representation of how my day went."

She shook her head and stared down at the message again. "You want to forward that to me?" she asked absentmindedly.

He looked at her quizzically but quickly complied. "Why? What are you thinking?"

"I have no idea what I'm thinking," she admitted. "There are really no thoughts. My mind's a blank, and, at the same time, it's quartered, with all the bits and pieces from today, yet none of it makes any sense. None of it is clear-cut or logical. None of it is anything." She groaned, raised both hands in disgust. "Your friend may or may not have committed suicide, and yet from that email? ... It sounds like he didn't."

"What jumps out at you?"

"I am split on the subject. Maybe he did it deliberately to set up his wife," she suggested, turning to face Simon.

He stared at her with a jolt. "Christ, I didn't even think of that." Simon shook his head.

Kate shrugged. "If he was pissed off and angry, completely fed-up, and saw his own world collapsing? ... I don't know that I wouldn't seriously consider that as an option too, as well as the more obvious alternatives."

Simon nodded. "As I said, I hadn't considered that as an option. Just not something I would have thought about."

"No, I understand." She sighed. "You are too good to have considered that option, and, at the same time, it's quite possible that Eleana found out that Bartlett knew what she'd done. So Eleana decided that Bartlett needed to disappear very quickly. She was the only witness to him going over the edge."

"Right," Simon confirmed, "which could go either way."

"Exactly. If she did or didn't know about his children, either way again, maybe she determined that none of the money should go to them."

"Exactly, and, from his email, it sounds as if she was aware of that trust and the foundation and just hijacked both."

Kate sighed. "So we'll just have to see where the investigation goes."

THE NEXT MORNING everything was pretty much out of Simon's hands, except for the actual business part of it. The cops had been brought in, the email analyzed and then dissected, and a series of meetings began. By the time he walked into a board meeting with the shareholders at noon, he was pretty fed up and totally exhausted. Throughout the whole thing, he tried to hold back his inner feelings, as several of the members looked at him and frowned. He nodded, introduced himself, and announced that he had been appointed by Bartlett to handle the next steps for the company.

Eleana got a chilly reception when she walked into the meeting room and stared at Simon in a fury. "What are you doing here?" she snapped.

He gave her a cordial smile. "Maybe I should ask you what you're doing here?"

"It's my company." She sneered at Simon, as she turned to security and said, "Get him out of here."

"That won't happen," Simon replied, and the security guard hesitated, looking from one to the other. "So, you can either sit down and shut up, or I'll have you removed." She gaped at him, and he nodded. "I'm here at Bartlett's insistence, and the company is in for a hell of a few shocks coming up."

"No, no, no," she snapped, "you have no business being here at all."

He picked up a folder and passed out enough copies of the letters from both lawyers for all the board members to see.

At that, several of them looked from her, back to the letters, then at Simon, and asked, "What the hell's going on?"

Deciding the blunt approach was best, he took the bull by the horn. "The company's broke, and it'll be going into receivership, as we attempt to clear debts, hoping we may end up with something, with anything left at the end of the day."

Several of the members gasped, and Simon nodded.

"We're also opening an investigation into Bartlett's death because there are some indications that he didn't commit suicide." He deliberately did not look over at Eleana Mayfield Morris, who sat, frozen, staring down at the papers in front of her.

"Everything has already been put into motion. Nothing is to be decided here, and no meetings will happen to discuss the restructure of the company, which is in progress, nor any bankruptcy filings, if needed," he stated in warning. "There are, however, an awful lot of debts to be paid to vendors and taxes to be paid. Therefore, assets will be seized, and that is currently ongoing as well."

"Jesus Christ," one of the men muttered, staring at him in shock. "You just come in here out of the blue and dump all this on us?"

"I'm doing that because neither Bartlett nor his father-in-law are here to do it," Simon stated. "Believe me. I would like to be anywhere but here, and this is the last thing I need on my plate. However, I do owe Bartlett to handle this for him."

"You don't owe Bartlett anything," Eleana said, still sneering at him.

"Whether you like it or not"—Simon turned to stare down at her—"your milking the company dry has stopped. Your bank accounts and credit cards have been frozen, and, if you're lucky, you'll have one house at the end of all this, and you better be grateful for that, even if it doesn't happen," he stated coldly. "In the meantime, you need to get the hell out of my way, while I do the job that I need to do. The police will be very interested as to why and how you were the only person left there to see Bartlett at the end of the day. Not to mention, they are looking at you as an accessory to murder."

"He is my husband," she snapped, glaring at Simon. "Of course I was the last person to see him alive."

"In the same room where he apparently jumped."

"Why? You think I picked him up and pitched him out the window?" She laughed hard, waving her arms. "Do I look like I could do that?"

"Actually you do," Simon confirmed, with finality. "I know perfectly well that you go to the gym and lift weights, and Bartlett was not a big man. He was a beanpole of a man and didn't weigh more than 165. So, if you caught him by surprise, it's definitely possible. I don't know that you would have thrown him out the window, but there is a very good chance that you pushed him."

She stared at him in shock, as the blood rose up over her cheeks, and she opened her mouth.

He snapped at her before she could speak. "Don't even bother starting anything here. In fact, you can get out right now," he stated, with a wave to the security guard. "All your access to this building and any of Bartlett's companies has been rescinded, and the entire company setup is under lockdown right now, and nothing comes in or goes out. As for anything else, the detectives will be in touch with you." Simon glared at Eleana, as she was escorted out the front doors.

Simon turned to face the shareholders. "All of you deserve an explanation, and you will get it as soon as I have a better idea of the core problems in the company. I can tell you that there is no money and that bankruptcy and restructuring is imminent." He noted all the angry, flushed, and sorrowful faces around the table. "Any access to files any of you have had has also been rescinded, while we look at embezzlement and other potential criminal charges."

"Against whom?" asked one of the shareholders, staring at Simon. "According to you, nobody is left."

"We don't know if Mr. Mayfield was operating alone in this company. He did quite a job of wiping out as much money as he could from the company himself, funneling that company money to his daughter," Simon explained. "So it'll take quite a bit of time and effort to sort through just how much damage has been done and how much we can salvage."

"Good Lord," muttered one of the men, staring at Simon. "I feel sick just thinking about it."

"So do I," Simon stated in agreement. "I only heard

about this a few days ago, when Bartlett came to me for help."

Another of the men asked, "That may be, but what are your credentials to take this on? What makes you qualified to take this into your hands?"

"It doesn't matter what my credentials are," Simon declared, turning to face him. "To your advantage, I am a successful businessman, and, if nothing else, I'm dead honest, and that's why Bartlett came to me. Rest assured, I have brought in a full team with all the expertise we'll need."

Simon grabbed his folder and announced, "So, ladies and gentlemen, the shit show begins now." He got up and walked out of the boardroom, leaving everybody in stunned shock behind him.

He knew it would be a long process but a fairly simple one. The company needed to be streamlined. It had very good earnings, just that people had been helping themselves to the pot and had been embezzling a lot of money. Simon needed to stop the bleeding as fast as possible, so that everybody would get paid.

Several of the board members raced behind him. "Hey, hey, you can't just run out like that."

"I can," Simon stated, turning to frown at them. "Do you have a question?"

"Yeah, I have a question," one member declared in an outburst, full of anger and frustration. "What's happening with the staff? What about all the creditors?"

"That's one of the reasons why we're doing what we're doing," Simon explained, "so the staff can get paid and so the creditors will end up getting something back too."

"Seriously, it's all gone?" he asked, the bluster about gone now.

"Yeah, it's all gone," Simon repeated. "I won't sugarcoat it. It's bad."

"What the fuck. How did Bartlett let it get to this point?"

"Because Bartlett wasn't running it, his father-in-law was," Simon stated. "The facts remain to be seen, but, so far, what I suspect is that, somewhere along the line, he starting stripping money out to support his lavish lifestyle, and that continued to snowball over time. He had had a significant tax problem as well. At some point in time, the old man decided things were going badly, and it would be so bad for the company that he would just bleed it dry. So that's what he did. When he more or less knew that he was done and was in worse trouble and there was no way out, I suspect he took his own life. But even that is in the hands of the police at this point too."

"What the hell," the baffled board member muttered, as he looked around. "It's a massive company."

"It is a massive company, and it had massive profits, all of which people took great advantage of. And none of us want to hear that, but, at the end of the day, there's really no other option or conclusion to come to. We'll get through this, and, with any luck, the company will continue to thrive."

"That could go bad as well."

"Yes, it could," Simon agreed. "I can tell you that there are a lot of assets, but they'll be seized and sold in order to get things back in balance. The company will continue to run—unfortunately under my direction."

"Unfortunately?" the other man asked in a dry tone.

"Yeah, unfortunately for you." Simon smiled coldly. "I already have plenty of my own business projects going on.

This certainly isn't what I want to be doing, but I won't let Bartlett down now."

The other man walked beside him, speaking right to his face. "I've heard something about you. You pick up all these old buildings and fix them up."

"Yeah, I do. That's at least some of what I do." Simon sighed. "I run a bunch of businesses, which is why Bartlett came to me." Even as they watched, the forensic team moved around the building. "I've got to meet with the staff and reassure them that there is sufficient money for them and that the company will continue business as usual, until further notice."

"But is it?" the same man asked, looking around. "I've never been involved in something like this."

"I gather it's not your money that you invested initially then."

"I inherited the shares," he replied, "but I always wondered at the way it was run."

"In what way?"

"The shareholder's meetings would be canceled, and every time we'd get this quick update saying, *Everything is great, looking good.* We'd get these reports that honestly looked great on paper, but they always seemed off somehow."

"Do you still have those?"

"Yeah. Do you want them?"

"I do. So, if you can forward them to me, that would be great because I'm not sure exactly how much paperwork has been left behind for me to find. I suspect a lot of cleaning house was done before Bartlett stepped in. What I can tell you is that the restructuring process will be hard and swift, but, at the end of the day, if you stick by the company and don't sell your shares, it will make a profit again someday."

"Will it though?" he asked, looking at Simon with suspicion etched on his face.

Simon looked at him and smiled. "Oh, it will," he declared. "Nothing is wrong with the company. It was the people helping themselves to the profits and the generally poor management that took it down this road."

"What about Eleana Mayfield Morris? I mean, she seems pretty shell-shocked."

"Yeah, she is, but that's because her candy jar has just run dry," Simon declared, with a wry note. "Believe me. She's one pissed-off woman right now."

"Is it really dry though?" he asked, looking back at the parking lot. "I'd hate to see her with nothing."

"She's run through millions," Simon corrected the guy, "and lots of what she has squirreled away on the sly belongs to the company, so don't feel sorry for her. She's a huge part of the problem." And, with that, Simon turned and walked right back out.

CHAPTER 16

KATE WOKE IN the middle of the night, bolting out of bed, instinctively reaching for her weapon, as she spun around looking for the threat. The room was in complete darkness, and yet a shadow moved, not at her side but against the wall. She stepped cautiously forward, recognizing Simon's shape, his nude body gleaming in the moonlight, as he bent over something on the floor.

"Simon," she whispered questioningly, but there was no answer. She watched as he proceeded to tie something, and yet nothing was in his hands, and she realized what was happening. She quickly put down her weapon and walked closer, trying not to disturb him, yet wishing that she could pull him out of this vision, out of this nightmare that she knew would torment him afterward.

She took another cautious step forward, but he didn't notice; he was caught up in whatever vision he was in, and she knew instinctively it was one involving the church. When he reached for an imaginary tool, for a moment she thought she saw a stake, but that may have been her imagination, as he got it up off the floor and raised it over his head and then slammed it down.

She winced, seeing only a fraction of what he was seeing, but imagining it all too clearly—a sledgehammer driving a stake through a victim's hands.

When he reached down to steady something, she stared in horror, as he appeared to struggle to hold something in place, something that was moving.

She swallowed hard, wondering if her killer had gotten to the point of staking his victims while they were still alive. The horror of it stuck in her throat, and she wanted desperately to pull Simon from the vision and back to consciousness, but, if he could find out anything, maybe see something, she was desperate to hear what it was he had to offer.

"Simon," she whispered in a low tone but direct. "Who is he, Simon? What's he doing? Why is he doing this?"

He shifted, almost like a head jerk to the side in her direction.

Then, keeping her voice low and steady, she whispered again, "Try to get as much information from him as you can. Find out what he's doing, his thoughts. Can you find out what church he's in?"

Simon did nothing but stared, his eyes glassy.

"Can you tell me what victim he has? A male or a female?"

Again his head jerked to the side, as if some internal struggle were going on, and then Simon stood and, in a sudden scary move, he turned and pinned her in place with his silvery eyes. Then he slowly sank to his knees and then face down, almost in a smooth dive as he collapsed to the floor. She bolted toward him, reaching down to touch him.

He was alive. His pulse was there, slow and steady but way too faint to make her happy. She tried to roll him over with great effort, but he was out like a light, heavy and floppy. She finally got him rolled onto his back. She smacked him gently across the face. "Simon, wake up, wake up."

When she got no response, she hit him harder and then harder again. Finally he jolted awake, and he glared at her. She stared down at him in worry and then leaned over and kissed him hard. "You sure as hell better be back," she snapped, "because I do not want to be kissing a ghost."

His lips curved into a smile beneath hers, and he pulled her into a tight embrace and flipped them over, so that he was lying on top of her. Then he kissed her in a completely different manner. She felt her body soften under his passionate onslaught, and she slid her hands up, grabbed him by the ears, and tugged him backward to glare at him. "Not until I'm sure it's you."

"It's me," he confirmed quietly. "We'll talk later."

"What if I want to talk now?"

"Too damn bad," he stated. "I need to remember why the hell I'm not taking myself out, if this is what my life is like."

"Because taking yourself out would hurt a ton of people," she murmured, pulling him down and giving him a kiss of love and compassion.

He soaked up her kiss and all the emotions she had to give, then gave it back to her tenfold, his lips moving down her throat and across her collarbone to suckle at one breast.

Her body was tense, still warring with the fear, nervousness, and shock from earlier.

"Forget it. It's okay. Forget about it for now. We'll talk about it later."

That was a little too close to the word *Forgive* in her mind, but knowing that she needed to switch from work and the horrors, she let Simon lead her down the path of delight and joy. When she finally exploded in his arms, she collapsed and whispered, "We really should have moved to the bed."

He chuckled. "My knees will have carpet burns."

"My ass too," she retorted.

Chuckling, he shifted onto his heels and pulled her up slowly. "Now, how about getting some more sleep?"

"Or we could talk."

"Sleep first," he muttered, and she watched as he staggered the few steps toward the bed and realized that he was still caught up in the energy throes of whatever had happened. He collapsed onto the bed and, within moments, was out cold.

For her though, that was a much harder thing to do. She grabbed a notepad and wrote down the little bits that she had seen, knowing there needed to be a heavy conversation with him about it. She checked her watch and winced when she saw it was five o'clock. She normally got up at six, so five just meant an earlier-than-normal morning.

She had a shower, headed to his kitchen, put on coffee, and, with that dripping, she sat down on the couch and stared out at the beautiful scenery in front of her, but her eyes didn't see the beauty. It had been a long time coming, but lately she only saw the underbelly, and knowing that this killer had yet another victim—and potentially one who wasn't dead before being crucified—was horrific.

Her mind was still caught up in it all and in full work mode, so she opened up her laptop and brought up her notes. She quickly updated them with everything that had happened yesterday, and then Simon's most-recent vision. The notes were for her eyes only, and she would modify them for her report. The last thing she wanted was anybody knowing the details of Simon's visions. They were personal, private, and already torturous enough for her to not want to see him have to divulge one of those with anybody else, knowing what he went through on a daily basis.

When a sound came nearby, she looked up to see Simon, leaning against the bedroom doorjamb, staring into the main living room area. He was smiling at her.

"You couldn't go back to sleep," he said with certainty, as if he knew her all too well.

She shook her head. "No, you were out, so I let you sleep. I went and had a shower, and now I'm having coffee. There's more if you want some." He walked over to the coffeepot, and she realized he'd pulled on a simple pair of cotton pants, nice and loose, relaxed even, more like pajama bottoms. He had nothing on his upper body, and his muscles flexed, lean and smooth. She watched him move in fascination.

With a cup of coffee in hand, he sat down crossways on the couch, cuddling the cup in his hands as he stared at her. "So, how bad was it?" he asked in the same conversational tone.

"Bad enough," she admitted. "I bolted out of bed and grabbed my weapon, thinking we had an intruder or something." She shook her head. "I just don't know what to do about these paranormal intruders into our lives."

"Yeah, well, if you ever come up with an answer, let me know," he murmured.

"I did try to talk to you," she said, "seeing if you could get any other information."

He looked at her in surprise, then slowly shook his head. "I don't remember that. … I do remember hearing something though." Frowning, he stopped and gently stroked his cheek. "I am sore for some reason."

She smiled and nodded. "That would have been me."

"Ha, I should have known."

"Do you remember what he was doing?"

He looked at her and nodded slowly. "He was staking another victim, and then …" He hesitated, as he blew gently on the hot coffee.

She looked at him, searching his face. "And?"

"Something is different this time."

She nodded. "I think I saw that, as I watched you."

His gaze flew up to study hers intently.

She gave him a wry look. "Honestly, from what you were doing, it seemed like you were trying to get the legs and arms to stay in place because the victim wasn't dead enough."

He winced and nodded. "There was blood, like lots and lots of blood."

"Any idea where he was?"

"In a church. I don't know what church though. However, I saw this deep-burgundy carpet, and the blood ran into it, but it just seemed to be rivers and rivers of it," he whispered.

"Did you see anything interesting, anything identifiable? Like his hands. Could you see his hands?"

He held out his left hand and turned it around to stare at it. "Hairy, large, white."

She nodded. "Wristwatch, bracelet, tattoo?"

He shook his head. "No, none of those. Well-cared-for hands, definitely not a laborer."

"What about the right hand?"

He switched the coffee cup to the other hand and stared down at his right hand, frowning, as if he were looking past his own hand to that of another. "More bruised up, more damaged." Then he winced. "From the damage he inflicted himself."

"Ah, so the victims were tortured, beaten."

He corrected that thought. "Not a sexual beating, not as a punishment, maybe as …" He stopped, looking for the proper word, and dropped his head, like he was falling short.

"Part of his salvation?"

"Something like that, yes. It's almost as if he couldn't beat himself, so he could only beat them."

"Why can't he beat himself?"

Simon shook his head. "I'm not sure, but there's something. … Somehow he's not allowed to hurt himself, not that he's special but that he can't. He doesn't have the strength, not physically but morally or spiritually. … He doesn't have …" Simon considered it. "He doesn't have the courage to take his own life, to whip his body to death," he explained quietly. "So he's doing it to others and asking them to forgive him for it."

"Ah," she said on a long-drawn-out breath. "So, the *Forgive* means forgive *him*, not for any sins that they may have inflicted on him."

"I think so," Simon replied, "but honestly I can't be sure. This right hand is the same. … No jewelry, no scars, no tattoos."

She wasn't surprised, but she was disappointed. "To be expected," she muttered. "Just that, every once in a while, it would be nice if something were identifiable."

He gave her a ghost of a smile, as he whispered another soft breath across his coffee, cooling it down.

"Did he say something?" she asked Simon.

"The word *forgive*. He keeps asking them to forgive him, but he can't forgive himself."

"Why can't he forgive himself?" she asked curiously.

Simon shook his head. "I think, in a twisted way, it's for

what he's doing. He's choosing them over himself because he doesn't have the courage to do it to himself. At the same time, he can't forgive himself for his own lack of courage."

"Interesting," she murmured, as she thought about it. "Did you recognize the victim?" she asked silently.

He shook his head and then whispered, "It's a woman."

Kate winced. "Of course it is," she said, "but so far it's been pairs."

"This is a pair, but I'm not sure they're a true pair, as in together."

She froze, slowly turning to look at him. "Meaning?"

"I don't think that they are necessarily together. It's a pair, and there's a man and a woman, but I don't think, at least I'm not getting any impression, that the killer got them together. Maybe that's part of his frustration this time too. He has them, but they're not quite right, and he's making them fit. There's also …" Simon looked up and, in a voice that had a warning tone, added, "There's a huge red flag of anger flying through him. I don't get any understanding as to why he's doing this or why he's picking these victims, but it's almost uncontrollable, and the more he does it, the worse he's getting."

"So, it's not easing off when he does this," she noted. "Normally a serial killer appeases part of whatever it is that needs appeasing when they kill, and then they'll stop. For some serial killers, it could even be years before anything triggers it again."

Simon shook his head. "Not this one. With each kill, he's just getting angrier."

"Angry at himself?"

"I don't know. Maybe."

She groaned and then nodded.

"Red toenails," he said suddenly, out of the blue. She looked at him in surprise, and he winced. "That's completely useless, since there are probably one million women within a few miles of here that have red toenail polish on."

She nodded. "And the feet?"

"Long and narrow, a tall woman, her feet are well-kept, the legs are smooth. … I mean, this is a judgment on my part, at least I mean it to be, but she looks well cared for."

"And again, many women around here will be the same, well groomed, pedicured, lotions, things like that," Kate noted. "Clothing?"

He shook his head. "He was looking at the legs, as she kept moving them, and it kept pissing him off. Then he kept hitting her legs to stop it, and eventually he did get the one staked the way he wanted it." Simon looked at her. "She wasn't awake, but, with the pain, this guttural groan came from her throat, as if she were waking up. That in itself disturbed him, I think. Actually I think it made him angrier."

"So, he wants his victims to submit, is that it? He doesn't want them to fight?"

"I don't think he wants them conscious," Simon said, "and yet he doesn't want them dead either."

She just stared at him, struck by the complete conflict in what he was saying.

Simon added, "I think he's catching the couples in their car, which is where he is torturing and killing them. So this time is different because the blood is at the church."

Kate frowned, as she grabbed her laptop and tapped in this last bit of info. "We haven't found their cars yet, so we'll keep on that angle."

Simon frowned. "I think he needs them to suffer. He

needs them to suffer because he can't suffer himself."

"Ah," Kate noted. "So, it's all about him and finding a surrogate for his own salvation, yet he's not happy that he has to do so."

"Exactly." Simon quietly stared down at his coffee and then reached out a hand and held it out to her, palm up. She placed hers in it, and he whispered, "Please find this asshole soon."

DETERMINED TO KEEP his day straight and on a regular pathway, avoiding as much confrontation with Bartlett's board and company as he could, Simon headed to his first rehab building of the morning, only to find things were running more smoothly than he had any right to expect. A couple hours later, he slipped down an alleyway to the women's shelter, dropped off a roll of bills with Lisa, then carried on to his second rehab.

By 11:30 a.m., Simon began to feel like he would get through the day okay after all, until a phone call came from Bartlett's wife. He groaned. Simon walked away from the site a bit to have some privacy, as he listened to Eleana Mayfield Morris go on and on. "If you would stop shrieking at me," Simon interjected, "I might understand what you're saying."

Her voice rose yet again, as she blasted him. "You've got no fucking right to take over my company like you are," she screamed at him.

"Yes, I do," he stated. "Your husband had already drawn up the paperwork. I get that you're not happy. Welcome to life."

"I'll get you for this," she vowed, her voice dropping into a hard, ugly threat. "You're not fucking ruining my life over some godforsaken dead husband who hated this whole world so much that he popped himself," she muttered. "I've already got the lawyers on it."

"The lawyers are more than welcome to be on it," Simon noted, "and we'll talk about all you've embezzled at the same time. That is something the cops will want to talk to you about too."

She gasped. "I didn't embezzle anything," she argued. "That's my company, my money."

"Newsflash," Simon quipped, with a note of amusement that he didn't even bother trying to keep out of his tone. "You don't get to just take money from a company without paying the taxes on it."

There was an odd note in her voice when she added, "I have every right to my money."

"In case you didn't realize it, your father was stripping the company dry the whole time, but you don't give a shit, as long as you get to keep doing it too, right? I mean, let's not do anything to keep the company alive and well."

"You're wrong," she spat. "My father would never do that."

"Your father's been doing it steadily for the last few years. Right up until he finally committed suicide because he knew the gig was up, and he knew he would be facing jail time for it. Not to mention the fact that he would have to face you. You've been spending money like it was candy for years, as if you had full rights to the jar, but you didn't. Not to mention not paying the taxes on it or paying your creditors, so there is a bigger reckoning coming, and how it all ends up at the end of the day will be on your head."

"You can't talk to me like that."

"Eleana, I will say it once, and you better hear me well.

Cooperate, and you'll end up with something, possibly a house to live in at the end of it. Don't cooperate, and believe me. … I'll make certain that every single creditor gets their money first, and you will damn well be at the very end of the line."

"That's the problem with business assholes like you," she screamed again. "You think you're some holier-than-thou and better-than-everyone-else asshole. Businesses are not something that I have to be worried about. I'm fully aware that there are taxes to pay, but I'm allowed to take whatever it is I want to take from the company," she spouted. "And I don't give a shit about any creditors. They shouldn't be doing business, if they can't afford to take a loss here and there."

"But that's also something for you to remember then, isn't it? You shouldn't be in business, if you can't afford to take a loss, and believe me. That loss is coming. So get out of my way, and we'll leave a company behind, maybe still intact. But, if you don't get out of my way, I'll do my best to see you in jail." And, with that, he hung up.

When his foreman looked at him in surprise, Simon shrugged. "A very ugly deal somehow ended up on my plate. You know how people love to spend money that isn't theirs."

He winced and nodded. "Yeah, I've been hearing rumors about a company like that."

"Yeah. Bartlett just went out a window but set up all the paperwork for me to take over and to handle everything but didn't tell his wife. The company needs to declare bankruptcy. I made it clear to her that she needs to stop treating the company as her own personal bank account, and then a few other weird shenanigans are going on too," Simon noted, "so that's my world at the moment."

"Sorry, man. That sucks. Why would you even want to take that on?"

"I didn't. I helped Bartlett out for a few minutes, looking over his business records, explaining to him just how bad things were. He didn't realize his father-in-law had been systematically stripping the company of all the money, and nobody understood just how bad things were. So, as a result of helping out Bartlett and telling him what he needed to do, he went to his lawyer and legally put me in charge. So, *boom*, that's my life now."

He stared at him. "He didn't even have your permission to do that?"

"No, … he didn't ask me. He sure as hell didn't. Anyway I've put a good team in place to try to save the company, and, if we can, we can, but, if we can't, we can't." Simon shrugged.

"And yet you're such a softie, you'll do something."

"Rest assured, I'm not putting my money into a bad deal like this one. I bought one property from him to help out and because it's one I've been eyeing since forever. But that's it." Simon groaned. "We have to get through all the smoke and mirrors first, then figure out what shit everybody was involved in. Bartlett might have been blind and stupid, but he also might have been complicit. Truth be told? I don't even know for sure that Bartlett was innocent in all of it."

"Got it," his foreman noted quietly, "and that really sucks."

"Let's just carry on here and see if we can come up with something that's a whole lot less stressful."

"Everything here is going well at the moment," his foreman shared, as he nodded. "So, if you need to go off and handle that shit, … go ahead."

"I don't want to handle any of that shit," Simon declared forcefully. "That's why I put a team in place."

"Yeah, I'm not sure a team will be enough," the foreman stated. "That sounded like a pretty major threat coming from her."

"Sure, but she would have to know somebody to hire in order to knock me off," he stated, with a smile. "Not sure she's got that clout."

"No, but, where there's a will, there's a way," he pointed out. "Remember that."

"*Thanks*, but regardless I do have other work I need to do, so if you're good here?"

"I am, so go, take off, and do something useful," his foreman said with a smile.

With that, Simon headed toward the downtown area once again. He wanted to look at a couple buildings there, not the least of which was a church in that area. Just something about it nudged him, when he'd woken up with that particular image in the back of his mind, wondering if that had to be something.

There was a sense of familiarity to it, but he hadn't ever been there, so why the hell would it seem familiar? The only thing he could think of was the killer was familiar with this church. However, Simon didn't have enough, or anything really, to tell Kate about that, without sounding ridiculous. Plus enough of that shit was going on that he didn't want to deal with any more of it.

Twenty minutes later, he walked into the front of the church, surprised that he could just walk into a place like this. It was stunningly beautiful—the artwork on the walls, the stained-glass windows, and the view of the medium-size garden—everything just seriously stunning. Simon walked up to the very front altar, where there were candles, and looked down at the carpet. It was red, bloodred. Actually, if he were honest, it was more of a burgundy than what he'd expected in his night vision. And yet Simon noted no sign of anything amiss or of this church being picked as a dumping ground.

Frowning, he wondered if it were possible that he was ahead of the killer for once, that maybe Simon was seeing something *before* it happened. He stared around, his hands on his hips. It felt right. It looked right, but he had no way to know if it *was* right.

When his phone rang while he stood there, he knew it would be Kate. No way it wouldn't be. She was developing an uncanny ability to know when he was either confused, perplexed, or dealing with something that involved one of her cases. And, if he were truthful, it was all about her cases.

He picked up his phone and spoke right off the bat. "Yes, Kate. What's up?"

She hesitated, then asked, "Are you okay?"

Worry was evident in her tone. "Uh, maybe," he replied. "I'm standing inside a church that had a familiar sense to it. So I made my way down here, but I really don't know why."

"Where are you?" she asked, her tone sharp.

He winced, then gave her the name of the church and the general area. "I don't even know what street it is on," he admitted, pondering that.

"Fine," she said. "I've got it up on Google. I'll grab a taxi and be there in a few minutes."

"Hey, hey, hey, but I don't know that this has anything to do with anything."

"Nope, maybe not," she admitted, "but I'm on my way." And, with that, she disconnected.

He stared down at his phone, then stuck it in his pocket. When he heard a voice behind him, he was startled.

"May I help you, young man?"

He turned to see an older priest, smiling at him. "I just came in for a few minutes, Father."

"And you're welcome to be here," he said, a benevolent smile on his face.

"This church hasn't been hit by the same string of nastiness that the others have, I understand?"

"No, and God willing it won't be," he stated, with a serene quality to his tone. "We do good works here."

"But maybe that's why the killer is bringing them here," Simon suggested.

"There is much to speculate, or we can keep ourselves in the realm of truth only."

Simon smiled at the priest. "That would be nice, but I'm not sure that most people have the ability to detach like that."

"Maybe not," the priest agreed, "but gossip is never good."

"No, it isn't, but what's happening in the churches is seriously ugly."

The priest nodded. "That," he said in sorrow, "is unfortunately very true. Have you …" He stopped and then asked in a sympathetic tone, "Have you lost somebody special?"

"No, I have not, at least not in this instance anyway."

"When there is seemingly no other place to turn, people will still eventually turn back to where they belong, and that, of course, is here."

Simon wouldn't argue with the priest. Simon just wondered if this priest knew of people in need in particular. Simon wanted to know if somebody came to mind who might be doing something like this, but Simon couldn't quite figure out how to even formulate the question.

"It bothers you, doesn't it?" the priest asked, staring at him intently.

Simon smiled. "Yes, I'm associated with the police, and my girlfriend is the one investigating these murders," he explained. "Don't worry. I'm certainly not the killer."

The priest relaxed ever-so-slightly and added, sympathy in his tone, "I'm sorry about your involvement. It obviously bothers you."

"Anything like this should bother anyone," Simon stated. "I would hate to think we could get so complacent in our lives that killings like these would be considered normal."

The priest nodded again. "Your words are true, and I believe your heart is in the right place as well."

"It has been many times," Simon murmured, "but I'm no saint, and there is much in my world that I could improve."

The priest chuckled and gave him a benevolent smile. "Now that just shows that your heart is really in the right place, since you are still looking to improve, looking to help yourself and others."

"How do you know I'm here to help others?"

"Because you're here asking questions and because you're wondering if there's some connection. But, of course, there is no such connection here because we just don't have people like that here."

"I believe the priests at the other churches would have declared the same thing."

"Sure, they would. We do acknowledge that there are troubled souls. We do our best to help, but sometimes even our best isn't enough to hold back the gates of evil." He looked up to see Kate walking in the front doors, her boots clacking the tiles with purpose, before reaching the carpeted area, as she walked toward Simon.

Simon smiled, then nodded toward the priest. "Father, this is my girlfriend, Detective Kate Morgan." He turned and reached out a hand, as she grabbed his, stopping beside him.

"Good day, Father," she said. "I believe you are on the list of potential churches for our unfortunate current case."

He smiled at her. "If it is God's will, then it will happen. The troubled souls are coming home," he stated, "not always by the front gate, but, when called, they come any way they can."

CHAPTER 17

THE PRIEST HAD walked off, leaving Kate and Simon alone. She looked over at him, and, stepping closer, she whispered, "What is it, Simon?"

"This is the next church," he said in a soft voice.

She stiffened and turned to look at him in surprise, a question on her lips as she whispered, "Are you sure?"

He gave her a look. "No, of course I'm not sure, but anything could happen. This is the church that seemed familiar to me. It's one that the killer's been in several times, I bet. It's one that he really seemed comfortable with."

"Why this one?" she murmured.

"I don't know, but I'm sure there's a reason."

She thought about it and nodded. "We were linking the three churches to date in a circle, and this location does fit into those parameters," she muttered. "We had a list started of ones to keep an eye on."

"This needs to be on your list," Simon stated.

"Yes, it does," she agreed, as she looked around again, frowned, and then turned to Simon curiously. "And you came here on your own?"

"I did because I wasn't sure."

She nodded. "So, you just let your feet do the talking?"

"Something like that, yes," he said, with a half laugh. "I know that, to you, it all sounds very strange."

"It is *all* very strange," she agreed, "but I won't turn down any data. I just have to make sure that it's reasonable as to how we got to this point."

"It's reasonable enough," he stated, "because it'll be within your locations, as one of many."

"Right," she muttered, with a nod in the direction of the priest. "What did you talk about?"

"Only that this church could potentially be targeted. He seemed to think that it wouldn't happen, but, if it did, … it was God's will."

"Of course," she groaned. "Everything is God's will when we come down to it, is it not? I mean, at what point in time do we have a sick mentality, somebody who needs help, without making it all about God's will?"

"I think that's all part and parcel, especially in a church setting," Simon pointed out. "The priest certainly didn't argue that it could happen here, but he just wouldn't project it."

"Of course there's probably no security or anything."

"I don't think so."

"In that case, I'll bring it up with the team in the office, which is where I'm heading just now. Hopefully we'll set up some surveillance."

"You have to understand that, if you do that, the killer won't come in."

"No, I figured that. I'll talk to the team about it, and we'll come up with an answer."

"Of course," Simon said, with a smile.

She looked at him, noting the tension around the corners of his mouth and his general fatigue, and nodded. "You're struggling with this whole thing too, aren't you?"

"This and Bartlett," he muttered. "Then there was the

phone call from his wife, outraged that I would do anything to curb her spending habits. She's currently sending her lawyers after me."

"*Great*," she muttered, "like you need that crap."

"No, I really don't, but apparently a lot of other people are involved too."

"What about Bartlett's children? Did you ever hear more about that?"

"No."

"And, with all this going on, and Bartlett having ties to one of the churches, do you really think there's any connection between that case and this one?"

"I don't know," he admitted. "I would like to think not, but I don't know."

"Right," she said, noting that for the future, "and, until we get to the bottom of it all, anything is open for interpretation."

"It always is," Simon declared, "and that's part of the problem. We get a few answers, but we don't get enough, not until something else happens to help crack the case."

She smiled, squeezed his fingers, then dropped his hand and said, "I'll talk to you in a little bit." And, with that, she spun around and headed back out, noting that the layout was very similar to the other churches they had been to with this killer's victims. Even the great big beams on the side of the wall would still present quite an effective challenge to hoisting up anybody on a cross.

There were still a certain number of challenges that this killer was dealing with, and, not for the first time, Kate wondered if there was a chance that this involved more than one killer. Maybe it was a pair of killers, and yet why? ... And how?

She pondered that, as she headed back to the office. She walked in on an impromptu meeting, where everybody, even Reese, their analyst, was standing around in a circle, looking at the whiteboard. "What did I miss?" Kate asked, as she joined them.

"Not a whole lot, but we just got the forensic report in, and those traces of broken fibers? Some appear to be from the trunk of a Camry built in 2001, and the carpet's blue."

"Okay, wow, that's great," she said. "That's huge."

"Yeah, except that there are over two thousand of them in town."

"Sure," she agreed, "but at least we have something. We need to knock those numbers down, so we can track them though." She winced, wouldn't add Simon's theory regarding killing these couples in their own cars, but she did add, "Of course we could start with stolen ones from the last three weeks."

"Why three weeks?"

She shrugged. "I don't really have any reason for that, except that we don't want to cut the time period too short. If he had any previous planning for this, he would have needed some time to put the whole mess together, and maybe he stole a vehicle well before it was used too."

"I'll start with that," Reese offered, as she quickly headed down the hall to her office.

"I also have news from Simon, and you have to take it with a grain of salt."

Silence reigned, as everyone turned to look at her. "What did he have to say?" Rodney asked.

"He had another vision last night, a pretty rare and difficult one," she noted. "I saw it, saw him caught up in it, and I saw him staking his latest victim, so our killer already has one. According to Simon, there are two again, a male and female, but he wasn't sure that they were partners, as in he wasn't sure that they were connected. As if our killer had grabbed them from different places. They weren't quite right, but he was trying to make them fit."

"Oh, now that is interesting," Owen stated, looking at her in admiration, "because, really, how many victims can he find to do what he needs to do, before he morphs into taking people for other reasons, or when he loses the basis of his requirements?"

"I think we're there already," she hesitated, then told them what Simon had suggested about motivation.

"Christ," Lilliana muttered, staring at Kate in horror. "You guys must have had quite the night."

"Yeah, well, it wasn't exactly peaceful and calm. I'll tell you that," she shared, "not when he gets caught up in something like this. Honestly it's pretty scary to see. I bolted out of bed, grabbing my weapon, thinking we were dealing with something completely different, and there he was, stabbing at invisible people with a stake." She winced to see her audience completely engrossed. "Oh, and by the way, he doesn't seem to think that the victim was dead at the time, and, from the pantomimed fight I saw, I would agree."

"What?"

"Holy shit."

Everybody stared at her in shock.

She nodded. "But today I called him and he said that he felt a sense of familiarity to a church, when he'd been walking around town, checking on his building projects. He made a point of stopping by, and, as far as he's concerned, it'll be the next location."

THE REST OF Simon's day passed fairly quickly, and once again he was drawn to return to the same church. As he sat down on one of the pews, just trying to get a sense of why people came, he felt a certain calmness within his own soul, reaching and responding to the peace and the solace evidently on offer. He saw other people around, a couple obviously in love, their arms wrapped around each other, another couple quite content, seemingly happy to just be beside each other, a single woman off to one side, and several men in individual pews.

Simon wasn't sure what brought them all, but he doubted that it was the same purpose that had brought him here, but you never know. He studied them carefully but didn't see anything, didn't sense anything, not that there was any reason to, of course. It's not like he knew how it felt to connect to a serial killer, but he would like to think that something telling would be there, something tangible that would allow him to see that person, before it came to a meeting with a literal stranger, and yet there was no way to know.

As Simon sat here, he watched as a few people came, and several people went. It was a calm and private setting, people coming and going for their own purposes and on their own schedule. A woman sobbed gently off to the side, dealing with a loss, a pain of some sort. Yet others just appeared to be sitting here, praying.

It was a foreign concept to him, having been raised the way he was. With the abilities he had, he knew there was life after death. Simon just wasn't so sure that it was a *kind* life after death, not when everything on this planet was so torturous.

He stayed for another fifteen or twenty minutes, and

then got up. As he walked past a pew, he froze because there was that energy, and yet, as he looked from one side to the other, nobody was there, only remnants of energy. He strolled outside, casting his mind back to who was there, to who had been sitting there. Was it even someone that he could have seen or was it from earlier that day? The energy was literally cold, cold enough that he couldn't fathom who it was or when.

Swearing to himself, he called Kate, as soon as he got back outside. And, pacing the huge staircase, about the tenth step down, he walked back and forth until she answered. "They were here," he said.

"Who was where?" she asked in a calm and patient voice.

He pinched the bridge of his nose. "I'm at the church, and, as I walked back out again ..." He was almost rambling, though he couldn't control his rant. "I sensed the same energy, and I could feel that presence."

"Are they still there?" Her tone was sharp, as if she suddenly understood just how important this was.

He replied in exasperation, "No."

"Did you see them?"

He winced and whispered, "No."

She let out a noisy breath. "What did you see?"

"Nothing," he snapped. "Christ, I'm sorry. I don't even know why I called you. It made perfect sense at the time, and then, all of a sudden, once I'm talking to you, I realize I have absolutely nothing, and it makes no sense at all."

"Well, of course, you called me," she said in a soothing voice. "There's no reason not to call me, and obviously you're not trying to pull the wool over our eyes or make this up. Sure, it would be lovely if we could get more information, but listen. The fact that you sensed the energy there, what does that tell you?"

"That this is the place, that this one is next."

"And that's fine. I can confirm that church is definitely within our circle of potentials," she replied. "I'm talking to the team right now about what we can do to get coverage. If nothing else, I'll spend the evening there."

He hesitated, and then, his voice barely a whisper, he said, "But, if he sees you, I don't think he'll come in."

"No, I would have to come through another avenue," she noted, "some other way so he doesn't know I'm there, then try to hide somewhere."

He pondered that. "Maybe you should talk to the priest first."

"I will," she said, "I would need permission to get in from another direction, so I could hide."

"And, Kate, please don't go alone," he snapped. "You'll need backup."

"Why do you think that?" she asked.

"I don't know," Simon admitted. "But the energy I felt in that pew was of a couple."

Her voice was soft, as she whispered, "Are you saying there's two of them? Two killers?"

"I don't know," he whispered, his voice equally soft, "but it just occurred to me that it's possible."

CHAPTER 18

SIMON HAD HIT on one of the possibilities that Kate had yet to explore with the team. She turned to look at Lilliana, as Owen ran up beside her. She brought them both up to speed. "Simon was just at the same church, and he's pretty sure he found the energy signature of the killer, but the killer wasn't there at the time, or, if he was, he had just left. The only reading Simon got was of that energy alone, so he wasn't able to give us a description."

"Given his abilities, that's not all that hard to understand," Lilliana noted, as she looked over at Kate. "What do you think?"

"I don't know what to think," Kate admitted, "but I definitely think we need to stake out that church tonight."

Lilliana nodded. "I'm up for it. Is anybody else?"

"I'm up for it," Kate stated, "but we need to get inside another way, not by the front doors, in case the killer's watching who arrives and is making notes that everybody's gone before he goes in."

"You're saying *he*," Owen pointed out.

"Only in the sense that we know somebody is carrying these bodies around, and that can't be an easy thing."

"Absolutely true," Lilliana agreed, with a nod. "And statistically of course …" She let her voice trail off.

"Yes, statistically we have way more male killers than we

do females, but that doesn't rule them out. Nor does it rule out more than one person doing this."

"No, sure doesn't," Owen noted in a clipped tone.

Kate looked at her watch. "I'll contact the priest now. I may have to go down there in person and see if there's one way I can get in and maybe another way out at another time." She frowned as she pondered it. "Do you think ten o'clock?"

"I would go earlier," Owen suggested, "and I'd go myself, but it's not a good time."

"No, it's fine." Kate waved her hand. "Lilliana, are you good to go?"

"Yeah, I'm absolutely good to go," she stated, her voice hard.

"I also checked into our Mr. Lampard and Julie Lampard on the sly. Turns out he has an alibi for the night in question. He was working nights, and his job supervisor can vouch for him."

"Shit, and he looked like such a great option," Kate muttered.

"That's only because you can't stand him," Lilliana said. "Although I'm not sure."

Kate scrunched her nose, like she got a whiff of a bad smell.

"You're right about that too," Lilliana noted, with a mock smile.

"If your friend needs help getting out of that marriage," Kate mentioned, "Simon has good contacts for places she can go."

"I don't think she's ready for that," Lilliana shared, "but I don't know."

At that, Kate nodded, then turned back and asked Rodney, "What about you tonight?"

"Right. … How about we do shifts? I'll show up at midnight. If you're there from nine, we'll see what it looks like three hours later." He gave her a look. "I'm absolutely in, and we can also call in a couple black-and-whites, if you want."

"Maybe," she muttered, as she looked at Lilliana. "What do you think?"

"Definitely," she agreed, "let's not be heroes."

With that decided, Kate sent Simon a text. "I'll be at the church tonight on watch, so don't expect me over at your place." And she got back to her paperwork, sorting out the details of how to get into the church, so that nobody else could see them, plus figuring out where the hell they would hide.

SIMON LOOKED AT the message and swore.

Of course it would be Kate who went. Of course—and in a way—it was impossible to expect anything else. She would take it as being Simon's information, and it would only be of value if his data could be verified. Therefore, the job of verifying it was up to her.

Not to mention this asshole was killing people indiscriminately at this point it seemed from Simon's latest vision, and he needed to be stopped. However, the fact that it would be Kate on the frontline was what disturbed Simon. He knew, if he mentioned anything, she'd get outrageously pissed off at him, leaving him with no option but to sit back and to decide what he would do about it.

He couldn't just barge in on her stakeout; no way that would work. She would take that as interfering in her job, especially when undercover. If the situation were reversed, he would take it the same way. It's just that … it wasn't him; it was her. And somehow that made a difference. In his mind he understood her viewpoint, but he wanted to protect her regardless. Yet somehow, being the person he was, going out with the person who she was, that was the wrong thing to do.

He groaned as he sat back, only to see several people watching him with amusement. He remembered he was in a coffee shop still. He smiled. "You know, some days are just bitches."

"Lots of days are bitches," the woman beside him said with a laugh, and she smiled at him as she got up. "Hope you have a better day."

And that was the thing, wasn't it?

Hope you have a better day. Just that thought shared with him, from a complete stranger, was all it took to put a smile on Simon's face. It wasn't so much about *making* it a better day because so many people had so little control over their day that they assumed it was a case of fate stepping in and either giving them a good day or a shitty day. Instead of realizing that so much of the world was under their control, they just didn't believe it and had no way to prove it or to see the proof of it, so they turned away from such concepts.

And with that bit of wisdom, he got up, pocketed his change that had been sitting on the table, then grabbed his wallet and laptop, slipping it into the carry case he packed around with him all the time, as he headed out to his next meeting.

As he walked outside, a woman called out from behind him, "Simon."

He turned to see a woman glaring at him, then felt a

sharp pull on his shoulder. He stumbled back a step. The crowd around them screamed and bolted, as he stared at Eleana Mayfield Morris. "Seriously?" he asked, feeling the pain setting in his shoulder. "You shot me?"

She looked at him in surprise and then immediately dropped the gun, her hand going to her mouth. "Oh my God, oh my God." She started to scream. "I didn't mean to. I didn't mean to."

"No way in hell," he muttered, as he slowly sagged down to the cement as the pain took over his heart and mind. "No way in hell you didn't come here, intent on doing this," he whispered.

"What have I done?" Eleana was screaming in hysteria, and he heard her wailing.

The last thing he thought of was Kate, and he scrambled to get out his phone and to text her. He had no idea if he hit Send or not, ... then he hit the pavement face first, and everything around him went black.

CHAPTER 19

KATE BOLTED TO her feet, as she stared down at the message. She phoned him immediately, as she snatched her jacket and called out to the others. "Simon's been shot. Find out where he's been taken and call me."

She raced to her vehicle, Rodney on her heels, wishing Simon would answer his damn phone. The team soon found out that Simon had been taken to a hospital nearby. Rodney drove her there, ignoring her protests.

As she got to the hospital, she raced inside and asked about Simon and where he was.

The woman at the intake desk checked her computer. "I don't have a file on him. Are you sure you have the right hospital?"

Terrified, Kate looked at her and asked, "What? He just came in on the ambulance."

"Oh, in that case, he's probably still down in emergency, and they haven't had a chance to get him entered into our system yet," she explained, but her last words fell on deaf ears, as Kate was already racing to the emergency department.

As she got there, a gurney was being rolled in through the big double doors, and there was Simon. She stared at him in shock. "He's unconscious?"

"Who are you?" asked the ER attendant.

She held up her badge. "This is my partner."

He stopped and looked down at Simon. "I'll let you know in a minute."

"Can you tell me the details?"

"No, only that he's been shot."

"He sent me a text saying that he'd been shot, but nothing else."

A nurse joined them but didn't say anything. Simon was whisked into a room, and a medical team came to work on him.

Kate stepped back, letting them work, even as her phone started to buzz, with the rest of the team asking her what was going on. All she told them was that he'd been shot and that she didn't have any more than that just yet. Seeing the medical team working on him, she let out a deep breath, as one of the doctors stepped over to her.

"He's alive, and it doesn't appear to be life-threatening," he shared. "He's out, unconscious, but it's likely from the pain and the blood loss. The wound looks to be high in the shoulder. So, nothing major was damaged, and all his organs are intact."

"Thank God for that." Kate sighed, brushing her hair off her face, the relief making her shoulders sag and her heart calm.

"Do you have any of the details?" the doctor asked her.

"No, I don't. He just texted me, saying he'd been shot."

The doc nodded and didn't say anything, but then he looked at her curiously. "I guess it's pretty rough when it's your own partner, isn't it?"

"Yeah, you're not kidding."

Just then he got called back, and he bolted again into Simon's room.

She watched, and it seemed like it was a discussion more than anything. Soon afterward Simon was wheeled out. She stopped them and leaned over, when she got up abreast of him, and kissed him gently.

"I'll be here when you wake up." She had tears in the back of her eyes, but she was afraid to let them spill over, unsure if she could make them stop.

His eyes opened, but they weren't seeing anything, and he very quickly shut them again.

She stepped back, and the doctor added, "They'll go into surgery to take out the bullet."

"Do that," she replied in a pleading tone, "and let me know. We need that bullet."

"Got it." Then they quickly raced Simon to the operating room.

She pulled out her phone and called Owen. "Simon was shot, and I don't have many details. He's been taken up to surgery to remove the bullet, and they say it's not life-threatening. It's high on his shoulder and missed everything important, thank God," she added.

"Christ," he muttered. "Do we have any idea what happened?"

"No, I don't even know who the attending officer is," Kate noted. "Nobody has shown up here yet. If you could get that information, it would be helpful."

"I'm on it," he said, then hung up.

She sat down in the waiting room, and, when a cop bustled in, she stepped up and identified herself. "Are you the one assigned to the shooting?"

He nodded. "Yes." He frowned and asked, "Are you Kate?"

"I'm Kate," she confirmed, with a nod. "Detective Kate

Morgan." She pulled out her badge to show him.

"He was telling me to contact Kate." The cop smiled. "In between passing out."

"He contacted me himself," she explained, with a smile. "He sent me a text, though brief and unhelpful. It did the job, but I didn't get any details."

He nodded. "Not a whole lot of details were available. Apparently some woman shot him. She called his name outside of a coffee shop and shot him, point-blank."

"What?" Kate stared at him in shock.

"We had plenty of eyewitnesses and have her in custody, so it won't be an unsolved case by any means. Yet, as to the motivation, I have no clue. The woman has been hysterical, and she had no ID or anything on her. We are also running her prints as we speak."

Kate knew he was doing everything that she could think of, so it was all good.

"If you're the girlfriend, maybe it's an ex-girlfriend," he suggested, looking at her hopefully.

"I have no idea, but it seems unlikely."

He got a call, stepped away to take it, and, when he returned, he had the shooter's name. When he gave it to Kate, she winced and nodded.

"Oh, *her*, know of her anyway," Kate said in exasperation. "Her husband committed suicide just this week, and her father committed suicide not that long ago, maybe just a month ago, but I'm not sure." She hesitated a moment, then added, "I don't know. You will have to get the timeline on all that, but the company? Apparently her father had embezzled a good share of the funds, and they're broke now. Her husband, Bartlett Morris, asked Simon to look into the finances of the company, and Simon immediately identified the problems and told him to get a team on it right away in the hopes of stopping the bleeding and saving the company. But then Morris committed suicide, which I understand is under investigation too. Simon got called in by Morris's lawyers and found out that Morris had signed over management of the company to him, asking him to do what he could."

"So, this Simon has the control?"

"Yes, so far, he put the board on notice and froze the company assets. He's doing what is needed to be done to try and save what could be saved. Apparently Eleana had taken embezzling lessons from her father and has been spending the profit pretty heavily, with zero thought to taxes or creditors or anything else, so she was really pissed at him."

"She was pissed at whom? Simon?"

"Right," she said, with a nod. "She was really angry at Simon for stepping in and for raining on her parade."

"He doesn't have a choice though, if it's to that point," the cop noted, shaking his head.

"Please," she replied, handing him her card, "if you'd keep me in the loop, I would appreciate it."

"She's down at the station," he shared, checking his watch. "I'll be interviewing her in a little bit."

"I'm staying here," Kate noted, as she looked toward the hallway, where Simon had disappeared. "They've just taken him up for surgery to take the bullet out of his shoulder."

The cop winced. "Sorry, that's a shit deal all around."

"Yeah, especially considering he was put in a shitty position, one that he didn't ask for, or never really had a choice in the matter," she noted quietly, "so he's treading gently himself in this case."

"Yeah, you know, sometimes people are just shits," he

said, giving her a gesture of condolence. "What can a guy like him do in that situation but try to bail them out of their trouble and hope that everybody else gets a paycheck at the end of the day? He damn sure shouldn't have to worry about getting shot though." And, with that, he shook his head. "I'll come back to get the reports from the doc here, so I'll talk to you in a bit." With that, he was gone.

Kate walked over to the waiting room and just collapsed back down again, wondering what she was supposed to do at this point. Wait until Simon got out of surgery for sure, but then what? She didn't want to *not* go to the church tonight, but if they were releasing Simon? … No. She stopped at that thought because that was bonkers.

They wouldn't be releasing Simon.

He would be in overnight, no question about it. In a way, that was an easy answer for her because then he wouldn't interfere in her investigation. She winced at that thought, wondering what was wrong with her that she would even consider it here and now.

But it was true. While he was in the hospital, and hopefully at least partially sedated, he wouldn't be asking to come on the stakeout with her, something she had dreaded since first telling him. She shouldn't have mentioned anything to him, and it would have been easier to deal with the fallout after the fact, but, as it was, there wouldn't be any fallout because the poor guy would be stuck in the hospital, trying to get over getting shot and the subsequent surgery.

Swearing at the world around her, she stepped outside and contacted the rest of her team to let them know what was happening. Rodney was on the other end of the phone call, having returned to the precinct, after dropping her at the hospital with her car.

"You stay there at the hospital," he told her. "I can go on the stakeout tonight."

"Simon will have to stay overnight anyway," she replied, "if not for a few days. However, tonight he'll be stuck for sure. So, I'll go on the stakeout. I'll stay here until he's safely out of surgery. As long as everything goes well ..." She took a deep breath. "I'll go on the stakeout. Simon will be fine here in the hospital, and nobody'll get at him either."

"You sure about that?"

"They caught the woman who shot him, right in front of witnesses. It was Bartlett's wife, Eleana Mayfield Morris. Apparently she didn't like anything Simon had to say or the changes he's making," she explained, with a groan. "I wonder if Bartlett had any idea what he was asking Simon to take on."

"Probably not, otherwise he would have asked instead of just dumping it on him."

"Isn't that the truth," she muttered.

Anyway, with those arrangements made, she returned to the waiting room and sat down to wait until Simon came out of surgery. She waited and waited and waited, until finally she couldn't stand it any longer. She hopped up and walked over to the nurses' station. "How do I find out how the surgery is going?"

"Somebody should have come and contacted you, if they're out already," she explained, tapping on the keyboard in front of her. "It looks like we had a couple other issues come up on other surgeries, so his was pushed back a bit, as it wasn't life-threatening."

Kate winced and nodded. "Okay, so where are we at now?"

"Let me pop up there and check it out, and I'll let you

know what I find out." She pointed Kate to the waiting area. The nurse disappeared, and, when she came back five long minutes later, she said, "He should be out in another few minutes. I was told they are just about done."

Kate nodded her thanks, then sank back down. When the doors opened, and Simon was wheeled out, still under sedation. She raced to his side, leaned over, gave him a gentle kiss, and looked up at the doctor.

The doctor was positive that he would make a full recovery. "Listen. He won't be awake for several hours, so go do what you've got to do. He's not going anywhere, and, in here, he'll be fine."

And, with that good news in her heart, Kate turned and bolted out to deal with the rest of her chaotic world.

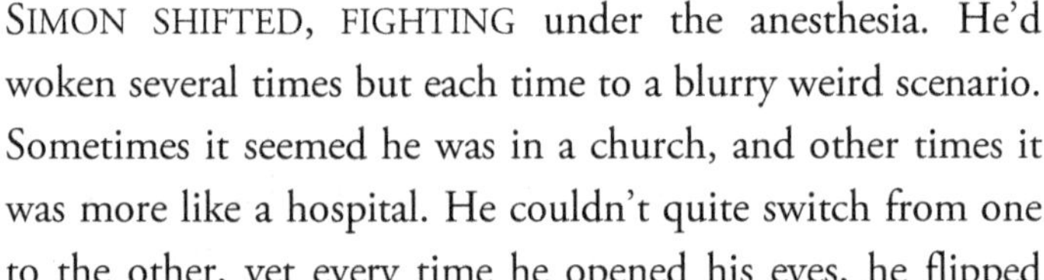

SIMON SHIFTED, FIGHTING under the anesthesia. He'd woken several times but each time to a blurry weird scenario. Sometimes it seemed he was in a church, and other times it was more like a hospital. He couldn't quite switch from one to the other, yet every time he opened his eyes, he flipped from one world to the next.

He shuddered in place. as the pain racked up and down his body, reminding him that, no matter what had happened, some way, somehow, his body was reacting to pain. Whether it was his pain or someone else's, he didn't know, and he sure as hell wished to God he did. If he knew which, it would make it easier to deal with. He almost laughed at that because it wouldn't make it easier at all, nothing would, and the whole thing was just bullshit.

Once again he was reminded of his grandmother, her voice in the background warning him about starting down this pathway. Still, there hadn't been enough of a warning to keep him from going one way or the other. Yet he couldn't blame her because she could have only told him so much anyway. His experience was different from everybody else's experience. So, as much as he wanted somebody to blame, there wasn't anyone. This was just the reality, his reality.

He opened his eyes and found himself in what appeared to be a hospital room. He blinked several times, not wanting to drift back under, not without any answers.

A woman walked over to stare down at him, immediately reaching for his hand. She spoke in a soothing tone. "I'm glad to see you're awake. You've had quite a turbulent ride."

He blinked at her several times.

"It's all right. You've been shot, but you'll be fine."

He stared at her and whispered, "Who shot me?"

She winced and shook her head. "I'm sorry. I don't know. I'm a nurse at the hospital, but the police did want to be called when you're awake."

He shifted ever-so-slightly and then cried out again.

"Yes," she noted, as she held him down. "You had surgery to remove the bullet, and you are going be just fine, but don't move too much and you'll do better. You will be very sore, so try not to move. If the pain is too much, let me know, and I can raise your pain meds a bit."

He cried out, "No, no, no, don't."

But the pain meds immediately reached for him and dragged him under.

When he woke the next time, he swore to God it was only a minute later, like no time had passed. Maybe there hadn't been any passage of time. He didn't know. He was so damn confused.

What confused him even more was that now he was in a

church, staring around at the incredible artwork. He couldn't tell what church it was, but he felt a sense of peace, and, at the same time, a sense of absolute anger that inherently just twisted through him. He groaned in agony, not sure if it was his ire or the person in front of him. Then, almost with a flip of a switch, he was tossed out of the church again. He opened his eyes in the hospital and whispered, "Dear God, somebody help me."

Almost immediately he heard footsteps and a woman, the same woman, walked over and smiled at him. "Hey," she said. "You're having quite the nightmares."

He stared up at her, feeling the sweat dripping off his face. "You could say that," he whispered, and he struggled to speak, asking for water. She immediately brought over ice water. He sucked back a big drink and then relaxed back down again. "Kate?" he asked. "Where's Kate?" The nurse frowned, and he stared at her. "She's a cop and my girlfriend. She should be here."

"Ah, that would be the woman who's constantly phoning."

"Yes, that would be her," he said, but the disappointment ate at him. "She couldn't even be here?" He thought it, but, when the nurse looked at him in sympathy, he knew he had spoken it out loud. Even though he'd been shot? The thought was cutting into him.

"She had to leave for work, and the doctor did tell her to leave because it would be quite a while before you resurfaced," she explained in a soothing tone. "I understand she was here for quite some time, while you were in surgery and all, and I'm supposed to let her know as soon as you're awake again."

He gave a snort at that. "Sounds like her."

"I wasn't here while she was here, so I can't tell you how she reacted, but I do have pretty terse instructions, and I'm not going against her." The nurse laughed. "I don't suppose too many people are willful enough to try that."

At that, he couldn't help but smile because that absolutely was Kate. "Call her," he said quietly, "and, if I can talk to her, all the better."

"Oh, I don't think you'll get clearance for that just yet," the nurse replied cheerfully, "but I'll be letting her know you're awake." And, with that, she was gone again.

He groaned because he hadn't even had a chance to complete what he needed to say to her, but, even still, his mind was fuzzy and clouded. Was it the drugs or the visions?

The thoughts he had just kept slipping, and his mind was racing one million miles an hour. He didn't know and probably wouldn't know fully until he got his mind back again. At the moment that seemed like a distant option.

He couldn't understand why he was as groggy as he was, but something was holding him back or holding him in place. He looked down and he wasn't being restrained at all. He was just lying in the hospital bed. He sank his head back onto the pillow and groaned, wondering just what the hell was going on. Surely it wasn't possible that he was picking up on both a victim and the killer at the same time?

Could that be what I'm doing? he wondered, then stopped, confused as to why all this was washing in and out of him. He went from a flash of a church, to a flash of a victim, to his own injuries, and, with that, he realized exactly what had started all this.

Outside the coffee shop, Bartlett's wife had shot Simon, and he had slowly collapsed onto the sidewalk. He relived the moment several times, hating that he was incapable of stopping her before it happened, and yet apparently it had happened right there. Did anybody know? Had she been picked up? He searched for a phone beside him, but there wasn't one. He wasn't even sure if it had come in with him. There was a call button for a nurse, and he immediately hit that several times. When the footsteps came toward him, he whispered, "Where's my phone?"

"I don't know," the same nurse told him. "I'll check your personal belongings though."

"Please," he whispered, "it's important." When she hesitated, he opened his eyes again and stared at her. "It's really very important."

She frowned, then nodded. "I'll go take a look." Then she took off again.

The helplessness ate at him, but he didn't even know what it was that he was supposed to drive toward. He just knew that he had to move, that he had to drive somewhere, that he had to go somewhere. There was something, someone pushing him to do something. He blinked, feeling the drugs pull at him again. "No," he whispered. "No, I don't want to go under again."

The nurse arrived and held up a phone. "If this is yours, the battery looks like it's pretty dead."

"*Great,*" he whispered, as he reached out an unsteady hand.

She frowned as she handed it to him. "Look. You know that you shouldn't be doing anything, right?"

"I know," he replied, "but I need to contact somebody."

"Is it about the shooting? I heard they caught the woman who did this."

He stopped, looked up at her. "That's something."

She smiled. "Right? That detective was pretty upset

about the whole thing."

He didn't want to nod or say anything to that because the *detective* could be anybody.

The nurse wouldn't leave him alone for a few minutes, as she checked him over and recorded his vitals, all while he lay here, irked that she wouldn't leave him be, while his phone was losing more and more power, yet not wanting to make the call while she was around.

Nobody would understand what he was trying to tell Kate. Hell, he knew there was a good chance he wouldn't even explain it well enough for her to understand. It was just too bizarre, but he had to try. When the nurse was finally done, he called Kate, only to have it go to voice mail.

He groaned as he laid back and sent out as many strong messages as he could, but he knew his psychic messages weren't going anywhere. He was in a heavily doped state for the pain, and, while he knew that much, he didn't know how to combat it. Something major needed to be done, yet he could do nothing.

He left a voice mail, his voice broken and harsh, and he knew that the message was coming out garbled, but it was the best he could do. Having done that, he collapsed back down. Feeling a lassitude and an exhaustion, he went back under. Then the chanting began at the back of his mind. He struggled, but the darkness took him, and he heard a whisper.

Too bad. Too late. She's mine.

CHAPTER 20

K ATE WALKED INTO the back of the church, studied the area, having memorized where she would move and could find a hiding place to stay put. She quickly took up position and then frowned, not sure she liked the lack of advantageous viewing. She had Lilliana over on the far side, and two cops were outside in surveillance vehicles. It would be a long night. She didn't have a cup of hot coffee with her, but a couple granola bars were stuck into her back pocket, if needed.

As she settled down, her phone buzzed, and she shut off the ringer, kicking herself for having left it on that long. She hoped it was early enough that nobody had heard it, but it was a rookie mistake and one she was not happy about having made.

She checked the message and winced. Simon's voice sounded like he was completely under the influence of drugs, though the fact that he was even coherent was amazing. Yet the words that came across in the message didn't make any sense, something about a church and something about being tied up and restrained, and something about her needing to call him. She shifted deeper into her hiding spot, trying hard to be in a place where nobody could overhear her, and then quickly made a phone call. When it rang and didn't connect, she was almost relieved because she shouldn't be trying to make a call here as it was. Putting down her phone, she pondered his message and wondered if he was somehow connecting to the killer.

How did that work? Simon wasn't even mentally there, not with the drugs that they had given him. On the other hand, maybe that's why he was connecting. Maybe a wall separated here from there until the drugs took over, but, damn, that sounded insane. Maybe the wall was thinner just because of the drugs. Maybe his natural defenses were down and out, not in actual functioning order.

She listened to Simon's message two more times, trying to sort it out, but all that came across was that he woke up in a church, and he was tied up, and he woke up in the hospital and was getting confused, going from one reality to the other. He wasn't asking for help though. The urgency in his voice seemed to be more about trying to get her to understand something important. And yet how the hell could anybody understand anything important in that?

Groaning, she settled back when she got a text from Lilliana.

Problems?

Kate wasn't sure how Lilliana knew that there was a problem, but Kate sent back a **No.** Then she thought better of it, knowing Lilliana should be in the loop. **Just got a strange message from Simon.**

Do you need to leave?

No, he's still under the influence of the drugs, so the message was garbled.

She didn't get an answer to that for several long moments, and then Lilliana texted back.

Are you sure about that?

Yes.

She wasn't sure why Lilliana was making a big deal out

of it, except for the fact that Simon had been injured. Kate was not the worrying type and never one for nice talks either. However, in many cases, someone in her position would want to stay at the hospital, instead of being out on a stakeout, like she was, but then Kate wasn't everybody, and God help her for it.

Simon was also somebody who would have understood in a normal situation—but maybe not so much now. She chewed on her bottom lip as she contemplated her choices, and then sent Lilliana another text. **His message was about waking up in a church, but it doesn't make any sense because of the drugs. It's a garbled attempt to tell me something, without telling me something.**

So, I'm asking again, do you need to go to him?

No, he's under the influence of drugs, and he's not making sense, so me being there won't help. That seemed to satisfy Lilliana for a while, and then about ten minutes later she sent another text.

If you need to go in a little bit because he'll be awake, or at least call him, let me know, and I'll cover for you.

But I can't make a call from here, she reminded Lilliana because that would be too obvious, and somebody would hear her.

You can go to the church office and talk there, Lilliana reminded her.

Kate frowned, as she looked around. **We'll see.**

And with that, Kate settled down and hunkered in to wait some more. She wasn't the best at stakeouts, but she had a hell of a motivation this time, and they needed to stop this asshole. So, she was here where they needed to be. As it was, the hours ticked by in unrelenting drudgery. There was just her phone to surf on and a little bit of food to snack on, and, other than that, nothing. She checked in with Lilliana every half hour but still nothing to report.

Finally Lilliana texted her. **You're still solid on this?**

She winced, and, by this time, she was frustrated too. **Yes, I'm not ready to leave for a couple more hours.**

Good enough. We have Rodney coming in, if we need him. I just don't want to waste man-hours if we don't have to.

And, of course, that was the trick, trying to balance man-hours versus needs. Yes, it pissed off Kate because that was something that they needed to keep in mind, and yet, if this guy came, everything would be forgiven. If the killer didn't come, people would say she'd made the wrong call. Of course, making the wrong call was never popular, but, even if it was a wrong call, made for the right reasons, that just made life even harder.

She settled back, refusing to just wait and give it time, but, in her mind, she kept calling out. *Where are you, … you asshole? Get your ass in here, where I can capture you.* Then, of course, there was never any answer. When her phone buzzed again, she expected it to be Lilliana, but instead, as she looked down, she found a message from Simon again. This time he texted, and his message remained cryptic to say the least.

I hope you're getting this message, Kate. The killer is delivering his parcel, and I keep waking up at a church, but I don't know what church.

And that was the end of it. She swore and got up, looked around, but nobody was here. With nobody inside, she quickly walked over to the office, and, with the door closed, phoned Simon.

"Hey," he greeted her, his voice groggy. "I am glad to hear from you."

"I've been getting your messages," she noted. "I'm on a stakeout at the church right now."

"Yeah, and that's what I'm trying to tell you. I keep waking up at a church, but I'm not *in* the church."

"What do you mean?" she cried out in a frustrated tone.

"I don't know. I'm not *in* the church," he repeated, "and I can't tell you any more than that."

"Shit," she snapped.

"I know." And, with that, he hung up.

***

SIMON WASN'T SURE if he made it through to her or not. He tried again, sending her another text saying, **I'm serious.**

She sent him a thumbs-up.

He groaned, realizing that chances are, she really didn't get it. He relaxed back, drifted in and out, the pain kicking in. Then slowly easing back, he would roll over, and the pain would kick in. He needed to take more pain meds, but he was a little on the stubborn side. Besides, he also knew his abilities didn't work well when he was under the influence of drugs, and maybe that would be a good thing right now.

Or maybe my abilities were freed to work overtime under these drugs.

Maybe he could just sleep and, for the first time in a very long time, really relax, have a night of no nightmares, no subconscious or weird psychic visions kicking through his system, but instinctively he knew that was the wrong thing right now.

Something serious stirred out there, wherever *out there* was. He didn't even have wording or jargon for this mess. Sure, he probably needed to do some research into it, but it did seem more like an acknowledgment of something he was desperately trying not to acknowledge. Therefore, sending him in the wrong direction.

He slept for another few minutes, only to wake up once again feeling the pain kicking through his system. He checked his watch, and then went to pick up his phone but there was nothing. The nurse had been right; his battery was almost dead. He groaned once again and sent Kate a message. **Battery almost dead.** He got a response almost immediately, telling him to get off his phone then.

He smiled at that, and then again when another text came in.

I got this. Relax.

He decided that it was time for a decent sleep, and maybe he would be more cognizant once he woke up again. And, with that, he rolled over onto his good shoulder, propped up his sore arm on one of the pillows, and fell back asleep again. When he woke the next time, it wasn't an easy or a gentle awakening.

He slammed awake, crying out in pain, only to have everything in his world shifting from one vision to another, with absolutely no rhyme or reason.

A woman raced toward him and held him down hard. "Easy, easy, take it easy."

"I can't," he cried out, thrashing in the bed. "She has to get him! She has to."

"Hang on. Hang on. What are you talking about?"

Then his voice shifted, and he knew it was shifting; he could sense it. He felt something happening on the inside, something wrong, something seriously wrong.

"She's in danger," he whispered. "She's in danger. He knows. … Oh God, he knows. He knows. You have to tell her."

At that, the nurse held him down. "Hang on. Hang on," she repeated. "We've got this."

He heard other people coming toward him at top speed, but he didn't know what they were doing and tried to stop them.

Or he did know.

"No, don't knock me out. I have to help. I have to help her!" And then there was no more.

CHAPTER 21

KATE LOOKED DOWN at the phone ringing, wondering why tonight was such a mess of contacts. But it was the hospital, so, swearing, she got up and quickly snuck back into the church office and closed the door.

"What's the matter?" she asked, finally answering it.

"Hey," the nurse began. "You wanted to be told if there was any change in his condition. I just wanted to tell you that he woke up tonight, panicked, screaming something about you're not safe, and *He knows about you*, and I don't know what all," she said, then took a deep breath.

"I'm not even telling you all of what he said. It was freaky. He was completely incoherent for a while, and then it seemed like he suddenly got clear on what he wanted to say. So the message that I really think was for you is that *He knows, he knows, he knows*, and Simon kept saying it over and over again," the nurse explained, then sighed in exasperation, and then some.

"Christ."

"We upped his dosages, and he's asleep again, but honestly it got pretty crazy."

"No, I get it," Kate replied quietly, "and thank you for telling me."

"Did it make sense to you?" the nurse asked anxiously, "because he was pretty panicked that you should know."

"It does makes sense," she said, her voice gentle. "Thank you, and, if you can keep him asleep, that would be good for him and probably for the best."

"Yes, it would be, but he's fighting the medication."

"Of course he is," she stated. "Look. I'll try to get there as soon as I can. I'm on a job right now, and I can't get out."

"No, I understand," she replied. "When he wakes again, I'll let him know."

"Good enough." Kate pocketed her phone and stared down at her empty hand, wondering. To have been pulled out from the medications like this meant that he was picking up on something, whether he knew it or not, and, whatever it was, he was panicked, thinking that she was in trouble.

But he hadn't known when he was in trouble himself.

That was the problem with these kinds of abilities; he'd been so focused on her safety, and yet a woman came up and shot him at point-blank range. How the hell did that happen? Why was there not a warning for him? Why not something that would tell him that there was a hunter out there after him?

She sagged back into her hiding place and then bolted to her feet again, checking in with Lilliana.

Lilliana responded, saying, **I'm still here. You?**

Yeah, more craziness from Simon. I'm a little confused. I'll go out and check with the black-and-whites outside.

Are you sure?

Yeah, I'm sure.

Are we calling the stakeout then?

No. Instantly she frowned. Kate phoned Lilliana instead and, in a low voice, said, "I don't know what's going on, but it feels … I don't know, wrong somehow."

"In what way?" Lilliana asked, her voice sharp.

"I need to check outside," she declared, "and I don't know what the hell's going on, but this is wrong." She stood, already picking up her pace. "You need to move with me."

"Where are we going?" Lilliana asked, and Kate heard her moving through the phone.

"Out front, ... no wait." Kate stopped. "Not out front. Out back."

"Why out back?"

"Shit, shit, shit," she snapped, picking up her feet, running. "Because either he couldn't get in the front or he didn't like something about it, as in us."

"But how would he know?"

"Unless he saw us," Kate suggested, "or maybe saw one of the black-and-whites."

"Shit. Let's go," Lilliana said.

Kate burst out of her hiding spot and into the main part of the church, but, as she expected, nothing was going on, nobody was there, and her hollow footsteps echoed as she raced toward the back door. As she raced out into the night, Lilliana came from the opposite direction and stared at her.

"What the hell's going on?" Lilliana asked, but Kate was looking around, frantic.

She turned on her phone's flashlight and stared around in panic. "Have you heard from the black-and-whites?"

"No." Then Lilliana froze. "Shit, no, I haven't." At that, she pulled out her phone and started to make phone calls, checking in on the two policemen who were supposed to be out here.

Kate looked at her in misery. "It's too late."

"What do you mean, *It's too late?*"

"To call them," Kate muttered. "I just hope they're still

alive." And, with that, she bolted toward the back fence. She didn't even know what was driving her, but almost something from Simon, something he had said, something about a fence. As Kate raced to the fence, Lilliana was running to catch up with her.

"It would help if you would explain," Lilliana muttered in a tone that had a hint of an angry edge.

"I can't explain," Kate spat, raising her hands. "If I could, I would have, but I can't. So you're stuck with what I have to deal with too."

"Is this Simon again?"

"I don't know whether it's Simon or not," she muttered, and then her flashlight caught sight of something on the ground. "Shit." She raced forward, and there was one of the local officers, completely collapsed. She bolted beside him, checked for a pulse, then turned and looked back at Lilliana. "He's alive. Get an ambulance and get a team up here now."

Lilliana took one look, stepped away, and immediately made the phone calls.

Kate checked him over and found a bloody spot, and probably several blows to the head. She hoped he would be okay, but she had no way of knowing. His airway was open, and, outside of staying here to ensure he would be okay, she had a second officer to try and find. So, with Lilliana making the calls and standing guard over this one, Kate quickly searched the parking lot for the second one.

Close off to the side where they had their second surveillance vehicle parked, it was still there, but Kate noted blood on the ground nearby. All of a sudden, Kate realized who would be the next victim. She raced back to Lilliana, crying out, "He's gone. He's been kidnapped. I swear to God, our killer will use him as his next victim."

Lilliana stared at her in horror, and she went into a quick daze.

Kate continued. "There's blood at the second vehicle, and it's a long way away from this site. That's our second black-and-white. Whatever the hell's going on, our killer has now turned his attention to the cops because they were hapless enough to be seen."

Kate turned, then looked around and caught sight of something else. Clapping her hand to her mouth, she slowly stepped to the back wall of the church and stared in shock at the two crosses partially propped up against the dumpsters. On each of these simple crude crosses was yet another victim, and this time the blood flowed freely from the one, but the other one appeared to be long gone.

As she stared at the second victim, she felt the tears gathering in her eyes because this was her missing cop. He hadn't been kidnapped; he'd been crucified.

SEVERAL HOURS LATER Sergeant Colby walked over, nudged her gently on the shoulder, as she sat on the steps, staring off into the night. Colby stated smoothly, "It's not your fault, you know."

She glared at him. "And yet … it feels like it's my fault," she snapped. "We were here, and we were on the scene, and yet … he did this. Not only to the victim that he had ready to go but he also did it to one of ours," she stated, glaring at her sergeant.

He nodded. "But you weren't alone. They were on a stakeout as well," Colby pointed out, trying to calm her down. "I'm not sure what caused them to get out of the vehicle at the time, whether they were lured out or had to go to the bathroom. I don't know. Until the other one wakes up, it's not likely that we will know."

"Wakes up and is fine, you mean," Kate corrected, glaring at Colby. "Given those head wounds, he may never be fine, especially when he finds out what happened to his partner," she snapped.

At that, Owen stepped over and nodded at her. "What I can't figure out is why choose the one cop and not the other one?"

"Size," she stated immediately.

He blinked, looking at her with a confused expression.

"This guy, our killer, isn't very big, and he isn't very strong. So size is what made the difference as to which cop he killed. Maybe he would have killed both, but he could only have crucified the one because he was lighter and easier for him to handle."

"What would you think would be a reasonable size for our killer to do something like this?" Rodney asked, joining them now, looking at her curiously. "I mean, if you think about it, how big does somebody have to be to do this?"

"I'm putting him at about five-six, five-seven, in my head," she murmured. "And, no, I don't have any reason for that. Obviously I'll keep my options open, but I sure don't see him as being a hulky six-four."

"No, I can see that too," Rodney murmured.

"The only good news," Sergeant Colby noted at her side, his voice still low and calm, "is that we have more forensics this time. He was interrupted, and he did a rough job. So when you thought he'd taken away our officer, he had hastily put him up on the cross instead, which means he must have had the stakes with him."

"That's because he had the first victim already prepared.

What I want to know is, where is the other victim?"

"What are the chances that he only brought the one this time?"

"Not likely," Kate murmured, "not likely at all." When he turned and looked at her, she shrugged. "It would completely break his pattern." Then she turned and looked around nervously. "You know, guys," she said, almost frantic as she paced around the fence, but then her eyes lit up like a Christmas tree. "We need to check those dumpsters."

And, with that, she took off at a run. She really hoped she was wrong, but she didn't see that their killer would quit or would change his pattern, not without good reason. What he did this time was a break in pattern, if you wanted to look at it that way, but, more than that, it was sending a message, a message that was pissing her off.

She went through the dumpsters, checking, and knew that forensics would be all over the place anyway. At the last one, the one closest to the cop car, she flipped open the lid, then turned back to Sergeant Colby and whistled. Her team came running, and there inside the dumpster was a small male, dead from the looks of him, and probably had been for quite a few hours. She turned to see Smidge walking over toward her.

Seeing the look on her face, he barked, "You better not have more for me."

She motioned at the dumpster. "Unfortunately we do have one more for you. I suspect it's the original victim our killer brought to go on that cross. Then the killer chose to put our cop on it instead."

Smidge took one look and swore. "Christ, I'm not getting home tonight at all, am I?"

"Sorry," she muttered. "Doesn't look like any of us will."

He nodded. "Can't believe you guys were here and even then—"

"Yeah, don't remind me," she snapped. "We were right here, and that's why the cop was here too. We were on a stakeout, hoping to catch him in the act."

"So, in that sense"—Smidge turned to face her—"you had the right place and the right time, so what went wrong?"

"I don't know," she admitted. "Maybe he saw the cops. That's about the best explanation I can give, but really I have no idea."

"It's quite likely. He came here prepared. He's got the stakes and the crosses, and then, all of a sudden, he sees the cops. Did they contact you at all, you know, to say that somebody was here?"

"They didn't contact me, and I have to check with Lilliana, but she didn't say anything. So I'm assuming they didn't get the chance."

"So, what then? Our killer does whatever it is that he's thinking to do, then sees the cops, maybe by accident. Or maybe one got out to check what he was doing, so he kills him, or knocks him out, then realizes the one cop is probably not alone, then goes and finds the other guy at another vehicle, kills him, and decides to ditch his plans and put up his new victim instead? Why the hell would he do that?"

"It's a message," Kate suggested, "and chances are, the cop doesn't have a message on his chest. Am I close?"

"You're exactly right. He doesn't." Smidge eyed her. "Why not though?"

"Because his soul or salvation doesn't matter to our killer. This was an efficiency killing. The cop was in the way, and he would cause our killer trouble. Maybe it was a case of kill or be killed. He might have broken it down if he'd had a chance to even think about it, but he didn't. Our killer just would have reacted under threat, and that was it, and our guy was done."

"And yet two cops were inside the church, and two cops were outside the church," Smidge noted, glaring at her.

"That's right," she admitted, "and this guy took out the two on the outside, while we were racing out here to check."

"Why were you racing outside?" Colby asked, turning to look at her.

"Because I hadn't heard from them, from our cover unit, and it was just that ..." She hesitated, then shook her head. "I'll say the word, and you won't like it, but my instincts were screaming that something was wrong."

"You're right. I don't like it," Colby agreed, "but I've done the same thing many a time. We would like to have a more logical explanation for it, but we can't always."

"Simon also mentioned something about a fence in his garbled message, and what I found at the fence was our injured cop," she added.

"Great," Colby muttered, as he pinched the bridge of his nose. "This will be a hard one for the brass."

"And yet let's give her credit for what she's done so far," Smidge snapped, "because, as I said, right place, right time, just either wrong shitty timing that these guys were seen or one of them approached our killer without realizing that he could possibly be the killer."

"Why would he do that?" Colby asked.

"Either he knew him or assumed ..."

And just then something clicked in Kate's brain. She stopped and nodded, taking in her surroundings in a panic. "Maybe ... *assumed*, ... maybe because of his appearance that it couldn't be him, or ..." Then she turned to look at

Lilliana. "*Or* because he wasn't alone, and maybe the cop assumed that the killer would be solo."

"Yet *alone* is what you're going on for an assumption, correct?" Smidge asked in a quirky tone.

"I was initially," she explained, "but now I'm leaning toward it being a duo."

He winced at that and replied, "But this *could* be the work of a single person."

"I know. I'm just not sure …"

Sergeant Colby apparently heard the hesitation in her voice. He turned to her and said, "Spit it out, Detective."

She raised both hands. "I don't have any reason to back this up, so you can't hold me to anything. I'm just putting out ideas here." She took a deep breath and continued. "My idea is that it's a pair, and one of them is incapable of doing the job and needs the other one to carry out what has to happen, but it has to happen for both their sakes. I just don't know why."

"Shit." Smidge stared at her. "That makes a twisted sense. How the abused becomes the abuser."

"It does, but I don't have any proof of it," Kate stated bitterly, "so get me some proof, and then I can maybe find the assholes before they do this again. Because believe me. Nobody is angrier than I am that we got this close and once again they got away from us … and killed one of our own in the process."

"No, I get it," Smidge replied in understanding, yet the anger and sorrow was etched on his face, as it was on all of their faces. "So, go on, and get the hell out of my way, so I can do my work."

And, with that, he moved them away from the dumpster.

SIMON WOKE UP, this time his head clear, his body aching and sore, but he generally felt better. He pulled back the blankets, shifted into a more vertical position, gave his head a minute to stabilize, then got up and walked on his own to the bathroom. He looked at the shower and realized there wasn't much chance of them letting him have one, but he figured he could wait until he got back home again, and home was where he was going—and damn soon if he had anything to say about it.

When he stepped out of the bathroom, the nurse glared at him. "And hello to you too," he said by way of a greeting. "I'm feeling fine, much better as a matter of fact."

"You might be feeling much better," she declared, with an ugly stare, as if he were a viper that would strike at any time, "but we had to knock you out last night because of some reaction to the drugs. You were hysterical."

He just gave her a casual nod, knowing exactly where this was coming from. He had had the visions again. "That might explain some of the confused memories I have," he noted quietly, not willing to share anything about what he was remembering. He was just glad she was attributing it to a drug reaction, rather than him being batshit crazy or something equally inconvenient. He walked back to the bed and sat down. "How quickly can I see a doctor?"

"Will you really try to get out of here today?" Her eyebrows drifted down, as she waited for his answer.

"Yeah, I really am," he replied, with a forced smile. "I'll heal much faster at home."

"Yeah, but you're just out of surgery. I don't think he'll go for it."

"He must need a hell of a compelling reason," Simon

argued. "I never do well in hospitals."

She rolled her eyes again at that. "Come on. Let me do your morning check."

With that, he got back on the bed and she set to work checking his vitals. When she was done, he asked, "Any chance of a coffee?"

"Sure, but it's hospital coffee, so don't hold your breath."

"Another reason to go home," he muttered, giving her a sideways glance. "I'm sure the food leaves much to be desired, and the coffee definitely will."

She laughed. "Still, you're alive, and, for that, you should be damn grateful."

"I am, yet it was never a life-threatening injury."

"No, it wasn't, but, before you leave, the cop handling the investigation wants to talk to you."

"He can also contact me at home," Simon directed. "It's not as if I have to stay in the hospital because I'll leave town or anything."

"I'm glad to hear that they have your shooter," she replied, "and it's an open-and-shut case, as far as I understand."

"Probably," Simon noted, as he looked over at the door. "So, when can I leave?"

"I'll tell the doctor that you're anxious to leave, but I really wouldn't expect you to be released today, or honestly probably not for another forty-eight hours."

"That's nice," Simon quipped and waited for her to leave. As soon as she was gone, he checked his phone and saw that he had a little battery life left but not much. He quickly sent a text to Kate. **I'm awake. Help me get out of here.**

She phoned him instead, and he cut to the chase.

"My battery is almost done, but I really want to go home. Can you get me out of here?"

"How are you feeling?"

The concern in her voice made him wince. "I'm fine," he snapped.

After silence for a moment, then she spoke in a light tone. "But you don't sound fine. You sound snappy and irritable."

"Sure, but you and I have some things to talk about, and being under the influence of drugs with my ability is not exactly conducive to sleeping. If I stay here, you know perfectly well what'll happen, and I really don't want people to pick up on what's happening in my brain."

"You don't have to accept any medication while you're in the hospital," she pointed out. "It's there for your use, but you don't have to be tied to it."

"*Great,*" he muttered in frustration. "You know damn well how it gets. The minute it goes badly, they give me way more than I need, just to shut me up, and it all gets infinitely worse thereafter. The nurse was already looking at me sideways. Anyway, I'm getting out today, one way or another, so deal with it." And, with that, he hung up.

CHAPTER 22

K ATE WALKED INTO the hospital, just in time to see the doctor walking into Simon's room. She came in behind him, and the doctor looked at her in surprise, then at Simon, who just shrugged.

"She can stay."

She walked closer to Simon, then reached over and held his hand.

As soon as the doctor was done checking him over, Simon asked earnestly, "So, you'll clear me to go home, right?"

"I'd like to see you stay for forty-eight hours," he replied. "You just had surgery, and there can be some complications that aren't anything to fool around with."

"No, but obviously I'm struggling being here, and I don't want to stay," he snapped. He squeezed Kate's hand, and she looked at the doctor expectantly.

The doctor looked at her intently. "Do you stay at his house with him?"

"I have my own place, but I can stay with him," she offered. "I do have to work though, so if he needs to stay here, I understand that he needs to stay here."

Simon snorted. "You can't force me to stay, and I will be leaving. So, either we'll do this nicely or we'll do it in a more quarrelsome fashion, but I'm going home either way." The doctor stepped back and glared at him, as Simon nodded.

"Thank you very much for fixing me up," Simon added, "but I will heal much better and much faster at home."

"Not everybody has a phobia about hospitals, like you do," the doctor replied forcefully.

"Which is a damn good thing, since you already have plenty of cooperative patients to look after," Simon quipped, with a smirk. "Come on, Doc. I'll be smart and sensible, and, if there's any problem at all, I'll get it looked at immediately. I am perfectly capable of going home and looking after myself for the next forty-eight hours. I promise. I won't even get out of bed."

"Now if I thought that I could trust you to follow through on that, it would be a different story."

"He will," Kate confirmed quietly but firmly. "*That* I can make sure of."

The doctor stared at her as she pulled out her badge and held it up.

He pursed his lips as he thought about it, then shrugged. "Fine, but you'll have to sign a waiver, saying you're walking out of here against medical advice."

Simon nodded. "Not a problem." He sat up, looked over at her, and asked, "Is there paperwork that needs to be done?"

"I handled most of it yesterday. I think you just have to sign the release that he's talking about. Then we'll make a follow-up appointment to come back and see your regular doctor."

"You just need to see his family physician or even pop into a clinic to get checked out," the doctor shared, frowning at him, "but I would still rather you stayed."

"You would, and I've taken that into consideration," Simon said, "but I'm not staying."

The doctor swore at that and stepped back. "It's on your neck," he warned.

"Yeah, it always is, and that's one of the things I like about being alive and getting to make choices," he declared, with a smile this time. "If this kills me, then it kills me, but it's my problem, not yours." At that, he hopped up, looked down at his arm, which was now in a sling, and said a bit too enthusiastically, "Let's go home."

Kate wished he wasn't quite so stubborn, but, judging by the tilt to his head, she knew this was definitely something he would argue fully until he got out.

By the time he put on what remained of his clothes, and they got his discharge instructions, she loaded him into her vehicle and headed toward home. "So, what was really the problem?"

"The hospital," he snapped in an exasperated tone. "The fact is, it's a hospital, and people die there."

It took her several long moments of silence to figure it out. "Oh shit," she muttered, looking at him in shock. "Are you picking up other people?"

"I'm picking up all kinds of other people, particularly dead ones," he growled at her, "and the drugs are making it way worse. The hallucinations were godawful."

"Is that what you were picking up last night?"

"I think so," he muttered, as he closed his eyes. "Everything was disjointed, and just so many different people, things, and visions coming at me, all at the speed of light, but the only thing I could think of was that it was the hospital. I get it got pretty wild because I'd wake up screaming and talking crazy, so they kept giving me more and more pain meds. Finally they basically knocked me out enough that I could sleep, so my body could heal, although it's not the same as having a drug-free healing. It was awful, and so the best solution for me is the get the hell out of there."

"And you'll stay home in bed and look after yourself, correct?"

He rolled his head toward her, then smiled. "If you stay home with me, I'll definitely stay in bed."

"Rest assured there won't be any hanky-panky for quite a while, given your shoulder," she pointed out, "so staying in bed together might be an exercise in frustration."

"But it would still be better to stay in bed with you than to be stuck in bed without you and at the hospital," he pointed out, "so I'm willing to take the risk."

"That's nice," she quipped. "I, on the other hand, have a shitty case on my hands that still needs a lot of work right now, so that's not happening."

"Right," he said, shifting uneasily in the car seat beside her.

She looked at him and asked, "Do we need to get prescriptions filled?"

"I've got some pain meds at home," he replied, with a careless tone. "Otherwise I can place the order and have it delivered, or even have Edgar or Harry go pick it up."

"Right, the front desk guys would help out," she said, with a smile. "I keep forgetting that."

"Yeah, I've got people," he teased, with a smile in her direction.

"And it's a good thing to have people, particularly people who can do something for you," she noted, with a smile. She pulled up into the parking spot at his place.

"Let's go." Outside, he moved at a decent pace and with a smooth gait.

However, she felt the fatigue coming off him in waves.

"See? I'm fine."

"You're not that fine," she muttered, as they walked up to the front entrance. Edgar was there, and she walked over to him and explained the situation. "He'll pull some shit, but it'll be me that you answer to. He's your boss and all, but, in this instance, if he comes down that elevator, plans to leave, or in any way intimidates you over this, you contact me. Do you hear me?"

Eyes wide, he looked from her to Simon and back again.

Simon just groaned and turned to Kate. "Come on. You don't have to scare the hell out of him."

"If somebody lets you get out of this building without my permission, I'll do a lot more than scare the hell out of him," she snarled, turning to look at Simon. "First, I will deal with him, and then I'll tear a couple strips off you for trying."

"I promised I'd spend forty-eight hours in bed," he declared, glaring at her.

"Good answer, and just remember"—she turned back to Edgar—"Simon's been shot, and he needs bed rest, like no movement. So, if you see him down here, you can drag him back up. Bartlett's wife is the one who did this, and anybody related to Bartlett ..." She stopped and then added in a clipped tone, "*Nobody, no one* goes up to his place at all, do you hear me?"

Edgar stared at her, wide-eyed.

"No business, no nothing, no one goes up."

Again Edgar's gaze slid over to Simon and back to Kate.

She nodded. "Yeah, he's your boss, but, in this instance, you don't want to cross me." With that, she glared at Simon and said, "Now get your ass upstairs to bed."

He snorted. "I told you what would make it a far easier

job."

"That's nice," she said. "You're shot, and I am not coming to spend the day in bed with you. I'm simply taking you up and making sure you have everything you need."

"I don't need to be mollycoddled," he snapped, as they entered the elevator.

She looked back at Edgar and gave him a wink.

Edgar's grin flashed, and Simon noted it too, standing beside her, right before the elevator doors shut and moved upward. "My life would be easier if you weren't so damn popular with my staff."

"May I remind you that they're not really even your staff? They work for the corporation that owns the building," she stated smoothly. "They just happen to really like you."

"Sure," Simon agreed, "and that has a lot of advantages, at times such as these."

"Yeah, it sure does, and also when they know that you'll be a piece of shit about following doctor's orders too."

He glared at her, but she ignored him.

When the doors opened, she walked him straight through to the bedroom and quickly helped him out of his clothing. "Do you want a shower first?"

He looked at her gratefully and nodded. "Absolutely I would love a shower."

She hesitated but then nodded. "We have to keep the bandages and the stitches dry though."

"Yeah, you got a solution for that?"

"I do," she said, as she went to the kitchen, grabbed a plastic bag and some tape, and returned to the bedroom, quickly covering his bandages. "Now this won't work for very long, but let's give it a try." And, with that, she slipped out of her clothes, stepped into the hot shower with him, helped scrub him down, and, when he was done, dried him off and helped him into pajamas, then tucked him into bed.

"Jesus," he muttered, as he sank gratefully onto the pillow.

"Yeah, I know," she whispered. "That's also why they wanted you to stay in the hospital."

He just glared at her, and she smiled.

Kate announced, "Now, I'll make a coffee, put it in the carafe, and bring it in here for you, making sure you have everything else you need, but I can't stay, no matter how much I might want to."

He waved his hand and said, "Go. Honest to God, you've been a godsend already, and I understand."

"I don't know if you do understand," she muttered, patting his cheek. "Last night was a complete shit show. We lost one cop, and another is in the hospital." He looked at her in shock, as she explained, while she set about organizing his room, setting out things she thought he might need for the day.

By the time she was done, she looked back at him and added, "So, while your messages were quite convoluted, it did send me running. So hopefully we can save the one cop but the other one? Well"—she shuddered—"he was staked to the damn cross."

SIMON WAS TOO tired from the shower and from the move back to his bed to muster too much outrage over everything that had happened while he'd been trying to recover from surgery. However, now that he was starting to feel better after a nap, the outrage was settling in, deeper and deeper. Poor Kate. She had been right there, and somehow they had missed it, and yet he could see how. They were inside, focused on being quiet, so no way that they could have known that somebody was outside. The black-and-white unit was supposed to be their eyes and ears outside, and she was counting on them to provide the information they were missing, but instead their cover unit was taken down right under their noses.

The element of surprise or something else?

Simon pondered that for a moment, but he really thought that maybe Kate's idea of a pair of killers was better, and possibly correct, but, other than sense that energy of two people sitting in that area of the church, Simon hadn't the slightest idea. It was a logical means to an end that made him think Kate might be on to something. In all of his psychic scenarios, where he'd connected, he hadn't connected once to a female killer. It'd always been to a male killer. So, how the hell did that work? Though the twosome could have been two males.

Simon lay in bed thinking about it, wondering at the wisdom of trying to meditate and see if he could connect to one of their killers. Yet a certain element of fear was involved in that, mostly because Simon wasn't up to full strength, and what he didn't want was to have another strange scenario go off the rails, as had happened earlier in the hospital. That wouldn't do his own healing any good, or his stress level for that matter. Still, it sounded as if he was doing nothing but whining, and that wasn't what he wanted to do either. He wanted to help, but what was the best way forward?

Simon settled onto his bed, opened up his senses, and reached out to the killer, calling to him openly, calling him the cop killer from the church. He didn't even know how he was supposed to call somebody like this, suddenly worried that just might result in an angry response.

Almost immediately he slammed into a furious maelstrom of someone else's thoughts. A mind with so much anger that it was hard for Simon to accept. There was such a sickness to it, such a dark depravity, that it hurt just hearing him go on and on.

"The damn cop shouldn't have been there. He fucking got what he deserved. He didn't deserve to go to heaven. None of them fucking do. I'll kill them all. Nobody here on earth should have that right to heaven, not without forgiveness for their sins. I was doing fine. Everything was right. I had checked. Nobody was there. There was no need for the cops to be there."

Simon wanted to interject some calm and some sense into that railing mind, and yet no way to even get a thought in there, not with the guy going on and on. Plus his thoughts were not coherent. One came, and then suddenly it was crossed. He had the attention span of a child, but still Simon tried. The guy hadn't even considered that maybe it was simply a random security check on a church.

"I mean, who's to say why the cop was even there? There was no reason to think they suspected." With that thought there, almost immediately the guy seemed to calm down and sensed something about another option.

"Maybe it really was random. Maybe it was just a drive-by. Maybe a suspicious vehicle was around."

Simon heard the meanderings, something in the back of his mind, as if repeating the scene.

"Hey, did you need help?"

Then Simon realized a memory movie played out in the guy's mind of meeting the cop and how that came about. He had told the cop he was fine, just that some wood was here, which he could use. The cop had come over to inspect or to help, so the killer hadn't even given him any warning. He just reached up with a sledgehammer and slammed him one. It hadn't taken him long to realize that, chances are, as a cop, he wasn't alone, and that had him locating the other cop.

He called him out of the vehicle, saying that his buddy was in trouble. The second cop had hopped out instantly, and that was it. Being of a much smaller build, the killer had immediately chosen this guy over his other choice of victims.

And, with that, Simon watched as the killer's mind calmed somewhat, churning back and forth, wondering if he'd made any mistakes, before ultimately deciding he hadn't made any mistakes at all. It wasn't his fault. It was never his fault.

"It was their own fault, the cop shouldn't have been there. It was a case of wrong place at the wrong time and, therefore, not my fault."

Simon closed his eyes, as he listened to the poison spewing about in this man's mind, a mind obviously broken from whatever trauma had occurred in his past. So many people like this guy were out there that it was hard not to feel some semblance of pain for him, some empathy for what he'd gone through that had brought him to this point.

And yet, that empathy couldn't continue if Simon were to find an answer here. Yet what answer was he supposed to find? All he could do was see if there was anything, any message that he could pick up, any words, any clue.

When he heard a phone, he reached for his own, only to realize that he was still caught up in the vision, as the other man reached for his phone and answered.

"Hey, no, it's fine. No, don't worry. ... I've got it covered. It's fine. ... but it wasn't our fault. ... I'm sorry too, but it wasn't our fault. Remember that. He shouldn't have been there. It wasn't our fault," he stated in a firm tone, trying to reassure somebody on the other end.

"Look. I'll figure it out. Just give me some time, and I'll figure it out." And, with that, he hung up and swore, getting up and pacing around the room.

Simon felt his body lift off the bed and start to walk around the room, even though he could see it floating in bed. However, caught up in his twisted vision, Simon was still separated enough from it that he could see his body lying there, yet sense this other person pacing. All he heard was *Fuck, fuck, fuck* going on and on in the killer's mind.

Simon snapped out of the vision and reached for the phone to call Kate. When she didn't answer, he sent her a text message. **There may not be two active killers, but there's at least a second person in the know.** When she phoned him back a few minutes later, he quickly explained, and she sighed.

"Sounds like there was two."

"Yes, but we don't know what the relationship is."

"No, I know," she agreed. "So, if you get another chance, you—"

"Not likely," he said. "I'll rest now." With that, he shut off the phone and settled into the covers, wishing he could take another shower to wash away all that filth. That wasn't even an option, so he curled up on the bed and slept.

CHAPTER 23

KATE STOOD BESIDE the autopsy table and listened as Smidge went over the details on the cop who had been killed. His name was Mike Johnson, he was forty-four years old, small at five feet five, maybe 120 pounds, but he was wiry, strong, and, if he'd had half a chance and knew what was happening, he would have fought back and would have done a hell of a job. She wished he'd had that chance, not so much for the perp but for the family Mike left behind.

"Looks like two heavy blows to the head and a third one right through the face," Smidge described. "That's the one that killed him."

Kate nodded and looked away from the body, as Smidge went on. "The first one would have stunned him. The second one would have been enough to keep him down, and the third one finished him off. They would have been in quick succession," Smidge added.

She looked over at him, bit her bottom lip, and nodded. "I presume that, other than that, he was healthy?"

"Very," Smidge confirmed, leaning on the table, staring at the middle-aged man on his table. "It really sucks, since, in this case, it was definitely a wrong place, wrong time deal."

"For both of the cops," she noted, "and yet they should have been aware and wary. They were on a stakeout for a reason. How could they not be?"

He nodded. "They had their reasons. That's up to you to deal with."

"No, it won't be me. I'll deal with the killer," she snapped. "The rest? That's somebody else's headache, not mine. Mike paid the ultimate price if a mistake were made, and I'm not prepared to judge him and to say he made a mistake. For all I know, something else was happening." Groaning, she looked back over at the other victim and asked, "What can you tell me about her?"

"I have an ID because it was left on her." She looked at him in surprise, and he nodded. "Yeah, either he's getting sloppy or doing too many too fast and can't keep track of what he's up to, or considering there were IDs on the first three victims, he just doesn't care, but either way it's good news for us." He handed over the ID card. "I sent you an email, with ID information on the guy in the dumpster." He looked over at her and asked carefully, "How's Simon?"

She winced. "He's alive but insisted on going home."

"Already? He just got shot."

"I know, but he doesn't do well in a hospital environment, and well, … frankly, there are only so many people I can argue with at any one time."

"I can't imagine him being in the hospital with a gift like that." Smidge looked at her for a moment, adding, "People die, and for anybody who picks up on dead people, that's got to be hell on earth."

"Which is why I took him home, where he's currently in bed. But I have to keep checking up on him to confirm he stays there," she groaned, with an eye roll.

"Or you could take some time off to oversee his care and maybe get some rest yourself in the process."

She looked down at the cop on the morgue's steel table, gently flicking a lock of his hair off his face, then shook her head. "There are no rest breaks for any of us right now," she replied. "Our killer's really ramped up since the minute he hit the ground with the first one. He hasn't quit, and we're still playing catch up," she admitted, "but we did have video cameras near the church this time. We've got a sighting of the same vehicle that we were expecting to see, and, this time, we even got a little bit of a visual on the person as he attacked Mike. From what we're seeing, data says he's small, at the five feet five to five-six range, and also fairly lightweight. Which is why this cop ended up on the cross." She turned to ask Smidge, "Is that where he died?"

"No," the coroner corrected. "He was dead already."

"What about the one in the dumpster?"

"Dead for hours and his fingerprints are in the system."

She frowned at him.

He nodded and yawned. "I've been up all night. So, here are the sheets," he said, handing her the records on paper. "The rest of it is up to you, but I really don't want to see another one of these."

"You and me both," she muttered, as she walked out, studying the details. She phoned Rodney and said, "I'm on my way in. Anybody do notice to the next of kin?"

"Yes, Lilliana went and did the two civilians, and the sergeant spoke to the family of the cop."

"Right," she noted, really glad that she wasn't Colby. "That's good. We know why Mike was there and why he's dead," she stated, taking a moment, "but, as far as the other two victims, we've got nothing."

"No, and we need to get on it."

"We've been on it. We were close. We were so damn

close. We will track that car as far as we can, and we'll see if we can come up with any idea if there are two of them."

"I'm liking that idea more all the time, but Simon is the one who sent you to that church, isn't he? So it would help if he had something new."

"Not happening." She'd thought about it, but she didn't want him involved. "He insisted on being out of the hospital, but now he's in excruciating pain and is too damn stubborn to go back and stay there. So I doubt he'll be of any help to us. He needs to focus on healing. We need to take a look at all of the churches in that area. Plus I can't quite forget the idea that maybe he would go back and give this one a second try."

"No, it would be too risky," Rodney argued. "He almost got caught."

"That might be enough to keep him away. I don't know. If he's trying to balance out his victims, then he may still need to make this one stick. It's anybody's guess at this time," she noted. "I'll be there in about twenty minutes."

She disconnected, then headed outside and made the drive down to the station. When she parked, she got out and stretched, rolling her neck to ease out the kinks, then slowly walked inside to her desk.

Lilliana took one look at her and winced.

"Yeah, I look like shit. It's fine though," she lied.

Lilliana snorted at that. "I got a couple hours, but you look like you didn't get shit."

"I got a little," she muttered. "Though between that and dealing with Simon, who insisted on leaving the hospital this morning, and damn early at that, I'm definitely feeling like there's not quite enough coffee in the world."

"Hell, you always feel that way," Lilliana stated, with a

laugh.

Kate smiled and shrugged, conceding the point. "So, one thing did come up." Kate explained about the little bit that Simon had come up with.

"That follows along with your theory pretty well, doesn't it?" Rodney pointed out.

She nodded. "Yeah, but it's no confirmation. Plus anything he's getting is potentially skewed because of the drugs, so there's a limited amount of value to it."

"I'm sure he just loves it when you say that."

"Nope, he sure doesn't, but it's a little hard for me to just blindly accept information if I can't back it up," she stated, with a snort. "And we have to do that if we expect to put away this killer. We don't want to catch him only to see him walk because we can't back it up in court."

"No, you're right there," Owen agreed, as he walked over. "And to that end, I've been working on the city camera feeds, and I did track the vehicle back to a location. It finally disappeared at this apartment building." He walked over to the big map and placed a pin on it. "Yet the registration on this vehicle is not for that address."

Everybody hopped up and crowded around the city map.

Kate nodded. "That's a location I can get behind. It's right in the middle of all the churches so far, and," she added, taking a moment, "there's what? Four more churches in that general vicinity."

"Yes, but this one"—Owen pointed, as he pinned one that was the closest of the four—"is the most likely option right now."

She pondered that and muttered, "It's possible. I have to take a drive by and see how it looks from that perspective."

"What do you mean, *that perspective?*"

"From the perspective of somebody who's trying to un-load bodies and get them inside." She explained further in an exasperated tone. "So, in this last case, I suspect that he was planning on putting them in front of the altar, like the others, but may have built the crosses in the back of the church. Then carried the crosses into the church, unloaded the bodies at the back because it's closer to the altar. Maybe even using a trolley or something like a hand truck. I don't know. What do you use something like that for?"

Owen spoke up. "Bodies, fresh bodies anyway, would be soft and bendable, so something to carry them in, like a laundry bin. I don't know."

Rodney added, "If we get our thinking caps on, I'm sure we can come up with something that would transport a dead body from a vehicle to a church."

"Even a storage box, honestly," Lilliana suggested, stop-ping, looking at them. "You know those big ones with brightly colored yellow lids?"

Owen grimaced. "I understand what you are talking about. However, I don't know that the largest of those would work. Yet it wouldn't even have to close properly, except for transporting, you know? If you were pulled over accidentally by the cops, you wouldn't want to have a body hanging out."

"No, but they're big," Lilliana noted, "and then a hand truck to move them."

They all nodded.

Kate continued. "That is starting to make a whole lot of sense. So, one trip in with the wooden crosses, one trip in with the bodies, the tools could even go on the first trip, and then done and out. They don't even have to be from the same time or the same size."

At that, Rodney turned and looked at her. "What do you mean, not the same time?"

"What if they made deliveries? What if they were delivered in the back of the church? I mean, if the wood was taken there earlier, with those dumpsters around, for all we know, the wood could have been dropped off earlier in the day or even at another point in time, so that they were ready in advance."

"But then with the cost of lumber right now, you would think he'd be in danger of it being stolen."

Lilliana pondered that and nodded. "I guess so. That would make sense too, wouldn't it?"

Kate agreed. "It really does, but that doesn't mean he hasn't got some way to make a simpler version. I think he's probably still trying it out, still testing his process. So, in this case, he didn't get them inside. Whether that's because of the cops being there, so our killer needed to make it a quick fast job, or for some other reason, I don't know." Kate raised both hands in frustration. "Trying to see inside these broken minds isn't the easiest thing."

At that came a cough and the clearing of a throat behind her.

She turned to see Colby, glaring at her. "I know," she admitted. "I need to go talk to the shrink.'

"You sure do." Colby checked his watch. "We'll expect to hear your report in two hours." She glared at him, and he all but barked, "Get going."

She groaned, grabbed a notepad and a pen, and headed down to see if she could get a slot, while privately hoping against it. She had no real reason not to, except that she was still smarting from the last case, the pedophile psychiatrist, where it seemed pretty obvious that the last thing Kate wanted anything to do with was anyone in that profession.

As it was, his receptionist smiled at her and pointed. "You can go on in."

When she walked inside, he looked up, smiled, and said, "Wow, it must really be a cold day in hell if you're here."

She glared at him, and he laughed.

"Sorry, bad joke. Come on in." He waved to the chair and continued. "Have a seat and tell me what's wrong."

"What's wrong is that we have a dead cop, an injured cop, and a killer who keeps dropping more bodies in our lap." He stared in shock, as she nodded and confirmed, "Same case." Then she quickly brought him up to speed. "So, who is this guy?"

He stared at her, shook his head, and replied, "I mean, I can give you a part of the answer, but how sure are you that it's two people?"

"I'm not sure, not sure at all, but I keep thinking I'm sure."

"And when you say you're thinking you're sure …"

"I mean one person could have done this, in the sense that it's certainly possible." She gave him the rundown on the little bit that she had and then asked his opinion. "I don't really have any reason to think it's two, it's just … I don't know." She shrugged.

He looked at her over his glasses and nodded. "We need more than just your hunch or feeling or even input from a psychic," he stated, with an eye roll, and that told her how much he knew about her.

She stiffened and glared at him. "Obviously I don't have near enough," she snapped.

"No, you need more, then still more after that before it ever goes to trial."

"We must have it all locked down, so I was ordered to bring it to you to see what your take is on it."

At the word *ordered*, his eyebrows shot up. "You still can't come see me willingly, *huh*?"

"Not particularly, no," she admitted, "and, so far, you haven't helped as much as *my psychic* has, but maybe you could take care of that part of your job. Now."

"Absolutely," he murmured, as he stared at her. "I don't really want to be fighting with you all the time."

"That's good," she noted, "because I have no intention of fighting with you all the time either." She had said it so smoothly that it was almost too fast for him to catch on the first go, and he blinked. She withheld her smile and waited.

He looked down at his watch, not sure how to respond for a moment, then spoke. "Obviously your killer has a disturbed mind, somebody who's got a strong religious background, and is either trying to get people to repent and to forgive what was done to them or to forgive him for what he's doing to them," the shrink suggested. "We don't have enough to go on to determine which way that's working."

She nodded. "That's our take on it at this point, as well."

"In other words, I haven't added anything extra."

"Why the churches?"

"Forgiveness, the concept of heaven. Consider that he's trying to open the gates for his victims."

"And why these victims?"

"Have you found anything that connects them?"

"No," she said hesitatingly, "I thought we had because, prior to these last two, we thought BDSM was the connection, and that it was some bondage-gone-wrong thing, or people who enjoyed paying for sex, or even someone abused who turned to BDSM. It was a solid avenue for us. Our killer may be thinking that he's somehow locked into this and had a judgment against people who were involved, and it was his way of punishing them."

"And that's possible, but what about this one witness who was involved with some of them?"

"Billy Roy. He wasn't involved with the others at all," she pointed out. "Then we were looking at the husband of someone in a BDSM group who sounded right, but we can't put him anywhere close, and his alibi is rock solid."

"It may not have anything to do with him, but that doesn't mean he doesn't have asshole rights on his own."

"I'm pretty sure he does," she stated quietly, "but I can't do anything to help her if she's not willing to make a move on her own."

"Of course not," he agreed. "I see that all the time in my practice as well."

"Something I don't quite understand is why these women stay."

"They stay because they don't see any other option," he explained, lifting his head from the paperwork. "They stay because there is security in the devil they know, whereas the big bad world out there could be way worse, but it just hasn't gotten to the point where it's bad enough. You don't understand because you simply cannot get that kind of dependency or desperation or possibly just depression. You're an independent woman with the ability to protect and defend yourself, so the very idea strikes you as alien."

"*Not bad enough*," she repeated, her stomach churning, "yet bad enough that you would start psychoanalyzing me, so please refrain from that." The doctor raised his hand and nodded in apology, as she continued. "How can it not be bad enough when you get bashed around and you can't even think straight for the abuse that you're going through?"

"Because it's also what they know, it's what they've become accustomed to. A little nip here and there, and nobody really understands how devastating that can be, but, by the time there's another smack or two, they become prone to thinking they deserve it," he stated, with such sorrow in his tone that Kate felt the rightness of his analysis. "And that's all part of the insidiousness of this. These people are afraid that they deserve everything coming at them because that's what they've been conditioned to think. It's not like a choice, but, at some point in time, they just believe it. These guys are very adept at this kind of grooming. In fact, some of them are exceptionally good at it."

"Is there any way we can have a victim here who's following the orders of somebody else?"

He looked at her with interest. "Why would you say that?"

She shrugged. "I'm just back to wondering if we're dealing with two people."

"So, you're not thinking of two active people. You're thinking that somebody might have a hold on the other."

"I don't know if it's a hold but maybe a bond with the abuse but then broke free. And the one can't do this fantasy work on their own. But still having roots in the same abuse and fantasies of grandeur, they need somebody like this guy to do it."

"Yet he's not big."

"He's not big, but he's bigger than his victims, even than his partner in all this, which is why I'm wondering if we don't have a male-female or maybe a male couple here."

He nodded. "Considering that, up until this last case, we've had an established couple in each church, that kind of makes sense. … The death of a child could possibly have triggered it," he noted.

That struck home, as she had tried to forget about Daniel, when he had been a critical part of the equation.

"I'm pretty sure that all your answers will go back to those first three murders."

"Oh, I agree," she stated, with thoughts running rampant in her mind, "but the first cases aren't always that easy to sort through."

"No, that's true."

She stood up. "But I think you're right, and, if that was the trigger, who did it trigger and who did the triggering?"

"There had to be somebody who would know about the little boy's harsh existence. Plus how did the killer get the body out of the house, unless of course he was close by, either geographically or had befriended them. Don't you think?"

"Exactly." And before the shrink had a chance to add anything, Kate was already heading out the door.

Behind her, he called out, "Wait. You want a report?"

"Email it," she called back, already on the stairs, headed back to her office. She headed straight for the big whiteboard. She tagged the little boy's picture up on the board and spoke to the team around her in a frenzy.

"Daniel's the trigger, and, for whatever reason, what happened to him triggered all this," she muttered out loud. "So, we need everything we can find about that little boy."

"Sure, and we've got a lot of it already. The mother was devastated that she lost him. Apparently she was trying to get off drugs, but didn't manage to until she lost him. The father is also devastated that he lost him."

"Do we have any idea who else may have had the little

boy?"

"No, he never went into the system. Mary Brown just took over his care for her brother. In cases like that, it often happens, and we don't ever have any paperwork about it," Owen stated, coming up behind her.

"Let's check out every place that Daniel has lived in the last five years, while with his family, and let's track down more on the father. I need to know where he's been for the last five years too."

"Do you think he did it?" Lilliana asked, frowning. "That doesn't seem logical to me. He could have done it at any time while the child was living with him."

Kate sighed. "He might have effectively killed the little boy through abuse and starvation his whole life, and that is a big if, but that doesn't mean Daniel's father is responsible for all these killings."

"No," Owen agreed, "but it goes back to Daniel somehow. It goes back to this little boy, who was the trigger. So, who did it trigger, and who could still be being triggered by Daniel's abuse and death?"

"Somebody else who's been abused," Kate began. "Somebody else who barely survived the abuse. Somebody who watched and couldn't do anything about somebody else being abused," she suggested, turning to look at the team who was all standing there, staring at her. "There has to be something here that we're missing."

"There's always something here we're missing," Rodney stated in disgust. "Otherwise there wouldn't be as many victims as we have right now."

"Including two of our own," Owen muttered from the side.

"Smidge already had the ID on the woman but found

our victim from the dumpster in the system. So we need to check the report he sent out. We'll need to get the first family's pictures out and circulated, to find out where they lived and start putting this together."

Kate continued. "These people are connected somehow, even if only through the fact that they have the same killer," she announced, "but, once we find out what the bigger connection is, it'll all make sense."

Everyone watched as Kate worked in a frenzy. When she got like that, things tended to happen, and everybody raised their game.

"Are you sure about that?" Lilliana asked, staring at the board. "I don't see how this can make sense to anybody."

Kate replied, "What if the Billy Roy angle plays in with the intended couple at this last church?"

"*Oh-kay.*" Lilliana was nodding now. "That helps. Let me see. I'll call our torture dominatrix and run these names by him. Not the cops, but our couple."

Kate nodded. "Billy Roy doesn't think he's central to this, yet he may be a side topic of interest to our killer. This all makes sense to him in his demented mind. I know that I don't have any reason to say it, but keep your eyes open for the killer being a pair. I've still got just this suspicion that it's a pair of people, but, the more I think about it, the more it seems that this is not just an idea."

"But, if that's the case, one might just be an observer."

"Most likely," Rodney added in a clipped tone.

"Or a handler. Or somebody who can't do it on their own, and they need help, and he's doing it to help her maybe," Kate said, speaking slowly, sounding out the theory in her head. "Or maybe he or she, … whoever was abused, maybe this is payback somehow."

"By what?" Owen asked. "By killing all these people? That's not payback. That's a very sick mind."

"But we already know that," Lilliana piped up, turning on him. "It's got to be a very sick mind because this is not what sanity looks like. This is madness at its core, but it has to make sense to our killers." Lilliana held up a hand. "Our dominator is not answering his phone, probably torturing some poor woman as we speak. But he'll call back, as he loves being involved. Oh, one thing I found on our Billy Roy was a prior record. It didn't show up at first because it was opened and shut, no further action. Basically a cleared file or a purged file, so you have to go one layer down. Anyway he was arrested for his sexual proclivities. It didn't stick, since the only one complaining was some cop who stumbled upon it."

Kate's eyebrows raised. "Interesting. I want to talk to him."

"So do I," Lilliana agreed. "However, he's dropped off the face of the earth."

"Damn I forgot about that part." Kate frowned at that. "See what else you can turn up on the investigating officer." She then turned to Rodney and said, "I'm heading off to check out the apartment building where the car ended up."

"We don't know which apartment, so it's anybody's guess," Rodney warned, "and he could have just parked there anyway to ditch the vehicle."

"Let's go find out," Kate stated. "If I have to knock on every door, then it's still worth anything we can get from this." She turned to look at Owen and Lilliana. "Follow up on Roy and these latest victims, plus that missing cop, will you?" She pointed to the city map. "Also start mapping out with every address we have for our crucified victims, the churches and their homes, and see where that apartment building is as related to previous murders, while keeping an eye on the closest churches for future murders. The killers were interrupted last time, so it's possible they may go back to the places they're familiar with."

At that, Reese came in, and, having heard Kate's last words, announced to the team, "I already did the mapping. It's right smack dab in the center." She walked over to the map, placing pins in the locations for the homes of the first two sets of victims. "We also have an ID on our John Doe in the morgue. And my first look at him doesn't fit the pattern at all."

Lilliana hopped up. "I'll take a second look, do a deeper dive. I've got to find a missing cop anyway." She looked from Reese to Kate and Rodney. "You guys go to the apartment building and see what you can come up with."

With that, Kate nodded at Rodney and then looked at Owen and said, "Text us anything that comes up. This feels good. It feels right, like maybe we've got a break now finally. So let's get this asshole before he comes after another one of us."

And with that, Kate bolted out the door.

SIMON WOKE UP, stretched his good arm, then lifted his sore arm, wincing with pain. He knew it would be a while before he could even get into therapy to start working on that shoulder. He got out of bed, walked into the kitchen, and realized there was no damn food. He quickly placed an order at Mama's to have it delivered and then put on a pot of coffee.

As he walked into the living room, he sat down and

looked out at the beautiful scenery, yet slipped almost immediately into seeing four walls, just walls. They were not his walls but somebody else's. He froze and stared at the walls, but they were just this dark color, and yet he was at a doorway, looking around, and noted a bed, with somebody small on it.

He tried to see closer, but the vision kept shifting. When the voice from the bed rang in his ears, he flinched.

"Are you ready?"

The man in his vision murmured, "Yes."

"Are you sure?"

"Yes."

"Okay." The person on the bed shifted, sat up, and lifted her arms.

The man in the vision walked to her, bent down, and she looped her arms around his neck. He picked up this person, almost a child, carried her to a wheelchair, and plunked her down, then proceeded to wheel her out into the kitchen.

Simon studied everything he could see. The wheelchair was old, and the carpet was frayed, showing wear from the wheels. The windows were covered with a sheet, not curtains. The paint was dingy and peeling off the walls. As they pushed forward into the living room, Simon saw light from the living room windows, yet all he could see was another building across the road.

He peered at the building, trying to recognize something to distinguish it, but it was a rundown area, and the building was an off-green color, not any different than a million other old apartment buildings.

In the vision, the man pushed the wheelchair, which squeaked into the kitchen, and he proceeded to pull out the makings of a sandwich. There was restfulness in the man's mind, the anger having been burnt out, and a normal conversation took place about what to put on the sandwiches. She wheeled herself to the table on her own, and he joined her with the sandwiches.

Simon felt like a visitor, watching somebody's private life, as they talked about a TV show. *A TV show? What the hell?* Simon thought, thoroughly confused.

He wanted them to turn so he could see more about the outside, but he hadn't been able to catch a decent glimpse of the woman's face. As the man in the vision raised his sandwich to take a bite, he lifted his gaze and looked directly at the woman. Simon's heart froze as he studied it, trying hard to memorize the small heart-shaped face, the dark hair, the fatigue, and what looked like a lifetime of pain on her face. He winced as he realized that this was likely a brother and a sister combo, rather than a husband and wife or even lovers.

She was eating, but she was ripping pieces off and stuffing them into her mouth because it seemed like her jaw wouldn't open wide enough to take in the sandwich, even an open-faced one. She chewed slowly. Her sandwich was just peanut butter on one slice of bread, literally just being ripped into pieces and popped into her mouth. Whereas the man in this vision—who Simon embodied—watched her eat, while the man took great big gulping bites of his sandwich.

When she was only one-third of the way through her sandwich, she put it down again. When he glared at her, she shrugged, then sat back with a meek smile. "I'll keep eating. Don't worry."

"I do worry," he muttered. "You're not doing very well."

"I'm not likely to do very well ever again, and you know

it," she muttered. "My time's coming to an end, and you must make plans for yourself."

"I'm not making plans," he argued. "Besides, we've got our own plans."

She gave him a small smile, and then the smile fell away. "We messed up."

He shook his head.

Even in that act, it was hard for Simon to even keep his eyes open. Then Simon realized his eyes *weren't* open, and the vision was all encompassing.

"We didn't mess up," the man said. "That cop did."

"We killed a cop, who just wanted to help you." She stared at him, her face screwing up, not quite in tears, but in deep sadness. The ever-abiding sadness of somebody who saw an end in sight, but it wasn't an end that she liked.

"So what?" he snapped. "It was his fault." The anger flared on the inside, and his thoughts were escalating, just as they did the other day.

She groaned. "You can't always blame everybody else."

"We went down this pathway for the right reasons," he snapped, his tone like granite. "I'm not changing now."

"But maybe we should," she suggested softly. "It doesn't feel right anymore."

"Why not?" he asked, looking at her in surprise. "What difference does it make?"

"We killed a cop," she repeated, "an *innocent* cop."

"They're all *not* innocent," he pointed out.

"Yes and no," she replied. "We're trying to find people who needed saving, people whose lives were so difficult that they were better off dead, and that's not an easy thing. We were trying to save these people, but then—"

"*You* were trying to save them. However, I'm not sure.

Well, … I'm not particularly interested in saving them."

She stared at him.

"I'm doing this for you, you know? You've had nothing good in your life, so if this makes you happy," he explained, "I'm happy to do it."

"What do you mean?" she asked, her voice a soft and horrified whisper.

"I just mean that I'm doing this for you."

"No, no, no." She frowned at that. "You're doing this for you too."

"No, I'm doing this *for you.*"

She sat back, and Simon could only imagine the horror in her thoughts. These words were not what she wanted to hear.

She stared down at her sandwich and winced. "Maybe I won't eat more after all."

"Eat," he said softly, "otherwise you won't live very long."

"I won't live very long anyway," she pointed out, looking up at him in pain. "You know that. You're supposed to be making plans for yourself."

"I am," he confirmed, "just not necessarily the plans you want to hear."

"You can't keep doing this," she said. "You'll get caught."

"I won't get caught," he stated, with a shrug.

"It's not easy, to keep hiding what we're doing. It's not supposed to be easy. We're supposed to be helping people."

"No," he repeated, "*you*'re helping people, at least that's what you want to think. But really this is your anger that you're taking out on the world around you. I mean, maybe it helps you sleep at night to think that you're helping people, but you're not, and, deep down, you know it. The only reason you're having second thoughts is because of that damn cop."

"What if we get the wrong victims again? When we couldn't find the last one, and you just grabbed somebody, a man who may or may not have been the right fit?"

"It doesn't matter," he said, "because I have my own anger issues too, and I'm quite happy to get rid of them this way as well."

She stared at him, and tears came to her eyes.

Immediately Simon felt the man's remorse, as his hand reached across to hold hers gently.

"Sorry," he muttered, "but you know we have our own issues here, our own problems, our own needs. This is not just about you. It's about both of us."

"I know," she whispered, "but I was hoping that this would make me feel better." She stared at him, and her bottom lip trembled. "We're supposed to be helping them."

"By sending them home, yes," he said, as another wave of remorse washed over him, "but you can't know for sure that these people wanted to die."

"We know that little boy died in pain and agony, and he wanted to die a long time ago," she whispered, tears slipping free, "and we could have ended his suffering earlier."

He squeezed her hand, and Simon could almost hear him in the background crying too for the little boy.

"We could have," he whispered gently, "and we should have. It would have been easier."

"You know the rest of the world would say we should have called the cops," she added, "and that they would have come and helped him."

"But we also know about bad cops and know that even

good cops wouldn't have done enough, letting Daniel's abuse go on for years. Nobody looked after that little boy. His own family did this to him. Poor Daniel. … He suffered right to the end."

She nodded. "You're right, and that's why we started this. However, those people last night"—she choked on her words—"one of them didn't want to die. We know that."

"No, we don't know that," he argued in a snappish retort.

"That cop didn't want to die," she pointed out.

The man in the vision snorted. "He's a cop, so he wants to die," he declared. "When they take the damn job, they are ready to die. Those blue-blooded bastards are always walking into gunfights, so how is what I did any different?"

"Being willing to and wanting to are different things," she muttered, wiping at her tears.

"And that's what's changed it for you?"

"That plus the fact you literally just found somebody. Even though he wasn't in our parameters and wasn't supposed to die, and we weren't helping him at all. We were just killing him. We took something we shouldn't have. We took his life."

He just stared at her, then shrugged. "It's all done now, so I can't change it."

"No, you can't change it, but you also don't want to."

He looked up at her, smiled, and nodded. "No, you're right. Doing this, doing something, it feels good," he admitted, his voice turning harsh. "It feels so very good."

She winced but nodded in agreement. "You're right. It does. … It feels good, even if it's for all the wrong reasons— and that scares me."

"That's okay." He smiled, then proceeded to pat her

cheeks, wiping away the tears and gently cleaning her face with his hands, with affection. "You won't be around much longer, so you won't have to worry about it," he said. "So anytime you want me to fix it so that you're good and ready to go, you just tell me."

She sighed, then looked down at her little sandwich and shared, "Almost every morning I wake up and think it'll be today, that I'll ask you today, and then somehow I get through the day, and I'm thinking, … we'll see how I feel in the morning."

"So, that means you're not ready yet," he noted, "and I'm not pushing you. Believe me. I want you around for as long as you want to be."

"But really you don't. I'm a lot of work for you, and I know that."

"I'm happy to do the work," he stated firmly, his tone getting harder as he looked at her. "Don't you ever think otherwise."

She gave a long sigh and nodded. "You've been the best brother."

"We didn't have anybody else," he noted quietly. "It's always just been us."

"That's why I worry about what will happen to you when I'm gone," she admitted, looking at him and wiping her thin hair off her face. "I don't know what you'll do after I'm gone, but it worries me."

"Don't let it worry you one bit," he reassured her, with a smile that stretched across his face. *God, she is so naïve and innocent.* But he loved her and would keep her in the dark, so she could die happy. That was everything to him.

"This is making you feel better, but killing them? That's making me feel better," he stated with conviction, "and I have a right to feel better too. So, I'll keep doing what I'm doing, as long as I can."

"But we shouldn't be hurting people," she cried out softly. "We shouldn't be taking people, not like that. Not the ones who don't want saving."

"We are saving people because that's what you want," he repeated. "That's not what I care about. Still, I'm not doing anything outside of what you want me to do while you're alive and well," he stated, giving her a bright smile. "So, it's just more incentive for you to stay alive longer."

She laughed at that, picked up a bit more of her sandwich, and shoved it inside her mouth, struggled to chew.

She probably had had her jaw broken, and, with that, the mix in Simon's mind crashed, sending him tumbling back in time to his own living room.

CHAPTER 24

K ATE WALKED INTO the target apartment building, seeking the car that led her here, as her phone rang. She looked down to see it was Simon. "Simon?"

"Yeah. You got a minute?"

"I do. What's up?" She continued to walk in with Rodney, as he headed off to the manager's office. She walked behind him but a little bit away, so she could talk to Simon.

"I just connected," he said in an exhausted voice, "and it's kind of ugly, Kate. I feel like I have to wash inside out to get free of his thoughts."

"Of course it's ugly," she agreed, understanding full well how he felt. "Believe me. We're seeing the ugliness on this side. What did you get?"

She watched as Rodney knocked on the manager's door, and someone stepped out to talk to him. "We're at an apartment building right now, where we last tracked the vehicle involved in last night's murders at the latest church," she shared. "Finally we got a little help from some cameras."

"Interesting. I don't suppose another apartment building around you has a dingy greenish look, about a medium-rare parrot color. I don't even know how high it goes, but maybe less than ten stories?"

She looked around and out a nearby window. "Yes, there is one, why?"

"Because it could be that you're in the right place."

She stiffened, then looked around, noting the manager still talking to Rodney. "What else do you have to identify who and what we're talking about? Because remember, we've already got one cop down and another one in the hospital."

"I know. All I can tell you is ... I didn't see what *he* looks like, but I saw her."

"Shit."

"Yeah, she's crippled, handicapped in some way, with some debilitating condition, and she won't live all that much longer, based on the conversation I heard," Simon shared. "They're doing these killings because of her. She wants to save other people, before they suffer and die terrible deaths. He is doing it because of her, but really he's quite happy to murder because it gives him a vent for his anger."

"Well, shit, so that's why it was coming across with such a confusing motivation. There are two of them, and they're in it for very different reasons."

"Exactly," Simon agreed. "Listen. I don't have any idea what he looks like, but she's small, with a heart-shaped face and dark hair. I won't say hunched but very diminutive in stature. He picks her up out of the bed and carries her to a wheelchair. She can hardly open her jaw very well. Maybe it was broken at some time. She talks fairly well but struggles to eat. She was ripping off a little bit of peanut butter on bread and putting it in her mouth. I'm not sure she can eat more than that."

"So, her situation and her final wishes are what triggered her partner then?"

"No, no, because his plan is to help her out whenever she says she's ready. He's planning on killing her, to save her in a way. However, that first little boy is what triggered this.

They're upset that they didn't kill him and end his suffering much sooner. They were of the opinion that calling the cops would do absolutely nothing, so that was not an option."

"Well, shit," she muttered after ending the call. She turned to find Rodney asking for information on the tenants. She stepped up behind him and interrupted their conversation. "Do you have somebody here in a wheelchair?"

The manager nodded. "Yes, I do, a young woman. I can't remember what the problem is, but her brother looks after her."

"What's the apartment number?" she asked, her voice urgent. Rodney looked back at her intently, letting her do the talking, since she clearly knew something he didn't.

"Fourth floor." He frowned, obviously uneasy at the sudden questioning.

In a much harsher tone, she shook her head. "What number?"

He looked at her in surprise, then grabbed his paperwork. "It's 402. You just go up the main stairs, and it's the first one on the right."

"Good enough." Kate nodded and dragged Rodney out with her. Even as she moved, she dialed the rest of her team. As soon as Kate and Rodney were in the stairwell and had a little bit of privacy, she explained what she'd learned to all of them, overheard by Rodney, as they raced up the stairs.

"We have a good idea of who it is," she shared. "This last bit comes from Simon, but he identified a woman who is in a wheelchair, quite incapacitated, and a brother looking after her, as being our main acting perp, but both of them are in on the whole of it," she explained. "We'll go talk to them, but I need something, anything, to get us a warrant to get in there."

"You won't get it based on Simon's version," Lilliana said in exasperation. "And this won't help either, but here you go. That missing cop was reprimanded for his mishandling of the investigation in Billy Roy's BDSM activities, not too long before the cop went missing. And Billy Roy did intimately know both of our civilian victims in this latest church murder, which he was more than happy to share with me. He got his bi-fantasy and a three-way with them."

"That's what I mean. I need something on these two related to the murders and the car used last night. Find out anything you can about the occupants of 402," she stated, "including about the car."

At that, she hung up, and they raced upstairs. As they got up to the apartment, she stopped, just as a text came through. It was from Lilliana. "Warrant coming through, and we got it based on the vehicle. It's his, your guy in 402. And we got his and her name from the apartment lease."

Kate stopped, asked Rodney, "Why would they use their own vehicle?"

Rodney frowned and shook his head. "I'm not sure," he admitted in confusion. "It's quite possible that they're just arrogant enough to think it won't matter or …" He frowned. "But you're right. That's odd. They could have taken anybody else's vehicle or used a different one each time for that matter."

She nodded, and, as they walked up to the apartment door, she asked him, "How long do you think we'll have to wait for the warrant?"

"Depends," Rodney replied, "but I assume they'll be on this one really fast." They walked to the end of the hall and then back up again, checking things out. Through a window on the landing, she pointed out the apartment building close by. Sure enough, it was a green color, a mixture of light green and gray really, about the same height of the building they were in.

She sent a picture of it to Simon and got a thumbs-up back again. Something about this still didn't quite fit, but, as soon as Lilliana texted that they had the warrant, Kate walked to apartment 402 and knocked. There was no answer. Swearing, she knocked again and heard a faint reply coming from inside. Then slowly the door opened, being awkwardly moved backward by someone in a wheelchair.

Kate opened the door a little bit wider, smiled at the woman, and asked, "Hi, are you Sully?"

She nodded. "Yes, I am. What can I do for you?"

Kate looked at her with a big smile. "Where's your brother?"

The woman shrugged. "He's at work or he should be. He will be home soon enough though."

"Okay, and where does he work?"

The woman looked at her suspiciously. "Who are you? Why do you want him?"

Kate held out her badge and introduced herself and Rodney. "We need to speak with your brother and with you."

Sully eyed Kate quietly and then nodded in resignation. "Oh."

"We have a warrant to come in and to search the premises."

At that, the woman in the wheelchair grabbed her cell phone.

However, Kate stepped forward and pulled it from her hand, then read her the warrant parameters. She then raised the phone and declared, "You won't be making any calls.

And my partner will search the premises, per the warrant, while I ask you some questions." Kate nodded to Rodney, who took off to start his search.

"I need a lawyer," she snapped. "I want a lawyer right away."

"And you'll get one, once we take you down to the main station," Kate replied, "but right now I need your brother. Where is he?"

"You won't find my brother," she said, with a laugh. "He's dead."

Kate stopped and looked at her. Sully perplexed her by laughing and laughing and laughing.

"God, you guys don't know anything, do you?"

"We know lots of things," Kate corrected. "Maybe not everything but we're filling in the blanks as we go."

Sully just shook her head and collapsed back into her wheelchair. Almost a sense of relief took over her face.

"You're happy that it's over, aren't you?" Kate asked.

"Oh, it's not over. He won't stop."

"Who is he?"

Sully just stared and remained silent.

"Okay, so what happened to your brother?" Kate asked her.

"He died about seven months ago in a car accident. ... *Seven months ago.* That's when everything started to shift."

"In what way?"

"My brother's fatal accident involved many people, Mr. Brown too, and that's how we found out more about the little boy. We knew about Daniel's plight long before that because my brother had been a neighbor to Daniel, friends with him. After my brother's death, I reconnected with Daniel and his family, checking on Mr. Brown too, who had been involved in this same multi-car accident as well. But he survived and felt horribly guilty about it all."

"You say your brother is dead, yet you keep mentioning *your brother*, the one at work, who should be home soon." This was garbled and didn't make any sense.

"My brother was dead, so what could we do?"

Kate frowned, remaining silent, just letting her talk.

"Then we found out more about the little boy and saw how badly he looked. The poor little soul." Sully was in tears.

Kate just let her be.

"When Daniel died, I thought my heart would die with him," she muttered. "We'd gone over there to see him several times—well, to try and see him—but the Browns told us to leave and to never come back again. My heart broke, but we kept going back, kept trying to see the little boy, kept trying to do something, and then, all of a sudden, he was gone."

"Daniel had died?"

"Yes. We should have done something earlier, much earlier. Anything to end his suffering."

"Or you could have called for help," Kate added, staring at Sully in shock. Simon had been perfectly right on. "I mean, how can you even think that death was preferable when he had a whole life ahead of him?"

"A life of what?" Sully screamed.

That shrill reply still rang in Kate's ears.

"After all the damage that had been done to him? Have you seen him? Have you? He would be like me," she snapped, and then her voice broke, the bitterness over-whelming. "Do you think I want to be like this? This is what happened after my father beat the crap out of me, over and over again," she snapped. "I may look like I'm eighty, but

I'm only twenty-two."

In reality, Kate thought Sully appeared to be more like a child. However, Sully was right. She looked rough.

"I've been in such pain all my life," she bellowed in a bitter fit, "and it never stops."

"So, this man, … this man who helps you, he's not your brother."

"No, he's my partner. Somebody who loves me, … for who I am."

"Even if that love is twisted?"

"It's not twisted love," she cried out. "Love is love, Detective. He's got his own issues because he was abused himself. We are all broken here, and he understands what I'm going through."

"Of course, and what about all these other people, your victims? How is it that you can just decide to put them out of their misery? How can you make a judgment like that on their behalf?"

"Because obviously they're incapable of doing it themselves," she noted in surprise, as if Kate were completely naïve, "any more than I am capable."

"So, who is he?"

"He is my protector, like he tried to protect Daniel. He promised me that he'd take care of me when the time came," she muttered, with affection, "so you have to let him do that." Sully grabbed Kate's hand. "You have to let him do that."

"Why is that?" Kate asked, looking down at Sully. It was hard to find answers when Sully had unceremoniously made herself judge and jury, killing people mindlessly, without even a thought to who these people were and what lives they could have had. "You could have helped that little boy while he was still alive, but you didn't. You could have helped each of these people, could have done something positive to help them get away from their abusers. Instead you killed them."

"You had your chance, Detective, so you can hardly talk. You could have helped them all, but you didn't. The police don't care." Sully glared at her.

Kate was not sure how to respond to her allegation, as Sully continued.

"You people don't give a shit about children who are abused or about parents who are abusers or pedophiles, none of that. These men just walk out of jail again and keep hurting people, and you don't care. I mean, you think I haven't seen it?"

Kate had to concede the point, but the logic was twisted and turned. Yet something was here, so Kate let Sully vent.

"You think I haven't figured out that the cops rule and that it doesn't matter what the hell we do or say? That it doesn't make any damn bit of difference? Our lives are completely shot anyway."

At that, Kate studied her, and a horrible feeling crossed her heart. "Your dad, he was a cop, wasn't he?"

"Oh, yeah, he was a cop all right. He thought he was somebody special," she spat, with a sneer. "But we showed him in the end, and we showed him good who he really was."

"You killed your dad?"

She nodded. "Yeah, I did, though it took a bit." She laughed, and her expression turned almost cheerful, as she smiled so sweetly. "I mean, it wasn't planned. It was just one of those things that happened. I couldn't function anymore, but Peter finished it for me," Sully explained.

Peter. So they got a name for her partner in crime at the

very least, and now Kate needed the last name.

"We all lived in the same neighborhood back then. Where Daniel was too. Peter came in one day to visit me, when the beating was happening, and my father just wouldn't stop. I couldn't lift a hand. I was too terrified, and it's not as if I could have done anything anyway, but Peter ..." Her face lit up like a Christmas tree at the memory. "Peter just walked over and slammed him hard in the face a couple times, and that was it. His face just exploded. I mean, we didn't intend to do it, and Peter was protecting me, but we also knew that, if the cops found out, there would be no end to it."

Kate stared at her. "So, where is your partner now? Where is Peter now that you need him here?"

Sully shrugged and smiled. "It doesn't matter. ... I have to give him a chance to do his thing first."

"Really? So he gets to go kill more people just because he likes it now?"

Sully stared at Kate in horror. "How do you know that?" Sully asked in a hoarse whisper. "How do you know that he likes it?"

Kate's lips quirked. "I told you, Sully. We know a lot. We're just at the end stage of trying to stop you, to ensure that you don't go killing anybody else."

"We are not killing them," she bellowed, and Kate plugged her ears. "We're saving them. We are ..." Sully's voice broke, and she put a hand to her jaw.

The effort seemed to have exhausted her. She was nothing but a shell, and it showed.

"Anyway you're probably too late," Sully whispered in a hysterical voice.

"If you don't tell us where Peter is, he won't have any

opportunity to help you, and that's what you said you wanted."

"I do want it. I do," she wailed. "I don't want to go to jail like this. I beg you, … please let him. We have an agreement."

"No, I can't imagine that jail will be much fun," Kate noted, focused on Sully. "It'll probably be beyond nasty, but jail is where you belong, when you've killed so many people."

"You have to help me." She grabbed Kate's hand and squeezed hard. "You have to help me."

"I don't have to help you do anything," Kate declared, staring at her in disgust. "I get it. You have a shitty life, but you killed the one person responsible, and now, instead of being satisfied with that, you're off killing other people."

"I'm not killing them. I'm saving them. Why can't you understand that?"

"So, why carve *Forgive* on them?"

"Peter did the killings for me, to save these people. He added the *Forgive* to forgive him—because of all the things he was doing to them. He wanted to be forgiven."

"You know that he beats them first."

"Yes, of course," she confirmed, looking at Kate in surprise. "But he drugs them too. He found drugs on that first couple and took them, knew he could use them. I could use them too."

Kate sighed. Then again Sully was out of her mind.

"How else would these couples understand? Beatings are all they understand."

"The men too? The women maybe but why the men?" At that, Kate glared at Sully, a deep disgust rolling off her in waves.

Sully shook her head. "Not Roger. Peter didn't beat Roger because Roger was not an abuser."

"Yet he watched his own wife beat Daniel. How do you explain that?"

Sully went silent.

"I don't understand how the abused becomes the abusers. How could you do that? How could you become that? Is that all you understand, being beaten and broken?"

"Yes," she whispered. "The men? They didn't stop the abuse. Some liked the abuse. Others loved it."

"Does Peter beat you?"

"No, of course not. He loves me."

"These people you and Peter killed were also loved, you know?" Kate pointed out, shaking her head at Sully. "I have no easy answers right now for you. If you don't tell me where Peter is, and I mean damn fast," Kate said in threatening tone, "there won't be any help I can offer you at all. You'll go to jail, where you'll sit and suffer, until whenever you end up expiring naturally."

"No, no, no," she cried out, shaking her head.

"Then tell me where Peter is," Kate repeated, her voice hard. "You want me to help you, right? Why not help me to help you?"

"I can't. I can't. I won't."

At that, Rodney came back from the bedroom and held up a bag of drugs in one hand and a pay stub in the other, raising one eyebrow at Kate. "These drugs might match with what the coroner found in our victims. And this pay stub? Our guy works for a cleaning company."

Kate turned to Sully. "Does he clean churches, by any chance?"

Sully's face fell, and she nodded slowly. "Yes, he's part of the crew who cleans churches, and that's how he gets into all of them. He has keys to the storerooms and the basement doors."

She nodded. "And the car he drives?"

"It was my brother's," she whispered. "We figured that nobody would know."

"So, what then?" Rodney asked. "You just kept up the registration in a dead man's name?"

"You can do it all online now," she stated, looking up at him. "The pandemic changed all that, and apparently there isn't any need to declare his death."

"Shit," Kate muttered, turning to Rodney. "Just as our job starts to sort itself out, things get harder."

He nodded. "I'll call the cleaning company and find out where he is."

"You do that," Kate replied. "I'll just sit here beside Sully, and you can send in the forensics crew."

"They're on the way."

Kate smiled down at Sully and began with more questions. "So, do you want to tell me something else about all these killings? For example, how did you pick your victims? How did you find out what was going on in their lives?" And, with that, Kate sat down and tried to get as much information as she could. It was hard because, somewhere in her heart, she did find a certain amount of sympathy for Sully, this sad little figure, but Kate still couldn't condone what she'd done or the way she'd done it. "By the way, what was your father's name?"

"Why?" Sully sneered at her.

"So I can close the case, for one thing."

"You're not likely to find it open anyway. Peter put him in his vehicle and drove him off one of the highways on the coast toward the city. That was the last I ever had to see of his smug mug." She shrugged. "I don't even know if his body's ever been found. Good riddance."

"In that case I guess we'll have to go find it, won't we?"

"Or you could just leave him to his watery grave, where the bastard belongs."

"Maybe," she noted, "but I think there's been enough pain and torment. Why must the fish suffer too?"

Sully thought that was hilarious, and she started to laugh, until she broke down in hysterical tears.

SIMON ANSWERED THE phone and groaned, as he accidently reached with his bad arm.

"You shouldn't move that arm, you know? I told you that," Kate snapped.

"Hello, Kate. How are you?"

"Actually I'm doing much better, thank you. We have one half of the killing party in custody, and we're just about on our way to pick up the second half," she replied. "I just wanted to check in and see how you're doing."

"I'm fine, so tell me more."

"I can't really," she said, "but I'm heading off to grab her partner. After that, it'll be paperwork, and then I can come home."

"Oh, nice," Simon replied. "So you'll make it for dinner? I'll order something in."

"You mean, you haven't already?"

"Actually I have. I just finished ravioli and meatballs."

"Damn," she muttered enviously, "that sounds good."

"There's plenty. If all goes well, you should be here in what, two hours?"

"No, not sure I can make it that fast. ... I'll be lucky if I make it in four."

"I'll hold you to it."

"That's fine." Kate rang off.

Simon smiled, as he put down the phone, then took a look at the food and nodded. He definitely had enough leftovers, and he still had some decent wine. He walked over, put a couple bottles inside the fridge. As he closed the refrigerator door, he turned to see an entirely different church open up in front of him.

"Shit," he muttered, as he sank to the floor, caught up once again in a vision.

CHAPTER 25

K ATE DROVE TOWARD the church where Peter was scheduled to work today. She and Rodney pulled up and parked in the front. They walked in through the main double doors, several people were still around, enjoying the atmosphere of the church. She walked over to the priest, who stood to one side. She spoke to him quietly and asked if the cleaners were here.

He nodded. "Yes, the two men we have here on a regular basis are already hard at work in the back offices. Good guys."

She nodded. "I need this church cleared right now," she said quietly, "because we suspect that one of them is our killer from the recent church homicides."

The priest's eyes widened, and he quickly nodded, then took off. Gathering two other people, the priest quickly cleared the open areas of the church.

He came back to her nervously, and she nodded. "Let's go to your office and confirm you're all clear there," she explained. "Better yet, any chance I can convince you to walk out and to stay out for an hour or two?"

He shook his head. "No, Detective. I will stay here, safe in God's hands."

"Right, of course you will," she muttered, trying to hide her expression and to hold her tongue, not wanting to offend any more people than she needed to. "Let's go check your office, and then I'll lock you in there." She headed off, with him by her side.

"That's fine," he replied serenely. "I'm sure you can handle this."

"Oh, I plan on it," she stated, as he pointed to a doorway. She stepped inside and checked it out thoroughly. "I just don't know if we'll do it without bloodshed."

His eyes widened again, and he looked around nervously.

She motioned him into the office she had just cleared. And, with Rodney at her side, they locked him in.

She turned back to Rodney. "Let's split up, going in different directions," she suggested, as they headed toward where the cleaners were working.

She walked in to one office, where a man with a large commercial vacuum had a headset on. She stepped in front of him, smiled, and waved her badge.

He pulled off the headset, then looked at her expectantly. "What's the matter? What can I do for you?"

"Is your name Peter?"

"No, I'm not Peter. He's on the other side, probably at the kitchen area by now."

"Good enough," she replied. "I need you to come and answer some questions for me." At that, she led him outside where the police were gathering and the rest of her teams were arriving.

She quickly informed them that Peter was still inside, but he was the last one now. With that, she headed toward the sacristy, hoping to catch up with Rodney, before he ran into Peter. She was held up for a minute, as she checked to make sure no one was behind her. As she got closer, she saw

Rodney awkwardly kneeling in front of a cross.

She let out a little whistle to get his attention.

He looked up as expected, but she knew there was trouble when she saw the look in his eyes. Plus she now saw the man behind him with a sledgehammer. Her gun came out automatically. "Stop, police."

He froze as he looked at her, and then he laughed. "You can't stop me, not now."

"We've already got your girlfriend. We've got Sully. Don't you owe her something?"

"Nope, I sure don't. I've been there for her all this time, but she and I both knew this day would come."

"Sure, but weren't you supposed to do something for her instead?"

"Doesn't matter whether I was or not," he stated, with a broken laugh a glint of fury in his gaze. "You won't let me do it anyway, and no way I'm going to prison." And, with that, he swung the sledge toward Rodney.

She didn't hesitate and sent one bullet directly to his forehead, just as Rodney rolled to the ground, the sledgehammer missing his head as it clanged harmlessly on the floor. Meanwhile Peter pitched backward, staring up at the ceiling with blank dead eyes.

She raced over to Rodney, realizing he was hurt. "Are you okay?"

"Yeah, he took out my leg first. Then I dodged one, and he got my shoulder instead of my head. I'll live, but it hurts like hell."

"Okay," she murmured, "you stay down, and I'll get help." She helped him stretch out in a more comfortable position, as she called for backup. As the team raced in, she pointed out the killer on the floor, staring upward. "Rodney's been hurt, but I made it in time."

From the ground, Rodney added, "Yeah, she got here in the nick of time, all right. Christ, I don't ever want to come that close again."

She walked over and pointed out, "Hey, it could be worse. At least you don't have a message carved into your chest."

He groaned. "Yeah, don't remind me. I don't think forgiveness is anything I can see in that rat bastard's future."

"No," she agreed in good spirits, "but, on the other hand, you're not crucified, and your head didn't just get bashed in, and you will live to fight another day."

He looked up at her and smiled. "And you need to remember that you're not responsible for all the people this guy killed."

"Maybe not," she acknowledged, "and stopping him does go a long way toward making me feel better." She looked down at the dead man. "Fucking asshole. Boy, am I glad this one's done. What a crazy mess."

"Not quite done," Owen clarified, from behind her. "Just wait until Smidge finds out that you've got one more for him."

"Oh, he won't mind this time," Kate corrected, turning to grin at Owen. "This is the one Smidge wanted to see dead. Believe me. There'll be no court case for this one. For the girlfriend, I don't know. That'll be pretty nasty, ... if she lives that long."

"Do you know what's wrong with her?" Lilliana asked in a low tone.

"No, I don't. Sully had been severely beaten as a child, and that possibly caused her current degenerative condition, which is another task we'll have to deal with later on. Plus get this. Her father was a cop, and she and Peter killed him too, although in self-defense." Kate smiled at Lilliana. "I figure him for the missing cop who was harassing Roy. Funny how his own perversion was okay to act out, but this abusive cop thought Roy was out of line." Kate shook her head.

"Good enough." Lilliana nodded.

Owen said, "Let's get at it, everybody, and—maybe, just maybe—we'll sleep in our own beds tonight."

"I won't be sleeping in mine," Kate noted in a cheeky voice. "I'll go find a much fancier bed down in False Creek."

"Sure, but too bad he's laid up," Owen teased, with a knowing smirk.

"He is, but I'm not." Kate waggled her eyebrows at him, until Owen burst out laughing.

"Touché."

ONE MORNING A week later, Kate woke up, rolled over, and smiled at Simon in his bed. "You know something? A few days on a weekend cruise, some wine and good company, … all definitely what the doctor ordered."

"Right," he murmured, as he rolled over and pulled her close.

"You're on the road to recovery, but it'll still be a while."

"Yeah, shoulder injuries," he noted, shaking his head. "They're a pain in the ass."

"I would think so," she muttered. "Still, we got him."

"We got both of them."

"We sure did, and you'll have rehab to go through, plus the court case against Eleana, but Bartlett's company bankruptcy is looking good, *huh*?"

"It's getting there. It'll take a while, but now that we're

recovering the money from the fraudulent trusts, and Eleana's private stash," he noted, with a strong and hopeful tone, "there should be enough to clear everything up just fine. We might not even have to declare bankruptcy."

"Good enough," Kate said, as she yawned. "Man, I don't like those abuse cases."

"Neither do I," Simon agreed, "and they're deadly on you."

"They are," she murmured, "but you too. I'm so sorry, yet so glad that you always get mixed up in my cases." She curled up against him and snuggled closer. "Do we have to get up?"

"Nope, only if you want breakfast."

At that, her stomach grumbled, and she laughed. "How about breakfast in bed?"

"How about room service? We can do that, you know?" He smiled, his good arm roaming over her body.

"Or room service where we can get up and sit out on the deck and enjoy breakfast together out in the sunshine."

"Oh, now that sounds like the best idea yet." He leaned over, kissed her, and murmured, "I'm so glad you took a few days off."

"I needed them," she declared in all seriousness, as she looked over at him. "And so did you."

He tapped her lips gently. "We needed the time, this time we got to spend it together, and nothing is better than that." He leaned over and gave her another kiss. "Let's go get breakfast."

This concludes Book 7 of Kate Morgan: Simon Says…
Forgive.

Read about Kate Morgan: Simon Says… Swim, Book 8

Simon Says... Swim: Kate Morgan (Book #8)

Detective Kate Morgan is stumped, trying to decide when a case is really a case and when it belongs on her desk or someone else's. She's homicide and this? … This is something else, right? Following up the leads doesn't help, only confuses the issue—until someone slips up or slips away *literally*.

Simon wakes, choking on water, drowning in the darkness of his night, struggling to understand what madness he is connecting to now. As usual, he has few answers, and the ones he does find make no sense. Add in a young man in desperate need of assistance—yet hiding something—has Simon caught up trying to help someone, who maybe doesn't want help in the first place.

As Kate works her way through the details of multiple cases—or *not* cases—the realization is worse than anyone had realized.

Find Book 8 here!
To find out more visit Dale Mayer's website.
https://geni.us/DMSSSwim

Excerpt for Simon Says... Swim

Two Weeks Later, Second Week of November

KATE MORGAN WALKED into the station, a bright smile on her face. She looked around at her team, who had gotten up on their feet to clap and to cheer. "What was it this time? Three days and three cases closed? We're on a roll," she crowed.

Immediately came high fives all around her. "Right, and we needed it. Damn, we needed it," Lilliana stated.

"Oh, we needed some quick successes, all right," Kate agreed. "Just with so many open cases and more new ones happening all the time that it's almost impossible to feel anything but depressed."

"I know," Rodney agreed, coming up behind her, walking with the help of a cane.

She looked at him critically. "Are you back? How are you doing?"

"Oh, I'll survive," he replied, with a casual shrug, "and I'll probably walk with a limp for quite some time. That SOB got me good, and, thanks to that asshole, I'll suffer some for a time," he muttered. "Yet I'm damn glad to be alive."

It had been weeks since Kate had shot Peter, during his attack on Rodney, intent on adding yet another cop to his list of victims. That snapshot of Rodney's near-death encounter with their perp had given Kate a whole new perspective on Rodney, as he struggled to recover from the debilitating physical attack. She told him, "I'm just glad that you're doing better and that you're back. Doing without you and Andy was tough."

"I am back and better and thankful," he declared, with a smile in her direction, "and know who to thank for it."

"Oh, no, don't even go there," she said, with an eye roll. "That's the last thing I need."

"Yeah, what she said," Owen pitched in from the nearby desk, with a grin.

Rodney grinned at the joke and looked back at her, holding up a baggie. "Does that mean, if my girlfriend baked you some cookies, you'll turn them down?"

"I'll never turn down cookies," she stated, staring at him. "What do you think I am? A psycho?" And, with that, she snatched the bag from his hand and eyed it with a greedy expression on her face. Then it came to her. "These were for your lunch, weren't they?"

He burst out laughing. "Damn, I'm so busted."

She groaned and handed them back. "You can keep them." She smiled. "Besides, you're the injured person, not me."

"Ah, I'm not injured though," he added. "I just got re-leased to return to duty."

"Sure, but you still have to go to physical therapy, right?"

He glared at her and nodded. "Why did you have to go there and ruin my day? Do you know how painful PT is?"

"Oh, I do," she noted, with a satisfied nod. "Trust me. I absolutely do, which is why you're not getting out of it." He just continued to glare at her, and she chuckled. "Not happening." She pointed at his miserable face. "You need to get that leg back." Kate turned to ask her team, "Anybody have an update on when Andy is returning to work?"

Just then Sergeant Colby walked in. "So ..." he began.

Something about his tone of voice made Kate cringe. "What?" she asked cautiously.

He nodded at her. "We have the potential of something ugly coming up on the board—reports of a drowning up at Cultus Lake."

"That'll be up to the local law enforcement, right?" Kate asked.

"Yes, it's from a while ago, but yes."

"What do you mean, a while ago?"

"We have that case, and we have a couple other cases. Those others concern us because they probably link to that older one."

"Whoa, whoa, whoa," Kate said. "You're not making sense."

"I will, unfortunately," he replied, raising his hand to stop her onslaught. "Okay, listen up. I'll fill you all in from the top. We've had a drowning at Wreck Beach."

At that, Rodney whistled. "It certainly isn't from the weight of the bathing suits down at that new beach," he noted, with a smile.

"Maybe, but it happened early in the morning, off one of the rocks," Colby noted, with a sigh. "According to a witness, somebody out there apparently tried to help, supposedly tried to help, but the victim drowned and was carried down a ways, before being dragged to shore by the guy who had been trying to help. However, in hindsight, now our witness is not so sure."

Kate frowned at him in confusion. "I don't get it."

Lilliana snorted. "Thank you. I'm so glad you said that, though I never thought I would hear those words coming out of your mouth in one million years. And, Sarge, for the record, I sure as hell don't get it either."

"According to the eyewitness, this person trying to save our victim may have instead drowned our victim."

"So it could have been one or the other? That's hardly a solid witness account or a conclusive statement," Lilliana pointed out.

"Exactly, which is why it has ended up in our purview."

"So," Kate asked, "we don't have a body, or we do?"

Colby faced her. "As of twenty minutes ago, we have a body."

She groaned. "Okay, so we have a drowning victim. I'm still confused at how that has anything to do with us."

At that moment, their analyst Reese walked in, with several files in her hand. "Because," she interjected, as she passed out copies to everyone, "we have three other victims with eyewitness accounts, making it sound like somebody watched them drown and didn't do anything to help them. Or possibly tried to help them but failed."

Kate winced, then asked cautiously, "Watched them drown or actively helped them drown and then stepped back?"

"That's what you get to find out," Colby stated, with a nod in her direction. "We're taking it in the worst way possible, that they put this person in a position to drown and then stepped back and watched them drown. Now, if that's the case"—he gave them all a stare—"it's murder, and, therefore, it's ours."

"And if it's not the case?" Kate asked cautiously.

He shrugged. "Then it has nothing to do with us." She

glared at him, and he smiled. "All I can tell you is that this case is what has crossed our desk, so it's up to us to take a look."

"Okay then," Kate confirmed, "but it does sound …" Then she frowned and shrugged. "It sounds a little off."

"Which means it should be a perfect case for you then," Lilliana noted, with an eye roll. "Nobody does a *little off* like Kate."

"Regardless of who does it well," Colby butted in, "this is a serious case, and, as Reese pointed out, three other cases have similarities. No conclusive link but similar in the manner of death and in the eyewitness accounts."

"Why the hell would you drown anybody with eyewitnesses around in the first place?" Kate wondered out loud.

Colby turned, looked at her, and nodded. "Exactly, so see what you can come up with and get back to me as soon as you can."

She groaned. "Will do." She looked back over to the others. "I suppose you all have cases to work?"

"Yep, you're the one who took time off," Owen pointed out. "So guess what? You're it."

"Seems like I'm always *it* somehow," she mumbled to herself, as she walked over to her desk with the folders, wondering how the hell she would even start on this. Eyewitness accounts were notoriously unreliable, not to mention the fact that a lot of the time these convenient witnesses had ulterior motives.

As she looked down at the files in front of her, she had to wonder just what motive anybody would have for this.

Find Book 8 here!
To find out more visit Dale Mayer's website.
https://geni.us/DMSSSwim

Author's Note

Thank you for reading Simon Says… Forgive: Kate Morgan, Book 7! If you enjoyed the book, please take a moment and leave a short review.

Dear reader,

I love to hear from readers, and you can contact me at my website: www.dalemayer.com or at my Facebook author page. To be informed of new releases and special offers, sign up for my newsletter or follow me on BookBub. And if you are interested in joining Dale Mayer's Reader Group, here is the Facebook sign up page. http://geni.us/DaleMayerFBGroup

Cheers,
Dale Mayer

About the Author

Dale Mayer is a *USA Today* best-selling author, best known for her SEALs military romances, her Psychic Visions series, and her Lovely Lethal Garden cozy series. Her contemporary romances are raw and full of passion and emotion (Broken But … Mending, Hathaway House series). Her thrillers will keep you guessing (Kate Morgan, By Death series), and her romantic comedies will keep you giggling (*It's a Dog's Life*, a stand-alone novella; and the Broken Protocols series, starring Charming Marvin, the cat).

Dale honors the stories that come to her—and some of them are crazy, break all the rules and cross multiple genres!

To go with her fiction, she also writes nonfiction in many different fields, with books available on résumé writing, companion gardening, and the US mortgage system. All her books are available in print and ebook format.

Connect with Dale Mayer Online

Dale's Website – www.dalemayer.com
Twitter – @DaleMayer
Facebook Page – geni.us/DaleMayerFBFanPage
Facebook Group – geni.us/DaleMayerFBGroup
BookBub – geni.us/DaleMayerBookbub
Instagram – geni.us/DaleMayerInstagram
Goodreads – geni.us/DaleMayerGoodreads
Newsletter – geni.us/DaleNews

Also by Dale Mayer

Published Adult Books:

Shadow Recon

Magnus, Book 1

Rogan, Book 2

Egan, Book 3

Barret, Book 4

Whalen, Book 5

Nikolai, Book 6

Bullard's Battle

Ryland's Reach, Book 1

Cain's Cross, Book 2

Eton's Escape, Book 3

Garret's Gambit, Book 4

Kano's Keep, Book 5

Fallon's Flaw, Book 6

Quinn's Quest, Book 7

Bullard's Beauty, Book 8

Bullard's Best, Book 9

Bullard's Battle, Books 1–2

Bullard's Battle, Books 3–4

Bullard's Battle, Books 5–6

Bullard's Battle, Books 7–8

Terkel's Team

Damon's Deal, Book 1

Wade's War, Book 2

Gage's Goal, Book 3

Calum's Contact, Book 4

Rick's Road, Book 5

Scott's Summit, Book 6

Brody's Beast, Book 7

Terkel's Twist, Book 8

Terkel's Triumph, Book 9

Terk's Guardians

Radar, Book 1

Legend, Book 2

Bojan, Book 3

Kate Morgan

Simon Says… Hide, Book 1

Simon Says… Jump, Book 2

Simon Says… Ride, Book 3

Simon Says… Scream, Book 4

Simon Says… Run, Book 5

Simon Says… Walk, Book 6

Simon Says… Forgive, Book 7

Simon Says… Swim, Book 8

Hathaway House

Aaron, Book 1

Brock, Book 2

Cole, Book 3

Denton, Book 4

Elliot, Book 5

Finn, Book 6

Gregory, Book 7

Heath, Book 8

Iain, Book 9

Jaden, Book 10

Keith, Book 11

Lance, Book 12

Melissa, Book 13

Nash, Book 14

Owen, Book 15

Percy, Book 16

Quinton, Book 17

Ryatt, Book 18

Spencer, Book 19

Timothy, Book 20

Urban, Book 21

Hathaway House, Books 1–3

Hathaway House, Books 4–6

Hathaway House, Books 7–9

The K9 Files

Ethan, Book 1

Pierce, Book 2

Zane, Book 3

Blaze, Book 4

Lucas, Book 5

Parker, Book 6

Carter, Book 7

Weston, Book 8

Greyson, Book 9

Rowan, Book 10

Caleb, Book 11

Kurt, Book 12

Tucker, Book 13

Harley, Book 14

Kyron, Book 15

Jenner, Book 16

Rhys, Book 17

Landon, Book 18

Harper, Book 19

Kascius, Book 20

Declan, Book 21

Bauer, Book 22

The K9 Files, Books 1–2

The K9 Files, Books 3–4

The K9 Files, Books 5–6

The K9 Files, Books 7–8

The K9 Files, Books 9–10

The K9 Files, Books 11–12

Lovely Lethal Gardens

Arsenic in the Azaleas, Book 1

Bones in the Begonias, Book 2

Corpse in the Carnations, Book 3

Daggers in the Dahlias, Book 4

Evidence in the Echinacea, Book 5

Footprints in the Ferns, Book 6

Gun in the Gardenias, Book 7

Handcuffs in the Heather, Book 8

Ice Pick in the Ivy, Book 9

Jewels in the Juniper, Book 10

Killer in the Kiwis, Book 11

Lifeless in the Lilies, Book 12

Murder in the Marigolds, Book 13

Nabbed in the Nasturtiums, Book 14

Offed in the Orchids, Book 15

Poison in the Pansies, Book 16

Quarry in the Quince, Book 17

Revenge in the Roses, Book 18

Silenced in the Sunflowers, Book 19

Toes up in the Tulips, Book 20

Uzi in the Urn, Book 21

Victim in the Violets, Book 22

Whispers in the Wisteria, Book 23

Lovely Lethal Gardens, Books 1–2

Lovely Lethal Gardens, Books 3–4

Lovely Lethal Gardens, Books 5–6

Lovely Lethal Gardens, Books 7–8

Lovely Lethal Gardens, Books 9–10

Psychic Visions Series

Tuesday's Child

Hide 'n Go Seek

Maddy's Floor

Garden of Sorrow

Knock Knock…

Rare Find

Eyes to the Soul

Now You See Her

Shattered

Into the Abyss

Seeds of Malice

Eye of the Falcon

Itsy-Bitsy Spider

Unmasked

Deep Beneath

From the Ashes

Stroke of Death

Ice Maiden

Snap, Crackle…

What If…

Talking Bones

String of Tears

Inked Forever

Insanity

Psychic Visions Books 1–3

Psychic Visions Books 4–6

Psychic Visions Books 7–9

By Death Series

Touched by Death

Haunted by Death

Chilled by Death

By Death Books 1–3

Broken Protocols – Romantic Comedy Series

Cat's Meow

Cat's Pajamas

Cat's Cradle

Cat's Claus

Broken Protocols 1-4

Broken and... Mending

Skin

Scars

Scales (of Justice)

Broken but... Mending 1-3

Glory

Genesis

Tori

Celeste

Glory Trilogy

Biker Blues

Morgan: Biker Blues, Volume 1

Cash: Biker Blues, Volume 2

SEALs of Honor

Mason: SEALs of Honor, Book 1

Hawk: SEALs of Honor, Book 2

Dane: SEALs of Honor, Book 3

Swede: SEALs of Honor, Book 4

Shadow: SEALs of Honor, Book 5

Cooper: SEALs of Honor, Book 6

Markus: SEALs of Honor, Book 7

Evan: SEALs of Honor, Book 8

Mason's Wish: SEALs of Honor, Book 9

Chase: SEALs of Honor, Book 10

Brett: SEALs of Honor, Book 11

Devlin: SEALs of Honor, Book 12

Easton: SEALs of Honor, Book 13

Ryder: SEALs of Honor, Book 14

Macklin: SEALs of Honor, Book 15

Corey: SEALs of Honor, Book 16

Warrick: SEALs of Honor, Book 17

Tanner: SEALs of Honor, Book 18

Jackson: SEALs of Honor, Book 19

Kanen: SEALs of Honor, Book 20

Nelson: SEALs of Honor, Book 21

Taylor: SEALs of Honor, Book 22

Colton: SEALs of Honor, Book 23

Troy: SEALs of Honor, Book 24

Axel: SEALs of Honor, Book 25

Baylor: SEALs of Honor, Book 26

Hudson: SEALs of Honor, Book 27

Lachlan: SEALs of Honor, Book 28

Paxton: SEALs of Honor, Book 29

Bronson: SEALs of Honor, Book 30

Hale: SEALs of Honor, Book 31

SEALs of Honor, Books 1–3

SEALs of Honor, Books 4–6

SEALs of Honor, Books 7–10

SEALs of Honor, Books 11–13

SEALs of Honor, Books 14–16

SEALs of Honor, Books 17–19

SEALs of Honor, Books 20–22

SEALs of Honor, Books 23–25

Heroes for Hire

Levi's Legend: Heroes for Hire, Book 1

Stone's Surrender: Heroes for Hire, Book 2

Merk's Mistake: Heroes for Hire, Book 3

Rhodes's Reward: Heroes for Hire, Book 4

Flynn's Firecracker: Heroes for Hire, Book 5

Logan's Light: Heroes for Hire, Book 6

Harrison's Heart: Heroes for Hire, Book 7

Saul's Sweetheart: Heroes for Hire, Book 8

Dakota's Delight: Heroes for Hire, Book 9

Tyson's Treasure: Heroes for Hire, Book 10

Jace's Jewel: Heroes for Hire, Book 11

Rory's Rose: Heroes for Hire, Book 12

Brandon's Bliss: Heroes for Hire, Book 13

Liam's Lily: Heroes for Hire, Book 14

North's Nikki: Heroes for Hire, Book 15

Anders's Angel: Heroes for Hire, Book 16

Reyes's Raina: Heroes for Hire, Book 17

Dezi's Diamond: Heroes for Hire, Book 18

Vince's Vixen: Heroes for Hire, Book 19

Ice's Icing: Heroes for Hire, Book 20

SEALs of Steel

SEALs of Steel, Books 1–8

The Mavericks

Kerrick, Book 1

Griffin, Book 2

Jax, Book 3

Beau, Book 4

Asher, Book 5

Ryker, Book 6

Miles, Book 7

Nico, Book 8

Keane, Book 9

Lennox, Book 10

Gavin, Book 11

Shane, Book 12

Diesel, Book 13

Jerricho, Book 14

Killian, Book 15

Hatch, Book 16

Corbin, Book 17

Aiden, Book 18

The Mavericks, Books 1–2

The Mavericks, Books 3–4

The Mavericks, Books 5–6

The Mavericks, Books 7–8

The Mavericks, Books 9–10

The Mavericks, Books 11–12

Standalone Novellas

It's a Dog's Life

Riana's Revenge

Second Chances

Published Young Adult Books:

Family Blood Ties Series

Vampire in Denial

Vampire in Distress

Vampire in Design

Vampire in Deceit

Vampire in Defiance

Vampire in Conflict

Vampire in Chaos

Vampire in Crisis

Vampire in Control

Vampire in Charge

Family Blood Ties Set 1–3

Family Blood Ties Set 1–5

Family Blood Ties Set 4–6

Family Blood Ties Set 7–9

Sian's Solution, A Family Blood Ties Series Prequel
    Novelette

Design series

Dangerous Designs

Deadly Designs

Darkest Designs

Design Series Trilogy

Standalone

In Cassie's Corner

Gem Stone (a Gemma Stone Mystery)

Time Thieves

Published Non-Fiction Books:

Career Essentials

Career Essentials: The Résumé

Career Essentials: The Cover Letter

Career Essentials: The Interview

Career Essentials: 3 in 1